Risel (Davis)

Blaze Of

FURY

Book 3 of the
Mountains and Valleys of Life

Risel Buhler

FriesenPress

Suite 300 - 990 Fort St
Victoria, BC, Canada, V8V 3K2
www.friesenpress.com

Copyright © 2015 by Risel Buhler
First Edition — 2015

All rights reserved.

No part of this publication may be reproduced in any form, or by any means, electronic or mechanical, including photocopying, recording, or any information browsing, storage, or retrieval system, without permission in writing from the publisher.

A special thanks to the artist, Brenda Campbell for drawing the cover picture, just as I had describe to her. This picture cannot be copied without both artist and author's permission.

ISBN
978-1-4602-6902-2 (Hardcover)
978-1-4602-6903-9 (Paperback)
978-1-4602-6904-6 (eBook)

1. *Fiction, Christian, Romance*

Distributed to the trade by The Ingram Book Company

I dedicate my books in memory of my husband. If it weren't for his love and encouragement, I would not have written my books.

When this picture was taken I told him this is where I would start my first book. Our time together was too short but I thank God for the time we did have.

Chapter 1

When Austin drove into Calgary, he had made up his mind to set aside his problems. He had not seen his cousin Claire in quite some time, so when his parents told him that she was in the hospital, he decided to go see her. She had the most cheerful disposition of anyone he knew, and that was definitely something he could use right about now.

They were walking arm in arm, talking and laughing, as they passed the patient's lounge. Austin happened to glance over at the woman who, at the same time, looked at him. Their eyes met ever so briefly, but then she suddenly turned away. The color drained from Austin's face and his heart rate increased dramatically. Claire looked at him when, he did not answer her question.

"Austin is everything alright?" she asked.

"I'm sorry Claire. I think I just saw a ghost from my past."

When he and Claire got back to her room, he suddenly excused himself and darted back to the lounge. However the woman had evaded him. He began quickly to check the names that were posted beside each door. There was one name that sounded vaguely familiar, but the door was only slightly ajar and the curtain inside was drawn. He slowly walked back to Claire's room, hoping that he might spot this woman again. When he sat down on the chair near Claire's bed, it was like he was a million miles away.

"Are you alright?" Claire repeated.

"I'm sorry, did you say something?" Austin asked, trying to concentrate.

"Is something wrong as you seem, to be in a whole new dimension?"

"I'm fine," Austin replied despite trying to focus on what Claire was telling him, after a half hour, his attention waned, and he made up some lame excuse, and also told her that he had a lot of work waiting for him at home. He gave Claire a kiss on the cheek and promised her that he would do his best to keep in touch, and then he left.

As he leaving, Austin still held out hope of finding that woman, who now consumed his every thought. The room he thought could have been hers, was now unoccupied and the name by the door was removed. He walked slowly towards the elevator. The door was just closing when he caught a glimpse of her. Austin rushed over and pushed on the button, hoping that it would open, but it did not. When he turned, he noticed the stairs sign above the door. He quickly opened the door and ran down the stairs, but she had again eluded him.

Disappointed, Austin gradually walked toward the parking lot, all the while searching for his elusive lady friend. She had once again disappeared, just like she had so many years ago.

Austin struggled the rest of the day with his thoughts. Was this woman actually who he thought she was? After he finished his chores, he went back in his empty house. He didn't feel much like making himself something to eat, so he turned on the television. Austin could not shake off the memories that now flooded his mind. Did she recognize him? Is that why she looked away so quickly?

He had to find out if it really was Jan. He got up from his chair and walked over to the phone. He stood, scratching his head, while racking his brain. What was her married name? It was something like Nuts. "Nuts Nuts," he repeated to himself. Suddenly he yelled, "Nuss!" He quickly dialed information, and after getting the number, he called the hospital.

"Could you tell me if Anne Nuss is still a patient there?" Austin asked.

"One moment please," the receptionist replied. Austin could feel his heart beating in his chest as he waited.

"I'm sorry, but there is no one by that name registered here," she replied.

"She may be registered under the name, Jan Nuss," Austin said.

"Ah, yes, but she was released this afternoon," the receptionist informed him.

"Would you have an address for her or a phone number?" He asked hopefully.

"I'm sorry, but I cannot give you that information."

"Thanks." *So I was not mistaken he thought*, as he hung up the phone. His mind was working over time. He had to find out where she lived. *She is married*, he reminded himself. He pondered, what was wrong with finding out where an old friend lives? He would just like to talk to her again and know that she was happy. More then anything, he would like to know why she had left without a word. Austin dialed Claire's hospital room.

"Hi Claire, this is Austin again. I was wondering if you would do me a favor."

"Sure, if I can," she said.

"There was a woman that I saw in the lounge when we walked by there. I believe I know her. Her name was Jan Nuss, she is quite pretty with shoulder length blonde hair, and medium build."

"Yes I remember her."

"Did you ever talk to her or see her husband there?"

"Well cousin. I see you do have an interest in the opposite sex. I was beginning to wonder about you. Is this the woman you have pined over all these years?" She asked, laughing. There was silence on the other end of the line. Claire soon realized that what she had said was more truth than fiction.

"I'm sorry Austin," She apologized before continuing on, "I didn't mean to imply anything by what I said. I did talk to her briefly. All I can tell you is it sounded like she lives by herself on a farm near the town of Olds. I'm sorry, but she really didn't say exactly where. I will ask around, but I doubt if any of the nurses will give out that information."

"Thanks Claire, I appreciate it. Look after yourself," he said before hanging up the phone.

Austin checked the listings in and around the Olds area for Jan's name, but without any success. He had never forgotten Jan, but with the problems of trying to keep from losing his ranch, he had resigned himself to the fact that his dream life with her was never to be.

His finances had been very tight-plus cattle rustlers seemed to have targeted him, which made it even worse.

Austin paced the floor, wondering if she was seriously ill. Would he ever see her again? There was this haunting feeling, and hurt of not knowing why she had disappeared years ago without a word. Was she still married? Would he ever have the opportunity to tell her that he still care for her, or was it never to be?

Austin stepped out onto his veranda. The evening was warm with not a cloud in the sky. He looked up at the full moon. *With the right person, it would be a perfect night for a stroll*, he thought to himself.

As he stared up at the millions of twinkling stars, he was in awe at the vastness of it all. It had been a long time since he had admired the unbelievable beauty of God's handiwork.

Just then, a streak of light shot across the sky. *Make a wish*, he said to himself. It was then that he remembered the pact that he and Jan had made. Austin looked at his watch. It was five minutes to ten. Would she be standing outside right now looking up at the sky? Did she see the same shooting star, and if so, had she also made a wish? His thoughts drifted back to what seemed to be another lifetime.

Austin and Jan, along with their parents had attended the same church. He never did like going to church because he seemed to be always getting into trouble for one reason or another. The church did not allow boys and girls to get together, but when Austin happened to get near some of the girls, he would either complement them on how nice they looked, or tease them, for which he was severely disciplined.

There was one girl that stood out more then others, and she just happened to be the neighbour's daughter. Austin knew the rules, but he began to notice that she would often go for a walk down into the coulee. Then one day, as he watched her disappear into the valley, he decided to pretend that one of their cows had jumped the fence and he was sent to look for her. When he first caught up with Jan, she was very quiet and did not want to talk, but as he was very persistent, she soon opened up. It was not long before they found that they really enjoyed each other's company.

There was one bluff of trees that soon became their meeting place. It was a time that they both looked forward to. Austin and Jan knew that going out on a date would be impossible, as they were not allowed to date, so they made this pact that at ten p.m. every night they would, go outside and look up at the sky. It was the next best thing to being together, as they would be both looking up at the stars with their minds fixated on each other.

Austin was nineteen and Jan was seventeen when they began to talk about marriage and the dream of owning their own Ranch. They even planned what kind of house they would live in, but in all actuality, that was only a dream because owning that much land would not be allowed.

Austin told Jan that he would ask his parents to talk to the ministers about them getting married. From there, the ministers would talk to her parents, and the last part was easy, as he already knew Jan's answer. However when Austin's parents did go to talk to the ministers, they were told that Austin was not in good enough standing with the church to get married there, and they believed her parents would not agree to it. Part of the problem also was that he was adopted. Therefore his birth mother was probably never married, making him a bastard son. Then as they quoted the Bible verse," *that said the father's sins affected their children down to the third and fourth generation,"* he was marked before he began. He did know that not all of the people felt that way about adopted children, but that was his experience.

He remembered the numerous times that he had gotten into trouble with the elders. The first time was at a social function. He was about thirteen when his friend asked Austin to toss a bun to him, which he did. He was seriously reprimanded, as food was not to be played with. That was the first time he was told to go before the church to ask for forgiveness. Austin was very shy, and did his best to avoid doing that, plus he didn't think it was all that serious of a thing. He was glad that the ministers had not enforced it.

He and Jan had to be extremely careful not to be seen with each other, or they both could have been shunned. (This meant that family, and church, members would not eat with and or, talk to them.)

Then one day, Jan's family went away for the afternoon. That was the longest time that he and Jan ever spent together. Jan wept knowing that their dreams were never to be unless they ran away.

The next thing he knew, he was kissing her for the first time. They clung to each other, like it would be their last time together, and it was. He knew that they had gotten too emotionally involved that day, for which he felt guilty later. After that day he was never able to contact or talk to her. He caught a glimpse of her a couple of times, but she never again went for her walks.

It was a couple months later that he heard that she was to marry John Remple. He was ten years her senior. Austin couldn't believe what he had heard. He felt like there had been a conspiracy against him. She deserved someone much better then John. In his opinion, that guy was as dumb as a sack of hammers, and he told his parents that too.

Jan's parents told her that they felt John would make her a good husband. She tried to get up the courage to say no, but she was feeling the pressure coming from her parents, as well as from the ministers. Perhaps it was partially the fact that they thought they were protecting Jan from the sins that could carry over from Austin's birth family.

Once she sort of agreed, she could not go back, as that would have brought shame to her and her family. Jan began to pray that God would intervene and this marriage would never happen and five days later Jan left that area, and never returned.

A year after Jan left, her parents also moved away, temporarily. The last he heard was that Jan did not marry John, but an outsider, which was somewhat of a relief to Austin. He often wondered what had taken place, but everyone was very close-mouthed about it all.

Austin did not feel any remorse when he was excommunicated from the church. In some ways it was a relief. He was now free to marry whomever, he wanted. He was no longer constricted by all their rules and regulations. The only downfall was how this affected his relationship with his parents. The last time he was shunned, his parents also had to be careful as not to get caught disobeying the shunning. He remembered his Mother giving him his meals out on the step, because he was not allowed to eat with the family. Shortly after, he moved out of the area, never to return.

It was several years later that Austin accepted Jesus Christ as his personal Savior, and some of those old rules that he had been brought up with still seemed to resurface. The old teaching that once you were expelled from their church, you wouldn't make it to heaven, persistently came to his mind.

Not long after Austin inherited his ranch, a couple ministers approached him and said that they would accept him back into the church. The only stipulation was that he would, have to first go before the church and ask for forgiveness. This would, again, put him under the microscope for sometime. Austin told them that he was answerable to Jesus Christ and not them, and that they should mend their own fences. When he thought back to some of the trivial things in that church, and their opinions of what would get you to heaven, it angered him. It just wasn't right that the elders of the church had the power to demand what was right or wrong. It would have been acceptable to him if they could back it all up with scripture, but traditionally, this was rule, so there was no questioning it.

Austin believed in a God that loved him and who had sent his son Jesus to die on the cross for him, and when Austin messed up (which he often did), he could pray directly to God and ask him to forgive him and God would.

Austin smiled slightly as he thought about the day he bought Jan a pair of jeans, a western shirt, and a cowboy hat. The woman in the store must have thought he was just off the farm, when he tried to describe his girl friend's size, which he did get right.

Then one day, when he was in town, he ran into Jan. He very inconspicuously told her where to meet him and she did. He showed her the clothes he bought then, dared her to put them on. Thinking back, he probably was a bad influence on her, but he would have done anything to spend time with her. He was angry at the world and she was too. She took him up on the dare and hopped into his truck, than they went driving around the town. Shortly after, Jan's brother flagged them down, to see if Austin had seen Jan.

Jan quickly pulled her hat down to hide her face, while looking at a paper that Austin, had just picked up. Her brother would have never in his wildest dreams, believed that his sister would be dressed in such a worldly manner. Along with the change of clothes, Austin gave her the nickname Jan. Her family never did find out about their little escapade.

Austin's mind returned to the present. He was positive that Jan had recognized him. It was then that it struck him. She was not wearing the traditional dress. She must have left, and never returned to the old ways, but what had led up to that.

"I love you Jan," he said, trying to remember her face. He suddenly felt as if she was right there beside him. Perhaps, she to was looking at the stars. He was now more determined then ever to find out where she lived.

That night, Austin had a very restless sleep. He had dreamt that he and Jan were married, but then she disappeared into the forest and he couldn't find her. He woke up with a jolt when he heard someone banging on his door.

Austin looked at the time before jumping out of bed. He quickly slipped into his jeans and ran his fingers though his unruly hair on the way to opening the door.

"What, still sleeping, are you? I thought you would be chewing me out for being late." Ted said, stepping into the house, as Austin went back to his room.

By the time Austin got back into the kitchen, the aroma of coffee filled the room.

Ted looked up from the magazine he was reading.

"Yah still going out to check the cattle this morning," Ted asked.

"I plan on it," Austin replied, starring at the coffee pot.

Ted looked over at Austin. It was unusual for him to still be in bed at this hour. Normally he would have been chomping on the bit. Something must have happened to put him in this strange mood.

After a few minutes of strained silence, Austin filled their cups with coffee before placing them on the table.

"Have you found any leads into the cattle rustling yet?" Austin asked. Austin and Ted had become good friend, since Austin moved into the area. He was grateful to Ted for all his help on the Ranch. He sometimes wondered what he would have done without him. As a newcomer to the area, Austin knew that he was an outsider and had to prove to his neighbours that he meant business.

"No, but we are still working on it," Ted said laying down the magazine. Ted was a brand inspector, and worked closely with the cattlemen's association. There had been an over abundance of cattle rustling incidents lately, and besides trying to catch the culprits, they were working on how to prevent it.

Ted had a hunch that who ever was stealing Austin's cattle was not related to the rustlers that were causing the problems in other areas. There was a possibility that Austin's problem was more of a vendetta. There were rumors floating around town, that one particular neighbour of Austin's, was angry because, Austin bought some prime property that he had wanted. The neighbors hired hands, had been bragging of how they had inside information that Austin wouldn't be able to hang onto his ranch much longer. Soon they would be riding his range, as well as living in his house. It's amazing how some guys will shoot off their mouths when they get liquored up.

There was also talk about the probability of gas and oil exploration in this area, which could mean extra money in the ranchers' pockets. Although a lot of ranchers were not happy about oil and cattle mixing.

Ted loved working with cattle, and it gave him first hand information as to where the rustlers had been.

"Any more cattle missing lately?" Ted asked.

"Not since last time I checked why? You heard somethin'?" Austin inquired, taking a sip of his coffee.

"No, but you look like heck this morning."

"Oh, it's nothing," Austin replied.

"Ok, if you don't want to talk about it," Ted replied.

"Nope, let's get to work," Austin said, taking one more gulp of coffee before pulling on his boots. On the way out he put on his jacket and cowboy hat. "Yah coming?" he called as Ted began to stand up.

"Yes boss," Ted replied. He knew Austin well enough that if there was something he didn't want to talk about, there was no prying it from him. Actually, there was not a lot he knew about

Austin's past. He just refused to talk about his life. What Austin needed was a good woman, but that was another thing that was taboo with Austin. He was a heck of a nice guy, but definitely a tough nut to crack.

Austin and Ted spent the day separating the calves for shipment. He decided to keep twenty of the best heifers back for breeding stock. With the price being what it was, he should have more than enough to pay his loan and get him through the winter. There were also ten cows that he culled out for various reasons. It angered Austin when he thought of the ten cows and seven calves had gone missing. He had sold the three young calves that had been left motherless as the result. It was too much of a bother to have pail bunters around when the prices were good. The loss sure cut into his profit. If worse came to worse, he would get a part time job next spring to off-set his income

By the end of the day, both men were exhausted. Austin thought he would be too tired to think about Jan, but he was mistaken. The thought of her made him even more restless.

How could he go about finding her? Why had God put her there right in his grasp only to take her away from him again? A verse from the Bible came to mind. *You won't get it, because you haven't asked God for it.* But what was he suppose to ask for? He did not want to interfere in her life, if she was married. However if she happened to be alone, as Claire thought she might be, he would like to see her again. *Lord only you know what's going on in her life. You also know our hearts. Lord if it is to be, work it out. I am too stressed to take on any more right now. I leave it in your capable hands.*

When Austin's head hit the pillow, he fell asleep. He woke up early the next morning in a reasonably good mood. After all, God had graciously supplied the cattle he was about to ship this morning. He would have ample money for now. As for Jan, he could not get her, out of his mind, but at least he did not feel quite as down about it. He still wanted to find her but he had now left it in God's hands and when the time was right he was confident that they would meet again.

Chapter 2

It was almost a year since Jan had been in the hospital, but she could not get her mind off the day she left. If only her doctor had come in earlier to discharge her, she would never have seen him. She had been having some problems with her heart, so her family doctor had sent her to the city to have it checked out. It was unbelievable that their paths would happen to cross at that particular moment. She thought she had packed the memory of him so far back, that she'd hoped it would never surface again. Only, there were certain strings that were attached to that memory which seemed to unravel occasionally. She now wanted to stuff it back into that safe place and hope that it would not work it's way out again, but that safe place had been ripped open and seemed to be unfixable.

She was admiring the view from out of the patients' lounge window, when she turned at the sound of a couples laughing and talking. When their eyes met, she instantly knew who it was.

She quickly turned away as the color drained from her face. By his slight hesitation, she knew that he also recognized her. Paralyzed with fear she prayed that he would not approach her.

The moment she heard them move on, she escaped to the privacy of her room. From what she observed, he was probably happily married. He had matured a lot since she had seen him last. He was definitely what you would call "tall dark and handsome." If the clothes he had on were any indication of what he was doing, she would say that he either worked on a Ranch, or owned one. Not every man was dressed in western clothes with cowboy boots and hat. His tan was definitely an indication of a lot of outdoor activities.

Jan's heart ached when she remembered the clothes he had bought for her. *I wonder what he did with them,* she thought. Why couldn't things have turned out different?

She had gone to the safety of her room and closed the door most of the way, and had drawn the curtain around her bed. There was no way that she wanted to talk to him. After a few minutes she peeked around the corner. It reminded her of when strangers would come to visit her parents. Her and her sister would peek around the corner, then snicker and run back to their rooms. Only this time, when she saw him checking the names by each room, she was not snickering. She was quite sure that he would not know her married name. Not only that, she no longer went by her given name, which was Anne. After the disillusionment with her family, she had taken on the nickname Jan which was the Austin had called her.

Jan backed into her room, and was leaning against the wall when her doctor walked in.

"Are you all right Mrs. Nuss?" he had asked.

Jan nodded her head then gave him some lame excuse that didn't really make much sense to even her, but he accepted it and told her that he would sending her test results to her family doctor who in turn would contact her in about a week or so. Jan was relieved when he told her that he was discharging her.

Jan was relieved and glad to finally be able to leave. Only she had to be careful to not run into Austin. She thought she had caught a glimpse of him just as the elevator door closed, but she could not be sure.

That evening the moon was full and the air was quite warm, so she decided to go and sit on her swing. It took her back to her youth and the silly pact that her and Austin had made. She remembered how she used to go for walks down into their coulee. It was so peaceful down there. Then Austin showed up looking for a cow. Now that she thought of it, he hadn't looked very hard. After that, Jan looked forward to the days Austin would meet her, and was terribly disappointed when he couldn't. It became almost a regular occurrence. They began to talk about marriage, but fate had different plans.

Just a couple of days before Austin's parents came to visit, another family that she barely knew had come to talk to her parents. She was extremely upset when her parents had, more or less, indicated to her that they had agreed that this family's son would make a better husband for her than Austin would. She had never before gone against her parents' wishes. She wondered if her parents had suspected that her and Austin had been secretly meeting, and it was clear to her now that they had. She had told her parents that she did not want to marry this other man, but as her parents had agreed to this union, and it would bring shame to her and the family if she did not go through with it.

She allowed herself to remember the last time her and Austin were together. Jan had fallen into his arms and wept. They even talked about running away together. She shuddered as remembered the warmth of his body against hers, as he held her close. He kissed her, tenderly at first, which made her whole body tingle as their passion heightened.

Someone in their district must have suspected that she had been meeting Austin or had seen them coming from that general area at different times, because she was never allowed to go for her walks again.

It was then that a shooting star streaked across the sky, breaking into her train of thought. It was if she could hear Austin say, *"Quick make a wish."* She did, but what good would that do. She looked at her watch. Did Austin remember? Jan stood up quickly. It was not good for her to be dredging up old memories. They must go back to that far away hiding place. If only she could wipe them away totally. Either way, that was the past, and it was not likely their paths would cross again.

Book 3 of the *Mountains and Valleys of Life*

* * *

Spring had finally arrived and Jan was beginning to feel restless. She felt life had dealt her a raw hand, and she desperately needed to get out of the rut she was in. She had been married to a wonderful man for five years, when his life was snuffed out in an accident. That was a year and a half ago. She very much wanted children, but that did not materialize. Perhaps God was still punishing her because of her past sins.

She was thankful that Don had the foresight to have insurance on their farm loans as well as having a sizable life insurance policy. At least she did not have to worry about how she would pay back all their loans. She had a farm sale, sold all the machinery, and rented out the section of cultivated land, because she did not feel capable of doing the farming herself. The home quarter was mainly pasture. She had a notion to put a few cows in there.

Jan stood looking out her kitchen window. After its winter hibernation, the green grass was now weaving its way through the dry brittle grass stocks of last year. The tulips along the fence now waved gently in the soft breeze, as they stretched out to absorb the warmth of the sun. Jan was beginning to get cabin fever after being cooped up most of the winter.

The announcement on the radio of a cattle sale at the local Auction Market caught her attention. *She had been contemplating whether it was better to have her own cows on the pastureland, or should she just rent it out with the rest of her land. She decided that it would be best that she check out the price of cows, so she could make a reasonable decision.*

Jan quickly changed her shirt then slipped into a clean pair of jeans. She ran a comb through her hair, and grabbed her jacket on the way out, just in case she needed it. She generally drove the car, because it just seemed easier to drive, but for where she was going, it was more appropriate to take the pickup. She wished she had someone to go with, but most women she knew either had no interest in going to a cattle auction, or they went with their husbands. Oh well, she needed to work on her independence. She had been at this Auction Mart with Don several years ago, but now that she was alone, she felt like a fish out of water.

It was about a forty-five minute drive to her destination. She rolled down her window ever so slightly, as the sun began to heat up the cab. Time passed quickly as she listened to the country music on the radio.

When she drove into the parking lot, it was full of pickups hooked onto stock trailers. After finding a place to park, she began to have second thoughts about coming. Well, she had come this far she, might as well take the next step.

There were a lot of people milling around outside and in the lunch area, but what surprised her was, there were not a lot of people in the sales area. She chose a seat on the far end of the second row, and it didn't take long for Jan to realize that cows were selling at a premium. She took out her pencil and note pad and began jotting down the prices of the young heifers, but she was aware that there could be a problem at calving time. For a while Jan lost herself in the entertaining part of the auction. She was mesmerized as she listened to the mixture of words and mumbling fillers, of the auctioneers' sales pitch, as he continued on waving and pointing at each perspective buyer.

Occasionally a wild cow would be brought through, at which time the person in the ring would duck behind a protective wall. Those were definitely cows that she didn't want.

Jan had not paid any attention to the comings and goings of the people around her. She was sitting up against the wall where she could be as inconspicuous as possible. She had lost track of time, when suddenly someone from behind tapped her on the shoulder. He stepped over the seat and sat down beside her. She was sure that he had mistaken her for someone else, as she was positive that there was no one here that would know her.

"Hi Jan," he said as he sat down beside her.

Jan's mouth dropped open and she felt a bit faint.

"I thought I recognized you when you came in. Are you selling or buying today?" he asked.

Jan swallowed hard as she tried to speak. "I-I just came to check out the prices," she sputtered, staring at him in disbelief. The twinkle in his eyes had not changed. If she could have mustered up the strength to move, she would have escaped. Instead she was numb with dread and wished that the ground would open up and swallow her. This was not how she expected her first meeting with him would be.

Austin always had a way of making Jan relax, and that was exactly what he was doing now. It was not long before he had her telling him where she lived, and about the loss of her husband.

"I am really sorry to hear that Jan, I had heard that you had gotten married," he said, but the twinkle in his eyes had now disappeared.

Time flew by, and before she knew it, the sale was over.

"If you aren't in too much of a rush, why not let me buy you some lunch?" he said, laying his hand on hers. The warmth of his hand sent a shock wave through her body.

"I don't think that is a good idea," Jan said, while pulling her hand away.

The tone of his voice changed, and the look in his eyes was now cold. "Why not?" he asked.

"If there are people around that know you, they may get the wrong idea. You know how rumors start. I don't want to cause any problems between you and your wife," she said, standing up.

"My what?" Austin questioned, stepping over the bottom row of seat before, offering his hand to her.

When she stepped over the bottom seat, her legs felt like jelly under her, and she would have tripped, if it had not been for Austin catching her. At that point she had to leave. She said a hurried good-bye, then headed out to her vehicle. Leaving Austin standing there, wondering what had just happened.

Once back in the safety of her truck, she took a deep breath. She had to get away before he tried to dredge up the past and ask questions that she did not want to answer.

She knew that he had tried to contact her before her parents sent her away because she had found one of his letters in the garbage, where her parents had thrown it.

Fear showed in her eyes as she put the key into the ignition. At the precise moment that she turned the key, someone jerked open her door. Jan gasped in shock as he grabbed her arm.

Her eyes were full of tears, which he chalked up to the loss of her husband, but right now he had some questions he wanted answered, before she disappeared on him again. He reached in, and turned off the truck, then took her keys.

"What are you doing?" she demanded.

"We need to talk," he said, pulling her out of the truck.

"About what?" she asked stupidly, while wiping the tears from her eyes.

"Leave me alone," she demanded, while trying to get him to loosen his grip on her arm.

Austin ignored her as he locked her truck, and placed her keys in his pocket.

"You don't want to cause a scene here in front of everyone, do you?" he said. His grip was beginning to hurt her arm. When she saw the look on his face, she shuddered. He was angry, and she had a good idea why. Jan noticed some people watching them, and wondered what they were thinking. She reluctantly went with him, as he led her towards his truck. Then after opening the passenger door, he ordered her to get in.

"Austin, please let me go," she pleaded.

"Just get in!" he demanded.

She finally did as he said. Before shutting the door, he saw a fearful look on her face. His voice softened. "You know I would never harm you. All I want is answers to some questions. Then I will bring you back."

Book 3 of the *Mountains and Valleys of Life*

When they drove out of the yard, Jan saw a police officer talking to the people that had watched the whole scene play out, between her and Austin. They had only driven a few blocks down the road, before she heard Austin swear softly to himself. It was then that she noticed the police car approaching from behind, with the lights flashing.

"Now what?" he said pulling over.

Jan turned as white as a sheet. She had a good idea why he was being stopped. Austin apparently had not seen, what she had in the parking lot. How was Austin going to explain this one? What would she say when the officer asked her, if everything was all right?

Austin opened his window as the officer approached. The first thing he asked for was Austin's drivers license, then after looking at it, his eyes met Jan's. "Are you all right, Miss?"

"Y-Yes sir," she said, now very nervous.

"Would you please step out of the truck, Sir?" the officer said to Austin. He then led him back to his car, and ordered him to get in the back seat. After a few moments, the officer returned to talk to Jan.

"Mam, do you know this gentleman?" he asked.

"Yes Sir, I do," she replied.

"Can you explain to me why he forcibly took you?"

"I'd rather not, but I don't want him to get in any trouble. He is really a good man. It is just that it all stems back to our youth," she said in a trembling voice.

"Would you like me to take you back to your vehicle?"

Jan hesitated for a moment before replying, "No Sir. I guess I do owe him some sort of an explanation. Maybe then we can both rest easier."

"All right Mam. If that's what you want, I will let him go," he said, before taking down her phone number and address.

When the officer opened the door and let Austin out, he said, "Sir, I will be calling the lady later on to be sure that she got home safely. If not I will come looking for you."

"I told you that all I want to do is talk to her," Austin replied.

"Well next time, I'd suggest you don't cause a scene in public," the officer told him and then returned to his car.

Austin was embarrassed, but it was no ones fault but his own. He definitely had handled this badly. Maybe he should just take her back and forget about Jan her.

When he got back into the truck the first thing Jan asked was if he was ok.

He looked at her and then burst out laughing.

"What's so funny?" she a bit annoyed.

"Well, I can either laugh or cry" he said. "I'm the one that took you forcibly and almost got thrown in Jail, and you're the one that is asking if I'm alright. I love you Jan," he said not realizing that he had verbalized it. When the officer drove by, Austin stopped laughing and turned to face her. "Jan, should I take you back, or will you please set my mind at ease, and answer some things that I need to know," he said pleading with her.

"I would prefer to go back, but perhaps we should just talk for a while. After all I wouldn't want you to get arrested, and have your wife ask you questions as to what happened," she told him.

"What's all this talk about my wife? Do you see a ring on my finger?" he snapped.

"Well, I just presumed that the woman in the hospital was…" she trailed off.

Austin looked at her then laughed. "Leave it to a woman to be jealous," he said.

"Jealous! Who's jealous?" she said angrily.

"Why, you! Who else?" He said, while reaching for her hand.

She immediately pulled her hand away. "Maybe you should take me back," she said, now wondering why she had consented to this.

"Sorry, Jan. I will behave myself, and by the way, I am not married. I do not have a lady friend, and the woman you saw me with at the hospital is my cousin. Does that clear the air between us now?" he asked.

Book 3 of the *Mountains and Valleys of Life*

Jan began to relax as they drove out into the country. She began to wonder where he was taking her, when he turned off onto a trail that looked like it would end at any moment. Then, suddenly, there was an opening that had the most breath-taking view of the mountains. Jan gasped at the beauty of it all. Austin stopped his truck then stared out the window. "It is something isn't it?" he said.

"It certainly is," she responded in total awe of it all.

They both sat in silence, neither one of them knowing what to say next.

With both hands resting on the steering wheel, Austin finally asked the dreaded question.

"Jan, why did you leave without telling me?"

A deep sadness settled over her when she answered. "I wanted to tell you, but my parents wouldn't let me out of their sight," she said, staring straight ahead.

"Why didn't you answer my letters?" he asked.

"I didn't receive them. I did find one of them in the garbage one day, but I didn't read it. It was already too late. My parents were sending me away the next day. Austin, please don't ask me to explain. It's all too painful, and I just can't talk about it now," she said biting back tears.

Austin turned to face her. When did you leave the church, and why didn't you contact me after you did? I gather the fellow you married was not of the same faith," he said.

Jan looked down at the floor of the truck and said. "Austin, you can't even begin to know what I went through since I saw you last. It was something that I would never have expected from the parents that supposedly loved me. I have never forgiven them, and I don't know if I ever can. It was about three months after I left, that I refused to wear those clothes. I will never again return to that," she said bitterly.

"It was through a mutual acquaintance that I met Don. I got a job in a restaurant, and we became good friend. Then when he asked me to marry him, I said yes." A smile crossed her face as she thought of him. "He was a good man."

"Did you love him?" Austin asked.

She looked at him in surprise. "I married him, didn't I?" she said sternly.

"That isn't what I asked." He said sternly. "Did you love him like… well…like this?" He said, suddenly grabbing her and kissing her hard on the lips.

She struggled to break free, at which time he released her. The twinkle that had returned to his eyes held her spell-bound. She knew she should look away, but she couldn't. Slowly he reached over and pulled her tightly against him. At the same time, he gently began to kiss her. This time she moaned, as she felt exhilarated by his kiss. Suddenly she pushed him away, breaking free of his grasp.

"Austin, please take me back now," she ordered.

Austin was taken aback by her reaction.

"I am sorry Jan. I didn't mean to upset you, but my feelings towards you have never changed, and I believe yours haven't either. I will take you back, and then at a later date we can continue this" he said.

"I don't think we should," she said as she moving away from him.

Austin never replied. He just reached over and gently ran his finger down the side of her face, before turning his truck around, and heading back in the direction they had come.

The parking lot was almost empty when they arrived. Austin parked his truck next to hers, then got out and opened the door for her. Taking her keys from his pocket, he unlocked the door of her truck, then leaned over and put the key in the ignition, and started it. Once she was seated safely in her vehicle, he bent over, kissed her gently on the lips then said. "Now drive safely, and we will talk again." He tipped his hat to her before closing the door.

He watched her drive away with a sinking feeling. How he wished he could have taken her home, where no one would ever hurt her like that again. What terrible thing had happened that would make her turn against her parents like that? Someday he would find out, but for now he would just have to be patient.

When Austin drove out of the parking lot, he caught sight of the police cruiser. Well, he was true to his word. He was keeping an eye out for him. He wondered if he had been watching when he said good-bye to Jan.

He was sure that both he and Jan would not sleep much that night. At least now he had a rough idea of where she lived. Later that evening, he called information to get her number. He dialed it, then waited for quite some time before she answered. He told himself that he was just making sure that she got home safely, but if he was honest with himself, the real reason was just to hear her voice again. Austin decided he would give her a bit of space for a while, but he was never going to lose track of her again.

Jan was surprised to hear from him, and told him that the police officer had called to make sure that she was all right. After a brief conversation, Austin told her that he had better call it a night, as he had a lot of work to do the following day. It was easier to talk to him on the phone because she didn't feel like she was under a microscope. Although she couldn't believe how much she had enjoyed talking to him. When he told her that he would call her again, she actually admitted to him, that she would like that. She had hesitated in giving Austin directions to her place. Later, she regretted it, as the fact was, she should have discouraged him from calling, because sooner or later he would want to know the full story. That secret must stay hidden. She did not want to leave him with the false hope of ever rekindling the fire that once burned between them.

CHAPTER 3

FOR THE NEXT MONTH, JAN was caught between never wanting to see Austin, and wondering if he would actually contact her again. A chill ran through her body. *What if someone in the old area actually found out about her past?* She wondered if he still kept in contact with the people from the area that they grew up in.

Well, why worry about what ifs? It was still hard for her to get through each day. Her life was so empty without Don. The couples they used to go out with still invited her along at times, but it just wasn't the same. She was now beginning to decline more of their invitations. She knew it was not good to just stay at home, but it was sometimes better to be lonesome at home, than to be lonesome in a group or a crowd of people.

Jan was just in the middle of making herself an evening snack, when the phone rang. It had been a gloomy day, and her hello must have reflected her feelings when she answered the phone.

"Anne, is that you?" the caller asked.

The old name caught her off guard at first. "Yes," she answered wondering, who the man at the other end could be.

"I was wondering if I could come see you some time," he asked.

"I'm sorry, but I don't know who you are," she replied.

"Oh, I guess I should have said who I was first. This is John Remple."

Book 3 of the *Mountains and Valleys of Life*

There was dead silence on her end of the phone. *It can't be him!* She said to herself. Just when she thought that things couldn't get worse, they did.

"Anne, are you still there?" he asked.

"Y-yes, I am still here," she said, wondering how he had found her number. He was the last person in the world that she ever wanted to see again.

"I know I probably surprised you, but maybe sometime you would let me take you out for supper," he said.

Jan was contemplating how she was going to get out of this one. She figured that, surely by now, he would have been married. Why would he be calling her now? That marriage had been called off long ago. The icy grip of fear engulfed her whole body. *What had here parents told him when, they sent her away.* Dear God, please don't let this be happening, she pleaded.

"I'm sorry John, but I don't think that would be such a good idea," she told him.

Now there was silence on his end. Jan gripped her chest and she felt her heart beat wildly. She grabbed a chair and almost fell on the floor, as she sat on the edge of the seat. *Why doesn't he say something?*

Then came the reply she did not expect. By the tone of his voice, she knew he was not happy, and she felt he was having a hard time controlling his emotions.

"Well, I will let you think on it for a bit, then I will come see you," he said before hanging up.

Surely he didn't know where she lived, and yet, he did have her phone number. How did he find her? Then a strange thought occurred to her. Austin surely wouldn't have told him, as he had disliked the man, more then she did.

The concern about John's phone call soon evaporated, as she was now concentrated on the pain that gripped her chest. When the teakettle began to whistle, she got up and turned off the stove. She slowly found her way into the living room, where she sat on the old rocking chair. She must try to relax. She felt like someone was sitting on her chest. When she moved her head, the room felt like it was spinning out of control. The doctor had given her a nitro spray to try if she ever had a problem, but it was in the medicine chest, and right now she didn't think she could make it that far. *Just relax*, she said to herself.

She laid her head back and closed her eyes. All she could feel was the pounding in her chest. It had done something similar to this once before, and it did eventually calm down, but she did not have this much pain with it. She reached over and grabbed a near by cushion then hugged it for all she was worth. That did not work, so she dropped it, and just rested her hands on the arms of the chair. *Relax*, she told herself again.

She thought that she heard a noise outside, but right now she was not about to get up to find out what it was. As she sat there, she could gradually feel that it was beginning to ease up a bit. It was then that she realized that someone was knocking on her door. Oh well, they would just have to come back another day. She was not going to move just yet.

Then a horrific thought came to her mind. Surely it wasn't John. *Don't be silly*, she chided herself, as her heart once again beat wildly. The pain in her chest was now horrific. Tears began to run down her cheeks, when she squeezed her eyes shut. It was then that she heard a man's voice call her name. "It can't be," she said softly.

Then she heard, "Jan, what's wrong?" Jan opened her eyes to find Austin kneeling beside her. She began to moan, and that was all she could remember, until she woke up in the hospital.

She could feel the warmth of someone holding her hand, but she was afraid to open her eyes. Who was the person that was standing beside her? She opened her eyes slightly.

"Austin!" she said trying to sit up.

"Just lie still," he said, pushing her back down. "You gave me quite a scare young lady. Don't you ever pull that again," he said with a concerned look on his face.

Jan felt like she was being strangled with all the lines and tubes that seemed to be attached to her. "What's all this?" she asked.

"You've had a slight heart attack, my dear. I knew I should have taken you home, so that I could keep an eye on you. What triggered this? Have you had problems like this before?" Austin asked her.

Jan suddenly remembered the phone call, and instantly her heart began to race as she began to look very pale.

"Calm down, Jan. What ever it is, I promise I will look after it," he said reassuring her as the nurse entered the room.

"Oh Austin. It was horrible," she cried.

The nurse quickly left the room while Austin tried to convince her that whatever happen couldn't have been that bad. "Jan, just tell me so I can help you," he said brushing some hair gently away from her face.

"I-I-I got a call from…" she stuttered.

"From who?" he said anxiously.

The sound of his voice seemed to be what got through to her. She must get control of herself. She said almost inaudibly. "From John Remple."

"Who is he?" Austin asked, just as the nurse came in to give Jan a shot to calm her down. Suddenly it struck him like a bolt of lightning, as he looked at Jan. "Surely not him?"

Jan just nodded her head as the quick acting drug began to take effect. Jan was not sure if she heard Austin correctly. Everything was beginning to get very faint. What she thought she heard was, "he will never again come between us." After that, she thought she heard the word marriage. She tried to talk but nothing came out as she drifted off into a deep sleep.

Once she fell asleep, her heart rate went back to its normal rhythm. Austin sat down on the chair near her bed. It was no wonder she was upset. It was like time had reversed itself, and the same thing was happening again. This time she was not going to disappear on him, and he would not let John disrupt their lives. He was going to take Jan home with him. He knew that she still cared for him, otherwise she would not have just said yes, when he proposed to her. He would, sooner or later, get her to tell him what had happened from the day they last met in the coulee, right up to the present.

Austin began to wonder what John's motive was for calling Jan. Had he never married, as far as Austin knew, and must have just found out that she was single again? Did he really believe that she would ever consider marrying him? Fat chance there was of that. From Jan's reaction she must have been extremely frightened by him. Well, soon that would be rectified if he had anything to say about it. He really did not want a big wedding, but they would have to talk about that once Jan was released.

The nurse told Austin that Jan would be asleep for quite some time, so he decided to go back to Jan's farm. He had been working long hours at the ranch lately, and could sure use some rest. It also struck him that he had not locked up Jan's house. He was sure that she would not mind if he stayed there.

On his way, he called Ted. He was glad that all the cows had calved, but still, they needed to be checked. Austin had only told Ted that he had taken a friend to the hospital, and that he would be away for a few days. Just until he knew that everything would be fine. Austin would fill him in later, if or when he felt like it.

When Austin walked into Jan's home, he instantly felt like he had stepped back in time. Her furnishings were modest, and everything was clean and in order.

It was the picture of Jan and her husband that made him uncomfortable. He picked it up to take a closer look at the man she had married. He was slightly taller than Jan, and was not a bad looking fellow either. Austin felt a twinge of jealousy when he thought of her being with another man. *Never again*, he said to himself.

He placed the picture back on the table. There were a couple of pictures of an elderly couple that he did not recognize. He presumed they were of her late husband's parents. When he looked around, he realized that there were no pictures of her family. He knew that cameras were frowned upon, but the occasional picture would have surely been taken at some point. It was like she had cut all ties with her side of the family.

Austin was worn out from work and, now, the added stress. He laid down on the couch, and the next thing he knew he was waking up with a jolt, just as the sun was beginning to set. It took him a few moments to finally figure out where he was. He was beginning to feel rather hungry, seeing as he had not eaten anything since breakfast. Suddenly his thoughts went to Jan and her health problem. He grabbed his hat, which he had laid on the kitchen table. Then on his way out, he spotted some keys hanging on the side of the cupboard. He grabbed the ones that he thought looked like possible house keys. *Wouldn't you know it?* He said to himself, as the fifth key out of the six finally turned the lock.

When Austin walked into Jan's room, she was as surprised to see him, as he was to see her sitting up on the edge of the bed.

He went over and took her hand in his, as he bent over to kiss her on the forehead.

"You are looking better than the last time I saw you," he said, releasing her hand, before sitting down on the chair.

Jan sat the silently, as she finally realized that what she had thought to be a dream, was actually true. He had rescued her in her time of need.

After you went to sleep, I went back to your place and had a bit of a nap myself. I hoped you wouldn't begrudge your future husband a bit of rest," he said winking at her.

"My what?" she blurted out.

"I told you before I left, I would never let anyone come between us again, and when I asked you to marry me, you said yes. Now don't tell me you don't remember that!" He said, joking with her.

Blaze of Fury

Jan put her hand on the side of her face. It seemed to be getting very warm. She remembered most of what he had said, except for the part about the proposal. "Austin, I-I…" she stuttered.

"Don't tell me you don't remember?" he said.

"Austin, I do remember some of what you said, but I don't remember the last part," she said apologizing.

Austin moved his chair closer to her. He took her hand in his and looked into her eyes.

Jan looked away, but Austin put his hand under her chin and turned her head so that she had no choice but to look at him.

"Jan, look at me and tell me you don't still love me," he said.

She could never look at him and lie, because he always seemed to be able to know if she did.

How she would have loved to throw her arms around him, and tell him how much she still cared, but instead tears filled her eyes as she said, "I can't."

"Well then, if you still love me, there is no reason why we shouldn't get married. You know how I feel about you, and I can't keep an eye on you, if you're here and I'm at the ranch." he told her.

"Austin, please. There are some things that you…" she said squeezing her eyes shut. Austin, it's to soon."

Austin let go of her hand. When Jan opened her eyes, she saw that devastated look on his face. She had hurt him deeply once before, and she could not bear to see that look again. She reached over and laid her hand on the side of his face.

"Austin" she said slowly, "I don't think there has ever been a day, that I haven't thought about you. I do love you very much, but there is something that happened years ago, that I couldn't forgive myself for. Not only that, you may not be able to forgive me either." Tears streamed down her cheeks as all those memories flash back.

"Jan, I don't care what happened years ago. All I know, and care about, is that I love you and you love me. When, or if, you ever want to tell me about it, I know our love for each other will get us through." Austin got up and stood beside Jan. He looked at her for a moment, then bent over and kissed her gently on the lips.

"Jan, I will not pressure you if you really feel that you don't love me enough to marry me. I want you to know that there is nothing that you could tell me, that I would not forgive you for. If God can forgive us, what right do we have not to forgive one another? Besides, after we are married, you don't have to worry about John calling again," Austin said.

The colour drained from her face. "I don't want to ever see, or talk to him," she said, as laying back down.

"Let's forget about him. First things first, I will not leave here until I know you are feeling better. I was wondering if you would mind if I stayed at your place, while I your here. Then when you get out, if you have no one to stay with you a few days, you will come home with me," he said.

"Of course you may stay at my house, but really, I will be fine. You really don't have to worry about me. I am sure you have a lot of work to do at home," she insisted.

"I guess I should tell you a bit about myself, and where I live," he said.

"Well, I gather from looking at you, that you are either working on a ranch, or you own one." It was then that she saw the strained look on his face. "I'm sorry Austin. I feel that maybe you have enough on your plate without worrying about me," she told him.

"Just say yes to my proposal, and that would take a big load off my shoulders," he said, squeezing her hand.

"Austin, please give me some time. It has been a while, and maybe we shouldn't rush into this." How she wished that she could share that one dark secret with him. Then, perhaps, she could say yes. On the other hand, though maybe he would change his mind about her.

Austin spent half his time in the hospital, and the rest of his time fixing things in and around Jan's house. He was disappointed knowing he must go home soon. Before he left, she told Austin that her neighbor's, seventeen, year old daughter would be staying with her for the next five days. As she told Austin, it would not be appropriate for her to stay with him, even if he promised to behave himself.

However, she did promise that she would someday come to see where he lived.

* * *

It did not take Jan long to get back to her old self. Only now, she walked with a spring in her step. Maybe life was worth living after all. Austin called her almost every night, and for the nights he missed, he had apologized. One afternoon, Austin told her that he was going to be in her neck of the woods, and wondered if she would meet him at the restaurant on the highway just east of Carstairs. He could not give her an exact time but somewhere between eleven and twelve.

She was so excited to see him again, that she got there well before eleven. She sat there drinking coffee, while looking out the window. There was a man that came in around eleven fifteen and, as they were both alone he struck up a conversation with her. He asked if she was there by herself, and at that moment she was glad that she could truthfully say that she was waiting for someone. However, he picked up his cup of coffee and joined her at her table.

Jan felt a bit uncomfortable with this situation, but he did seem harmless. He had a short, neatly trimmed, beard that sort of reminded her of the men back home. She decided that he was probably just looking for someone to talk too. They had been chatting for about fifteen minutes about the weather and farming, until Austin walked in.

Austin's reaction to seeing Jan sitting with another man was one of jealousy. "Hi Jan," he said bending over to give her a brief kiss on the lips before sitting down next to her. *That should be enough of an indication to this guy as to what the relationship was between us.* "I see you had someone to keep you company while you were waiting," he said, laying his hat on the chair beside him.

Jan was taken aback by his public affection towards her, but that special look Austin gave her made her feel all warm and tingly inside.

"We were just chatting by the way, I don't even know your name," she said, looking at the man across from her.

Austin's eyes met the icy stare of the other man. He could see nothing but hatred in them. Either he was not impressed with Austin kissing Jan in public, or he had not expected a man to interrupt his time with her.

He quickly picked up his cup, then turned to Jan and said, "Nice takin' to yaw," before going to pay for his coffee. He left without a backwards glance.

Austin had an uneasy feeling about that man. He looked vaguely familiar, but he couldn't place where he had seen him before.

He warned Jan about talking to strangers, and even though he and Jan kept busy talking, he could not get this man out of his mind.

Austin asked Jan, if she would consider coming out to his ranch. "I may put you to work, if you feel up to it," he told her.

"Doing what?" she asked.

"Well, after me and Ted get back from moving cattle, it would be nice to come home to a good home cooked-meal," he said, then quickly added, "I don't mean to imply that is the only reason I want you to come."

"Well, they say the way to a man's heart is through his stomach," she said smiling.

Austin reached for her hand. "You have already reached my heart." He said that with that twinkle in his eye.

Jan quickly changed the subject.

"Who is Ted?" she asked, looking at him.

"He's is a friend of mine. He helps me when-ever, I need an extra hand," he replied.

"Would I be able to go riding with you?" she asked.

"Well, maybe later, but a full day for riding would not be advisable. I don't want to haul you back into the hospital again," he told her.

"Tell you what. If you promise to let me go riding with you, I will cook your meals," she teased.

Austin could hardly believe what he was hearing. He had hoped against hope that she would come, and now he finally got the answer he was waiting for.

"Let's see. Today is Tuesday so I will come pick you up Thursday night, then we can get started early on Friday morning. Pack some warm clothes if you want to go riding - the weather can still be chilly," he told her.

Jan sat quiet for some time.

"Jan is something wrong?" he asked.

"It's just, well, I never considered the overnight thing," she admitted.

"Jan, I have a good sized home and a couple of spare bedrooms. I told you before, I promise I will try to behave, and who do you plan to meet that will care anyhow? I'm sure the cows won't mind, he added.

"It's just that... oh, Austin I'm just afraid," she said.

"Hon, I love you, and would never do anything to hurt you. You surely know that by now," he told her.

She looked up at him, when he used that term of endearment, "I know that Austin, but I don't want to hurt you," she said.

"Jan, I know you well enough, that you would never intentionally do that," he told her.

"It's a date then," he said, taking her hand in his.

"All right Austin, I will come," she said with some reservation.

Austin suddenly looked at his watch. He had not realized how late it had gotten. He had a couple of bulls in his trailer, and it was high time he got them home.

After making a few last arrangements, he told Jan to finish her coffee, but he had to go.

When Austin went to pay the bill, he asked the waitress if she knew the man that had been there earlier. She told him that he came in occasionally to meet a lady, whom she believed to be his sister. As for his name, she said the lady called him by a strange name, something like Ho-Hon. Austin thought for a while then, quickly said. "You don't mean Johan?" (Johan translation to English, is John)

"That's it!" she replied.

Austin could feel his blood pressure rise. He knew there was something familiar about that guy. It must have blown John away, when Austin walked in and gave Jan that kiss. John had probably recognized him, henceforth the hatred in his eyes.

Not once in the past four or five years, had Austin ran into any of the people that he knew from his childhood. Why did it have to happen now? Jan had definitely not recognized him, and he wasn't about to tell her now. It would only upset her again. He was glad that he had told Jan to get caller display on her phone, so that she could monitor her calls.

Austin walked over to Jan and gave her a good-bye kiss, then whispered, "I love you," in her ear. Then he was gone.

Just as she waved good-bye to Austin, she had the strange feeling that someone was watching her. She turned her head to see who it was. "Oh, did you forget something?" she asked, as the same man that had sat with her earlier stood glaring at her. Only now, the look on his face frightened her. When he sat down beside her, she wanted to get up and run. Instead, she wrapped her hands around her coffee cup, like her life depended on it.

"Anne, stay away from that man. He is no good for you," he said.

Jan's mouth dropped open at the use of her old name, she hadn't been called that since she left the place she had grown up in. Who was he and how did he know who she was?

"I heard your man died. I think it would be good for you to come back home, and make it good with the church, and with me. It is time you held true to our agreement. I will still take you for my wife, even after what you did. I will teach you how to be a good wife, and mother to our kids," he said going on and on about how he would make her into the wife he thought she should be. She began to wonder if this man had escaped from some institution, or he had her mixed up with another person called Anne.

Suddenly, something about him made her look closer. She quickly, got up and headed for the door. She had taken a couple of steps outside, when he caught up to her. When he grabbed her arm firmly, his finger dug into her flesh. "Let me go!" she cried, bumping into someone behind her as she tried to pull free.

"Having a problem, Miss?" the man behind her asked.

Jan knew she had heard that voice before. "Yes. This man won't leave me alone."

"Let go of her, Sir!" came the voice behind her. The authority in his voice made her look up. *Oh great, it would have to be, the same police officer that tried to rescue her from Austin.*

John's hold tightened on her arm. "This is between us," John snapped, pulling her towards him.

"Let me go! You're hurting me," she said now almost in tear.

It was then that Jan heard the sound of gravel flying, as someone slid to a stop near by.

"Mister I would suggest that you let her go. The officer said, looking directly at Jan.

"Yes please!" She said now fearful that something terrible would happen, if John got her alone.

"You'd better let her go John, if you know what's good for you," Austin said from behind her.

The officer gave Austin a direct order to stay back, while watching John's every move. Austin had a hard time trying to control, himself.

"Mister, if you don't want to get in trouble with the law, you'd better let her go," the officer said sternly as he walked over to loosen the grip that John had on her arm.

John's face reflected the anger that he had for both Austin and Jan, when she rushed to Austin's side. In one swift move, he took a swing at Austin, only to miss and hit Jan, knocking her to the ground. Austin quickly checked to make sure that Jan was not hurt. He was about to take a round out of John, but the Police officer had already hand cuffed him, and was now leading him to the police car.

Jan tenderly placed her hand over the right side of her chest, where John's fist had struck her. Austin led her over to his truck. Once there, he opened the top button of her shirt before she could stop him. "What do you think you are doing?" she snapped.

"I'm just checking to see that you are alright." Jan careful opened two more buttons, then slowly pulled her shirt to the side, trying not to reveal too much. Austin moved her hand away to see a large red mark on the upper part of her breast. There was a slight break in the skin from the metal clip of her bra. Austin swore under his breath as she closed up her shirt. "I should never have left you here. I thought I saw him standing beside you when I left," Austin said.

"Did you know who he was?" she asked in surprise.

"When I left, I asked the waitress if she knew who he was. I thought there was something familiar about him. He must have a sister around here somewhere. The waitress said she had called him Johan, that's when I realized who he was. I was sure that he had left, other-wise I would never have left you here alone." Austin said, just as the police officer walked towards them.

He looked at Jan. "I hope all my time won't be taken up rescuing you from all your suitors. Can you explain what just happened here?" he asked.

It was Austin who gave a brief explanation of their past, and how John fit into the picture.

The officer then asked Jan what John had said to her just before, she tried to leave.

After Austin listening to what she told the officer he began to fear, for Jan's safety.

Jan did not want to press charges; all she wanted was to never see him again.

"Well, all I can do is take him to the station, finger print him, and give him a possible assault charge, then let him go. Maybe a few hours in jail, will cool him off," the officer said.

"Most likely it will make him even angrier then he already is," Jan replied.

"By the way, Sir," the officer said, turning to look at Austin very sternly, "I want to warn you never to drive that way in a parking lot again. You could have hit someone."

"I'll watch it next time," Austin said.

"There better not be a next time," he said turning to walk back to his police cruiser.

Austin turned to Jan. "Just stay here a minute," he said closing the door to his truck.

Jan wondered what he was up to. It was some time before he came out of the restaurant. Then he walked over to her truck to make sure that it was locked. When he got back to his truck, he told her to get in, which she did without thinking. When inside Austin stuck his key into the ignition, and started it.

"Have you got the keys for your truck," he asked.

She checked in her purse then told him that she did.

"You're coming home with me. I need to get these bulls home, and I won't take the chance of John coming after you tonight."

"I can't Austin. I don't have a change of clothes or, any other personal things," she told him.

He put the truck in gear, not willing to listen to any excuses. "Any personal items you need, we can pick up in town later. As for clothes, you can wear some of my shirts, and maybe even some of my jeans. You may have to cinch up the belt a bit more so they don't fall off. If the belt is too big, there is always a chunk of bale twine," he said, glancing at the scared look on her face.

He reached over and pulled her closer to him. He placed his arm around her, and gave her a squeeze before placing both hands back on the steering wheel. "It will be fun, you'll see," he said with a big grin on this face.

It was that look that he gave her that put her at ease. They drove through Calgary and headed south down along highway 22. She had no idea where he lived, or what to expect when they got there. The ordeal with John had taken its toll on her, and she finally resigned to her situation. Without realizing what she was doing, she laid her head on Austin's shoulder, and he responded by placing his hand on her leg. It was all so natural.

Never before had Austin wanted anything as badly as he wanted Jan. He must convince her to marry him and soon.

Jan dozed off for a while. She did not wake up until they stopped at a little store in town.

"Sorry to disturb your nap, but this is our last stop, before we head out to the ranch." He pulled out two twenty- dollar bills from his wallet and handed them to her. "Go pick out some things that you will need for the next five days or so," he said.

"I don't want your money. I have enough to get what I need," she said sliding over to the door.

"Take it!" he said sternly.

When their eyes met, Jan decided that perhaps she should appease him, even though it felt strange taking money from another man. She would buy only the things she knew she really needed, like toothpaste, a toothbrush, shampoo etc. That way she would be able to give him back the change.

"I hope you won't be too long, because I got these bulls back on solid ground." he told her.

When Jan got back fifteen minutes later, she could see how restless Austin was. His day had not gone as well as he'd planned. There were a few things that had to be done before his day was over, which meant his time with Jan this evening would, be limited.

When they left town, they headed west. Jan sat back, all the while looking at the sights around her. She wanted to ask Austin how much farther they had to go, but he seemed to be deep in his own thoughts. She decided to just pay attention to the road, in case she had to find his place again. The rest of the trip was driven in silence. The closer they got, the more nervous Jan became. What if Austin found out about her secret? Would he be able to forgive her? Those questions continued to haunt her. She knew, only too well, that she would have to tell him before they got married. That was if he still wanted to marry her, once he found out.

Jan's breast, was now getting quite sore, and just as she laid her hand gently on the bruise, Austin glanced over at her.

"Is everything all right?" he asked.

"Yes, I am fine. It just stings a bit," she said.

"We'll have to have another look at it when we get to the ranch. It's just a couple miles farther now," he said.

"Thanks, but I think I can look after it myself," she told him.

"Bashful, are we?" he asked.

When their eyes met, Jan could feel her face getting warm as it took on a rose colored glow.

Chapter 4

When they finally reached their destination, Jan was not prepared for what she saw.

She had noticed that the lay out of the land, since they left town, was unique. It went from gradual slopes, to large cliffs, to beautiful valleys. The farther west they went, the trees were in more abundance. The area was definitely ranch country. It was obvious that drilling was prevalent in the area, because of the numerous pumps, which she related with sucking the life out of the earth. Yes, she knew that in this day and age it was a necessity, but here it spoiled the countryside.

"Well, does it meet with your approval?" Austin asked stopping near his house.

Jan was so shocked that she was speechless. All she could think was, *Austin must be well off to have a place like this.* There, on the side of a hill that overlooked a long gradual valley, sat a very large log ranch style house, with cedar shakes on the roof. It fit perfectly in its setting. There was a bluff of trees that shelter the house, but not enough to obscure the view.

"Would you like to wait here at the house, or help me get these critters unloaded?" he asked.

She did not want to go into his home alone. "I'll give you a hand," she told him nervously.

Austin continued down the trail that sloped off to the left. Jan was speechless at what she saw. It was like driving into another farmyard. There were a couple of large shops, and a large hip-roof barn with numerous corrals. It was then that the horses in the small pasture next to the corrals caught her eye, but one in particular. He was black as midnight and as the late afternoon sun shone on him, he gave off a bluish shimmer.

"He is beautiful," she said softly.

Austin looked at her, then in the direction of her gaze. He swelled with pride when he said. "Yeah. He is something, ain't he? But don't ever go near him alone. He can be dangerous until he knows he can trust you," Austin cautioned her.

Austin backed his trailer up to one of the empty corrals. He was about to get out to open the gate when Jan stopped him. "No, let me get it," she said jumping out of the truck. Austin backed the trailer up after she opened the gate. Jan started to unlatch the trailer door, when Austin stopped her.

"Let me do that. Just stand back because I never trust a new batch of animals, especially bulls. Even if they seem calm enough, once you put them in a strange place anything can happen," he said, waiting until she was a safe distance away. Once the trailer door swung open, the first bull slowly made his way out. When Austin opened the center gate of the trailer, he was surprised to see that bull down. He was sure that both bulls were sound when he picked him up. *I should have checked them before we left the restaurant*, he said angrily to himself. He then got in and gave the bull a kick with his boot a couple of times before it slowly got to its feet. He was stiff, but it looked like he would be fine.

"Will he be alright?" Jan asked.

"Yes, he will be just fine. I should have checked them before," he said.

"I'm sorry, Austin," she said blaming herself for the delay.

"Why should you be sorry?" he said, closing the trailer door.

"You would have had them home long before this, if it weren't for me," she said.

"Don't be silly. How were we to know what would happen. Besides, John did me a favour," he said, smiling.

"How do you figure that?" she asked.

"Well, you're here, aren't you?" he said before moving his truck ahead.

She stood there, staring at the trailer, when suddenly she realized that the bulls were heading in her direction. She quickly grabbed the gate and swung it shut. *Wow that was close* she though, while sliding the iron rod securely into it's slot.

"Get in. I'll unhook the trailer then, take you back up to the house. I have a few chores to do before I can give you my full attention," he said, parking his trailer in its rightful spot.

It was obvious from what she saw, that Austin liked things neat and in order. When they got back to the house, Jan got very quiet. It just didn't feel right to stay in a man's home, without being married.

"I hope you find everything to your liking," he said when he swung open the front door.

Jan was about to step in when Austin scooped her up in his arms and carried her into the house.

Jan was taken aback by what he had done. All she could do was wrap her arms around his neck. When he set her down, just inside the door, their eyes met. Austin bent over, and gave her a brief kiss before she quickly removed her arms from around his neck.

"Why did you do that?" Jan asked.

"Do what? Carry you in, or kiss you?" he said looking at her with that sparkle in his eyes.

"The first one," she said looking away.

"Well, that is what you are supposed to do when you bring your life partner home," he said.

"That's for when you bring your bride home," she said, not wanting to look at him.

"Well, let's just call this a practice run," He said, putting his arm around her as he led her into the kitchen.

Jan couldn't believe what she saw. Something here felt oddly familiar. The kitchen had lots of cupboards and counter space. It also held a good-sized table, which so many kitchens of the day lacked. The living room was spacious, with a large rock-faced fireplace that went up though the vaulted ceiling. This room was definitely masculine. It had a beautiful leather couch and chairs, accessorized with large wooden end tables, and a matching coffee table. What caught her eye first was, the view from the living room window. There were a lot of cattle grazing in the valley below, and just beyond was a hill mainly covered with trees. The most breath taking view was watching, the afternoon sun glisten on the snow covered peaks of the Rocky Mountains.

"Oh Austin, it's so beautiful, it just... well, there are no words to describe it," she said.

Austin placed his arm around her waist as he stood beside her. "It is something, isn't it?" They both stood there in silence for a few moments. "Come, I'll show you the rest of the house," Austin told her.

He showed her the two spare bedrooms, of which he told her the latter was hers for the duration of her visit. "Unless you wish to stay with me here," he said leading her into a bedroom that she instantly knew was his. The smell of his aftershave and cologne filled the room. This was Austin's domain, and she felt very uncomfortable here. There were a few pairs of dirty Jeans and socks lying on the floor, and on the chair were some shirts, also in need of a washing. One thing his bedroom had, that the other didn't, was a full bathroom.

"Sorry. I hadn't planned on company," he said.

"Don't worry about it. I am amazed at how clean your home is... for as busy as you must be," she said.

"It helps to close the doors and use as little space as possible," he said.

All the bedroom furniture was sturdy, but the rooms lacked proper curtains and bedding.

Austin showed her a very large bathroom, which included a big Jacuzzi. He gave her quick instructions of how to operate it, before leading her to the laundry room. Here, again, there was ample cupboard and counter space, but it was definitely in need of some TLC. *Well, the least I can do while here, is to do some cleaning*, she said to herself.

"There is a basement also, if you care to go exploring. Just make yourself at home," he said, taking her in his arms. "I'm glad you are finally here," he said looking deep into her eyes.

Jan, now spellbound, as she placed her arms around his waist. Her heart raced when he kissed her. At the same time, a sharp pain shot through her bruise breast. She moaned as she returned his kisses.

Austin released her and backed away. " I'm sorry Jan. I promised you that I would behave myself. I better get my chores done, and then later we can talk," he said, running his finger down the side of her face, before heading out the door.

Jan stood there thinking. *This was wrong. I should have gone home before...* Then she remembered the look John gave her, and the words he had said. She shuddered to think of what would happen, if she were ever alone with him.

The pain in her breast brought her back to the present. It felt hard to the touch.

Jan found her way back to the bathroom, and took off her shirt and bra. She was shocked to find the entire top of her breast swelled up and black and blue. There was also a streak of dried blood that had come from a cut in her skin, near the metal piece on her bra strap. She found a clean cloth in a drawer. She soaked it first in warm water, then carefully wiped away the blood.

Then after soaking the cloth in very cold water, she placed it over the swelled and hardened part of the bruise. She squeezed her eyes tightly shut as it was now, very painful. She was thankful that his fist had not struck her in the face. She stood there with her head leaned back, hoping that the cold would ease the pain and swelling.

Suddenly she felt as if she was being watched. Jan opened her eyes then, looked towards the open door. Jan was now angry with herself, as she quickly grabbed her shirt to cover up. She had being so used to living alone, that she had been so careless as to not close the bathroom door.

Austin went over to her and once again pulled her hand away from her bruised breast.

"What, do you make a habit of doing this?" she demanded covering it up again.

"I am just checking to see how bad it is," he said, taking a pouch from the drawer. "Here fill this with ice from the fridge," he said handing it to her. "I'm use to dealing with all kinds of problems with my cows," he said, reaching for his old hat that lay on the end of the counter.

"I'm not one of your cows," she yelled after him as he headed back outside. Jan heard him laugh as he closed the door. She quickly shut, and locked the door before getting dressed. She then picked up the pouch and went to the fridge to fill it up. While walking around the house, she held the ice pack on her bruise. She was now feeling restless, so she decided to go to work cleaning up the laundry room. Once that was done, she wondered if Austin would mind if she went into his room to get his dirty clothes. *Well, if he felt he had the right to check on her bruise, then there should be nothing wrong with my going into his room to gather up his dirty laundry.*

From habit, she first checked out his pockets, which held some change, a half pocket of fence staples, a few screws and bolts, and even an unused condom. She dropped it on the dresser next to the other objects. It hurt when she thought that perhaps he had brought some other women here, otherwise why would he have it. Things were moving too fast. She had to keep her distance from him. Then she remembered the secret that she withheld. She had keep her mind occupied, or she felt that she would break.

She had cried enough tears in the past, and she didn't want that wound opened that wide again.

It was almost suppertime, so after Jan placed the second load of clothes in the washing machine, she went to check out the fridge. She found some steaks in the fridge and potatoes in the crisper, and frozen vegetables in the freezer. She was sure that Austin would have worked up an appetite by the time he got back. She had not asked him when he would want supper, but he had told her that afternoon that he had plenty of work to do. While waiting for supper to cook, she folded up the first load of clothes and placed them neatly on the chair in Austin's room.

By the time the sun began to set, she had cleaned up the laundry room and the main bathroom and had finished two loads of laundry. She had cleaned most of the kitchen, and was now waiting for Austin to come in for supper.

Jan stood looking out the living room window, watching the changing colors of the amazing sunset. She did not hear Austin come in behind her.

Austin's heart ached to hold her as he stood watching her, but he knew that he had to keep his distance. They loved each other and that he knew, but something was keeping Jan from totally being at peace with their relationship. He had to find out what it was, and soon. The thought of, what would happen, when or if, John ever caught up with Jan, scared him. Even though the men in the community where they were brought up were, the dominant person in the relationships, most of them were good to their wives. However, he had seen and heard that some were very cruel, violent, and very possessive, when it came to their wives. From the statement that Jan gave the officer, about what John had said to her, it was quite likely that he fit in that category. It was a Godsend that she had left the area for whatever the reason was. It made him shudder to think of what her life may have been like, if she had stayed to marry that man.

"Beautiful, isn't it?" Austin said.

Jan jumped at the unexpected sound of his voice.

"Oh, I didn't hear you come in," she said, watching the last of the pink and orange turn to a dim glow.

"I'm sorry to be so late. It sure smelt good when I came into the house," he said.

"I figured you would be hungry," she told him, now somewhat distant.

Austin looked at her. "What's wrong Jan," he asked. She had been so happy earlier. What could have happened since he left?

"Jan, are you upset because of what I did and said, in the bathroom?" he asked.

"No, not really. Although you were out of line," she said looking at him.

For a moment he thought she was back to her usual self, but then he saw the sadness in her eyes. She now became very quiet.

"Jan, are you going to tell me what I've done?" he asked.

"No, your business is your own," she said, going out into the kitchen, and began to put the food on the table.

"It looks good Jan. Thank you," he said, before giving thanks to God for the food, and for their protection.

They ate in virtual silence until Austin could take it no longer.

"Jan, if we ever plan to make a life together, we have to be able to communicate, and if there is a problem, we have to be able to talk it out," he told her.

"You are pretty sure of yourself, aren't you?" she said, starting to clear the table.

Austin jumped up, grabbed the plates out of her hands and dropped them in the sink. Then grabbing her by the shoulders, he looked into her eyes. "Jan, I love you and I know that you love me. I want you to be my wife, and I want to know why you won't commit fully," he said.

"You have to give me time, Austin. You don't know me, and apparently there are things that I don't know about you," she said sadly.

"All you have to do is ask, and I will tell you anything you want to know," he said touching the side of her face.

The thought of the condom in his pocket made her turn away. "I have dishes to do," she said.

"I'll help you," he told her.

She wanted him to leave her alone, so she did her best to convince him that things were better and that he should just let her do her job. He could just sit down and rest and tell her about what he had been doing. That way, if he did most of the talking, she could just listen. It seemed to have worked, although at times she began wonder if he had caught on to what she was doing. Occasionally, she did get caught up in his conversation and forgot that she was angry with him. When she was done he looked at her and said. "I knew you couldn't stay mad at me forever."

"I'm not mad, just disappointed," she said instantly sorry for what she had said.

Now it was Austin's turn for silence. He had no idea what she was talking about. Austin left the room for a while then returned, with some shirts and a few pair of jeans that were too small for him. "Here are some clothes you should be able to make due with while you are here. I'll just throw them on your bed. It will be an early day tomorrow, so I think I will turn in early. If you like to read, there are some books on the shelf in your closet," he said.

Jan took that as a hint that they were done talking for tonight. She went first to the washroom, and then to her room, while Austin locked the front door and turned off the lights.

Jan decided to use one shirt as a nightshirt, but she wondered what she would use for undergarments. She could wash them out, or go without a bra, but tonight she did not want to do that. She went through the pile of clothes, and was surprised to find a couple pair of new mans briefs. She found this embarrassing, and wished that she could go home. Not only that, she had to get her truck. It was not safe to just leave it sitting there. She would tell Austin tomorrow that it was best for her to leave. She couldn't hide from John forever, and besides, she was certain that he did not know where she lived.

Jan opened the closet and found some hangers to hang up the clothes that Austin had laid on the bed. Then, after getting undressed she put on Austin's T-shirt. It was then that she thought of Don. He was a good man, but there was one big difference between him and Austin, and that was the passion between them. If she had been actually honest with herself, she would have had to admit that Austin was, and always would be her only true love.

Jan opened the other door of the closet to look for the books that he had told her about. Her mouth dropped open at what she saw. She slowly reached in unhooked the hanger, and looked closely at the shirt and pair of jeans. She reached up to take down the cowboy hat and placed it on her head. On the floor were the boots. She laid them on the bed, before sobbing into her pillow.

Suddenly, there was a knock on the door. Jan quickly sat up but before she could say anything, the door sprang open and Austin walked in. He flung the condom at her and said,

"If this is what you are mad about, I just want to inform you that it's not mine. I picked it up down by the corral. It probable fell out of Ted's pocket, and if you don't believe me, you can ask him tomorrow. I thought you knew me better than that," he said, now angry with her for believing the worst of him, and at himself for not throwing it out.

It was then that he saw the clothes lying on the bed beside her. Jan's eyes were red from crying. "Jan," he said now at a loss for words. Jan turned to sob into her pillow again. He came over and laid a hand on her shoulder. "Maybe I should take these things out of here," he said picking up the shirt and hat.

"No," Jan said, hanging on to the jeans, "Just leave them," she said trying to get herself under control. "Those days were the happiest days of my life until..." she said, biting back tears. "Why did you keep them?" she asked sadly.

"Probably for the same reason, Jan. I never did get over you either." Austin pulled down a box that was up by his hats. "Look in here Jan," he said handing it to her.

Jan wiped away her tears, than opened the box. She unfolded the paper that was in it and studied it very closely. "It can't be," she said. "Maybe that is why I thought something was vaguely familiar about your house." She looked up at him with a faraway look in her eyes, and said, "This is actually our dream house?"

"Yes Jan," he said, "It is."

Jan stood up, threw her arms around him and cried. He just held her as his eyes, too began to fill with tears. They should have built this ranch together, but at least she was here now, and he hoped that she would stay. "I love you, Jan," he said softly.

"Oh Austin, I have always loved you, and I always will. I have to tell you something, but… I just can't because it hurts to much," she said.

"Jan, I don't care what it is. I know that when the time is right you will tell me. I just want you as my wife, and I will never give up until you say yes," Austin said.

Jan reached over to pick up a Kleenex to wipe her eyes. "Austin I want to say yes but…"

"No buts Jan wait here." He said leaving the room. Jan finally regained her composure. Her thoughts were of that day, when Austin told her to put on these clothes, that he had bought for her. She hung her old jeans and shirt back in the closet, than returned the hat and boots to their rightful places. Lastly, she placed the drawing of the house back in the box and laid it carefully beside the hat. It was all so unbelievable.

Austin returned with something in his hand. This time, when he looked into her eyes, it was if he was looking right into her soul. That, along with his smile, was more them she could resist. Austin took her hand in his, than knelt down on one knee.

While still looking deep into her eyes, he said, "Jan Nuss, will you promise to marry me?" he said, slipping a beautiful diamond ring on her finger next to her wedding band.

Jan could no longer resist. "Oh, Austin. You know I want to say yes," she cried.

Austin held her tight. The pain in her breast was worth it, just to be near him.

"Austin, I promise to tell you why I left. You must know before we get married, other- wise it could ruin our whole relationship," she whispered.

"Would you like to talk about it now?" he asked.

"Austin, I don't want to spoil this moment. All I ask is that you pray for me, and us, so that our hearts will be prepared for what may happen after I tell you," she said.

"Well, either way, I will take this as a yes," he told her.

"Yes, Austin," she said quietly, and he kissed her gently on the lips.

"Is it really that bad?" he asked.

"To me it is, and I just have not been able to forgive my parents, or myself for not being able to do something to have changed the whole situation."

Austin touched the side of her face.

"Nothing can dampen the joy I have within me now that I know that you will be my wife. We will have to discuss wedding plans," he said.

Jan was quiet for a few minutes. "Austin, I don't want a fancy wedding," she told him.

"I will agree to that, if you agree to marry me soon, say next week?" he said watching her very closely.

"Whatever you say," she said in unbelief.

Austin took her in his arms and kissed her, then slowly released her. "I must be on my best behavior, even if I don't want to be. Tomorrow will be a long day and soon, very soon, you will join me in the other room. Good night hun, I hope you sleep well, and with pleasant dreams," he said, winking at her."

"The same goes to you, Austin." She placed one hand on either side of his face while looking at him. "Remember, I will always love you," she said.

"The same goes for you. I better go now." He said, removing her hands from the side of his face. "Goodnight, Jan." Then, with a backwards glance he said. "By the way, that shirt looks better on you than it did on me." He closed the door behind him as he left, leaving Jan standing there, wishing she had told him everything.

Austin laid staring up at the ceiling and praying in earnest, for both Jan and himself. Jan was finally in the house that he had built with her in mind. Only, in his dreams, they were spending their night in the same room. Well, at least they were under the same roof, and he had gotten the answer he had wanted.

He remembered the feeling of loss when she disappeared, and then the hopelessness of it all when he found out that she was married. Well, that was all behind them now, but what was this dark secret that she found so difficult to talk about?

He had heard the old rumors of her being sent away because she had shamed the family. That could only have meant one thing, but he knew Jan better then that. He had even overheard his parents talk about it.

That brought up the concern of what his parents would say, and their reaction to his marrying her. Well, either way they had to accept her, or reject them both. He knew deep in his heart that, God had brought them back together for a reason, and no one could convince him otherwise. It was not just a coincidence that over the years, their paths had never crossed. Than suddenly it happen twice, first at the hospital, and again at the Auction Mart. With that revelation, he fell asleep.

CHAPTER 5

WHEN AUSTIN WALKED OUT OF his bedroom, the aromas of coffee and bacon filled the air. He stepped into the kitchen where Jan was busy making breakfast. He had to pinch himself to make sure he wasn't dreaming. She was actually here. Even though his clothes were too large for her, she had definitely made them look great. She had tucked the shirt in, and cinched the pants together by braiding some bale twine to fashion a belt.

Without turning around, she said, "your breakfast will be ready in a minute. By the way, how do you like your eggs?"

"You're up early." Austin said, grabbing her from behind, then kissing her on the neck. "Over easy, just like you. Firm on the outside, and softhearted inside, he added.

"Not sure if that's a compliment, she told him. This was all new to Jan. She never got this warm and fuzzy feeling when Don touched her. She cared very much for Don, but with Austin it was so different. It was as if life would come to an end, if she lost him now. This was what love was supposed to feel like and she liked it.

Austin was at least six feet tall, which made him four inches taller than her. The shirt she wore was loose, so when he looked down, he noticed the bruise. "Is it still quite sore?" he asked, staring at it.

"Austin, behave yourself," she said quickly, putting the pan down to adjust her shirt. "Well, how is it?" he asked, now with a concerned tone to his voice.

"Yes, it is still quite sore, but given time it will heal," she told him.

Austin released her and went to pour himself a cup of coffee. "Just the thought of John makes my blood boil," he said.

"Austin, let's not talk about him, please?" she said.

Austin never replied. He just sat down with his coffee and watched her. He could easily get used to this lifestyle. Then suddenly he said, "You know Jan, it's a good thing that Ted is coming over to help this morning, or I may not have been able to keep to my promise."

"What promise?" she asked, looking at him. "Oh!" she added, turning away when she saw that look in his eyes.

Jan quickly changed the subject, "What does Ted do?"

"He is a brand inspector. We've become good friends since I moved here. He likes to work cattle, so he doesn't mind coming over when I need help. He can be quite a ladies man, so be forewarned," he said.

Jan glanced at Austin when she heard the change of his tone in his voice. She placed a plate with, a few pieces of toast, on the table. She than went back to the stove where, she made sure that the bacon and eggs were, done before putting them on the plate. She then, placed them in front of Austin.

Jan placing her hand gently on his shoulder, and said, "Austin, don't get all jealous on me. Nothing can change my feelings towards you. Where there is true love, there is no room for jealousy; for with true love comes trust, and forgiveness," she added.

"You're a wise woman, Jan. Where is your breakfast?" he asked.

Jan got herself a cup of coffee, than sat down across from him. "I don't eat much for breakfast. Toast, and coffee are about it," she added.

Austin reached over and took her hand in his, before giving thanks for the food.

After a brief moment, Jan asked. "What will you be doing today?"

"We'll be checking the herd, as well as moving some cows to a different pasture" he said hungrily, eating his food. "This is good Jan," he added.

"Austin, is there any reason that I couldn't join you today?" she asked.

Austin looked up in surprise. "Well, no. Have you ridden a horse before?" he asked now realizing how little he really knew about her.

"Not recently, but yes, I did ride a bit," she replied.

At first he was hesitant, a tenderfoot out amongst cattle can sometimes mean nothing but trouble. Seeing she was soon to be a rancher's wife, there was no time like the present to break her in.

"Alright, but you'd better eat more than that, if you plan on putting in a days work." He told her.

Jan quickly washed the dishes, while Austin sipped his coffee. "I suppose I should be buying some groceries," Austin told her.

"That might be a plan, if you want to eat properly. I could run into town tomorrow if you like?" Jan said, putting away the last pan.

"By the way, thanks for washing my clothes and for cleaning up my mess," he said.

"It's the least I can do. I better get ready now," she said, disappearing in the direction of the bathroom. When she looked at herself in the mirror, she was amazed at how much her hair had grown. It seemed like just a short time ago since she had gotten it cut. She quickly braided it than let it; fall down the center of her back.

When Jan returned to the kitchen, Austin was talking to his friend.

Ted looked at her in surprise. He had no idea that Austin had company. The biggest shock was that it was a woman, and a real looker to boot. He walked over to her while looking her up and down. "Well, hello there," he said in the same flirting tone of voice, that he used when talking to the women he wanted to get to know.

"Back off, Ted," Austin said standing up.

"Where did you find this young filly? You sly old dog!" he said to Austin, while touching Jan's arm.

"Back off, Ted!" Austin said again, now getting very protective of his woman.

Ted looked at Austin with a smile on his face. "Gonna try to keep this one for yourself, eh?"

Jan was beginning to feel uncomfortable, as she took a couple of steps towards Austin.

She was not used to his kind, and shied away from his advance. Austin sensed her discomfort, and in one stride, he was beside her. He put his arm around her shoulder and said, "Ted, this is Jan. Her and I are getting married next week. Jan, this is Ted he's my friend that, I was telling you about last night. He then looked directly at Ted. "That is, if he learns to keep his hands off of other men's women," he added.

Ted's mouth dropped open at the bombshell that Austin had just dropped. He stepped back, while raising both hands in the air, as if to say, *I'm backing off*. "Well, this is a shocker. I guess this means congratulations are in order." He looked at Austin and said, "When did this all happen? Yah think yah know a guy, and he throws you a curve ball. Go figure." He shook his head. "Well, either way Mam, it's nice to meet the woman that finally lassoed this guy," he said tipping his hat to her.

Austin looked down at Jan. "You ready?" he asked. She indicated that she was. Austin grabbed one of his newer caps and placed it on her head. She adjusted it to make it fit, while he found a jacket that she might be able to wear. "Here, take this one. It might get cold out there," he said, before putting on his almost worn out jacket.

Ted thought something seemed amiss, and he now noticed the clothes that Jan was wearing, but one other thing he sensed, was the love they seemed to have for each other, and he prided himself on being a good judge of people. How did Austin manage to keep this one a secret? Suddenly it hit him. This was probably the friend that he had taken to the hospital. He would have sworn that Austin was a confirmed bachelor. *Well go figure* he said to himself as he stepped outside.

The three of them hopped into Austin's truck then headed to the corrals below.

Austin parked the truck, then winked at Jan as she slid out after him, but he showed no other affection towards her while Ted was around. Austin whistled once, and Jan saw the black horse raise its head. The second whistle brought the black horse galloping in their direction. It also got the horses in the next pasture running towards them.

When the black horse got to the fence, he whinnied and shook his head up and down before he put his head over the top wire. Austin offered him the sugar cube that lay in the palm of his hand. After the black horse had nibbled it up, Austin stroke the front of the horse's head.

"Jan, this is Midnight. Move towards me very slowly," he said, reaching out to her. Austin slowly put his arm around Jan. Midnight flared his nostrils at the intruder, while waving his head up and down. "Easy boy." Austin said, reaching out to his horse.

Ted stood back, watching what was about to unfold. Midnight was very protective over Austin, and vise versa. Again he watched as Austin ran his hand down the front of Midnight's head.

"Easy boy." Austin said, calming midnight while, holding Jan tight against him. Midnight turned and ran back some distance, then reared up. It was obvious that he did not like the intruder.

"Come on, boy," Austin said, trying to coax him back.

Ted finally realized what Austin was trying to do. Jan was now part of Austin and he wanted to let his horse know that she could be trusted. He wished him luck, but he very much doubted that it would work.

Finally, Midnight returned. When he sniffed at Jan, "Austin told her to not to move, but to just let him get her scent. Again, Midnight snorted, ran back a distance and shook his head, before walking slowly to the sugar cube in Austin's outstretched hand.

Austin patted the side of Midnight's neck. "Easy, boy. You are going to have to get used to her, because she isn't going to go away," he said calmly.

Jan stood motionless beside Austin as she listened to the affectionate tone in his voice. There seemed to be a mutual understanding between the two of them.

Austin took Jan's hand in his then said. "Just lay your hand on mine as I reach out to him." She was very nervous.

Austin sensed her fear. "It's oaky, Jan. He won't hurt you while you are beside me. Just relax," he said.

Midnight sniffed at their hands. There was the familiar smell of his master's hand, and yet, something else too. He snorted as he shook his head.

"Easy boy," Austin said again, carefully touching him just above his nose. Jan had to step closer, as her arm was not as long as Austin's.

Midnight immediately began to rear up, at which time, Austin grabbed Jan and pulled her out of harms way. This time, Austin spoke with authority as he scolded Midnight for scaring her. It was almost comical, as Midnight seemed to sulk at his owner's disapproval. Austin was not one for giving up. They went thought the motions again, and this time, Midnight grudgingly, let Jan touch him ever so slightly.

"Good boy," Austin said, offering Midnight another sugar cube, and giving him a good pat on the side of his neck.

"It's high time we get to work," he said, before turning to Jan. "I don't want you to go near him when I am not around, understand?" he said, using the same tone of voice as he had on Midnight.

Blaze of Fury

"Yes, Austin," she said softly. Then she looked up at him with a pleading look in her eyes. "Do I get a sugar cube too?" she asked.

Ted burst out in laughter. "I think you've met your match, buddy," he said.

By then, Austin had caught on, and gave Jan a tap on the backside, grinning from ear to ear. Life would not be boring with Jan around. He kind of liked their bantering.

Austin hooked the halter shank onto Midnights, halter and lead him into the stable, while Ted lead his Paint horse in the same direction. Next, Austin brought in a beautiful copper colored horse. "Her name is Hope. She is a very good-natured horse, and easy to handle. She now belongs to you, Jan," he said, watching Jan walk over to pat Hope on the neck, before running her hand along her side. "Why did you call her Hope?" Jan asked

"Do you have to ask?" he said as their eyes met.

"She is beautiful, Austin. Thank-you," she said, going over to give him a slight kiss.

Midnight snorted and pawed the ground. "He is jealous," Ted said as he placed the saddle blanket on his horse.

"When did you ride last?" Austin asked.

"It was before I got married," she replied.

Ted was somewhat surprised, and her answer made him curious, but either way, a beautiful woman like her was quite a catch. He was dying to find out how the two of them had met, but he knew Austin was a very private person, and he was not about to tell anyone unless he wanted to.

Jan saddled up Hope, under the watchful eye of Austin. He was surprised how well she had done. It was then his turn to saddle up Midnight, who, by now, was getting impatient. Next, Austin grabbed a pair of chaps that hung in the tack room, and strapped them on. Jan could not take her eyes off of him. She had always known that he was a very handsome, muscular man, but looking at him now, in his getup, she realized how proud and blessed she was to have a man like him, that loved her.

It was then that the lectures, which she had heard as a child, on pride came back to her. When she was growing up, there were so many rules to follow that it seemed like there were more "wrongs" than "rights." No slacks or fancy dresses, allowed for the girls. They wore mainly dark, and plain clothing. They weren't allowed too much property, and definitely no television or radio and it went on and on. She looked around at what Austin owned, and then at the clothes she was wearing. She could just imagine the tongues wagging back home if they saw her and Austin now. Especially with her staying here at Austin's home without being married. That wiped the smile off her face. She loved being here with him, but it didn't feel right to her either.

Austin was a bit concerned that, riding might be too much for Jan. Then again he may be just a bit over protective. She had told him that her heart had been doing fine lately.

"Jan, I want you to promise me that if you get any chest pains, you will tell me right away," he said.

"Austin, I am fine, so don't worry," she said, laying her hand on the side of his face.

Without thinking, he took Jan in his arms and kissed her, forgetting that Ted was watching.

"Get on your horse," Austin snapped.

"Yes boss," Ted said, snickering at Austin's embarrassment.

Austin helped Jan into the saddle, then patted her leg and said, "Be careful out there." He untied Midnight, then, putting his one foot into the stirrup he, swung himself up and into the saddle.

As they rode out, it was obvious that Midnight was a powerful, well-trained horse. Austin positioned himself between Ted and Jan. Ted was a good man, but he loved women. He knew how Ted operated, and he had no intention of allowing him to pull any of those stunts on his future wife. He knew the news of his up-coming marriage would get out, now that Ted knew. Gossip in small communities always spreads like a wild fire, so he was not about to tell Ted any more than necessary.

Blaze of Fury

As they rode out across the pasture, Austin explained to Jan that he was bringing home thirty cows that he wanted to sell. They were open cows, or, ones whose calves had either died, or disappeared, and also a few with nasty dispositions. It was the latter ones that they had to watch out for.

When they started out, Jan was very tense in the saddle, but after about fifteen minutes she was beginning to enjoy herself. Maybe it was like riding a bike, once you learn to do it, you never forget.

Austin could feel the restlessness of Midnight under him, so he nudged him slightly with the heel of his boot, and the power Midnight held back, was suddenly unleashed. It was Ted's turn next. He whipped his horse with the end of his reins, and at the same time used his spurs to get him going. Hope, not wanting to be left behind, bolted unexpectedly. If it had not been for her holding onto the saddle horn, Jan would have been lying on the ground. At that point, Ted would have made some remark about her having a lot to learn. Well, if those two wanted to know what she was made of, she would show them. She pulled her cap on firmly, now more determined than ever, while giving Hope free rein to gallop after the other two. Finally, Austin slowed Midnight down to a trot, letting the others catch up. Ted reined his horse in once he had caught up to Austin, but Jan was just beginning to enjoy herself. So instead of slowing down she nudged Hope on, and went racing on by. Austin and Ted looked at each other then, spurred their horses into action, and the race was on again. Jan could hear the beating of hooves coming closer, as the other two caught up to her.

Austin was very surprised at Jan's ability to handle her horse. Shortly after they caught up to her, she began to rein Hope in. The day was just beginning, and they were out here to work. She also knew that, by the end of the day, she would be feeling pretty sore.

"You did pretty good." Austin said, looking at Jan.

"Yeah, Austin, I think you've definitely got a keeper here." Ted said, quite impressed with Jan's abilities.

"Thanks, Ted, I believe you're right" Austin stopped and looked off to the left. "Ted, we've got trouble again," he said.

"What's wrong?" Jan asked, looking at the open gate.

"I think you are right," Ted said, riding over to check it out. He then got off his horse to look more closely at the ground. "It's the same horses," he said.

"Yeah, and I have a good idea whose horse it is, and where I would find it," Austin said, as his anger started to build.

"I'll check around out here while you two start rounding them up. I hope they are all still in there. I'll come join you after a bit," Ted said, as the professional side of him took over.

Jan was amazed at how different he suddenly became.

"I hope so to. Come on, Jan the fun is over and the work begins. There are supposed to be thirty cows in here that we need to round up, and take home," Austin said, riding into the pasture with Jan at his side.

The look on Austin's face was one of worry and stress. She had noticed a bit of that once before, but he did his best to hide it from her. She wondered what was going on, but she felt now was not the time to ask.

Austin and Jan rode up and down the hills, through dense bush, and through areas that reminded her of a park. It was in the park-like setting that they found what they were looking for.

Jan remarked how beautiful it was here, but Austin was not paying any attention to her. He was busy checking if all his cows were still there. Jan sat quietly on her horse while taking in every inch of the landscape. Here the trees were a good distance apart. It was the perfect balance of sunshine and shade, which made for lots of lush green grass. She had noticed earlier on that where, there was a lot of bushes next to nothing grew. However, those areas made good shelter from storms, and lots of places for the cattle to rub on.

"We are short eight head," Austin said, looking around. They had already checked almost every square inch of this pasture. Austin slapped his hand down on his chaps and yelled, "Yeah! Yeah!" At that point, the cattle began to head in the direction of the open gate.

"I hope Ted found them," Austin said, slapping his hand on his chaps to keep his small herd moving.

Austin watched as Jan nudged Hope off to the right when a couple of cows decided they wanted to take a side trip. She was definitely a natural. His chest heaved as he thought of holding her again. Only when others began to stray, did Austin nudge Midnight slightly, and his thoughts returned to the task at hand. It was not long before the lead cows headed for the open gate. At that point the rest seemed to fall in line, with Midnight and Hope following lazily behind. This gave Austin and Jan time to talk about the ranch.

Jan was enjoying herself out here in the wide-open spaces, with the man she loved by her side. God had blessed her even after all that had happened. If only her parents would have let her marry this man years ago, they would not have lost all these years. They would have probably had a family by now and... That was where she stopped herself from thinking about it. She had to tell Austin tonight. She needed to get rid of this burden once and for all.

When they neared the gate, Ted was waiting with five more cows. "Well I'm, still three head short. With any luck, they may have strayed in with the big herd," he said.

"That's a total of ten head missing so far this year," Austin told Ted.

"We will get to the bottom of this yet, I'll promise you that," Ted told Austin. The frustration showed on both of their-faces.

Jan rode quietly behind, listening to Austin and Ted talk, while they slowly moved their little herd home ward. Suddenly, one of the cows darted off to one side. Jan quickly rode after it, but just as she got that one back, another took off in the same direction.

Austin, now alerted to what was happening, spurred Midnight into action. He knew that cow only to well. His heart was beating hard with-in his chest, when he saw what was about to happen. Austin yelled at Jan to get out of the way, as he ran his horse right between her and the charging cow. When Midnight collided with the left shoulder of the cow, he did deflect the cow from hitting Jan and her horse. Only Midnight went down, sending Austin flying through the air.

Jan screamed when she saw what was unfolding right beside her.

Ted was there in a flash, waving his rope and yelling at the dazed cow with all his might. Ted continued chasing the cow towards the rest of the herd. The last thing he needed was for that crazy animal to go after Austin, who now lay on the ground. When Midnight got to his feet, Jan noticed that he had a mark on his shoulder, which was probably from the cow's horn. She jumped off her horse and ran over to Austin, who rolled over and then sat up. Then, with the help of Jan, he got to his feet. He stretched a bit then dusted the dirt off his clothes.

"You're hurt," she said, when she saw blood on the side of his face.

"I'll be fine," he said taking the bandana from around his neck, to wipe away the streak of blood that tricked down the side his face.

Jan picked up Austin's cap and handed it to him. "I'm really sorry, Austin. This is all my fault."

"It is not your fault, I knew that cow. I should have been watching her," he said, looking at her tear-filled eyes. "What's wrong?" he asked.

"You could have been killed," she said wiping the tears from her eyes.

"Well, I wasn't, so let's get back to work," he said, helping her back on her horse, than limped over to where Midnight stood. Austin spoke calmly to his horse, as he ran his hand down Midnights shoulder and leg to make sure he was okay.

When he swung up onto the saddle, Jan knew he was hurting.

Ted had been watching, but once he saw Austin get up, he kept the cattle moving.

"Everybody alright?" Ted asked when Austin caught up to him.

"Yes. Jan is a bit shaken, but she will be fine," he said looking back as she followed at some distance.

"What about you? That was quite a tumble you took," he said, noticing the blood trickling down the side of Austin's face.

"I will probably be a bit sore for awhile, but it will heal," Austin said.

"You better get that thick head of yours looked at when you get back home," Ted added.

Jan was not feeling well when she got back. The scare had sent her heart into a, frenzy. She took Hope over to the barn, and tied her to the ring in the wall before sitting down.

Austin and Ted soon followed, leading their horses. When Austin walked into the barn, the first thing he saw was Jan sitting on the bale. Her eyes were closed as she rested her head against the wall. He quickly tied Midnight to a pole, and rushed to her side.

Jan winced when Austin laid his hand on her bruised chest.

"Why didn't you say something?" he said angrily. He felt her heart beating as if she had just finished running a quarter-mile race. "I'm taking you to the hospital."

"No! I will be fine. Just let me sit here and rest for a bit. It was just the fear of what could have happened to you that triggered it. Just leave me alone, and go look after the horses," she said, wanting to be left alone a while.

Austin touched the side of her face gently, than slowly got up to do as she said.

"Is she all right?" Ted asked, keeping his distance from Midnight.

"No, not really. She has some sort of heart problem, and that scare must have affected it,"

Austin said, pulling the saddle off of his horse.

"I am sorry to hear that," Ted said, while taking his saddle and blanket too the tack room. *Austin really needs more stress in his life,* Ted said, to himself. He wondered why a God fearing man like Austin seemed to have more problems then that idiot neighbor of his.

After the horses were put back in their pasture, Austin drove the three of them back up to the house. Jan got washed up, before going to the kitchen to make some coffee.

"Jan, leave the coffee and go rest," Austin said sternly.

"I will in a moment," she said. Once she had the coffee started, she placed two cups in front of the men, before leaving the room.

Over coffee, Austin and Ted discussed the problem of the missing cattle. After a while they decided to call it a day. Tomorrow morning, the cattle liner would be there to pick up the cows they had brought home. Then, after that, they would go out to check on the big herd.

"Ted, do you have other plans this afternoon?" Austin asked.

"No, not really. Why? What's up?" Ted asked.

"I should go pick up Jan's truck from that restaurant, just north of Calgary, and I need someone to drive mine back," he said.

"Sure, I can do that. When do you want to go?" Ted asked.

"There is no time like the present. I'll go tell Jan and if she is ok, we'll head out," Austin said leaving the room. Jan was almost asleep, when he walked into her room. "How are you feeling, hon?" Austin said, bending over to give her a kiss.

"It's better now," She said.

"Will you be alright if I leave you alone for awhile? Ted had some free time and I don't like to leave your truck where it is. So if you will be okay, we'll go get it," Austin told her.

"I was just thinking about that. Maybe I should come too and go home from there," she said.

Austin was taken aback by her comment. He had never given it another thought that she would ever leave here. "I don't think it is advisable just yet. For one thing, you need someone to keep an eye on you, especially with that heart of yours acting up again… and…well…I still don't want you alone for the other reason, you know. Besides that, you look really tired, so get some rest. Where are your truck keys?" he asked.

Jan pointed to the dresser. Austin picked up the keys and placed them in his pocket.

"Austin, you better look after that cut on your head before you leave," She told him.

"I will, Babe," he said, winking at her as he left the room. He went to the bathroom and took off his hat. He washed his hands, then took a cloth and washed the dried blood off the side of his face and dabbed some from his hair. *Well, that would do for now.* He would deal with the rest when he got back.

On the way, Austin just needed to vent to someone about his frustration, and the fears he had about John. Ted did like to gossip, but there were some things that he knew to keep to himself. There was a lot that Austin had left out, but Ted did get the gist of why Austin's feared for Jan's safety.

Ted did agree that he had just cause to feel the way he did. By Austin description of this fellow, whatever happened to make Jan leave may have saved her life.

Ted began to wonder if that man was dangerous, or just plain stupid. Was he now stalking her? He turned to Austin and said, "He knows you took Jan with you, so… what if he sees you pick up her truck and follows you home?"

Austin was suddenly very quite. He had not thought about that. "What do you suggest?" he asked.

"What if we split up, and go different directions? We'll take a tour through the city on the way home," Ted said.

"That sounds like a plan. If we drive around some busy areas, we should have no problem losing him eventually. That's if he does try to follow us," Austin said, now satisfied.

"Why take the chance?" Ted told him.

When Austin reached his destination, he jumped out of his truck and right into Jan's. Ted got into the drivers seat of Austin's truck, and while he waited for Austin to leave, he tried to see if he could spot the man that Austin had described to him.

It was only of a couple of minutes until they were back on the road.

Ted looked in his rearview mirror as they drove out of the parking lot. There was a man standing just outside the door that he thought could possibly fit the description, of Jan's living nightmare. Well, if he did follow them, he would be in for quite a surprise.

It took them both about forty five minutes longer to get home but they, thought it was better safe then sorry. Austin arrived home ten minutes before Ted. Up until walking into the house, Austin had not even thought about food, but the aroma of a home-cooked meal reminded him that he hadn't eaten for some time. He'd had too many other things on his mind. "I thought I told you to rest," he said, walking over to Jan.

"I did, and then I decided I better have supper ready when you two got home. I figured that you had not considered the fact, that both of you missed lunch. Where is Ted?" Jan asked.

"Oh, he will be along shortly." Austin replied, as he grabbed her, when she was about to pour him a cup of coffee.

"Cap off in the house," she said, taking it off of his head then, dropping it on the floor.

Austin kissed her, which she willingly returned.

"Hey you two! Not when there is company in the house," Ted said, entering the kitchen.

Jan was embarrassed, as she quickly pulled away from Austin and pour out two cups of coffee for the men.

"Go get washed up for supper," Austin told Ted curtly, now a bit uncomfortable at the fact of been caught kissing his woman. He and Jan were both were raised to believe that the affection between consenting adults was not for public display.

Blaze of Fury

When they all sat down to eat, Ted was about to say something but Austin stopped him. Austin bowed his head and gave thanks for the food before saying, "you can now help yourself. How was your tour?" Austin asked.

"Not bad. I thought I might have had company for a while, but I may have been wrong. Either way, nothing exciting," Ted said.

Austin gave him a worried look and decided to ask later what he'd meant by that remark.

"This is great, Jan. She is a good cook to boot," Ted told Austin.

"If Austin changes his mind about you, I sure would take you home." Ted said jokingly.

Only, Jan did not find it funny. What if after she told Austin the whole story, he asks here to leave? *Please, God, may he understand*, she prayed under her breath.

"I'm sorry Jan, I didn't mean anything by what I said," Ted told her, when he noticed the look on her face.

"I know Ted. It's just... It's nothing," she said.

Austin reached under the table and touched her leg. When she looked at him, she could see the reassuring love in his eyes, and it made her smile.

Ted knew that whatever problems these two encountered, their love for each other would get them through it. For the first time in his life, he craved to have someone care that deeply for him.

Austin looked at Jan and said, "Would you like me to ask Ted about the package that you found in my pocket yesterday?"

Jan's face began to turn red as she began to blush. "No! I believe you," she said abruptly.

Austin wanted to make sure that she did, so he said, with that twinkle in his eye. "We'll make it clear now."

Ted looked at one, then the other.

"Austin, please, behave yourself," she scolded.

"Are you talking about what I think you are?" Ted asked. "Guilty," he said putting his hands up. "It was mine. I already got chewed out by your old man for leaving my stuff lying around." Then leaning back in his chair, he added, "That meal was delicious, Jan."

"Yes, it was very good," Austin, agreed.

The two men sat drinking their coffee, while Jan did up the dishes. She was almost done, when Ted decided it was time for him to leave. He told Austin that he would still be available the next day, but he could not promise anything for rest of the week. Austin followed him outside to talk in private. When he returned, Jan saw the worried look on his face.

"Is something wrong?" she asked.

"No, everything is fine now. Before I forget, here are your truck keys," he said, dropping them on the table. Jan sensed that he was not being totally truthful with her.

"I think I'd better get cleaned up," Austin said, leaving the room.

While Austin had his shower, Jan sat at the table writing up a grocery list. She also decided that it was best that she go home. It would only be for a short while, and if they were to be married, she had a lot of things to do.

Besides, it was not so much Austin's emotions that worried her, but her own. With each kiss, her body craved the oneness of married life. If they were to get married, she needed to get up the courage to talk to him tonight.

"Jan, will you come in here," she heard Austin say.

Jan walked over to his room, but he was not there. "Where are you?" she asked.

Austin opened the bathroom door. He had just had a shower, and was standing there with only his jeans on. Jan froze to the spot. She longed to kiss, and run her hand across, his bare chest. Her body tingled as she saw the muscles in his arms flex when he bent over to pick up the towel that had fallen on the floor. Her heart began to beat faster. It was then that she noticed some bad scrapes and bruises all over his back and arms.

"Oh Austin, you are hurt," She said afraid to go near him.

"I need you to check the cut on my head," he said dabbing up the blood that still oozed from the wound.

She wanted to go to him, but her feet just didn't seem to want to move.

"Well, are you going to help me, or not?" he asked.

When Jan walked over to him, he sat down on the lid of the toilet. Jan carefully began to part his hair. "Oh Austin! I think you'd better get this stitched up," she said, horrified at the size of the gash.

"I don't plan on going to no hospital. Just take a few stands of hair from either side and tie it shut. Do you think you can handle that?" he asked.

He had washed it quite well so the wound looked clean. She worked at it careful, trying not to cause him too much pain. However, he did jump and wince quite often while she was doing it. Finally she said, "That's the best I can do. Do you have anything that I can put on the scrapes on your back and arms?" she asked.

"No, they will heal." He said grabbing her. She was breathless as he held her against his bare chest. He bent over and kissed her hard on the lips. "I've been waiting to do that all after noon." He said.

"Austin, please, this can get dangerous."

"Oh Jan, let's get married now. I don't want to wait until next week," he said.

"Austin, we have to talk," she said leaving before things got out of control.

Austin slipped on his shirt, before following her into the kitchen.

"Okay, what do you want to talk about?" he asked.

"I think it is time I told you what happened years ago," Jan said.

Austin sat quietly looking at her. "I would like you to promise that you will not hate me after I tell you what happened, but I know that may not be possible. I only ask that you try to understand." She took a deep breath, than began.

"Do you remember the last time we met down in the coulee?" Austin nodded his head, indicating that he did. "Well, when I got back home that day, my Father was very angry. He had seen you coming from the same area that I had been earlier, and had suspected that we had met up. He forbade me to ever go down there again. I was promised to another man, and if any one found out that I was privately meeting up with you, the whole family would be shamed, or worse, shunned. Not only that, I would have had to go in front of the church to ask for their forgiveness.
"I could have been real bad."

Austin nodded his head. He knew, only to well what she would have been put through.

Jan continued. "After that, I was always under the watchful eye of someone in my family, so it was impossible to meet you again. I spent many hours crying, dreading my fate. I had no idea that you had tried to contact me, and I didn't think you cared any more because I saw no effort on your part, to rescue me from my dilemma. Then when I found your letter in the garbage, I was hurt and angry. I took it to my room, but I did not open it right away. That evening I need to find out what you had to say in your letter, but someone must have looked through my things, because it was gone. I tore my room apart looking for it, but it was hopeless."

Anger towards Jan's parents began to build within him, but he tried to remain calm.

Jan took another deep breath. She could not look at him as she started in on the most difficult part. "After a month or so, I began to get sick. My parents decided to take me to the doctor and...." Then she was interrupted by, the ringing of the phone.

"Just leave it," Austin said, but as it persisted, he decided that he had better answer it.

From what she heard from Austin's conversation, and the look on his face, Jan believed this call was quite important and distressing to him.

Austin asked the other party to hold on for a bit. "Jan, I am sorry, but this is really important. We'll talk after I get through here," he said before going back to his phone conversation. It was getting late, and she was now tired physically, and mentally.

Jan felt Austin needed his privacy right now, and she was just sick about adding more stress to his evening. Tears ran down her cheeks as she lay in bed, right up to the time she fell asleep.

Austin had not realized how long he had been on the phone, until he looked at his watch. When he entered Jan's room, he could see that her face was still wet from crying.

He just wanted to hold her and promise her that nothing, no matter how bad it was, would ever destroy their love. He picked up a blanket and covered her up. She stirred slightly when he bent over and gave her a kiss.

"Good night, my love. Sleep well," he said softly, before turning out the light and closing the door.

Chapter 6

Jan had a very restless night. In her mind, she had envisioned that after she told Austin her story, he would have taken her in his arms and told her that everything would fine. Next he would kiss her, and promise to not leave one stone unturned until well, nothing had changed. If only the phone had not rung.

The next morning, Jan almost spilt her coffee when Austin suddenly grabbed her from behind. "Sorry about last night," he said kissing her on the neck.

"Austin, you must stop scaring me like that," she told him.

"Sorry, I promise that tonight you will have my full attention. No more interruptions."

After breakfast was done, Jan began to clear off the table. While doing so, she told Austin that she planned on going into town this morning to buy some groceries. Austin poured himself a cup of coffee, before sitting down to wait for Jan to hand him his breakfast. He was quite enjoying his new lifestyle, but that was soon to change.

"Austin, I have decided to go home tomorrow. I am reasonably certain that John will not bother me again, and besides, I just don't feel that this is right. I am sure rumors have already begun to rear there ugly heads about us, and if we are to get married, I have a lot of things to do back home first," she said.

Austin felt like he had been run over by a Mack truck. "Why? I thought you would just stay here?" he said in astonishment.

Blaze of Fury

When Jan looked at him, she could see the disappointment in his eyes.

"It will be different once we are married, Austin, but we aren't yet. This isn't right and you know deep down what I mean. Sooner or later we may do something we shouldn't," she told him.

"Well, let's just go and get married now, or have you changed your mind?" He asked, grabbing her.

Jan placed a hand on either side of his face. "Austin, how many times do I have to say it? You are the only man that I have ever truly loved. Nothing would make me, happier then being, your wife, and to have your children." Suddenly, Jan burst into tears and went running out of the room.

Austin went after her. He took her in his arms, and held her until she quit crying. "Jan, what's wrong?"

"Austin, the reason I was sent away was because I was pregnant," she said, beginning to cry.

Austin quickly released her, "I don't believe it, I heard rumors to that effect, but I didn't believe that you..." he said walking over to the window.

"Was it John's?" he asked angrily.

Jan was in shock that he would even think such a thing. "Is that the kind of woman you think I am?" She said, now hurt, and angry at his insinuations.

Just then, they heard Ted holler. "Hey, you two. The cattle liner is here to pick up the cows."

"We will talk about this later," Austin said, giving the chair a boot, knocking it across the room, as he left.

Jan had never seen him this angry. She now felt that there was a good chance that this was the end of there relationship. She began to pray like she had never prayed before. Why had God brought him back into her life, only to have it fall apart again? Was she being punished for her sins? "Please, God, help us!" she cried.

Book 3 of the *Mountains and Valleys of Life*

After some time, Jan came to a decision. Austin desperately needed groceries, so that was the least she could do before she left. Then, if he still took the same attitude towards her after they had their talk, she would leave.

Jan went to the bathroom, and ran cold water over a facecloth. It felt so soothing when she placed it on her face. After doing it a couple of times, she looked at herself in the mirror. It had taken some of the puffiness, and redness, from her eyes. She went back to the bedroom and slipped into her own clean clothes. The excitement and thrill of the last few days were now replaced with heartache and emptiness. She would be glad to get home again, where she would have a change of clothes that actually fit her. It was not that she hadn't enjoyed the challenge of doing without, and the thrill of wearing clothes that had touched Austin's body. The thought of that made her tingle all over.

"Oh, Austin," she said softly. If their life together would never materialize, she would have the cherished memories of this time forever. Would she have to go through the same heart-wrenching feeling of losing him all over again? It was the phone that jolted her back to the present.

She let it ring a couple of times before deciding to answer it.

"Hello," she said slowly.

The man's voice on the other end seemed none to friendly, and very stern.

"Is Austin there?" he asked.

"No, I am sorry. He is busy outside right now," she replied.

The caller took for granted that she was Austin's wife. "Mrs. Klassen? This is Mr. Peterson, the manager of the bank. Would you tell Austin that if he isn't able to pay his loan soon, the bank, will have no other recourse, but to call in the entire loan. I would sure hate to have him lose his entire ranch."

Jan would have corrected him as to who she was, but the shock of what he said stopped her from doing so. "I will tell him and… ah, what was the exact figure of the delinquent loan?" she asked.

She knew it was none of her business, but maybe she could help. She couldn't bear to see this place slip through his hands. There was a moment of silence before he said, "For this payment, he will need $25,000 immediately, but if the loan is called, the full amount of $162,000 will have to paid back," he added.

"Alright, I will tell him," she said, making a note of it. Now she understood why he had chosen that number of cows to sell. He had probably hoped, that the thirty head that, he had culled out of the herd, would cover his loan. She hoped that the lack of the three missing cows would not be a problem. Did she dare to ask him?

Jan took the note she had written and placed it on Austin's bedroom mirror, where he could not miss seeing it.

When Jan left for town, Austin and Ted were still down by the corrals. On her way to town, she made special note of any landmarks, so as not to lose her way. She actually enjoyed shopping for Austin, but then the thought of never doing this again dampened her spirits. On her return, she told herself that she must have a positive attitude. Austin was a reasonable man. Surely he wouldn't just throw away everything that they shared.

When Jan drove into the yard, she saw a car parked near the house. Just as Jan picked up some of the bags, Ted seemed to appear out of nowhere.

"Yah need some help?" he asked, grabbing the rest of the bags.

"Thanks, Ted." she said, reaching awkwardly to open the door with the bags in her hand.

Jan sat the bags down on the counter, before turning to look at Austin. He looked a bit nervous. When she looked at the elderly couple sitting by the table, she turned very pale. Without getting up, Austin introduced first Jan, then Ted, to his company. Jan was very polite as she shook their hands.

"You look very familiar," Mrs. Klassen said to Jan.

Austin looked at Jan with a rather forced smile. "Jan was Abe Enns daughter."

"You mean you are Anne Enns?" His Mother said with a frown on her face.

Jan knew exactly what was going through her mind. *I might as well give them something else to talk about*, Jan said to herself, as she remembered the rumors about her that had spread through the old community.

"My married name is Jan" she began, and at which point she looked at Austin before finishing with, "Nuss."

"You mean you are married?" Austin's Father asked, now with a deep frown on his face. The look on Mrs. Klassen's face was not much different from her husbands.

"I was," she said, figuring that they couldn't think any less of her than they already did. Up until now, she had never really thought what it would be like to meet Austin's parents. All she could think of was that her and Austin were finally going to be together.

Ted did not miss a single detail of what was happening. What confused him was, why Austin had not come to Jan's aid. He was sure that Jan was almost at the end of her tether, when she suddenly bolted from the room. It was like they had forgotten that Ted was still in the room. Mr. Klassen turned to his son and said, now very agitated, "why is that woman staying in your home? I thought you knew she was a bad girl. She shamed her family by sleeping with other men, when she was promised to John Remple! Her family was so ashamed that they eventually moved away."

"Stop it. I know all about it. We were planning on getting married," Austin told them, sounding very unsure.

It was then that Ted saw Jan. She was obviously very upset as she slipped out the back door. He was positive that she had heard what they had said. Ted left unnoticed, while Austin's parents continued to degrade Jan. Why had Austin not stood up for the woman he loved? Why had he not confirmed that they were getting married? It sounded like he had changed his mind, and come to think of it, that was probably why Jan left like she had.

Ted stood leaning against his truck, until he heard the sound of a horse galloping.

Surely not, he thought, but yes, Jan had saddled up Hope, who was now galloping at breakneck speed towards the west.

Ted knew that Jan did not know this country, and at the speed she was going and in her frame of mind, it made for a dangerous combination. Ted drove down to the corrals. It was not too likely that they would be checking the cattle today. He knew Austin had no idea where Jan was, so he decided to hang around for a while until she returned. He puttered around for quite a while, and yet Austin made no attempt to find out what had happened to Jan. Ted was beginning to get concerned. He was cleaning out the tack room, when he heard the sound of a horse. He let out a sigh of relief. Only when he went to tell Jan how stupid she was for taking off like that, he was shocked to see Hope return without a rider.

That was it. Ted jumped into his truck and tore up the gravel road, all the way to the house. He ran into the house angrier than Austin had ever seen him.

"Austin, what the hell is the matter with you? Your parents show up and you abandon a woman like Jan?" He yelled, while glaring at Austin's parents. Austin jumped to his feet, knocking over the chair he had been sitting on. He saw Austin make a fist as if to hit him, but he knew Austin well enough to know that it was only a threat. "You'd better get your rear on that stallion of yours, and go look for your future wife. That is if you still have one," Ted said pointing to the front door.

"What are you talking about? Jan is in the other room," Austin said.

"Like heck she is. She heard what you people said about her, and so did I. Maybe your intention was, to get rid of her. You should all be ashamed of yourselves. I thought Christians were supposed to be forgiving, but I haven't seen any sign of that here today," he sneered.

Ted noticed both Austin's parents look down. He turned back to look at Austin. "Jan took off like a bat out of hell and now, Hope is back without her," Ted said, still fuming.

Austin was out the door and gone, before his parents knew what happened. Ted hung back, deciding it best that if Austin did find her, hopefully still in one piece, that they would sit down and talk out their problems, privately. He would just wait down by the stable.

Even though Austin felt betrayed by Jan, Austin could not stop himself from loving her. As for getting married, there were some things that he wanted her to clarify, first. What if something happened to her, and he never did find out the whole truth?

Midnight sensed, by Austin's one long whistle, that he was not in the mood for playing. He came immediately, and ready to go for a run. In no time at all, Austin had Midnight ready to go. With one quick movement, he swung himself up into the saddle. Then as Austin's spur dug into Midnight's side, the stallion now fully energized, as he burst into action. Austin was an expert horseman, and after giving Midnight free rein, they looked like one as Midnight raced west across the pasture. It was not long before horse and rider were out of sight, leaving only the faint sound of galloping hooves in the distance.

Austin's fear now, was that she might have ended up at the drop. That was what they called the hundred-foot cliff, along the trail. Surely she would not have gone out that far, and yet it was possible. Hope could have gone that way if given free rein. He shuddered at the though of finding her at the base of the cliff.

Austin was just a short distance from the drop, when he saw her. She was sitting on the big boulder near the cliff. From what he saw, she seemed to be fine. He had been running Midnight pretty hard, so he slowed him down to a trot, then a walk. When he got closer, he got off and led Midnight over to where Jan sat.

Blaze of Fury

She was deep in thought, and seemingly tuned out the world around her.

"Jan, are you all right?" he asked, first with concern then with anger at the thought of her being hurt. "By the way, what in blazes did you think you were doing taking off like that, without telling anyone?"

She made no indication that she had even heard him.

He sat down beside her and stared out across the valley. Finally, he could no longer stand the silence. He put his arm around her, and that was when she jumped to her feet. She stood staring down at him.

It was then that he saw the scrape down her face and arm. "It looks like you took a bit of a tumble. I had fears of finding you at the bottom of that cliff," he said.

"Would you have care if you did?" She said angrily.

"Jan, don't talk so stupid. You know I care," he snapped.

"Well, by the way your parents talked about me, I am no better than...than," she grabbed his fingers, before finishing with, "than the dirt under your finger nails." She said, dropping his hand. "And as for you," she said with tears in her eyes, "you sat there and acted as if you were totally innocent in this whole affair." When he took a step towards her, she stepped back towards the edge of the cliff.

With one swift movement, Austin grabbed her and pulled her towards him as the dirt crumbled under her feet. Jan clung to him as she heard the sound of rocks clattering and clacking as they bounced and slid right to the bottom of the cliff.

When she looked up at Austin, his eyes were dark and mysterious.

Austin could feel her body tremble, and the look in her eyes was one of fear.

He slowly bent over and kissed her. His kisses became more passionate and before they realized it, they were on the ground. She tried to push him away, but his kisses only enticed her more.

It was Austin who suddenly broke free and got to his feet. "You lied to me," he said.

Austin reached down and pulled her to her feet. Then after leading Midnight over to where she stood, he demanded that she get on.

"No, not until you tell me what, you meant by that remark," she demanded, now very hurt and angry. She could not believe the change she saw in him, since his parents arrived. Had they that much influence over him?

"Just get on," he said, grabbing her arm.

It was a different pain that Jan felt in her chest, and it hurt worse then any heart pain she had ever known. Her heart was breaking, because of Austin's insinuations. He couldn't have hurt her worse, if he had stabbed her in the heart and twisted it. "Oh, Austin," she cried in utter despair.

Austin let go of her arm. "Jan, for goodness sake, don't be so bullheaded and get on!" he said, now getting annoyed at her.

Looking directly at him, with tears in her eyes, she said, "Austin, I love you more than life itself. What I had feared has now come true. I had hoped and prayed that it would not end like this. I wanted so badly to keep my baby, I really did."

"I don't want to hear another word about your baby. It would be different if it was mine," he said now seething.

Jan stood there stupefied. She felt like he had struck her in the face. She couldn't believe what she was hearing. Had he not understood one thing she had tried to tell him?

With all that had happened up to this point, she had not realized that her heart was beginning to race out of control. She now felt very tired to the point of exhaustion.

"Austin, just go home to your parents, so you can run me deeper into the ground," she said very calmly, and defeated.

"Jan, leave my parents out of this. Now I have had enough of your childish actions. Get on right now, before I have to tie you onto the saddle," he said, glaring at her.

Blaze of Fury

Jan had all she could take. She stood her ground, glaring right back at him. Then in a slow, calm, clear voice she said. "Austin, until you can apologize to me for what you have just insinuated, I don't want to ever see you again. Now I want you to get on that stallion of yours, and go back home to your parents. I'll find my own way back, and I mean exactly what I said." With that she turned her back to him.

Austin stood there in stunned silence. It was his turn to feel the sting of rejection. Well, maybe she needed to be taught a lesson. He would just leave her to cool her heels for a while. He'd come and get her later.

When Ted saw Austin coming back without Jan, he was really worried. Something was not right here. Ted waited until Austin got down off his horse.

"Where is Jan?" Ted asked.

"Out by the drop." Austin said, beginning to remove the saddle.

"You left her there alone? Is she alright?" Ted asked now totally confused.

"If she wants to be so bullheaded, she can just sit there for a while. Besides, I don't want her talking to me about the kid she had from another man," he said, still outraged.

"You're a fool, man. Something doesn't sound right here, Austin," Ted said.

After Austin headed back up to the house, Ted saddled up both his horse, and Hope. There was no way that he was leaving Jan out there for the wolves and cougars or bears, which he feared could happen. He had every intention of getting to the bottom of this.

He had hoped that he might meet her on the way, but that didn't happen. He found her sitting on the boulder, crying.

"Jan, is there something I can do?" He asked softly. Jan got up, ran over to him, and wept on his shoulder.

"It's all over Ted, I've lost him again," Jan cried. Ted just held her in his arms for sometime until she got her emotions under control.

"I'm sorry, Ted. I didn't mean to involve you in this," she said.

When she backed away from Ted, he looked at her torn shirt. "Jan, what went on here? Did he hurt you?" he asked.

"Yes, but not in the way you are thinking, Ted." Then laying her hand on her heart, she said, "It's in here that it hurts."

"Jan, would you like to talk about it?" he asked, leading her back to the rock.

Jan had kept everything bottled up inside of her for years. The last time she confided in anyone was down in the coulee with Austin. That was a good many years ago, and what that got her was nothing but heartache.

After talking a while, she suddenly realized how easy Ted was to talk to. He was not at all the kind of man she first thought he was. He talked macho, but he had a soft spot in him. Before she knew it, she was confiding in him, but something's, still remained a secret.

Then the question came. "Jan, was Austin the Father?"

Jan nodded her head.

"I thought that much. Does he know?" Ted asked.

"I tried to tell him, but for some unknown reason he turns a deaf ear and wants to believe the worst." Then, as her tear flowed she said, "he said some hurtful things and I told him until he apologizes, I don't want to see him again."

"You still love him even after all that?" he asked.

"I will always love him, no matter what. I can't help thinking that he feels the same way. He just feels betrayed right now. If he would only listen to me, but even if he did, would he be angry at me for giving up our son?" She pondered, while she wiped the tear from her eyes.

"Jan, stop beating yourself up. There was nothing else you could have done in your situation. I will talk to Austin, and try to knock some sense into that hard head of his," Ted said, now ticked-off at his friend.

"No, Ted, just leave it be. I don't want to ruin your friendship. Austin deep down, is really a great guy," she said, with a far away look in her eyes.

"I can't believe you, woman! After all this, you still talk highly of the guy?" Ted scoffed.

"Ted, God has forgiven me for my part in this years ago, so I must do the same. But now I need to have Austin's forgiveness, for giving up our child without him knowing. When you truly love someone, you may be hurt and angry at them, but you still can't help but love them," Jan said sadly.

Ted sat silently trying to grasp what she had just said.

It was Jan that finally broke the silence. She took a deep breath. Her heart was no longer racing, but it was very irregular.

"Ted, do you know much about Austin's financial problems?" she asked.

Ted was very surprised at her question, because as far as he knew, Austin had confided only in him. "Why do you ask that?" he said, with a surprised look on his face.

"There was a phone call for Austin this morning, and from what I understand, he is in danger of losing his ranch. That can't be allowed to happen, Ted," she said, upset at just the thought of it.

"I'm afraid it may be inevitable. There is nothing we can do about it," Ted told her.

"Yes there is! You're his best friend, and you can talk him into having a silent partner," she said, pleading with him.

"That would never work and besides, I don't know anyone that has enough money to clear off his debt, do you?" he asked, not thinking that she had the answer.

"Yes I do, me. He would never listen to me if I offered him the money, so this is the only way," she said.

Ted looked at her in astonishment. "You!" he said in surprise.

"Yes me, I will do what ever I can to see that he does not lose this ranch."

"Where did you get that kind of money?" Ted asked, looking at her.

"From my husband's life insurance."

"Austin will never agree to taking your money," he told her.

"He is never to know where the money came from. Henceforth, the silent and unknown, partner, and I want you to swear never to reveal this to him. It would have to be a dire emergency before he is ever to know. Now promise me that you will talk him into doing this, before it is too late," Jan pleaded.

"Jan, I don't think I will ever understand you. Austin is a real fool if he lets you go. Now we better be getting back," Ted said helping her to her feet.

Ted saw Jan place her hand over her heart. "Jan, are you feeling okay?" he asked.

"I'll be fine."

"When we get back to the house, you better rest."

Jan stopped and looked at him. "Ted, I am not going back into that house. I am going to my home. When we get to the house, I want you to get my truck keys out of the bedroom that I stayed in. They are lying on the nightstand. I just can't face anyone right now," she said sadly.

"Well, in that case, I am going to follow you home. That way I will know that you at least got home safely. Otherwise, you will stay here," he told her.

Jan was not up to arguing and maybe it would be for the best, as she was not feeling that great right now. "Alright, I accept," she said, getting on Hope.

After putting the horses away, Ted drove her up to the house. He then went in for the truck keys while Jan waited outside.

"Where do you think you are going?" Austin asked.

"If you must know, I am getting Jan's truck keys." Ted said, noticing the surprised look on Austin's face, when Ted came into the room." He heard Austin's Father say that it was good that she was leaving, and Austin sat there not saying a word. Ted had it. He let fly with both barrels.

"Austin, you are either stupid, or a total fool to let Jan go without a fight," he shouted.

"Leave my son alone." Austin's mother said, now very upset.

"Pardon me, Mam, but you have the audacity to lay all the blame for this on Jan, when your son is as guilty as she is?" Ted accused furiously.

"Are you accusing my son of being the Father of her child?" she demanded, getting to her feet.

Ted looked directly at Austin. "You bet I am. It sure wasn't immaculate conception on his part."

Austin jumped to his feet. "Get out Ted!" he yelled.

"She still loves you Austin. Think about it, old friend. Don't make an even bigger mistake," he said, laying his hand on Austin's shoulder.

Austin shrugged it off, but by the look on Austin's face, the truth finally hit home.

Austin's mother never said another word. She just sat down and looked at the table.

"I'm sorry, but it had to be said, Austin. I'll see that Jan gets home safely, she isn't feeling very well."

Ted knew by the look on Austin's face that he was distraught. It was obvious that he was deeply in love with Jan. He had made a fool out of himself, and now he had to live with the consequences. Would he swallow that pride of his, and go to Jan? Only time would tell.

Ted had hoped that Austin would have gone out to talk to Jan before they left, but for some unknown reason, he had not done that. When Ted handed Jan her keys, he had a strong suspicion that she was not physically doing so well. He had offered to drive her home, but she insisted on driving herself. While following her, his mind was sorting out the bits and pieces that both Austin, and Jan, had told him. The puzzle was now all coming together. It was then that one piece of the puzzle caused him consternation. It was the piece that had ruined the rest of the picture.

He remembered the man that he had seen in his rearview mirror, when he and Austin had picked up Jan's truck. From Austin's description of this man, it had made him fear for Jan's safety. That was when his anger towards Austin burned with in him, even more. He had only known Jan a short while, but she was special. He had to guard his feelings towards her, because he knew he could fall for her very easily.

An hour and a half later, they both drove into a well-kept farmyard. Ted decided that, before he left, he would make sure that she was okay, and that everything in and around the house was as she left it.

Ted walked over to Jan's truck and opened the door for her, while she fumbled around in her purse looking for her house keys. When she got out, he could tell that she had been crying, but he said nothing. With keys finally in hand, she walked towards the house.

"Ted, would you like to stay for a cup of coffee?" she asked.

"Sure, if you don't mind, I would love to," he said.

Jan's hand was shaking when she tried to unlock the door.

"Here, Jan, let me do that," he said, taking the keys from her.

Once in the house, Jan went straight to the bathroom. She splashed cold water on her face, now glad for Ted's company. It was going to be very lonely after he left. She had no idea how she was going to face her future now. Her only hope was that someday she would find her son, but with the way things were going, she wondered if that would turn out to be another disaster.

While waiting for Jan, Ted made a quick tour through her modest home. Everything was fine, and there were no signs that anyone had been around while she was gone. He had no intention of mentioning his concern about her old suitor.

After pouring the water into the coffee pot, Jan took a few items out of the fridge and cupboard, and began to make some lunch.

"Jan, why don't you just sit down and rest," he said.

"I need to keep busy, and besides you haven't even had lunch today and it is already five o'clock." Then looking at him she added. "I bet you didn't even have breakfast this morning.

Did you?" She questioned.

Ted just shrugged his shoulders. She smiled at him and said, "You need to get yourself a wife, Ted. You are worse than Austin." The smile on her face disappeared, after she mentioned Austin's name. She quickly turned around to work on the sandwiches.

Ted was about to jokingly say that he would gladly take her, if Austin didn't smarten up, but he thought best to keep his mouth shut. He decided then and there, that he would stay in close contact with her as long as Austin was acting like a jerk. He only wished that she lived closer so that he could keep an eye on her. Jan had now given him the opportunity to do that, without her getting suspicious. That was if he was to be the go between, in Austin and Jan's partnership. It was not going to be that easy to get Austin to take on a silent partner, but he would try, for Jan's sake, more than Austin's. Then he began to think about things that he knew were dangerous territory.

What if he fell in love with Jan - then what? Oh, what the heck, he had been with a lot of women, and none of them had ever made him feel like settling down. Jan was just another woman, and he was here only to keep an eye on her until Austin got his head screwed on straight. The two of them sat talking, long after Jan had the lunch dishes cleaned up.

Jan learned a lot about Ted that evening and it was, all good. He was definitely a man that did not shy away from hard work, and he was very well educated. He once had a high up position with one of the major oil companies, but he was not happy there. He loved working with animals as well as being in wide-open spaces. He did have a quarter section of land, where he kept a few cows and a couple of horses. "Just enough to make a few dollars, but not enough to tie him down," he said. As he helped Austin quite often, he usually left his Paint horse there. He later took on the job as brand inspector, as well as working with the men that tried to catch the cattle rustlers. It was then that Jan found out that the problem with Austin's disappearing cows was different then she thought. There were never large numbers of cattle taken at one time. Ted had a strong suspicion that Austin's neighbor was the culprit.

He had been trying to buy that property from Austin's grandfather for years. He was furious when Austin took over the place.

Jan questioned Ted about Austin's grandfather. She was surprised that he would have had that much land. After all, growing up with the old ways, no one was to have that much property.

Ted explained that Austin had been adopted, and this land was from his biological grandfather.

Jan was shocked. She never knew that Austin had been adopted. That explained the jet- black wavy hair, and why he did not look like either his mother or father. She had wondered about his name many times. As a rule, the children took on the same names as their grandparents or parents. Apparently, Mr. and Mrs. Klassen had chosen to keep the name that Austin's birth mother had given him. Jan suddenly got very quit. Had her son been adopted out? If so, had they kept the name she had given him?

"Jan, are you alright?" Ted asked, as she suddenly got very pale.

"Yes," she said shaking off her thoughts.

"You know, Ted I am beginning to think that some of Austin's hostility may have something to do with him being adopted. I still wish I could have made him understand that the child I had, was his child," she said sadly.

"Oh, he knows now," Ted, informed her.

"What do you mean by that?" she asked, looking at Ted.

It was then that Ted, told her what he had said to Austin and his parents.

Jan was shocked. "Ted you didn't say that all in-front of his parents, did you?" she asked.

Ted indicated that he had.

"Oh, poor Austin." Jan said, now wondering what Austin was in for. Her mind went back to the treatment she would have gotten, if she had still lived in that old area. Well, he was clear of that, and as long as he continued to rely on God, he would survive what ever his parents threw at him.

"Poor Austin? How can you feel sorry for him after the way he treated you?" Ted asked.

Jan touched Ted's arm briefly, then said, "Ted, someday you will fall in love with a great women that you just can't live without, then you will understand. True love is something that you cannot just turn on and off." Ted shook his head in dismay

Jan and Ted now focused their discussion on the financial arrangement, that she wanted Ted to discuss with Austin. He told her not to count on it, as Austin could be stubborn enough to lose the ranch, before accepting help. It also had to do with Austin's pride, but Ted said that he would try. It was still better then having the bank take it all, leaving Austin to walk away with nothing but the clothes on his back.

He suddenly jumped to his feet when he realized how late it was. "Jan I have to get going. It is already after midnight, and I have a full day tomorrow. Are you sure that you will be alright, here alone?" He asked not comfortable with this situation.

"I've been here alone for some time, I'll be fine."

Ted wrote down his home, and cell phone numbers, than handed them to her. "Jan, make sure that you call me at any time, if you need help, or if you just need to talk. I am sure Austin will come around sooner or later." It was then that he saw the ring on her finger. Jan followed his gaze. Sadly, she showed Ted the ring. "He wanted to get married next week, but that's now off. I should have left it behind."

Ted looked at the deep sadness that seemed to engulf her. "Jan, don't take it off. As long as you keep his ring on your finger, it will remind you of the love you share. Then remember what you just finished telling me. If your God is real and Austin believes the same as you do, he will be going through the same emotions as you are."

"Thanks, Ted," she said.

"For what?" he asked.

"Your encouragement," she said. "Ted, when did Austin build that house?" she asked.

"A couple of years after he inherited the place. When he built it, I had asked him why he needed such a big house, and he told me that he had a special person in mind. He insisted that it had to be done just as on the scrap piece of paper he showed me," Ted said.

When he saw the look on her face, he knew.

"Aw, it was you he was talking about. Now I understand," Ted said in surprise.

Then in a very serious tone she added. "Ted, don't forget to talk to Austin about the money deal. He just can't lose that place, now that I know the rest."

"I'll keep in touch," Ted said, putting on his hat and walking out the door.

Jan felt so alone after Ted left. Her house didn't feel like home anymore. Jan slept very little that night. A good part of her night consisted of crying and praying. She did not fall asleep until she was to exhausted to cry.

CHAPTER 7

AUSTIN LAY ON HIS BED, staring blankly up at the ceiling. His day sure hadn't gone as planned. From the time Jan told him that she was going home, everything went down hill. His arms ached to hold her. He blew it big time. He remembered how hurt he was to find out that the rumors about her were true. He now realized that she had dropped enough hints, but he didn't have enough brains to clue in, to what she was trying to tell him.

Well, the wrath of God was unleashed on him tonight. Ted's outburst was plain and to the point. It wasn't as if he hadn't thought of the possibility, of him being the father of her child, when he first heard the rumors. He was so sure that he had been careful, and that nothing would happen. Boy, did he mess up. He remembered how guilty he felt after leaving the coulee that afternoon. It was wrong and he knew it, but they loved each other, and they both knew that there was a good chance that they would never be able to meet, like that again.

All the suffering that Jan had gone through in those younger years was his fault. He couldn't blame her for despising him. Especially after he accused her, up by the drop, of being with someone else besides him. He had no idea how she could say that she loved him in one breath, then in the next, tell him that she never wanted to see him again. He did owe her an apology.

Then there was the tongue lashing that he got from his parents, while he sat quietly taking it all in. He finally had all he could take, and asked them to leave. He needed to be alone.

The moonbeams now filtered into his room, replacing the sun that had disappeared under the horizon, quite some time ago. That was when he noticed the note that Jan had stuck on his mirror. He got up and pulled it off, then switched on his bed-lamp to see what it said. It was a note from Jan, but not what he had hoped. At first he was upset, but then he resigned himself to the inevitable. "Let them take the darn place. I just don't care any more," he said, crumpling up Jan's note, then throwing it across the room. The cheque he would get from the cattle he was selling, would go directly to the bank. He was concerned that it may not even cover his loan payment, but to heck with it all. Jan was better off with out him, as he would be penniless.

Austin went into the kitchen to see about eating something. He had not eaten anything since breakfast. He still did not feel hungry. He just needed something to occupy himself with. He opened the fridge to see what he could find. *There were still some leftover's from yesterday that he could eat, but...* It was then that he saw a six-pack of beer, way in the back. His first reaction was anger towards Ted. He had told him never to bring beer into his house, but occasionally, he would sneak it in.

Austin stared at it for a while. He hated the taste of the stuff. Not only that, the odour, of someone that had been drinking sickened him. During a hot day of branding, he had accepted a beer when there was nothing else to drink, but now he was tempted to see if perhaps you could drown your sorrow with it.

Austin closed the fridge door, while reprimanding himself for even thinking about drinking it. Only God could help him through this. Liquor would only make it worse.

He knew better. Austin went into the bedroom that Jan had used just a short while ago. There, on the bed, lay his clothes that she had been using. He opened the door of the closet and unhooked the hanger that held the clothes that he bought for her many years before. He held them for a moment, then fired them across the room, and went back to the kitchen. He opened the fridge, pulled out the six-pack, and then slammed the fridge door shut, at which time the Kleenex box that sat on the top of the fridge, fell down. He gave it a good kick, sending Kleenex flying everywhere.

Austin tried to put everything out of his mind as he downed the first can of beer, then the second, third, fourth and by the time he finished the sixth, he was almost out of it. He had eaten nothing all day, and not being used to alcohol, he was not feeling well.

The next thing he knew, there was someone shaking him.

"Austin, wake up."

Ted walked over to the cupboard to make a pot of coffee. Then, after putting a couple of slices of bread in the toaster, he sat down across from Austin.

"What do you think you are trying to prove, Austin? Even I know that this isn't going to solve your problems," Ted told him.

"What are you doing here?" Austin snapped. His stomach now aching like when he had the flu, and his head hurt like after he'd had his wisdom teeth dug out.

"Just thought I'd come to apologize for unloading on you like I did. It's not that I am sorry for saying what did. But I could have been more discreet, and not said what I did in front of your company. Now I am sorry for putting that six pack in there. I hope you won't make a practice of this. You have enough problems without that," Ted said, getting up to butter the toast. Ted waited until the coffee was done, before taking a couple of cups from the cupboard. He filled one, then took it, and the toast, and sat it in front of Austin, before getting himself a coffee.

Austin pushed the toast away. Ted pushed it back, saying, "Eat it, Austin, or I will force it down your throat."

"I'd like to see you try." Austin said sarcastically, running his hand through his uncombed hair.

"I am glad Jan isn't here to see you now," Ted told him, taking a sip of coffee.

"Don't ever mention her name in this house again," Austin said angrily.

Ted looked over at his friend. "Austin, are you mad at her, or yourself?" he asked calmly.

Ted sat quietly drinking his coffee, while Austin devoured the toast. Then, refilling both cups, Ted said, "Austin, I have a proposition for you. It's about the money you owe the bank. I think I know..." he began to say, when Austin jumped in.

"Forget it, I don't care anymore. Let them take the whole darn thing, I'm tired of fighting," Austin said totally distraught.

"Austin, you can't give up now. As I was saying, I know someone that is quite willing to pay off your loan," Ted said.

"You're the one that has been drinking, Ted," Austin said.

"There is only one stipulation. This person wants to be your silent, and anonymous, partner," Ted continued.

"Are you crazy? That can be worse than losing the place," he said, now sounding more like his old self.

"I know that, but this person will give you free rein of the place, as long as you continue to work the ranch as you always have, and they get their share," Ted told him.

"What's the catch? What percent do they want?" He asked.

"Well..." Ted said slowly.

"Yeah, I might have known. They figure that, seeing as I will lose it anyway, they could get half the ranch for next to nothing," Austin said.

"It's not that bad, Austin. You must consider the fact that you would have to sell every cow you have, and then some, to pay off the loan if they call it. Then you will lose it all, and from what I heard, that could happen any day. Not only that, Douglas would do anything to get the bank to foreclose on you, once he finds out that you are in serious trouble. That is if he hasn't already been pushing," Ted said.

"I know this person fairly well, and believe me, you will come out a winner. You never know, down the road, sh..." Ted stopped, hoping that Austin did not catch the near slip he'd made, when he almost said, she. Continuing he added. "They may even sell it all back to you when you get back on your feet."

"Well spit it out, what do they want?" Austin said, knowing he was pretty well whipped.

"They want twenty percent of the profits," Ted said.

"What's in it for you?" Austin asked, now suspicious of this sudden unexpected offer.

"Not a thing. I'm just doing it as a friend. I am still hoping that someday you and Jan will get back together, and you can share your dream house." Austin suddenly looked at Ted.

"What are you talking about?" Austin asked, wondering how he knew.

"It was just a good guess," Ted said covering his tracks.

It was some time before Austin broke the silence. "How is she?" Austin asked sheepishly.

Ted looked at Austin and said, "She was very upset, and in her words, she still loves you, and says that you can't just turn true love off and on. She said that deep down, she believes, or hopes, that you feel the same. I do believe she means it about the apology Austin, and I can't say that I blame her. I have to go now. I'd do some serious thinking about that offer, if I were you. Don't leave it too long."

Just as Ted was about to walk out the door, Austin, called him back. "What would you do in my situation?" he asked.

"Well…truthfully," Ted said, hesitating a moment before continuing. "I am sure I would be wary, but knowing what I do about both you and the other party, I'd say jump at it. I can't help but believe that this will turn out to be a good, and profitable deal for the both of you," Ted replied.

"By the way, thanks for making sure that Jan got home safely, last night," Austin told him.

"Glad to do it," Ted said not sure if he had done that for Austin, or himself.

Austin reluctantly picked up the Kleenex that littered the kitchen floor and stuck them back in the broken box, and set it on the table. The empty beer cans he threw in the garbage, before going into the bathroom to rinse out his mouth. The rotten smell on his breath almost made him sick. He preferred his stinky old socks to this. Even after gargling and brushing his teeth, that taste and odour still seemed to linger. He briefly ran a comb through his hair, and then headed outside.

He hopped in his truck and drove down to the corrals. First of all, he made sure that the two bulls had food and water before, whistling for Midnight. He went through the usual motions, but his heart was not in it. Jan was gone, and he was about to lose the ranch that his grandfather had given him, unless he did as Ted suggested. Then he'd be losing control of the ranch. He had wished for some time now, that he had not purchased those two bulls, even though he needed them for his heifers. He had bought them quite some time back, and therefore, did not feel right about changing his mind.

When the wind blew from the east, it generally brought rain or some sort of a storm. Even though the sky was threatening, Austin rode slowly out west to check on his cattle. Midnight was itching for his run, but today Austin was not in the mood. He jerked on the reins several times to stop Midnight from acting up.

By the time Austin finished going through his herd, it was beginning to rain. Just after closing the gate and heading back home, the rain turned into a downpour. Why had he not used his head and taken his slicker? He gave Midnight a nudge with his spurs, while putting his head down to keep some of the rain out of his face. All that seemed to do was deflect the water from his hat to his pants. Midnight burst into action, but the ground was now getting slippery. Austin hung on while giving Midnight his head.

Between the wind and rain, he was now beginning to feel the icy chill ripple through his body. *It wouldn't surprise me one bit if it snowed*, he said to himself. What he wanted was to be sitting in his warm kitchen, waiting for Jan to place his lunch in front of him. Halfway home, the rain eased up, and large snowflakes began to fall. It looked like a winter wonderland. Generally,

Austin loved to watch this type of snow, but he was cold, hungry, and worst of all, very depressed. By the time he got home, he had no energy to do anything. Austin brushed down Midnight, then checked his hoofs, before turning him out to pasture.

When Austin got up to the house, the wind had stopped, leaving the snow to pile up on where ever it landed. When he got into the house, he was so cold that he could hardly get his boots off. It didn't help that they were full of mud, and soaked with water. When he hung his hat on the hook a mixture of snow and water fell off, leaving a mound of slush on the mat below. It was like nothing mattered any more. His pants were soaked and muddy and when he made his way through the house to the bathroom, they left a trail of muddy streaks.

Normally, he would have taken his wet clothes off by the door, but instead, they lay in a pile with a puddle of water beginning to seep out from beneath the edges. Even soaking in a tub of very warm water didn't seem to take away the icy chill. When he closed his eyes and leaned back, all he could think of was Jan. They should be planning their wedding right now. He wondered if she was still wearing the ring he gave her.

Austin suddenly got a chilling thought. What if John found out where she lived? What would he do to her? Austin wanted desperately to hear her voice, and to know that she was all right. He knew he had to apologize to her, but that was something he had to do in person. Then the feeling of hopelessness set in again. How could he ever ask her to marry him, when he may not even have a home to bring her to? He felt he had also failed his grandfather, who had worked so hard for this place, and for what? So his grandson could lose it to the bank! Maybe he should consider Ted's friends offer. At least he would still own the bigger portion of it. What he couldn't understand was, how Ted had suddenly come up with this mysterious person with all the money.

Surely it wasn't Jan. No, that was impossible. She wouldn't have that kind of money, and if she did, he sure wouldn't take it from her. His pride would not allow him to do that. He knew that if things were to good to be true, they probably were. He was very fearful of taking on this unknown partner, but his other option was to walk away, with only the clothes on his back. He should be going to the sale, to find out if the cows he had shipped would, cover the loan payment.

The bath water was getting cold, when Austin finally stepped out of the tub. When he slipped into clean clothes, all he could think of was to pick up the phone and call Jan. He had to be sure that everything was still okay. He also needed to hear her voice and hoped that she would tell him that she still loved him.

He sat on the edge of the bed, staring at the phone on his nightstand. He picked it up several times, than laid it back down again. Her last few words still rang in his ears. He remembered it as clear as a bell when she'd said. "I never want to see you again." His heart ached at the memory of those cutting words.

He also remembered the scare he'd got when the ground gave way under her feet. *All he wanted was to love her like - like the last time? Then the thought of her making love to someone else angered him. Why had he accused her of trying to trap, him. When in all actuality, he had thought of doing that. He didn't want her to ever leave again.* He sifted through everything that she had said. Why was he so blind? It was so obvious what she had been trying to tell him.

He reached over and picked up the phone. This time he dialed her number. He let it ring for quite some time, and was just about to hang up, when her heard her voice.

"Hello," she said, sounding like she was out of breath.

Austin, now wondering why he had done this, as he was now stumped for words.

"Hello?" she said again.

It was then that he remembered the caller display.

"Austin? Is that you?" she asked. Her voice sounding like she was almost afraid to find out.

"Yes, Jan, It's me," He said, very distant.

"Is something wrong?" she asked quickly.

Austin could tell by the tone of her voice that she was sincerely concerned.

"No, Jan, I -I am doing as good as is expected in this situation. How about you?" he asked.

"About... the same." she said, trying not to cry.

"I just called to make sure that you haven't been bothered by... well you know," he said.

"Yes, I know and no, he hasn't called," she told him.

"Jan, I know - I owe you an apology, but I can't do it on the phone. I do miss you," he said, now sounding very distant.

"Austin, can I ask you a personal question?" she inquired, a bit afraid of how he might react to this.

"Go ahead," he whispered.

"How are things really going? I mean financially." She paused but he did not reply. "I didn't mean to pry into your affairs, but your banker phoned when you and Ted were loading the cows." He presumed that I was your wife, and gave me a message to give you. Is there something that I can do to help?" she asked.

"No, I have to go," He said abruptly before hanging up the phone.

Austin had just hung up the phone, when it rang.

He quickly picked up and said, "Jan?"

There was a silence for a bit before he heard Ted's voice. "No, it's Ted. I was wondering if you would come give us a hand here. It's a bigger sale then expected, and we are short handed today. It would do you good to get out and forget about everything for a while," Ted said.

Austin was quiet for a moment, than decided it was better than fretting over everything. Beside, he could use a couple bucks. "I'll leave right away," Austin said.

The roads were quite snow covered when he left. He wondered how bad his day could possibly get, but by the end of the day, he was thankful to Ted for getting him out of the house. It was a good day to sell his cows, as the prices were strong.

It was at least enough to cover his loan. The only worry now was, he had been in arrears for so long, and in three months, the next payment was due, again. Where would he get the money for that? Would he have to continue selling off his cattle until he had none left to sell?

For Jan, it was just the opposite. She had kept busy all morning, but after Austin called, she had no ambition to do anything. She felt very depressed. She knew that Austin still loved her, or he would not have called. She wished they could have talked longer. If only she had not brought up the topic of his finances. She realized that Ted was right. Austin would never take the money if he knew it was from her.

Jan's meals were far and few between. Since Don died she did not eat regularly. It was hard to make something just for one person, and since she got back home her appetite had diminished even farther. *Oh if only God would not have taken Don from me. Life would have been much more bearable.*

Jan looked out the window to see light snow flurries. If the weather had been better, she would have gone to Red Deer just to get out of here.

* * *

A week had passed, and Austin had not made any attempt to contact her. She was now doing her best, to face the fact that the life she had hoped to share with Austin, was never to be.

She jumped when she heard the phone ring. Perhaps Austin was calling her after all. She quickly ran out to the kitchen. She had her hand on the receiver ready to pick it up, when she glanced down at the caller display. When she saw the name, she dropped her hand to her side, and let the phone ring. Her heart began to race at the thought of him finding her. She had no idea what to do. Should she call Austin? There was only one other person that she could turn to, but she would call him later. She did not want to risk having the line ring busy, if John called again. By not answering, he would take for granted that she was not home. She would wait until at least 11 o'clock. Surely he would not call that late in the evening.

Jan monitored all her calls that evening. John called two more times, as did Ted. Jan was very temped to answerer Ted's calls, but she didn't dare risk it. She would call him later.

It was eleven fifteen when Jan called Ted back.

"Hello?" Ted said, half asleep.

"Oh, I am sorry Ted. I didn't mean to wake you up."

Ted seemed to come to life when he heard her voice. "Oh, hi Jan. I tried to call you earlier, but you must have been out," he said.

"No, I was home, but I had my reasons for not answering," she replied.

Ted sat straight up in his bed. "Jan, did John call again?" he asked anxiously.

"Yes, he called three times, but I didn't answer. That was why I didn't answer when you called. I didn't want to risk having him hear the busy signal. I hope he thinks that I am not home," she said.

Ted could tell by her voice that she was scared.

"Jan, why don't you go back and stay at Austin's. I'd ask you to stay with me, but that would be asking for more trouble. I don't think you should be there alone."

"I can't go back there, Ted and I don't want you to tell Austin about this either. He called about a week ago," Jan said.

"Really! What had he to say for himself?" Ted asked, a bit agitated.

"Not too much. He just wanted to know if John had called again. At that point, he hadn't. Then I asked him about his finances, and that was when he got upset. I should never have done that," she said.

"Yeah, that is a touchy thing to talk to him about right now," Ted said

"Did you tell him about the offer?" Jan asked.

"Yeah, I did shortly after you left. He was quite a mess when I got there. He had tied one on," Ted said.

Jan got real quiet. Maybe she didn't know Austin like she thought she did.

"Does he do that often?" she asked.

"Who, Austin? Are you kidding me? You could have knocked me over with a feather, when I saw him sleeping by the kitchen table. I guess it was my fault. Occasionally I slip some beer in his fridge, so I can have a drink, when I am helping him. He gets mad and tells me to get it out, and this was one time I should have listened. He must be hurtin' bad to have done that," Ted said.

It was then that he heard Jan clearing her throat and he figure she was trying not to cry. "I'm sorry, Jan. I should learn to keep my mouth shut. I wish I could be there for you, or that I could help you through this," he said.

"I'll be alright," she told him.

"Back to the finances, I think he will seriously look at it, even if he doesn't want to. He is close to getting backed up to the wall," he added.

"Thanks, Ted. Keep trying. He just can't lose his ranch. I'll go to my lawyer and get some papers drawn up so it can go through quickly, if need be. I have a terrible feeling that he may leave it until the last minute, or until it's too late. Either way, I am sure my lawyer can make some arrangement with the bank, just in case it comes to that. I better let you go back to sleep, Ted. I am sorry for bothering you. It's just that I needed someone to talk to," she said.

"I am glad you called, and don't hesitate to call again, even if it's in the middle if the night. I would feel better if you could find someone to stay with you." Ted said, his voice now full of concern.

"I may go away for a few days. If I do, I will let you know where I am," she said.

"You make sure you do that. I don't want to send out a search party, to looking for you," he said.

Jan felt better after talking to Ted, but it still did not relieve the uneasiness that she felt, when thinking about John. She decided that she would pack a few things in her suitcase, and go away for a few days. Where, she did not know. She would just get in her truck and go.

Before she turned in for the night, she glanced out of her bedroom window, and was relieved to see that it had quit snowing. She did not like to drive on bad roads, but taking in consideration the time of year, she was sure that by noon tomorrow, the snow would all be gone.

The next morning, Jan put the last few personal things in her suitcase, and then headed out the door, locking it behind her. Once in the garage, she decided to take her car. The roads were clear as she turned west onto the gravel road. When she reached the number two highway she turned north to Red Deer. She had a sudden change of mind and then headed west, aiming for highway twenty-two.

From there she turned south, seemingly lost in her thoughts. That highway, known as the cowboy trail, was her favorite highway. After Don died, she ventured out travelling north as far as Rocky Mountain House, and south to the number three highway. She loved the trees better than the wide-open spaces. There were picturesque areas, like when the majestic snow covered peaks of the Rocky Mountains arose in the distance. It was enough to take her breath away. Then she remembered the view from Austin's living room.

"Why, Lord?" she asked, looking at the ring on her finger.

After passing through Cochrane, Bragg Creek, and continued south, she began to wonder what she was doing. What if she ran into Austin here? She had no idea why she had come this direction.

When she got though the next town, she turned to the right. There was still some snow on the road as she headed west towards the foothills. She had no intention of going to Austin's, but there was a good possibility that she could meet him here on this road. Just as she past his turn off, she saw his truck approaching the main road. *That was close*, she thought, with tears in her eyes. She wanted so bad to have him hold her again, or even just to have a glimpse of him.

Jan had never been out this far before. It was a shame that so much of the ranch land was now being split up into acreages. And yet, she could understand why others would want to have the same taste of country life. She could accept that, only if they did not interfere with the true ranching way of life.

At one point, Jan stopped the car and took in the view. She sat there for some time, before turning around and heading back to town. She was not sure where she would go from here. Jan was half way between Austin's turn off, and town, when she saw him returning home. Surely he would not recognize her car. She looked down as they met. Then looking in her rear-view mirror, panic sat in when she saw his brake lights come on. Jan sped up, hoping that he would not turn around. Had he recognized her? She watched for a while, than finally the brake lights went out as he continued on.

That evening, Jan called Ted from Longview to let him where she was. He asked if he could take her out for supper, seeing as she was in the area, but to his disappointment, she declined his offer. She told him that, she was planning to visit a cousin of Don's in Nanton before spending a few days in Lethbridge. She would give him a call when she returned home.

* * *

Jan was weighing heavily on Austin's mind, as he headed home from town. He saw this dark metallic-green Honda car approaching, and was sure that he had never seen a car like that in this area before. It was then he remembered where he had seen one. It was in Jan's garage. When they met, he knew it was a woman, but she was looking down, and the position of her arm made it hard for him to see, if it actually was her. He slammed on the brakes and was about to turn around but instead, he stopped for a moment and watched for any sign of braking. If it had been Jan, she would have recognized his truck. *I had just wanted so badly for it to be her that, I'm seeing things,* he said to himself as he continued, his drive home.

Chapter 8

A COUPLE OF MONTHS HAD passed and Jan had still not heard from Austin. However, Ted had persuaded Austin to accept the offer, to save his ranch. Just in time too. Ted had gotten wind that Austin's neighbor was already making a deal with the bank, to take it over. Had he waited another week, he would have lost everything.

Austin, always looked after his animals, but as for his personnel appearance, he was a mess. His appearance now, did nothing to help when dealing with his financial institution. Ted appointed himself to be an overseer of Austin, just to protect Jan's investment. However, Jan had full confidence in Austin, but then she hadn't seen him lately. By the way his clothes hung on him, it was obvious that he had lost a lot of weight. Most of the time he was unshaven, and his home and vehicles, were now a reflection of him.

Ted knew that the only thing that would snap Austin out of his slump was, for him to get back together with Jan. But he had no idea how to arrange that. That was not the only problem arising. Ted had been in constant contact with Jan during the merger between her and Austin. He was now really beginning to feel like he was entering into a danger zone. Jan had offered Ted some compensation for bringing everything together. She also asked Ted if he thought it would be beneficial, for her and Austin to increase the herd by another fifty head. Austin would not be asked to put out any money as Jan would purchase them, and the same agreement still stood. The reason for that was, Austin had come into the agreement with a hundred head of cattle, so therefore, and she felt it only fair, that she contribute a few more cows.

Ted had discussed the deal with Austin when, they returned from checking the cattle. Austin was still skeptical of the whole agreement. It just didn't seem to make any sense for someone to do this, and yet he had still felt that he had lost a lot through this deal, considering the value of the land. Well, at least he didn't have the bank breathing down his neck. Instead, he was now being asked for his input. He had tried to find out who this partner of his was, but Ted was very close-mouthed about it.

They had just put their horses out to pasture, when Ted got a call on his cell phone.

"Oh, Hi there," he had said, apparently happy to hear from his caller. Then Austin heard him say, "Are you sure? Oh boy, how long ago?" Ted asked obviously frightened about something. After that, Ted disappeared around the corner to finish his conversation.

"Jan, I'll be there as quick as I can. I'm here at Austin's. I will bring him with me," Ted said, but Jan made him promise to leave Austin out of it, before she hung up.

"What's up?" Austin asked, after Ted told him that he had to leave right away. "I'll tell you sometime," he said.

Austin grabbed Ted by the shirt. "I heard you mention her name, and mine. Are you getting involved with her?" Austin said, now furious.

"Austin, don't be so stupid. You are the one she wants, so why don't you get your act together and go see how she is, instead of accusing me of something," Ted said pulling himself free, then running over to his truck. When Ted left, there was gravel flying all the way up the hill, and beyond. Austin knew something was wrong. He had a terrible feeling in the pit of his stomach, but he was so out of it lately, that he just couldn't think straight.

Book 3 of the *Mountains and Valleys of Life*

Again, it took Ted's words to make him think. Was he doing the same thing again? Austin had neglected God since Jan left. He now began to realize that only God could get him back on track. Right there, beside a bale, he fell to his knees and cried out to God for some direction in life. He asked for God's protection over who, or what ever, it was that was giving him this sick feeling that something was really wrong. He asked God to help him swallow his pride, and go to Jan and beg her for forgiveness. He knew he should have done it sooner, because the longer he had left it, the harder it got. He thanked God for sending him this partner at just the right time, so he did not lose his entire ranch. He also thanked God for bringing Jan back into his life, even if things were rough right now. He would trust God to allow him to bring her back as his wife, and then to someday be united with their child.

"God, be with Jan and protect her," he pleaded. He knelt there in silence for some time, with tears streaming down his face. He now realized what he had lost.

* * *

Jan sat huddled in the corner of the kitchen cabinets. At least he couldn't see her there. She had been in the living room, when she'd seen an older pickup drive in. The curtains were closed, so she didn't think that whoever it was, had seen her. Then she heard a knock on the door. Ever since Don died, she was reluctant to answer the door, if she did not know the person.

The house was quiet. Usually, the first thing she did in the morning was to turn the radio on, but for some reason this morning she hadn't. She stood there in total silence. There was nothing unusual about the first two knocks. The third rap on the door was a little louder and at that point, she thought maybe she should see who it was. When she recognized that voice, she froze to the spot

"Anne? Are you home?" he shouted.

Blaze of Fury

That was enough to send her into a fit of panic. Her throat got dry, as she began to hyperventilate, and her whole body began to tremble. She had to calm herself down, so she began to take some slow deep breaths.

Now he was pounding on the door, while hollering, "Anne, are you in there?" She heard him try the door. Thankfully, she had not gone outside yet today, so the doors were still locked.

She sighed in relief when she heard him walk away. Then she heard him on the other side of the house, she had a good idea that he was looking in the windows, to see if she was there.

She had to move and fast, without making a sound, before he got to the living room window. She quickly dropped to her knees and crawled into the kitchen. There she huddled in the corner, of her kitchen cabinets. He would not be able to see her there. Every once in a while, she could hear him as he circled the house. It got quiet and at that point, Jan was holding her breath, hoping he would leave. Finally, she heard him drive out of the yard.

That was when she made her way to the phone, and called Ted. She prayed that John would not call her when her line was busy, so she made her conversation brief and to the point. She sat huddled back in her corner for a good half hour, praying harder then she had ever prayed before. Why was God allowing this to happen? What would John do to her, if he did get in? She was hoping that he believe that she was not home, but her fear was that he would return. She took a deep breath, but could not get herself to move from that spot. Tears began to flow. She desperately wanted Austin to hold her, and tell her that everything was going to be fine. Why had she not allowed Ted to bring him? "Oh Austin," she whispered.

Maybe she should make the first move to see him. Even if he never asked her to forgive him, it didn't matter any more. Life was too short. They had already lost nearly seven years. It was then that she decided, that if she got through this problem with

John, she would call Austin and see, if he would be willing to sit down and talk to her.

Jan looked at her watch. It was almost an hour and a half since she had talked to Ted. *I wish he would get here soon* she said to herself. Just then the phone rang. Jan was afraid to answer it. She crept over to check and see who it was. She sighed in relief, when she saw Ted's number.

"Hello," she said quietly, now afraid that someone might be listening.

"Jan, are you all right?" Ted asked.

"I'm just afraid, but otherwise I am fine," she replied.

"Well, I will be there in fifteen minutes or less, so hang in there," he told her.

Relieved Jan stood up and said, "I will be so glad when you get here." Jan gasped in fright when she looked out the window.

"Jan, what's wrong?" Ted asked, now fearing for her life.

"He's back and I am sure he saw me." Jan said dropping the phone to huddle in her corner.

"Jan! Jan! Ted called. Then he heard someone banging on her door and hollering. Ted stepped on the gas now, hoping he would get there in time. Then he heard a crash, and the phone went dead. Ted quickly dialed the police, told them what was happening, and gave Jan's name and the directions to where she lived. His knuckles were white, as he gripped the steering wheel and tore up the gravel, the last couple of miles. Just before Jan's place, he slowed down. He stopped just out of sight, then grabbed his rope from beside him, and ran towards the house.

He could hear Jan screaming when he got out of his truck.

John had ripped the phone from the wall, the moment he walked in. Then seeing her huddled in the corner, he grabbed her by the hair, and he pulled her up.

"I've come to take you home with me, woman. Now go get some of your stuff," he demanded, his eyes dark with anger. "There is no one here to stop me this time," he said, with a smirk on his face.

Blaze of Fury

"Get out of here!" she yelled, pulling away from him. At which time, he backhanded her so hard that it sent her flying across the room. She slowly got up, wiping the blood from her mouth. She tried to make a dash for the door, but he grabbed her arm and twisted it hard behind her back. She screamed, as something in her arm cracked, sending a horrific pain through her body. He shoved her toward the bedroom, than grabbed the knife that lay on her counter She stood there in shock, not wanting to go into the bedroom for fear of what else he may try. When she refused to move, he punched, and beat her as she tried to fight back with her one good arm. Suddenly, she felt the blade of the knife at her throat. At which point, she had two choices. One was let him cut her throat, or she could do as he said, in hopes that Ted would get there before it was too late. If he did what she feared, she would be wishing that he had killed her. With the knife digging into her throat, she went reluctantly into the bedroom.

The first thing Ted saw when he gingerly entered the front door, was the drops of blood on the floor. He also saw John forcing Jan at knifepoint into the bedroom. He quietly crept into the kitchen only to hear, Jan screaming as John cut open her shirt with the knife that he held in his hand, which ultimately cut into her arm and then the side of her face. John than threw the knife on the floor and threw himself on top of her.

Jan began to black out with all the pain and yet, she did her best to fight back with her good arm. *She would fight to her death*, she said to herself. Suddenly, she was free of him. She took some deep breaths as her blood began to stain her bed. Jan heard things crashing around her, and a lot of cussing as she drifted in and out of consciousness.

Ted and John were almost the same height, but as for weight, John at least seventy-five pounds heavier. John had worked hard on the farm ever since he could remember, so he was very strong, although Ted was no slouch either. He was strong and quick, and he was hopping mad. They fought until John, with his added weight, could fight no more. When Ted got the upper hand, he was ready to kill him, but he stopped just short of doing that. He grabbed his rope and tied it around John's feet and dragged him outside. Than he tied John up so tight, that it would take some real undoing, to get him lose.

He then ran into the bedroom and took Jan's pulse, to make sure that she was alive. "Thank God," he said. He grabbed a blanket and covering Jan, to give her some sense of dignity, when he heard the police arrive. At least Ted gotten there before John could strip her totally of her dignity. Ted quickly got a cloth to hold against the large gash on the side of her face, as he hollered at the police, to call an ambulance.

When the first officer entered the house, he saw blood and the result of the scuffle. It was when he saw the unconscious woman lying on the bed, that he quickly called out for the other officer to call for an ambulance, as soon as possible. When Jan began to come around, Ted brushed her hair from her face, before saying, "Jan just lie still. He is gone and won't hurt you again. I promise you that."

Jan suddenly realized that her shirt and bra did not feel right. She reaches down to her jeans and found them still intact. She could barely see out of her swelled eyes as she turned to Ted. "Ted did he... she asked, not able finish the sentence for two reasons. One, was she couldn't bring herself to say rape, and secondly because of the swelling, from John hitting her in the mouth.

"No, sweetie, he didn't. You will be fine. Just rest the ambulance will be here soon," Ted said calmly.

Jan slowly turned her head to look at the police offices standing on the other side of her.

It was hard to see now, but she was sure she knew his voice. With great difficulty, she said, "Well, officer, you must be my guardian angel, because you always seem to be coming to my rescue."

He looked at Ted, and asked, "I see you have a different friend this time. Who is this one?"

Blaze of Fury

"I am just looking after the interest of a friend of mine." Ted said, stroking Jan's hair.

"Well, I think your friend may be in danger of losing his interest," the office told him, as he watched the way Ted was looking at Jan.

When Jan tried to move her right arm, she cried out in pain. "Jan, don't move," Ted said, holding her down. It was obvious, by the position of her arm, that it was broken.

Ted sat beside Jan, holding her hand, when the police officer went outside to join his partner. It was some time before they came back into the house. "Is the ambulance here yet?" Ted asked.

"It's coming now. You tied that guy up pretty tight. You could have killed him, you know that?" The officer said.

Ted looked him right in the eye and said, "He is darn lucky that I didn't hang him from that tree out there."

After looking at Jan, he heard the second office say quietly to the other, "It sure would have saved us and her, a lot of trouble, if he had." At which time, the paramedics came rushing into the room.

Ted stepped back and watched them work on her. He felt sick inside. He couldn't even picture telling Austin about this. He had been beating himself up enough lately. This would just send him over the edge. He would tell him much later, but then he had a horrifying thought. What if this gets on the news? Lately though, Austin hadn't been watching much TV, or reading the paper. Austin had said that, he was depressed enough. Well, God seemed to let them both get close to the edge, but never over the edge. Maybe there was some reason for that.

Ted couldn't believe that he was even thinking about God. Maybe some of what Austin and Jan had told him was rubbing off.

When Jan was ready to be moved, she asked if Ted would come with her. "I will be following close behind, Jan. I promise. Are you sure you don't want me to call Austin?"

"No please, not yet. I don't want him to see me like this." She said, with great difficulty,

"Okay, now don't try to talk," he said, bending over to give her a kiss on the forehead, and that was the last thing she remembered.

When Ted stood up, he saw the officer looking at him. "Not a word out of you," Ted sneered.

The officer shook his head before saying, "We will need a statement from you."

"Can it wait until later? As you heard, I promised to be there for her," then added, "because her fiancée was unable to be here."

"I will meet you at the hospital then," the officer told him.

"Try to close the front door before you leave. I'll be back later to do it properly," Ted said heading out the door.

Ted saw John in the back of the police cruiser, when he ran over to where his truck was parked. He wondered what still lie ahead for Jan. Would they both have to go to court to testify against him? It would definitely have been less trouble for them, if he had strung him up. Their troubles would be over. Well, maybe not.

* * *

Jan's summer had consisted of several surgeries on her arm, as well as plastic surgery to try to fix the ugly scar on the side of her face. Her ribs hurt a lot, even though the x-ray showed that they were not broken. Ted had come to see her quite often to up-date her on what had been going on at the ranch. As for Austin, he was slowly beginning to get his act together. He had accepted the fact that he now had a partner in the ranch. Ted had told her that Austin had been trying to contact her, and was beginning to think that she had intentionally not taken his calls.

One morning, when Ted came to see how Jan was doing, she got a phone call. To her surprise, it was from John's lawyer. He told her that John wanted to make amends for the pain that he'd caused her, and asked if she be willing to come to the jail to talk to him. Ted saw the color drain from her face. He quickly went to her side, and took the phone from her hand. "Jan, what's wrong?" he asked, as she stood there, looking like she was ready to faint.

"Who is this?" Ted asked. Ted listened to John's lawyer, while Jan considered the request. Jan touched Ted's hand.

"If under supervision, I could make it clear that he could never come near me again. It may be worth it. I can't live in fear of him forever. I have to try something," she told him.

"Forget it, I don't trust him," Ted said sternly.

Jan took the phone from Ted. "I'll do as he asked, Ted." In a few minutes, they had a meeting arranged.

"Jan, what the heck do you think you are doing?" Ted blurted out, as was now very angry with her.

"Ted, don't you understand. I have to make it clear to him while, under supervision, that I will never be his wife and that he, is never to come near me again. Right now I fear the day that he will be released. I want this whole thing to be over with. I also want a restraining order."

"Jan, there is no reasoning with a guy like that," he said, grabbing her by the shoulders.

When she looked at him, she suddenly had a sinking feeling in the pit of her stomach. She should have seen this coming. Maybe it was just her imagination.

Ted quickly let her go, when she looked away. Had she suspected that he was falling in love with her? "Okay you can go, but I am coming with you. I won't take no for an answer," he told her.

Jan had second thoughts about coming, when they arrived at the jail. Ted had given her the option to back out, but she was determined to go through with this.

Ted and Jan were escorted into a room where there was a table in the center with a couple of chairs on either side. Jan was very nervous, as the guard told them to have a seat. Jan sat down, but Ted went and stood back against the wall. This was between Jan and John. He was there only for support.

After a few minutes, the door opened and the guard escorted a now clean-shaven man in his late thirties, into the room. Jan stood up when he walked over to the table.

She couldn't believe this was the same man that had attacked her. He was actually rather attractive, until she saw those eyes. The eyes she would never forget.

John sat down, all the while watching her, as she slowly sat across from him. Suddenly, John saw Ted. He jumped to his feet, and at the same time, the guard put his hand firmly on John's shoulder.

"What's he doing here?" he said angrily.

"Sit down," The guard demanded.

John hesitantly obeyed.

"He is here to support me, John. Anything we have to say to each other can be said with him here," she said, surprisingly calm. "What did you want to say to me?" Jan asked.

John looked up at Ted as if wondering if he should just walk out, but when he looked at Jan he changed his mind. "You're a beautiful woman Anne. If you would have married me, I would have made you a good husband." He looked at the cut and the bruises that were still prevalent on her face and arms. "I want to say that I am sorry for what I did, and that I really feel that we could make a go of it, if you give me the chance."

"John, I am sorry that things did not work out the way you hoped. I know you feel let down, because it was decided that I should marry you. It was my parents that felt you would make me a good husband because you were a hard worker, not me. I was in love with someone else." She could see the anger building up in his eyes, which sent a chill down her spin, but she remained calm.

"It's that Austin Klassen, isn't it? He is the one that should be punished for what he did.

"If he cares so much for you, why has this guy been hanging around?" he snarled, pointing at Ted. "What kind of woman are you?" he probed, his eyes dark with anger.

"I wouldn't go there, John. It's not Austin's fault. If anyone is to blame it is I, because I should have stood up to my parents, and flat out said, no. You mentioned at the restaurant that I should go before the church to ask their forgiveness. I will never step foot in that church again, and if you think I owe you an apology for not marring you, that will never happen either. The agreement was between my parents and you. They knew who I, wanted to marry, and it was not you. If you think what you did was right, I pray that you never have a wife to abuse. If anyone should, to go before your church to ask for forgiveness, it's you John. Marrying you will never happen," she emphasized.

John's eyes seemed to get darker the more she talked.

"I have asked God to forgive me for what I have done in the past. I feel sorry for the people that have stayed steeped in tradition. I know very well that you all feel that, I will never make it to heaven, since I left the church. When in fact it could be just the opposite for those that just use that church, for their advantage. You better read the Bible and find out what is truly right and wrong. Not only that, you tell me that you would make me a good husband." She lifted her arm that was still in the sling. "Is this what a good husband does? No! A good husband is, loving and trusting, and does not rule with an iron rod and fist! God said to love your wife as you love yourself. Would you do this to yourself?" she asked John, but he did not answer her.

Ted was surprised at how Jan took charge. When he looked at the guard, he could see that he was enjoying the tongue lashing that this man was getting, from the woman that he had abused. Jan continued.

"I have heard that some men in the church treated their wives badly. Yes, the Bible says that the husband is to be the head of the house. If the husband loves his wife like himself, his wife would in turn love him, and want to please him. That still does not mean that they won't have their disagreements, but that can be rectified through the love they have for each other. I suggest you think back to how you were brought up. If you feel that beatings are the way to get a woman to do what you say, I think you'd better get yourself some help," Jan said, as she saw John clench his fists.

"My father was a hard working man," he snapped, while banging his fist on the table.

"I don't doubt that, but was he a loving husband and father?" Jan asked.

Jan stood up. She looked into his eyes and said, "John, what was in the past is over.

Read your Bible and you will find what I said, is there. I'm sure that God will help you over-come your temper, and forgive you if you ask him. I will not be your doormat."

John stood up and grabbed Jan's left hand. Ted immediately stepped forward, and pulled his hand away, and at the same time, the guard yelled at John and pushed him down into the chair. John glared at Ted, then turned to Jan, after he saw the ring on her finger. "So you are promised to another man, are you?"

"Yes, John. I am getting married to a man that loves the Lord just as much as I do. Someone who loves me, and treats me with kindness and compassion, and because of that, I love him more than you can imagine. Good-bye John," Jan said, walking towards the door that the guard opened, for her and Ted as they left.

When they got into Ted's vehicle, he turned to her and said. "That was quite a sermon you laid on him back there. You even made me think," he said while driving her back home. "But do you actually believe a guy like him will listen?" he asked.

Jan was quiet for some time before she said, "Ted, I have decided to sell my farm and move away. I don't know how John will react when he gets out, and I am not about to wait and find out. With the money I will get from the sale of my land, I want to purchase land somewhere else. I don't know if it is a good idea, but I was wondering if there was some land close to Austin's ranch. For now, I plan on moving out of the house, even if I have to rent for awhile, until I decide which way to go," she said.

Ted noticed that her hands were shaking. Her voice was calm, but he knew she was scared. "I thought you were getting married. That's what you told John," he said.

"Austin hasn't asked for his ring back yet. I was thinking about giving him a call. I don't want him to think that I am avoiding him," she said.

After Ted left, Jan went over to the phone and dialed Austin's number. She let it ring for some time, but there was no answer. She tried a couple more times, but still no answer. Oh how she wanted to hear his voice, to feel his gentle touch, and his passionate kiss. "Oh Austin, I miss you so much," she said with tears streaming down her cheeks.

She sat with her head resting on the table. Her arm was aching as much as her broken heart. When the phone rang, Jan jumped and banged her arm on the table. She gritted her teeth as the pain in her arm was excruciating.

She looked at the caller display, not believing her eyes. "Hello," she said not knowing what to expect.

"Hello, Anne. This is Mrs. Klassen, Austin's Mother."

"Yes," Jan said, not knowing what else to say, and wishing that people won't call her by that old name.

"I am sorry for not calling you sooner. Both my husband and I wish to apologize for what we said about you, when we were at Austin's house. We were totally in the wrong. Will you forgive us?" she asked.

Jan was quiet for a moment. What was she to say? Finally, she said. "It is very difficult for me to say yes, but I know that as I have been forgiven, so must I do."

"I understand, Anne. I thought that perhaps you and Austin might have gotten married by now. I had hoped that, if you hadn't, that you would consider inviting us, when you do."

"Haven't you talked to Austin lately," Jan asked, rather surprised.

"No. He asked us to leave just after you left. Didn't you know?" Mrs. Klassen asked.

"No, I haven't seen Austin since I left his place. He did call once, but we only talked briefly. I was trying to call him tonight, but I haven't been able to reach him," Jan told her.

"Oh, Anne, I can understand why you feel the way you do towards us. I must say we must earn your forgiveness. I really would like to get to know you, and I also wanted to say how sorry we were to hear about your terrible ordeal with John. If there is ever anything we can do, don't hesitate to call," Mrs. Klassen told her.

Jan, and Austin's mother had a good long talk about Jan's decision to sell and move, which Mrs. Klassen said may be wise. She also suggested using a different name in the phone directory, so he would not be able to find her, if he decided to try it again. By the time they finished talking, Jan decided that Austin's mother, was not quite as bad as she had first thought. Apparently God was working a change in their lives also. She wished that her mother would talk to her, but neither of her parent would have anything to do with her, because she had turned her back on their way of life.

A couple of weeks later John, was sentenced to a year in Jail, which meant, with good behavior, he could be out in half that time, or less. Jan decided to ask her neighbor, if he was still interested in buying her land, and he said that he was. So while he made arrangements to get a loan, Jan began to look for a place to live. She really did not want to live in town, although she may have to consider that for the time being. But which town or city should she move to? She had tried several times to contact Austin, but to no avail. Not only that, she still needed some minor surgery on her arm and her face. She had been quite upset by the vicious scars that John had inflicted on her. Her hope was that, after this next surgery, it would be barely visible.

Blaze of Fury

Jan had not seen Ted for a while, which she felt was for the best. She had a feeling that he may be falling for her, and she did not want to hurt him. He had not accepted any compensation for all he had done for her, but she hoped someday, to find a way to repay him.

Chapter 9

Jan felt very depressed when the movers took out the last box. She walked around the empty house, thinking of the years she and Don had spent there. All of them were good memories, except for the ending, and John had seen to that. Now she would be moving on, leaving this house for someone else to make new memories.

As winter was coming up soon, she decided that this was not the best time for her, to move out into an unknown area. She decided to rent for a while because she still hoped to find a place in the country.

When she walked out, she never looked back. It hurt too much. For a very brief time, she had looked forward to the move, but now she wondered if she and Austin would ever resolve their differences. She looked down at the ring on her finger. Ted had told her once, that she should wear it because it meant that there was still hope, but it was beginning to fade.

Well, she'd better get going. It would take her a good two hours to get to her temporary home. She wanted to get there before the moving van arrived. Not only that, she wanted to be there before Ted, and his friend arrived, to help her unpack some of the heavy boxes.

She decided to take her car. Ted said that he would bring her back later on to get her truck. Ever since the day she went to talk to John, Ted had made himself scarce. He had called twice a month in the first two month but only once in the past month, and that was when he'd asked if she needed help moving into her new place. Jan hopingly had her last surgeries on both her arm and her face a few weeks before, so she still had her arm in a sling, but the bandage on the side of her face had been removed. It had left a red line, which she was told, that would fade within the next month or so. The bruises had all cleared up long ago, except for one stubborn one, just next to her right eye.

* * *

Ted had told Austin the night before to look presentable when he picked him up the next morning. Ted had to admit that lately Austin's attire was, some what improved. He at least dressed proper for church and business affairs, but for most part, it was below par.

As for looking after the workings of the ranch, there were no problems. Austin loved the great outdoors and always took care of his animals. They were his first and only priority now that Jan was gone. After losing Jan and almost losing the ranch, Austin's home and truck had been severely neglected. Once Austin accepted the fact, that he had no other choice but to take on this partnership, he did now occasionally do some house cleaning, as well as occasionally washing his truck. However it was still far from being up to the standard that Ted was accustomed to seeing, before Jan was in the picture. Jan's name was never mentioned, other than the one time when Austin attempted to contact her. When Ted picked Austin up the next morning, he was in his, who cares, attire.

"That's what you're wearing? We aren't going to clean out the barn," Ted told him.

Austin just shrugged his shoulders.

The reason Ted's calls to Jan were seldom now, was because he unwittingly, had felt he was falling in love with her. He knew that there was no future for him with her. She was in love with Austin, and nothing would change that. He wanted to see her happy and the memory, of Austin and Jan together, was something he never forgot. They belonged together.

When Ted got to Jan's new apartment, the movers had placed the furniture where Jan had told them to, but she needed help with moving boxes. Before Ted went into the kitchen, he told Austin to tuck his shirt into his pants, which he sort of did.

"Hi, Jan, how's the arm?" Ted asked.

"It's getting better slowly. I haven't heard from you lately. How have you been doing?" she asked.

"Oh, I am still keeping busy. I may have found some land for you, if you are still interested," Ted told her.

"I just might be, but I'd want to know more about it first." Then, after a hesitation she asked. "How is Austin doing?" Whenever Jan talked about Austin, Ted could sense that deep hurt with in her.

"You will have to ask him yourself," he said.

"You know I can't go there. I've tried to call him, but he either doesn't answer the phone, or he is outside," she said turning at the sound of approaching footsteps. She was shock to see Austin standing in the doorway. They both stood there in stunned silence. Neither one knew what to say. They knew that Ted had planned this. Austin quickly tucked the rest of his shirt into his pants, now wishing that he looked more presentable, as Ted had told him to.

The first thing Jan noticed was that he had lost a lot of weight. Secondly, he had a couple days growth of whiskers. This was definitely not the Austin that she remembered.

Austin too was shocked by her appearance. Her right her arm was in a sling, and there was something else. He walked over and looked first at her eye, then turned her head to see the scar down the side of her face.

Ted noticed the look in Jan's eyes when Austin touched her. Even though his heart ached, he had a smile on his face. He knew that even the slightest touch of Austin's hand made her happy.

"What happen to you, Jan?" Austin asked running his finger down the side of her face.

Jan was surprised that Austin had not heard about it, as it was on the news.

"He has been out of touch lately with world affairs," Ted told her.

"We will talk about it later, but first of all Jan, what do you want us to do?" Ted asked, feeling that now was not a good time to talk about John. Austin and Jan needed to be gradually reunited. They all went into the living room. When Austin moved some books out of the way, a small blue Bible fell on the floor. He picked it up then, slowly opened it. Jan turned around just as Austin opened the front cover. She held her breath.

Austin stood, staring at the picture of a tiny baby with black hair. Then he read the inscription: **Austin James Klassen, born March 20**. Austin looked at Jan with tears in his eyes.

The look on Austin face tore at her heart. She walked over to him, and put her good arm around him. Austin put his arms around her as a tear ran down Jan's cheek. Austin also fought back tears as, he thought back to how it should have been. It took this picture of his son, to really make it hit home. This was the child that he and Jan should have been able to raise on their own, but instead they had no idea where he was now.

Ted quickly left the room, knowing that they needed their privacy.

After several minutes the pain in Jan's arm became unbearable and she pushed Austin away.

When he saw her massage her arm, he said, "I'm sorry Jan, I didn't mean to hurt you."

Austin led her to the couch, where they both sat down.

"Jan, I want to apologize for saying what I did when you were at the ranch this spring. I should have picked up on what you were trying to tell me, but I was so wrapped up in thinking the worst. I guess God used Ted to set me straight, followed by a lecture from my parents. I've been a real fool, and I really wouldn't blame you if you didn't want anything to do with me, but I do love you. I have missed you more then you will ever know," he said, looking for some indication that she had forgiven him.

"I missed you too, Austin. I should have just come out with it, plain and simple, instead of beating around the bush. Will you forgive me for not being able to protect our child? I was so afraid that you would hate me for giving him up, but my parents refused to let me keep him, or even try to contact you. When they took our baby away, I refused to go home. When I left that place, a young lady that worked there helped me get a job. I couldn't face you after all that. Later, I met Don. He was good to me and I liked him a lot, but you were my real true love," she said, sadly. "Well, you know the rest," Jan said playing with her ring.

"Jan, I do not hate you for giving up our child. There was nothing else you could have done. I promise you, that we will someday find him and bring him home again," he said, reaching for her hand. "I see you are still wearing my ring."

"I never took it off, Austin. Ted told me that, as long as I wore it, I should never give up hope that someday we would be together again," Jan said.

"Ted said that? Maybe there is hope for him yet," Austin said with a smile on his face.

Jan smiled. That was more like the Austin she remembered. "Ted has been a good friend to both of us, Austin. I'm sure you can't deny that. By the way, where is he?" she asked, looking around.

"I guess he decided we needed time alone," Austin said, now grateful to him for bringing them back together.

"Jan, what happened to your arm and face?" he asked touching the bruise near her eye. Suddenly he grabbed her good arm, and pulled up her sleeve. The knife wounds on her arm were healed, but still visible. "Jan, what are these marks from? Were you in an accident?" he asked.

"No, Austin. I don't want to talk about it. It's over and done with. Let's just forget about it," Jan said, pulling some ornaments out of a box.

Austin was about to pick up another box, when the paper that had fallen on the floor caught his eye. **JOHN REMPEL SERVES TIME**. Austin dropped to the couch as he read the article.

Then he went in search of the page that was supposed to show a picture of John's victim. Jan walked into the room, just as Austin looked at her, then at the picture. He glanced at it again then, said. "He did this to you? Why didn't you call me?" he said feeling totally helpless.

"Austin you'd already had all you could handle. Ted helped me a lot," she told him.

"So that's why he took off like a wild man? He should have told me, the idiot," he said angrily.

"Don't blame him. He wanted to, but I said no. When I was huddled in the corner of the kitchen cabinets, I regretted it. I just wished that you would have been there to hold me and tell me that it would all be okay, but then… she stopped as her tears began to flow at the thought of what happened next.

Austin took her in his arms and held her. Only this time, he was careful not to put any unnecessary pressure on her arm. Austin took his finger and wiped away her tears. "Now I understand why I had such a terrible feeling that something was wrong after he left. So that is why you are moving. You're afraid that he will come after you again," he said, lifting her head by placing his finger under her chin. Jan just nodded her head. He stared into her eyes. "Jan, my life has gone down-hill since you left, I need you back. Will you still consider marrying an unshaven, sloppy, old rancher?" he asked.

Jan ran her hand across his unshaven face, than said, "Kiss me first, then I will give you my answer."

Austin bent over and gave her a brief kiss, than he held her tight as he began to kiss her like there was no tomorrow.

"Okay you two. We came here to do some work," Ted told them.

When Austin released Jan, the first thing Jan saw, was the look on Ted's face.

Jan turned to Austin. "Would you mind getting the two boxes out of my car, so I can make some coffee, please?" Jan asked, handing Austin her car keys.

When he was out of sight, Jan walked over to Ted. "Ted there, will always be a special place in my heart for you," she said, placing her hand over her heart. "I will never forget all you have done for us, Thank-you," she said laying her hand against the side of his face.

Ted reached up and put his hand over hers, as he pressed it tightly against his face. He wanted to remember this moment. He then took her hand, and put it up to his lips. He kissed it, before slowly lowering her hand and then letting it go. All the while, he did not stop looking into her eyes. Jan smiled up at him, than quickly went into the kitchen.

That was where Austin found her, when he returned with the boxes that held the coffee pot and coffee. Then taking her in his arms, he said, "Now, where were we when we were so rudely interrupted? Oh yes, you were about to give me your answer." Jan noticed the twinkle was back in his eyes. "Well, if you shave off that stubble, I will marry you," she said. "Oh! By the way, your parents are coming to our wedding."

Austin stepped back and looked at her. "What did you say?" he asked.

"Your mother called to apologize for what they had said about me at the ranch. She said they hoped we would invite them to our wedding. I told her that I hadn't talked to you, and she was quite surprised. As was I when she told me that you had asked them to leave. We have some fences to mend Austin."

"Yes, I know. By the way, were you out my way a while back?" Austin asked. Jan thought for a moment before replying. "Yes, I was. I had a feeling that you may have suspected it was me when I saw the brake lights come on."

"Why didn't you stop?" he asked, with a hurt look in his eyes.

"Probably for the same reason that you didn't come to see me," she replied.

Austin took her in his arms and said, "Jan, we have wasted too much of our lives being stubborn. We have to over-come that, because I never want anything to come between us again."

"Agreed, but I think, by now Ted is probably wondering if he should go home, because we aren't getting anything done," she told him. At which time, Austin reluctantly left her side. Jan was now wondering how she would tell Austin that she was his partner in the ranch. She couldn't take the risk of him getting angry with her again, but secrets were what caused the last problem.

When Jan got the coffee started she joined Austin and Ted in the living room.

"Austin tells me that congratulations are in order. Well, I might as well get started by being the first one to kiss the bride," Ted said, sounding like the lady's man she'd thought he was when they'd first met. He came over to her and winked, before bending her backwards and kissing her a little too passionately for her liking.

"Alright Ted. Back off," Austin said sternly, tapping him on the back.

Ted let her go, leaving her blushing. "If you want to be my best man, you keep your hands off my woman! Understand?" Austin said, glaring at Ted.

Ted knew, by the look in Austin's eyes that, he was none too happy, and as for Ted, it hurt to know that it was the only time he could ever kiss her.

"Sorry, Jan. It won't happen again," he said, walking away.

When the coffee was ready, Jan brought out some cookies that she had baked.

"Jan, why don't you just move in with Austin? It would save everyone a lot of work," Ted said.

Jan reminded him that they were not yet married.

"It looks like I may be in for one of her sermons," Ted told, Austin.

"What's that mean?" Austin asked.

Austin sat silently as Ted told him, almost word for word, what Jan had told John when they went to see him in prison.

Austin smiled. "She is feisty, isn't she? I question if he will ever change. Hopefully that, once he knows we are married, he will stay clear," Austin told them.

"Well, I wouldn't wait too long. I sure don't want to continue babysitting you two forever. I have a life too you know," Ted said.

"You wait until you find that right woman, then we will see how you react," Austin told him.

For a brief moment Ted and Jan's eyes met. Then in his usually joking manner he said, "Who says I haven't already found her."

"I'd like to be the first to meet the women that tames you," Austin told him.

Ted just smiled at Jan, as he said they better get to work because he had a meeting to go to that evening.

* * *

After Austin's chores were all done, he sat at his table. The picture of Jan that he's seen in the paper was etched in to his mind. He clenched his fist and then got up and kicked his chair, sending it flying across the kitchen. If John were here now, Austin would have finished him off. How dare he do that!

Austin then focused his anger on the ones that seemed to have control over, who would be an acceptable marriage partner, and forcing their unwed daughters to give up there children, without talking to the father of that child. How dare the elders of that church, and her parents, ruin their lives! They aren't God! God loved the little children! He did not say to get rid of them, like throwing out garbage. It was their grandchild and yet, it was just to save their pride and family name.

Austin didn't sleep much that night. He tossed and turned, as thought of all the plans that he and Jan had made so many years ago. They had lost many precious years.

After chores, he was still angry and just needed to get it off his chest, once and for all. He showered, got dressed in his usual western clothes, and headed out. He did not know what he was going to say when he got there, but he was sure he'd figure it out. The weather was cold, but the roads were good. When Austin was nearing his destination, he began to wonder if this was such a good idea, as it was not just one person that he wanted to voice his opinions to. When he drove by the church, there were several cars there, even though it was not a Sunday. Without a second thought, he turned around and parked right in front of the church. Austin figured it must be some kind of meeting. Therefore, the preachers would most likely be there. They were the main ones he was aiming for. It was his turn to talk, and let them know what he thought of all their rules and regulations.

Austin walked up to the door, and all the old memories came flooding back. He took a deep breath and said, "God, help me," then open the door.

When he walked in, everyone turned to see who had disrupted the meeting. He took his cowboy hat off and carried it with him to the front of the church. The one minister started to reprimand him, but Austin stopped him and told him it was his turn to talk.

He started with, "Everyone here knows who I am." He then grabbed a Bible that lay near by, and opened it to the New Testament. "You guys call yourselves preachers, but I don't believe that you know that there is such a thing as the New Testament. We are no longer under the law, especially your laws. Jesus died for us, and we are now under Grace, and we can now go directly to God to ask him to forgive, and he does forgive. No more just having a bunch of busybody preachers making up dumb rules, just because they like the power they have over everyone.

He heard gasps from some people behind him. He continued, not letting anyone else speak. "And yet, how many of you," he said, shoving the Bible into the hand of the minister that was well known for mistreating his wife, "have read that you should love your wives as you do yourselves? Your wives are people, not and old rugs you beat on."

"I wonder how often you have interfered and ruined, young couple's lives, by not allowing them to get married? Of course, it would be a major sin in your eyes, to allow your kids to go out on a date. As for marriage, it should be the decision of consenting couples that love each other, without your interference." He then glanced over the people behind him and said. "As for you parents, your children should be free to marry, the ones they love. I wonder how many married couples in this church, will never know what true love is like. It shouldn't depend on the status of a person, or who their birth parents, might have been. These are your daughters, and if you loved them, you wouldn't treat them like a car that you trade off because it has a scratch in it. I know you are not all against adoption, but I also remember what one elder told me, when I was younger."

He then turned back to the ministers. Heaven help those that break one of your precious rules, even if it isn't biblical. You men act like you can actually control who will make it to heaven, and who will or won't be forgivin'. Who made you guys God? It may be a shock to you, but you aren't going to be the only people in heaven. I do hope that someday you will open your eyes to what is biblical and what is traditional. I often wonder why anyone here would adopt a child when some of you don't care where your grandchildren end up, after hiding a daughter's pregnancy. If the couple had been allowed to marry, some of these things may not happen, but when it does, the baby is given up as garbage."

Blaze of Fury

He turned around, looked at the people, and said, "Yee who are with out sin, cast the first stone." he said, pointing to his chest. "I am sure there are people in this church that have sinned, in different ways, and never got caught." Austin knew it disrespectful for a man, to wear a hat in church, but when he turned to leave, he put his hat on his head. Austin took one step, when he saw John sitting there.

"What are you doing in here?" he shouted, walking over to him. He grabbed John by the shirt, pulled him up to a partial standing position, and said. "If you ever try what you did to Anne again," he said, using Jan's given name, "or even if I see or hear, that you tried to contact her, I will do to you like I do to my bull-calves, and then you can go and join the women singing soprano." He said, now extremely angry. He shoved John back in his seat, before walking out.

When he got back in his truck, he sat there for a few moments. He took a few deep breaths, then started his truck and headed home. He looked in his rearview mirror and saw a couple come out of the church and drive away. He wondered if it had something to do with what he had said. He felt reasonably calm. In all reality, he was not sure what he had actually said, but he felt better.

Oh boy. The whole county will now hear that I went crazy in the church. They will say that the devil, must have got hold of me and I will never make it to heaven now for sure. Especially after talking to the preachers as I had," Austin thought.

Austin took another deep breath, then said, "God, forgive me if I said things I shouldn't have, but if I did say something that they needed to hear, may their ears and eyes be opened." Well it was over, and that would be the last time he would enter the doors of that church. His biggest surprise was seeing John there, especially after what he had done to Jan. There may have been a bale agreement, for him to be under the watchful eye of the church. He was surprised that he wouldn't have been shunned for a time, or did they actually believe he was in the right, as

Jan parents had agreed that he could take her as his wife? That he rather doubted, but then again who knows. All he knew was that John was warned to stay away, or Austin's wrath would be unleashed.

Austin was at peace as he drove back home. Jan would soon be his wife. What more could he ask for? All he could say was, "Thank you, God." Then it struck him. What would Jan say about what he had just done? Well, maybe she would never hear about it.

* * *

Jan was relieved to finally be able to use her arm. She was told not to do anything to strenuous for a couple more weeks. To Jan's delight, Austin now spent every available moment with her. As for their wedding, it was to be a week before Christmas. Only immediate family and a couple of their closest friends would be invited.

Jan had two older brothers and a younger sister. From what a distant cousin had told her, they were all married and had children. They were still attending the same church, so she knew that none of her family would come, but Austin insisted that they should send them all an invitation, just in case they had a change of heart. He now wondered if any of their family members had been in the church, when he was there.

Jan was very nervous the first time she met Austin's brother. He was the minister in one of the local churches, but her fears were unfounded. Jake his wife Dianna, and their three children, welcomed her instantly into the family. They told her that they were thrilled to see Austin so happy. Jake told Jan told her how devastated, Austin had been after she had been promised to John. When that had not materialized, Austin never gave up hope that they would someday get back together. He said he believed that God had a hand in reuniting them.

Her and Austin had decided not to have all the fancy frills like most weddings. Their dreams revolved around the ranch, so it stood to reason that they would dress western. Ted was happy about that. He didn't own a suit, and he sure didn't want to wear no penguin suit, which is what he called a tuxedo. As Jan had no one in her family to stand up for her, Austin suggested his cousin, Claire. Jan remembered how jealous she'd felt when she first thought that Claire was his wife. She was hesitant about having her, as maid of honor, because she thought Claire was the prettiest, women she knew. When she first met Claire, Jan had stood back and watched while Claire and Austin chatted. She instantly felt the jealously rising up in her, which she told herself was plain stupid, as Austin and Claire were cousins. Suddenly, with out her realizing what had happened, Claire had pulled her into the conversation. Claire told her about all the times, she and Austin had gotten into trouble, when they were children. For the rest of the evening, the three of them were laughing and joking with each other.

* * *

It was the first of November, and the weather had turned cold. It was overcast with light snow falling, but Jan's spirits were soaring. She was anxiously waiting for Austin's arrival. He had told her that he had a few plans for the afternoon, and then later he had to run home to do a couple of chores, before taking her back to her house.

When Jan saw him coming, she grabbed her coat and laid it on the bench, before opening the door.

"Boy, it's cold out there today. You better bundle up, and it may not hurt to take some warmer clothes along, just in case you want to go to see Hope, when we get home," he said.

The thought of her calling his place home was soon going to be reality. She remembered how hurt she had been, when she'd left there. However, she decided to do as he had said, seeing as the clothes she had on, were not exactly chore clothes.

Jan had no idea what Austin had in mind when they left, but she was soon to find out.

"Jan, I know you have been fretting over what you should wear for the wedding. I hope you don't mind me showing you, what I would like to see you in."

"Shirt, jeans and cowboy hat," she said, teasing him.

"That might not be a half bad idea, but not this time," he said, laughing. "Just wait and see," he added.

Jan was wondering where he was going to take her. It was not long before he pulled up at a western shop.

It was obvious, that he had been there before. He walked over to one particular rack, while Jan wandered around, looking at all the different kinds of clothes.

Austin motioned for her to join him. What he pulled out of the clothes rack was a beautiful, light-tan leather top, with matching long skirt. Austin watched her every expression, with pleasure. "Oh Austin! This is beautiful," she said, as she ran her hand across the soft leather, before fumbling with the tassels that formed a V in the front of the waist-length top. There were turquoise, southwestern designed pieces of leather, strategically throughout the top and skirt.

"Try it on. I think I can still pick out your size," he said, holding it up against her.

Jan looked at the price. "No, Austin. This is far to expensive," she said, looking at the five hundred dollar price tag.

"Humor me. Go try it on," he said, leading her to the dressing room.

"By the way, what size shoes do you wear?" he asked.

"Size eight, why?" she asked, but he did not answer.

Jan pulled on the skirt, and was beginning to slip on the top, when Austin knocked on the door. "Open the door Jan, I want you to try these on," he said.

"I'm not dressed yet," she told him.

"Well, just open it a bit and I'll hand them to you," he said.

When Jan began to ease the door open, Austin nudged it a bit, which made the door swing wide open. Jan quickly pulled her blouse up to cover herself. Austin reached over and touched her bare shoulder.

"Please, Austin," she said feeling the blood rush to her face. Jan could hear Austin let out a long sigh as he dropped the boots in front of her, before she closed the door.

Jan loved the feeling of the soft leather against her skin, but it did not compare to the sensation she felt when Austin touched her.

The look on Austin's face was one of awe, when she stepped out of the dressing room.

"Well, are you going to say something?" she asked.

"I-I don't think you would want me to tell you, what I am thinking right now," he said.

"So, in other words, you like it?" she asked.

Austin went over to her and ran his hands down either side of the three quarter length sleeves. Then taking her hands in his, he said, "Oh Jan, that was made for you. You are the most beautiful woman I have ever met. Do you like it?" he asked.

"It's beautiful, but to expensive. Besides I believe the groom is not to see the bride in her wedding dress, before the wedding, she told him.

"I don't believe in that stuff for a moment," he said.

Austin reached over and pulled the pins out of her hair. "Jan, don't wear your hair up anymore," he said, as she shook her blonde hair, letting it fall down her back.

When Austin laid his hands on her shoulders, Jan could feel Austin's hands begin to tremble. He leaned towards her as if to give her a kiss, but then as if having second thoughts, he said, "Jan you better take it off before I... Well. Just go take it off." Then he walked away.

Jan couldn't understand what had come over him, but she did as he asked. When she came out of the dressing room, the woman from the store took the leather outfit from her.

"Jan, I shouldn't be telling you what to wear for our wedding. You tell me if I should back off and let you do what you want," he said softly.

"Oh, Austin. I love that dress, but like I said, it is way too expensive."

"Just wait here," he told her, returning shortly after with a box under each arm.

"Austin, you shouldn't have spent all that money on me!" She said.

"Just open the door, woman," he said, grinning from ear to ear.

The snow was falling heavier when they left the store. "We better get home, so I can do my chores before it gets too nasty," Austin said. The snow was beginning to drift across the road, as the wind picked up. One thing that Jan disliked was, driving in bad weather. She had to admit that Austin was a good driver, but at the sight of an oncoming semi, Jan held her breath while digging her fingers into the seat. Austin did slow down, but not enough for her liking. When they met, it was like running into a snowdrift. She said nothing but when she took a quick glance at Austin. His knuckles were white and he had his hands wrapped firmly around the steering wheel.

Austin took his foot off the gas pedal, while he kept the truck going straight, hoping that when the snow cleared he would, still be on the road.

Jan had no doubt that Austin was a bit nervous during that time, but he showed no emotion. All he said was, "It looks like we are in for a snow storm."

Jan was glad when they finally reached the ranch. "Maybe you'd better stay inside while I do my chores," Austin said, going to change his clothes.

Jan couldn't believe how different the house looked since she left. He used to keep the place exceptionally clean compared to what it was now.

"Sorry about the mess, Jan. I have been working on it lately, but I sort of let everything go after...well. You know," he said rather embarrassed.

"Maybe you are marrying me just to have a house keeper," she said.

As he got ready to do his chores, he replied with, "Yes. Plus a few other fringe benefits." Austin ran his finger along the side of her face. Then placing his finger under her chin, he tilted her head up and kissed her lightly, before going to slipping on his coat, boots, and cap. "See you later," he said.

"Be careful out there." Jan told him, before looking to see what Austin had in his fridge, and pantry, that she could use to make supper. Once supper was under way, she began to clean up the kitchen. Jan had spent quiet a bit of time and yet, Austin was still not back. She glanced out the window and was horrified to see nothing but a wall of white. Would Austin even find his way back to the house, in this storm?

She had to keep busy to keep from panicking. She cleaned the bathroom, before going on to the laundry room. It had been dark for several hours and yet, Austin had not returned. She began to pray. If only the storm would let up. It was ten thirty, when she heard a noise outside. Jan ran to the door and opened it, only to be met by a blast of cold wind, and snow, that took her breath away. She tried to cover her face as she called out Austin's name again and again. She was just about to shut the door when she saw him. He stumbled towards the door, his face covered with snow. Jan grabbed him and pulled him inside.

Austin's breathing was heavy, as he leaned against the wall. He was covered from head to foot with a blanket of snow and ice.

"What happened?" Jan asked.

"I got off the trail on the way up the hill, so I decided to walk. It's darn hard to find your way out there. I hope the cattle will be alright," he said brushing the snow off his face.

"You get out of those clothes off, before you catch a deathly cold, while I run you a warm bath." Jan said, heading for the bathroom. Austin could smell the food, but she was right. He needed to get warmed up first.

It was hard for Austin to take off his wet clothes, as his fingers were so cold. He then slipped on his housecoat. His iced up clothes made, a crackling sound when, he dropped then on the floor by the washer. He looked around and realized something looked different, and so did the bathroom. Jan had filled the tub with very warm water, and had gone into the kitchen to see how their supper was faring. "Hey Jan? What did you do to my laundry room and bathroom?" he asked.

"I cleaned it. Why?" she asked.

"Oh, that's why it looks different. Oh, by the way, I may messed up the laundry room already," he said as he walked into the bathroom.

When Jan walked into the laundry room, she knew she was going to have her hands full with him. *The first thing I am going to buy is a large clothes hamper. I might as well do another load of laundry while I wait*, Jan said to herself, as she threw his wet clothes into the washer. Jan then began to wash up the puddle of water, and ice chips that spread across the floor.

When Austin walked into the kitchen, he was wearing jeans and a T-shirt. "Sorry about messing up the laundry room, after you worked so hard to clean it up." He looked around the kitchen. "You have been busy," he said.

"You must be hungry, so sit down. It may be a bit dried out, after being in the pan this long," she told him.

When Jan came back to the table, Austin pulled her down on his knee. "I missed you, Jan. I wish we were married already, because I am afraid of losing you again," he said.

"I will marry you, even if I get mad at you," she told him.

"Is that a promise?" he asked.

"Only if you agree to the same," she replied.

"Agreed," he said, sealing it with a kiss. "And by the way, you will have to spend the night with me again. There is no way of travelling in this. If this storm lasts any length of time, you may be stuck with me even longer. It will be at least noon before I can pull my truck out of the snow. I'm hungry. Let's eat." he said.

Later, Austin even helped Jan with the dishes. He had noticed how tired she looked.

"Jan, is everything okay?" he asked, while running his hands up and down her arms.

When he saw the scars on her arm, he thought of what John had done to her, and it made him furious. Maybe it was better that, he was not there when it happened, or he may have done something that he would have regretted.

Austin picked her up, and carried her to her room. "What are you doing?" Jan asked.

"I think you'd better get some rest. I don't want to have to dig my truck out tonight to take you to the hospital." He said, laying her on the spare bed.

Austin sat down beside her, and they began to talk about the ranch. Jan had to be very careful not to give away any secrets. How would he react if she told him that she was his partner? Jan moved over to make room for him to lie beside her. It was then that he began to tell her about having to take on a partner to stay afloat. However, he had to admit that even after his partner had gotten their cut, he was finally able to save more money then before. He told her about the fifty cows that his partner had added to the existing herd. His fear was that there may-be some ulterior motive for the generosity of his partner.

Jan rested her head on Austin's shoulder. She was totally exhausted. While the cold icy blast of the winter storm raged outside, she could feel the warmth of Austin body beside her. It made her feel so safe and secure. It was not long before she drifted off to sleep.

When Jan did not answer him, he glanced over to find her sound asleep. He did not want to disturb her, so with his free arm, he carefully reached for a blanket that lay on the chair beside him. He did his best to cover the two of them, before kissing her gently on the forehead. He lay there, thinking of what their future together would be like. It was not long before he too, was sound asleep.

When Austin woke up the next morning, Jan was still laying on his arm.

His arm had fallen asleep, and was aching something horrible. He desperately needed to move it. He did his best to slip it out without waking her, but it did not work.

Still half asleep, Jan said, "Okay, Don. I'll get up," she said, turning over. Suddenly, she sat up, when she realized where she was. Austin was sitting on the edge of the bed with a hurt look on his face. "Oh, is it morning? I must have been dreaming," she said.

"I hope that dream will fade," he said standing up.

"What's wrong?" she asked.

"Nothing," he said, walking towards the door.

"Austin, don't do this again. Tell me what's wrong," she snapped.

"You called me Don," he said, turning to look at her.

"I knew I had seen that look before," she said softly. "You have to face the fact that I was married to him for five years, Austin. I remember Don had the same look on his face when I call him..." She stopped.

"You called him what?" he asked.

"Well, whenever I dreamt about you, I would call him Austin. Even after the dreams stopped, I never forgot about you. I hope you will forgive me if I do that again. He knew about my past, and was a very loving and understanding man. Remember, Don was a part of my life for five years and I did care for him, but it was different," she said.

Austin tried to understand, but it hurt to know that she had been with another man. She was right. He had to face that fact. There was no way of rectifying what, was in the past.

"Austin, did you spend all night in here?" she asked suddenly.

He looked at her and winked. "Don't you remember?" he said.

Blaze of Fury

    The shocked look on her face, made him confess that nothing had happened. He explained that she had fallen asleep on his arm, and he hadn't the heart to wake her up. Jan sighed in relief.
    "Would that have been so bad?" he asked.
    "Yes, Austin. This time I want it to be right," she told him.
    "I promise, as before, I will behave myself," He said, leaving the room.

Chapter 10

The evening before the wedding, Ted, Austin and Jan, along with Jake and Dianna, were all at the church waiting for Claire. Ted was feeling a bit uncomfortable, as the only times he darkened the door of a church were at weddings and funerals, which didn't happen that often. When the door opened and Claire walked in, Jan had to keep from laughing when she saw the look on Ted's face.

Claire was not shy, and never hesitated to say, exactly what she thought. After saying hi to everyone, she walking over to where Ted stood. "Well, hi there. Austin sure kept you a secret." Then, turning to Austin, she said. "Why didn't you tell me about this one? If I had known that you had a friend like him, I would have made, more of an effort to come visit you," Claire than reached out to shake Ted's hand. Claire made a face at Austin, before turning her attention back to Ted. "Nice to meet you," Claire said.

All Ted could say was, "like-wise." There were no-off hand smart remarks, as he had used with Jan when he first met her. He was utterly speechless, which really surprised both Austin and Jan.

Austin saw the surprised look on Ted's face, and said, "Claire, this is my friend Ted Jackson. Ted, this is my cousin, Claire. You will get used to her after a while. She can be a real pain, but we decided as a family, that we would keep her around anyhow."

When they all went to the restaurant for coffee after the rehearsal, Jan was very quiet. Then she excused herself. Austin watched her walk out the front door. He knew something had upset her, but he had no idea what. Claire was true to form, so while she had everyone talking and laughing, he decided to check on Jan. He found her standing outside with tears in her eyes.

"Jan, what's wrong?" he asked.

Jan immediately put her arms around Austin, and then laid her head on his shoulder.

"Oh, Austin. I had so hoped that at least one family member of mine, would have acknowledged the fact that we were getting married. You would think, by now, I would be used to all the rejections," she said.

"Honey, I know it has to be hard for you. I promise that after we get married, we will do our best to try and break down some of these barriers, but we can only do so much. God has to speak to them, because we both know that, without his help, we can't change them," he said, holding her.

"Austin, I love you so much," she replied.

"I love you too. Now, do you feel up to joining the party, before everyone thinks we abandoned them?" He asked wiping away her tears with his finger.

Jan was glad when the evening was over. Claire was spending the night at Austin's, even though Jan had told her that she was welcome to stay with her. Right now Jan was glad for that, because she just wanted to be alone and rest. Her heart had been acting up, and she knew she was not up to chatting for hours.

After Austin took her home, she went straight to bed. She was glad that she had everything ready to take to Austin's the following day. They had decided it would be easier to get dressed there, but Claire had insisted that Austin should go to Ted's, as the groom was not to see the bride before the wedding. Austin had consented. He knew there was no use arguing with

Book 3 of the *Mountains and Valleys of Life*

Claire when she had her mind made up. Arrangements had been made for Ted, to use Jan's car to take them to the church.

The next morning, Jan went to pick up Claire for their hair appointment. She had hoped to see Austin that morning but he was busy somewhere. The morning had gone by quite quickly.

Jan's hair was slightly longer than Claire's. Only Jan's was blonde, where as Claire's was dark brown. Claire had tried to convince Jan to wear her hair up, but Jan remembered what Austin had said. As a child, she'd always worn it up. However a compromise was found. They would wear their hair up on one side, with ringlets dropping down the back and other side.

When Jan got dressed, she began to feel very nervous, she then pinch herself to make sure this was real. Her dream of spending the rest of her life with Austin was now coming true. She looked up and said. "Thank-you God."

Claire wore a western-style light blue outfit, which really brought out her blue eyes.

When Ted walked into the room and saw Jan, he just stood there for a moment before going over to take her hands in his.

Jan also noticed how different Ted looked when he was dressed up. She would not have recognized him, if she had seen him on the street, dressed like this.

"Jan, I envy Austin. I hope he knows how lucky he is," Ted stated.

"Thanks, Ted," she said, pulling her hands discreetly from his grasp. Just as Jan was about to slip on her coat, Ted took it from her and helped her put it on. "Thank you, kind sir," she said before catching that look in his eyes. Jan was relieved when Claire walked into the room. Again, Ted was spell bound.

"Wow, this is my lucky day. Two of the most beautiful women in the same room! My luck may be changing after all," he said helping Claire with her coat.

When they were about to walk down the isle, Claire saw the sadness in Jan eyes. "Jan are you all right?" she asked.

"It's just that I wish I had a Father to walk me down the isle," she replied.

"I know it must be hard. I believe that with God's help, and a lot of prayer, things will someday change. Austin is one of my favorite cousins, and I know he loves you very much. Just concentrate on the man that you love, and are about to marry. That's better," Claire added, when she saw the sparkle return to Jan's eyes.

Claire picked up her flowers, which consisted of white daisies and baby's breath. Jan had chosen a small white Bible, and on it, was a blue rose with blue and white ribbons dangling from it.

When Jan walked down the isle, her eyes focused on Austin. He had on a white shirt, with black pants, and a longer black jacket. She had never seen Austin in anything but work, or casual, clothes. She had a hard time believing, that this handsome man, would soon be her husband.

Jan was so nervous, that she went through the motions without remembering doing them. Although she did remember the tingling sensation she felt when Austin took her hand in his, while saying their vows. It was when they slipped the rings on each other's fingers, that it finally struck her that this was very real, and not just a dream. When Austin kissed her, she could feel his body tremble when he placed his arms around her.

Austin couldn't wait to get out of the church. He just wished they could have a quiet supper and then go home. They'd decided not to go on a honeymoon until the following summer, as there were all the winter chores that, needed to be done. The main thing was, that they were finally together.

Jan had met Austin's parents briefly before the wedding, so their relationship was not quite so strained. Although, she often wondered if they still had reservations as to whom, he had selected to be his wife. *Old habits die hard*, she said to herself.

Both Austin and Jan had to admit that their small reception at the restaurant turned out quite well. After it was over, Ted took Claire back to Austin's to pick up her vehicle, as she had no intention of staying with the newly-weds. She made the decision to go back home to Calgary, but not before she and Ted had decided, when they could get together again.

On the way home, Austin began to tremble with anticipation. Jan was now his wife, which for so long, he had believed would be impossible.

Jan looked over at him and said, "Austin, are you alright?"

He pulled her close and said, "I will soon be."

Jan began to blush, and with that, Austin pulled her even closer as he sped up. "You are still the same Anne that I fell in love with," he said, smiling at her. When Austin looked at her, he said. "Maybe I shouldn't have, said that."

Jan laid her head on his shoulder. "Oh, Austin I wish things would have turned out differently years ago."

To which Austin replied, "So do I hon, so do I. I can hardly believe that you are now my wife."

They drove the rest of the way in total silence. Even in their joy, a shadow hung over them, as they both had heavy hearts, when it came to not knowing where their son was. When Austin turned onto the last stretch of gravel, Jan sat up. Austin placed both hands on the steering wheel as the truck began to fish tail on the slippery road. Jan's whole body became rigid, as she dug her fingers into Austin's leg where her hand had been resting. Austin glanced over and realizing Jan's fear, he gradually slowed down.

When he stopped in front of the house, Austin sat staring at Jan.

"Is something wrong?" she asked.

Austin ran his finger down the side of her face. "No. It is just that…I still can't believe that you are my wife," he said, pulling her tight against him, as he pressed his lips hard against hers and the passion began to build. There was no denying that Jan was a willing participant.

Finally, Austin released her. "We better go in before we freeze," he said.

Blaze of Fury

When they got to the door, Austin opened it, but just before Jan was about to step in, he scooped her up in his arms and carried over the threshold. Jan quickly wrapped her arms around his neck, as he used his foot to close the door. "See? I told you that I needed a practice before the real thing!" he said, laughing. Austin put her down inside and they both took off their shoes and coats. Then, again, he scooped Jan up in his arms and carried her to his bedroom. Austin laid her on the bed. "I love you Jan," he said, before bending over and giving her a kiss. He had pretty well given up his dream of sharing his home with Jan, but it had now come true. God was good and faithful to them both.

Jan felt like she was dreaming, as she returned Austin's kiss. If someone would have told her a couple of years ago that she and Austin would be getting married, she would have never believed it. "Oh, Austin, you have made me the happiest woman in the world. I have always loved you," she said. Jan inhaled the masculine scent of his aftershave, as he kissed her again. The feeling of Austin's touch rippled through her, as he kissed her with more passion than she had ever known before. She could feel the power of his emotions, as he lay beside her. Never, in her wildest dreams, could she have imagined how beautiful it would be once their love for each other could finally be unleashed.

* * *

When Jan opened her eyes the next morning, there was a brief moment where she was not sure where she was, but then it all came flooding back. She could feel the warmth of Austin's body as he slept behind her, with his arm wrapped around her waist.

Jan glanced at the clock, and was surprised to see that it was already ten o'clock. She did not want to wake him just yet, even though she knew that the chores had to be done. She had no idea how sound a sleeper Austin was, as she lay there, gently running her hand across his. Austin was very strong and he had a fair sized hand to go with that strength, but there was something special in his gentle touch.

Austin moaned, then turned over, when Jan gradually lifted his arm and squeezed out from under it. She gently reached over to cover him, before going into the bathroom.

She looked at herself in the mirror. Her hair was a mess, but she felt more alive than ever before. It was so different from her first marriage. She bowed her head and prayed.

"Thank you God, for your loving guidance. I know we have a lot of adjustments to make, but our love for each other, has never change. What I do know is that you have brought us back together for a reason. Help me to be a good wife, and to accept him for who he is and I pray that he will do the same for me."

When Jan returned to the bedroom, she picked up their clothes that were strewn around the room. After putting the clothes away, she got dressed then, went into the kitchen to make breakfast. Jan was just about to set the table, when Austin wrapped his arms around her waist. After he kissed her on the neck, she turned to face him.

"I didn't hear you get..." she began only to be cut short, as he bent over to kiss her.

"Good morning, Mrs. Klassen," he said.

"Oh Austin, that sounds so good," she said clasping his face in her hands.

As he held her tight, she could feel the arousal within him. Then he backed away.

"I would like to stay here with you all day, but I have chores to do. It's going to seem like a long day," Austin said, before pouring himself, a cup of coffee.

"Sit down, and I will finish making breakfast," she said after agreeing with him.

While Austin watched her, his body quivered as his dream of loving Jan as his wife, had finally come true. When Jan sat down to join him for breakfast, he took her hand in his and thanked God for the food, and for answered prayer. He asked for a blessing over them, their home, and their son, and if God was willing, then future family. When he finished, he looked at Jan and gave her hand a squeeze.

They ate in silence for the first few minutes. They had never talked about having children, but she knew Austin had wanted some. During her previous five years of marriage, she had never been able to have a child, so she had no reason to believe that things had changed. Would Austin be angry with her, if she could not give him the family he wanted? Jan decided to talk about something other than children, so the best thing was to ask what had to do today.

After talking about all the things that needed to be done, she offered to help him. He told her that he would take her up on the offer later on, but not today. He would do only what was absolutely necessary. He told her that he had made arrangements with Ted, to do the chores for the couple of days, so that they could spend some time away from the ranch. Jan got up and threw her arms around Austin. She had wished that they could spend a bit of time together without all the work, and it had come true. Austin sat her on his knee and gave her a quick kiss. When he looked into her eyes, he said, "Jan you have made me the happiest man alive." Austin released her as he stood up. "Now, like it or not, I have to get to work," he told her.

Chapter 11

Austin and Jan had now been married for four and a half glorious months.

As Jan sat across the table from Ted and Claire, she thought back to the first time that they had met. Jan was relieved that Claire had become the focus of Ted's affection, because Austin had been obviously annoyed by Ted's steady attraction towards his wife. Now that Ted was so enthralled with Claire, Austin was more accepting of him.

Jan excused herself, as she had not been feeling well the past few days.

Austin followed Jan into the other room, seeing how pale she had gotten.

"Are you all right, hon?" he asked, laying his hand on her forehead.

"I am fine. I just need a bit of a rest," she said.

Shortly after Claire came to ask if there was anything that she could do before she and Ted left. To which, Jan replied that a little rest was all she needed. Jan had her suspicions of what was wrong, but she was not going to say anything just yet. She had a doctor's appointment coming up, but she had not told Austin. She was sure that if she told him, he would not let her go out riding, the following day. She loved to ride, and it was especially enjoyable during calving season. She loved to see the baby calves romping around in the pasture.

Blaze of Fury

That afternoon, Austin told Jan that he had to run into town to get some minerals for the cows. He asked if she wanted to come, but she told him that she had some baking to do.

Jan really didn't feel much like baking, but she knew that tomorrow would be a full day, so she needed to do it now. All the while she worked, there was one thing that weighed heavily on her mind, and that was that she had not told Austin, that she was his unwanted, silent partner in his ranch.

When Austin got home, he was none to happy as he chucked the mail on the table.

"What's wrong, Austin?" Jan asked.

"It's another letter from that darn partner of mine. It makes me angry every time I think about them," he said, throwing his hat on the floor.

"What does it say?" she asked.

"Just read it for yourself" he snapped.

Jan wondered what her lawyer was doing, as she had not instructed him to do anything, for quite some time.

Jan sat down on the chair next to Austin. She picked up the letter that lay on the table, while Austin went to get himself a cup of coffee.

"Austin, what has your partner done that makes you so angry? Have they interfered in the running of the ranch in any way?"

"No," he said, sitting down by the table.

"So what makes you so angry at them?" she asked.

"It's just that I don't feel that I have control any more. Whenever they ask for something to be done, I feel that I have no choice but to do it," he said.

"You could say no, if you don't feel that you want to do as they ask. After all, you have the biggest share," she said.

Austin looked up at her. How would she have known that, unless Ted had talked to her about his business?

"What would have happened if you hadn't taken on this partner?" she asked. Austin did not reply, as he knew full well that he wouldn't be here at all.

Jan sat reading the letter, and was not happy with her lawyer. These were instructions that she had given him before they were even married. Without thinking she said, "This was to be done some-time ago."

Austin looked at her strangely, as he said, "What did you say?"

Jan looked at him in shock. What had she done?

"Ah.. I really don't think what is said in that letter is so wrong. After all, Ted has helped us out a lot," she said, going to get herself a cup of coffee. She knew her face was getting red. She had no idea how she was going to get out of this, other than to tell him the truth. She already knew that Austin suspected that she was hiding something.

"Jan, get over here and sit down. You know more about this, than you are letting on," he said sternly.

"I'm just saying, that if your partner buys the cows, to give to Ted, it won't cost you anything. You know full well that Ted had never asked for any pay, and he comes to help whenever we need him," she said, still facing the cupboard. Jan was a bit upset at her lawyer. This could have been done without involving Austin.

Austin got up and turned her to face him, before saying, "Jan, I want some answers. You know who my partner is, don't you?"

Jan laid her head on his chest. "Austin, I don't want you to hate me again."

"Before we sit down to talk about this, I want you to remember that we promised each other that even if we got mad, we would never stop loving each other," she said. The look on his face softened.

"I'm not mad at you Jan. I just want some answers," he said.

Jan took his hand and led him back to the table. Jan did her best to change the subject. "I want to talk to you about that property just to the west of yours. The owner has given me until the end of the month to make up my mind, if I want to buy it. What do you think I should do?" she asked.

Blaze of Fury

"I thought that was already sold to Douglas," Austin said in surprise.

"No it hasn't. He wasn't that keen to sell it to him, so he is giving me first chance to buy it." She said continuing nervously. "He also has eight years left on a sixteen hundred acre government lease, that could be transferred over to me at the same time."

The look on Austin's face was one of confusion. "How did you know about that property?" he asked.

"Ted told me about it, just after I sold my land. I wanted to put the money I got from the sale of my land, into some other property. He told me about it when he first got wind of it. I don't think too many people knew about it just then."

The look in Austin's eyes scared her when he said, "It sounds like you and Ted got pretty chummy."

"Austin, don't do this again or I won't tell you any more," she said wishing that Austin would not always insinuate, that her and Ted were more than just friends.

"Yes, Ted helped me with a lot of things after I left that day," she said, remembering it all too vividly. "I realized that you were having financial difficulties, the day you got that phone call, so don't blame Ted. While out at the drop, I pried it out of him. He indicated that it was a concern, so I asked him to intervene if there was no other way."

"Are you telling me that you are my partner?" he said standing up.

"Would that be so bad?" she asked, going to him. He pushed her away, and then grabbed his hat and left. Jan stood there feeling totally devastated. She had no idea what to expect next.

Austin did not come in for supper, and Jan had already gone to bed when she heard him come in. Only he did not come to bed. Jan got up and found him sitting on his recliner, staring out the window.

"Austin, are you coming to bed?" she asked. He did not answer her. "Austin?" she said going to lay her hand on his shoulder, which he shrugged off. Jan knelt down beside him. "Austin, we have to talk. We can't leave this alone or it will only get worse."

He looked at her, but she could not read his expression. "Please, Austin. All I wanted to do was, to be sure that you did not lose your dream. I didn't think you would have taken the money if I had offered it to you. It was I who persuaded Ted to convince you into taking on a partner. I just couldn't let the bank take this from you. It was also my idea to give Ted some cows, because I do owe him something for all his help," she said.

"Where did you get that much cash?" he asked coolly.

"It was from Don's life insurance. Please, Austin, I am sorry if I have hurt you," she said.

"Do you want me to believe that there wasn't something more going on between you and Ted?" he said, his eyes now showing his distrust in her.

"Austin, is that what this is all about? Do think that I am the kind of person that would jump into bed with any man I meet? I thought you knew me better than that. I love you, not him. If I was that kind of woman, I would have gone to bed with you when I stayed here before," she said, now annoyed at him, as she stood up. Jan pulled her hand away, when Austin reached out. It was with a heavy heart, that Jan headed back to bed. She was tired and still not feeling that well, when she lay down. It was all out now. There was nothing more for her to say. It was Austin that had to over come his jealousy and pride. He had to accept the fact, that there are times that you need help.

She turned on her side, as tears began to flow. She had almost fallen asleep when Austin came to bed. He did not say anything, but lay down behind her, then wrapped his arm around her waist. That was probably as close as he would come to saying that he was sorry. A few minutes later, she placed her hand over his, as he snuggled closer. Then with a feeling of relief, she finally fell asleep.

The next morning, Austin did his best to cover up his dispirited feelings, but Jan knew he was still not happy. Jan made a special effort to change his mood. She could not stand to have any tension between them. When he came into the kitchen, she went to him and wrapped her arms around his neck. "I love you, Austin." She said before giving him a kiss.

She looked into his eyes, knowing full well that he was holding back. She stood staring into his eyes for a moment before saying, "Do you forgive me for not telling you about the partnership?" she laid her hand on the side of her face.

Austin looked at her for a moment. He loved her very much, but he felt like less of a man for having accepted money from her. He forced a smile, than said, "I am working on it."

"Austin, I have one more thing that I better tell you," she said.

She could feel his body tense up, as he prepared himself for another blow, but he relaxed slightly when he saw that twinkle in her eyes.

"Do I sit down for this?" he asked.

"Well, you may want to," she told him.

Austin walked over to the chair and sat down.

"Austin, I have a doctors appointment coming up," she started only to be quickly interrupted, by Austin.

"Why? What's wrong?" He asked jumping to his feet.

"Well, I think that I might be pregnant," she said as Austin stared at her in disbelief.

"Are you sure?" he asked, grabbing her by the shoulders.

"No, but I haven't been feeling that great lately, and I have had my suspicions that is why. I wanted to surprise you when I knew for sure, but after last night, I didn't want you feeling that I was hiding something else from you. Will you be happy if I am?" she asked, watching his every expression.

"Why wouldn't I be?" he said, wrapping his arms around her.

"Well, I just don't seem to be able to do anything right lately," she said sadly.

Austin stood quietly looking at her. "I am sorry, Jan. It is just that I feel strange about the fact that you bailing me out. As the man, I feel that it is my duty to support myself and my family," he said.

"Austin, please don't go back to the old ways. You know that a marriage is supposed to be a partnership. To me, you are still the head of our home, and you have worked hard. Sometimes things happen that we have to accept help, but I also believe that we should be lovers, soul mates, and best friends. Which should, in turn, lead us to be partners in everything through- out our lives. I can't even begin to tell you how much you mean to me. There are no words to express the feelings I have when you hold, or love me. Whatever I have is also yours. Will you accept that?" she asked.

"If you are talking about your money, then no. That belongs to you," he said sternly.

"I am not talking just money. I want everything that I own to be put in joint names, because it is not just mine alone. We are now one, and possibly even three, and then well, who knows. We are partners in marriage, as well as everything else in our lives. Don't you understand?" she said pleading with him.

"I said no!" he said firmly.

"No you never, you said you would not accept the money, I want to do this Austin. We are already partners, and I want you to be my partner in this new property too. Please? And I still think we do owe Ted something, and I want you to think about that," she told him.

Austin looked at her, then, laying his hand on her stomach, he gradually smiled and said, "All I can say is, I will think about it."

"That's at least a start. Now, let's eat before Ted shows up." Before she walked away, Austin grabbed her and kissed her. Then as he released her, she said, "Thanks, Austin."

"For what?" he asked.

"For just being you," she said going to finish putting their breakfast on the table.

While Jan and Austin ate, Jan's mind was focused on the son that her arms ached to hold. Would they ever find him? She knew that Austin was ecstatic in knowing that in, a few months, he could possibly be a Father.

"Maybe you shouldn't go riding today," Austin said, now being very protective.

"Austin, I'm not an invalid. There is nothing wrong with me riding, she said.

* * *

It was another week before her doctor appointment. She was looking forward to the doctor confirming her diagnosis. Not only that, she needed him to know that her heart was beginning to acting up. She also needed her prescription renewed, and hoped that the medication would not affect their child. She knew that Austin had his suspicions that she was not totally truthful about how she was feeling.

Austin had gone to pick up the mail and some salt blocks, while Jan did some grocery shopping. Austin came into the store, just as she was paying for her groceries.

"How are you doing?" he asked when they walked out to the truck.

"I am fine, Austin. I wish you wouldn't worry about me so much. I am still going out with you to check the cattle this afternoon," she told him.

"I don't think that will happen," Austin said.

"Austin let's not get into this again."

"You know full well that it isn't a good idea," he said firmly.

"Look, Austin, you can't keep me bottled up in the house. House work can cause just as many problems for me, if not more, than sitting on a horse," she told him.

Austin did not reply. He just handed her a letter from her lawyer, but Jan did not open it until she got home.

Austin sat there watching her, as she opened and read the letter. She then handed it to Austin.

After reading it, he looked at Jan. "So, you are going ahead with the purchase of that land," he said, pushing the papers across the table to her.

"Austin, I asked for your input, but you refused to discuss it. You know that I have to roll the money from the land I sold into another property, or I will be paying a lot of taxes. Apparently something has come up, and it will be several months before it will be finalized. We have to sign these papers so the deal cannot be changed. You know as well as I do, that this land would be a great asset to what you already own, and if we don't do this, Douglas will take it. We both need to sign these, and send them back as soon as possible," she told him.

"It's your deal. I'm just the hired hand," he said marching out of the house.

Jan sat down with her head resting in her hands. She could feel her heart beginning to race wildly, so she went into the bedroom and lay down for a bit. Some-how she and Austin would have to straighten this all out, or it could lead to an even bigger problem between them.

Jan wiped the tears from her eyes. It seemed that she could never do things right. She was about to go do laundry, when she suddenly doubled over. She moaned in excruciating pain, as she hung onto the table. Suddenly, someone grabbed her and helped her to the chair.

"Jan, what's wrong?" Ted asked.

"I don't know. It just happened all of a sudden." She said as the pain eased slightly.

"Where is Austin?" he asked.

Suddenly, Jan yelled. The pain got so bad, that she felt like her insides were being torn apart.

Ted ran outside and laid on his truck horn. He then went back into the house, where Jan sat, now looking very pale. "If Austin doesn't show up in the next few minutes. I am taking you to the hospital," Ted told her. He was sure that she could pass

Blaze of Fury

out at any moment. He picked her up in his arms and headed for the door, where Austin met them.

"What's going on here?" he demanded. He took one look at Jan's life limp body, and then took her from Ted.

"Let's get her to the hospital. My truck is just outside," Ted said, opening the door for Austin and Jan. Jan began to stir and moan, before slipping back into unconsciousness.

* * *

The next thing Jan remembered was, waking up in the hospital. She was cold and trembling. Austin took her hand in his.

"Hi, Babe. So you finally woke up," he said.

"What happened?" she asked.

"You gave me a darn good scare, well, not only me. You scared the daylights out of Ted, too," he said.

"Do you feel better?" Austin asked.

"My stomach hurts. It must be something I ate," she said.

"I don't think so," Austin said, pushing her back, as she was about to sit up. "The orders are total bed rest for at least a couple of weeks," he said.

"But why? I am fine," she said.

Austin placed his hand on her stomach, while saying, "You have to look after our off- spring."

Jan's eyes lit up. "Do you mean, I am…"

"Yes. We are going to have a baby, eventually. That is if you behave yourself," he told her.

"I can't believe it!" she said, laying her head down on the pillow.

"Well, according to the Doctor, it is true." Austin said, with a big grin on his face.

"I can't believe it's true," she said again.

"What's the matter now?" he asked.

"Well what?" he asked.

"Well, Don and I had wanted a child, but after five year's it just didn't happen. I didn't think that I would ever have any more children and now, after just a few months, I am really pregnant," she said.

"Is that a bad thing?" he asked, not understanding her.

"Oh no!" she said, trying to sit up, but Austin again pushed her back down. "I couldn't be happier, but well... he was my husband and wanted a child. I just feel that I disappointed him," she said sadly.

Austin sat there quietly, and Jan began to wonder what he was thinking.

Jan pulled him closer to her and then, as their eyes met she, cupped his face in her hands and said, "I am so glad that I went to the auction that day. Other wise, we may have never reconnected. I hope that you can understand that I did care very deeply for Don, but there is that guilt that I carry with me because I love you more. Oh, Austin, I just love you so much," she said putting her arms around his neck, as she pulled herself up to him. It was then that the pain again, rippled through her body. She let go of Austin and fell back on the pillow. She pulled her knees up, and clenched her arms tight around her stomach until the pain eased off.

"Should I get some help?" Austin asked, now feeling helpless, and looking rather pale himself. He was at a loss of how to help her.

"No I will be fine in a moment. Austin, I can't lose our baby. What if it is my last chance?" she said, grabbing his hand.

"I've been thinking, Jan. Maybe God was saving you for me after all. I wouldn't worry about that, I just know that we will have more. If something does... well...you know," Austin could not bring himself to say lose this one. "We'll have another, and another, and another," he teased.

"Hold it Austin, I'm not sure I'm ready to have all that many," she replied, while trying to smile, as the pain began to ease off.

"Well, we do need some ranch hands, don't we?" he said, with a grin on his face.

"You are something else, but I still love you," she said.

"I love you too, Jan. I hate to leave you right now, but I have to get back home. Ted is coming back this afternoon. We are going out to check the cattle," he said, as he bent over to give her a couple of lingering kisses. "Now, I want you to obey orders, and look after yourself and our young one," he said gently placing his hand on her stomach.

"I'll see you later Mommy," he said.

"Ok, Daddy," she replied.

Jan could see the happiness in Austin's face, as he winked at her before he left. She closed her eyes and began to picture their son working along side his father. She opened her eyes when she heard someone walk into her room.

"Are you young Austin Klassen's woman?" the man asked.

Jan recognized him. Austin had pointed him out to her one day when they were in a restaurant.

"Yes, I am his wife," Jan replied.

"My ranch hand, that's next door, said that he thought he saw your man in here. Well, tell that man of yours, that he should have sold me his land when I asked him earlier, and not to count on buying the neighbors place, or he may find that he will have more problems than he can handle," he sneered.

"Is that a threat, Mr. Douglas?" Jan asked.

"Call it what you want. He is a dreamer and someday I will get his place. I'll guarantee you that," he said.

"We are both dreamers, because that land will someday go to our children," Jan told him, firmly.

"I don't know where he got his hands on that money to keep him going, but I know, sooner or later, he will go broke," he said with a snarl on his lips.

"I am sorry, but you are barking up the wrong tree. We are doing quite well financially, and have nothing but a good future to look forward to. Now, if you don't mind, I would like you to leave," Jan said firmly. She was surprisingly calm, but fuming inside.

Book 3 of the *Mountains and Valleys of Life*

Jan spent a long week of total bed rest in the hospital. Between the pains in her stomach, and her irregular heartbeat, the doctor and Austin were both very worried about more problems arising. However with a lot of prayer, her pains began to disappeared, and her heart was now, back to normal. She was finally allowed to go back home, as long as she rested and did not over do it. Jan was positive that it was all the stress that had triggered her problems.

* * *

Jan put on a warm jacket then, slipped on her cap. She knew there was a chill in the spring air, even though the sun was shinning. While riding in the sun, it felt warm, but as soon as they got in the shade of the hill or the trees, it felt cool. Jan was glad that she had put on a pair of gloves at the last minute. As the three of them rode out together, Jan listened to Ted and Austin as they discussed the continuing problems of the missing cattle in the area. They had not had any cows stolen lately, and she hoped that the theft would not start up again.

Austin asked Ted about the lease next to his. That was when Ted glanced over at Jan. Ted had not seen Jan since the day they took her to the hospital. That was nigh three weeks ago, and she was definitely looking much better. She was happy, and he was glad for the both of them. When Ted congratulated them, he saw the glow in Jan's face. He told them that it couldn't have happened to a more deserving couple. *Maybe this will compensate for the child Jan lost,* Ted said to himself. He still had an ache in his heart because he still cared very deeply for her. At times, he wished he were in Austin's shoes.

"It's ok, Ted. He knows that I am his partner, and I have told him about the land and the lease," she said. At which time, Ted shared freely all he knew about the property that was next to theirs.

As they rode out to the far part of the pastures, she was deep in thought as she tried to envision what her son would be doing now, and what he would look like. She was sure that he would look much like his father. She laid her hand on her stomach, and she wondered whether it was a boy or girl. She was feeling real good the past few weeks, and was sure that the worst was now over.

"Jan! Jan!" Austin shouted at her.

"Oh, I am sorry! I was lost in my own thoughts," she said.

"Well, I want you to be careful out here," Austin told her.

"Why, what's wrong now?" she asked.

"Ted just informed me that Douglas has been asking questions about us. I want you to be careful just in case he, or his hired goons, step over the line," Austin said.

"Yes, I thought he might," she said.

"Why do say that?" Ted asked.

"He came into my room when I was in the hospital. He more or less indicated that he was going to try to find out who backed Austin financially, and that he would someday find a way of laying his hands on this land," she said.

"What did you tell him?" Ted asked.

"I told him that would never happen, and asked him to leave."

"Why didn't you tell me?" Austin asked, with a worried look on his face.

"I had more important things on my mind," she said, placing her hand on her stomach.

"Well, you be careful, and don't go riding very far from the ranch when you are by yourself," he told her firmly.

"I doubt if Douglas would do much by himself, but I have heard of other ranchers having problems with a couple of his hired goons. I firmly believe that you should listen to your husband on this," Ted said, making eye contact with Jan.

Jan could see that Ted was genuinely concerned about what was going on here.

She said that she understood as she looked away.

They decided to split up while riding through the pasture, but Austin told her not to wander off too far. If she found a problem, she should not try to do anything on her own, but come and get one of them. She agreed, as she took the middle area. When Jan came upon a small herd of cattle, she took her time watching the calves, as she walked Hope through them.

Everything seemed to be fine. She took special note of the ear tags of the cows that had not yet calved. When she rode back towards the gate, she saw a couple of riders in the distance. She must have taken longer than she had realized, for Austin and Ted to be waiting for her. When she got closer, she saw the color of the horses and there were now three riders.

Suddenly, she recognized the older man. What was Douglas doing on their property?

"Is there something you want?" she asked when they reached her.

The two younger men looked at each other, then at her. Jan suddenly felt very nervous, as Ted and Austin's warnings began to haunt her. She knew instantly that the three of them were up to no good.

"Well, Austin really did find himself quite a prize," the one rider said as he rode over to her. He reached over and gave her braid a flip.

Jan backed her horse away from him as she asked again, "What are you doing here?"

"We don't need a reason, but I think we just found one," he said, looking at the man on the horse next to Mr. Douglas. Mr. Douglas was enjoying watching his men taunt her.

"You'd better leave before Austin finds you here," she told them.

The other man rode over, positioning Jan between the two of them. At that point, Jan began to fear for her safety. A noise in the bush distracted them briefly, which gave her the opportunity to kick Hope into action. Her only chance was to ride as fast as she could to get away from them.

She prayed that someone would come to her rescue, as she heard the beating of the horses' hooves behind her.

Blaze of Fury

Austin and Ted were taking their time on the way back, when they saw Jan galloping at full speed with two riders in hot pursuit. Instinctively, both Austin and Ted jabbed their spurs hard into the side of their mounts, and were soon racing at top speed towards Jan and her pursuers. "I'll kill them if they hurt her," Austin yelled.

It was then that Ted saw a third rider turn, and head in the opposite direction. Ted saw Austin reach for his rope, and he decided to do the same. As they got closer, Austin was horrified to see Hope stumble, which sent Jan soaring through the air. The two riders dismounted, and then walked over to her.

Jan yelled, "Leave me alone," as the one man grabbed her arm.

Ted grabbed for his rifle and shot into the ground near them. They both stopped dead in their tracks. Austin leapt off Midnight before he came to a full stop.

"Are you all right, Jan?" Austin asked when he reached her.

"You two better bite the dirt, or I will fill you both full of lead," Ted yell at them.

Austin and Jan both looked up at the angry tone in Ted's voice. Jan had never seen Ted this angry. She feared that he was mad enough to do exactly as he'd said.

Both men seemed to sense it, because there was no argument. Ted threw his rope towards Austin and said, "Tie them up."

"When I'm through with you two, you will wish that you never stepped foot on my place," Austin told them.

"You want exercise? You're going to get it," Ted said, as he grabbed the end of the ropes and began leading the men toward the ranch.

Jan was now as white as a sheet. "Jan, are you alright?" Austin asked again.

"I think so," she said slowly.

"Would you rather ride ahead, or do you want to ride along with us?" he asked.

Jan was suddenly not feeling very well. "I think I will ride with you," he told Austin. Austin helped her back on her horse, before mounting Midnight. No one spoke as they headed back to the ranch. Ted had just used his cell phone to call ahead for the police to meet them, when Jan turned to Austin.

"Austin, I think something is wrong. I don't feel very good." Austin took one look at her, and told her to hang in there as he quickly rode over to Ted and asked for his cell phone.

"What's wrong?" Ted asked.

"It's Jan," he said, dialing 911.

Ted turned to see Jan slump over the saddle horn. Austin, too, noticed what happened. He quickly handed the phone to Ted. He got to Jan just in time to catch her as she slid out of the saddle.

Ted finished the call to 911 then, told Austin that he would be back to pick them up with the truck. His two captives had to substantially pick up their pace the rest of the way.

Austin tapped Jan on the cheeks, trying to wake her up. He was now beginning to panic.

Jan slowly came around then, moaned in pain before passing out again. He had a good idea what was happening. With tears in his eyes, Austin held her in his arms until help arrived.

* * *

Austin was sitting on the chair beside Jan's bed when she began to stir. He took her hand in his, while lightly stroking her hair. Sleepily she began to, open her eyes before drifting off again for a few minutes. Then slowly, she began to wake up. She looked around and then suddenly tried to sit up, only to be restrained by Austin. She placed her hand on her stomach. Something was not right. She took one look at Austin then, burst into tears.

Austin just held her hand as she cried. He also wiped several tears from his eyes. His emotions were running wild. The bitterness and hatred towards the ones that did this overwhelmed him. He should have stood firm and not let Jan go riding, but he could not dwell on that now, as he felt he had to console Jan, and to encourage her that there would still be a next time. She suddenly with drew from him. He continued trying to get her to talk to him, but when she finally did, she was very upset.

"I'm sorry Austin. It's all, my fault, and I don't deserve to have children. I have now lost both of our children. In fact, you would be better off without me," she said, as tears ran down the sides of her face.

Austin got up and grabbed her firmly by the shoulders. "Jan, don't you ever say that again, as neither one was your fault. And yes, I would like to have a family, but I would never give you up. Besides, we do have a son, and I promise you that we will someday find him. I still have faith that God will give us another child, and the doctor said there is no reason that we can't have another one. It was Douglas's fault, and he will pay for this," He said in a burst of anger.

Jan looked at Austin, and what she saw scared her back to reality. "Austin, promise me that you won't do something stupid. Please?" she said, pleading with him.

Austin walked over to the window and stared blankly outside. He was so looking forward to having this child, and now it was gone.

Chapter 12

Austin laid charges against Mr. Douglas and his two hired hands for trespassing, and harassment of his wife, ultimately leading to the death of their unborn child.

Life did not return to normal for them, as Jan no longer let Austin get to close to her. She was afraid of going through this all over again. Austin confided in his brother, Jake, about their problem. He was sure that she was blaming herself for not being able to protect her children. Jake had told him to give her time. He also suggested that perhaps Dianna, his wife, could get Jan to open up. She needed to talk to someone that she trusted, and if she held it all in, it could lead to other problems.

The day of the trial was especially hard, as Jan had to testify against the three men. It was the ruthlessness of the lawyers that concerned Austin. Would she be able to deal with all the stress of the questions that would be thrown at her? At first, she refused to testify, but when other ranchers wives, approached her about having been harassed by the same two men, Jan decided this must come to an end. During the days leading up to the trial, Jan talked very little. She relived the fear of what may have happened, if Ted and Austin had not been there. The mountain of evidence against these two men was over whelming, and because Mr. Douglas had done nothing to stop his men, he also was charged.

Jan looked pretty frail and tired by the time the trial was over. She was relieved when the charges were read. The two men were sentenced to two years in jail, and Mr. Douglas was sentenced to one month in jail or a one thousand dollar fine. There was also a restraining order in place, stating that he and his men were not allowed to have any contact with Austin or Jan, and were ordered to stay off of their property. This was far from compensating for the life of the child that Jan and Austin had lost.

When Mr. Douglas was led out of the room, he threatened Austin that he would pay for all this. Upon hearing him, the Judge immediately added another thirty-day jail sentence, with a special notation of his threat.

Jan had never seen a man as angry as Mr. Douglas, when they took him away in handcuffs. She suddenly feared for their lives.

Jan had a lot of nightmares after that, but she never disclosed them to Austin. She would always wake up in a cold sweat. Austin was very worried about her. He could not help her if she did not talk about it.

The day that Mr. Douglas got out of jail, she did not leave the house. She desperately needed someone to talk to, so she called her sister-in-law. Dianna was very sympathetic to her plight, but told her that if she and Austin did not confide in each other, their marriage would continue on a down hill spiral.

Jan loved Austin very much, and she knew that things had deteriorated to a dangerous level. He sometimes did not come to bed until long after she was asleep.

After Dianna prayed with her on the phone, Jan felt a peace like she had not felt since her and Austin had gotten married.

For the first time since the trial, Jan told Austin that she was going to town to get some groceries. Austin was quite surprised, and now had some hope that things may be returning to normal. When Jan picked up the mail, she was shocked to find a letter there from her parents. She was so excited, that the moment she got into her car, she tore open the letter. Only it was not at all what she expected.

Her mother began by say that she was sorry to hear about what had happened between her and John. She then proceeded to tell her that they had hoped that one-day, Jan would come to her senses and return and ask forgiveness, especially after her husband died. They had hoped that maybe she would come back and make it right with John. She wrote that they were very disappointed when they'd heard, that she was going to marry Austin, after he had shamed them so. She finished by saying that her dad had said that her sins were too great to be forgiven.

Jan was hurt very deeply. How could they turn on their own child for what she had done, and yet condoning what John had done to her? Her happiness meant nothing to them. She crumpled up the letter and threw it into one of the grocery bags.

Jan cried most of the way home. She had hoped that someday she would be able to at least talk to one of her family members, but that seemed very unlikely, especially now with her father's attitude towards her. She knew him as a stern but fair man, but she was now changing her mind about the word fair. She now question whether he believed that there were rules for the women but not the men.

Jan was glad that Austin was not around when she returned home. She went straight to the bathroom to splash some water on her face. Austin was in the kitchen when Jan returned. In his hand, was the crumpled up letter from her parents. He could see that she had been crying, and from what he had just read, he could understand why.

Austin took a few steps toward her then stopped. Jan stood there looking into the eyes of the man that she loved. She needed him to just hold her. She ran over to him and threw her arms around his neck. Austin held her tight, which she hadn't allowed him to do for some time.

"I'm sorry, Jan. I know life doesn't seem to be fair," Austin told her.

Jan felt so safe in his arms that she did not want him to let her go. "Just hold me Austin," she said.

Blaze of Fury

They stood there for some time, before Austin released her. He looked into her eyes, and then slowly leaned over to give her a little kiss. Finally, Austin had a glimmer of hope that things would return to normal.

Austin sat down with the latest newspaper, while Jan finished putting away her groceries. Austin then thumbed through the rest of the mail. He found an envelope addressed to both him and Jan, from her lawyer. He first handed it to Jan, but she told him to open it, as she was busy. It was the papers for the purchase of the neighbors land. Austin was about to get into another discussion over this, but decided that it wasn't worth the fight. If that's what she still wanted he would, reluctantly, give in.

"Jan, are you sure about this?" he asked.

"Yes, and please don't start with that again," she said with that pleading look.

Austin shook his head as he laid the paper on the table. Jan was preparing herself for another argument, but instead he said. "Where's the pen?"

She handed him the pen, and they both signed on the appropriate lines.

Austin was surprised at how happy it seemed to make her. He could no longer deal with the wall that had been building up between them, as he grabbed her and pulled her down on his lap. He looked for some indication that she wanted him as much as he wanted her. He slowly leaned towards her and gave her a slight kiss. To his pleasure, she responded.

The tension between them was now fading away. Shortly after Jan fell asleep, she began to toss and turn, which woke Austin. He was about to go sleep in the other room, when she began to talk in her sleep. She was pleading with someone in her dream.

"No! No! Please don't hurt him," she yelled.

He tried to wake her, but she pushed him away. "Please, don't hurt him!

Austin! Austin!" she said, as she began to cry.

Austin began to shake her lightly, trying to wake her up. "Jan! Jan!" he said, tapping her lightly on the side of her face. Jan suddenly woke up in a cold sweat. She stared at Austin for a moment then, threw her arms around him.

"Jan, it's alright. I'm here, it was only a dream," he told her.

"Hold me," she said, now shaking like a leaf.

"It was only a dream," he said again, while brushing a strand of hair back.

Austin leaned over and kissed her as she clung to him. The dream of losing Austin was so real, that she was not about to let him go.

Austin did not ask about her dream until the next morning. From that point on, things seemed to take a turn for the better. It took a while but she started to go out riding again. Austin and Jan enjoyed working together on their ranch as a team, but Austin did not allow her to ride too far from home, when she was by herself. Jan even said the she wanted to participate in the branding this time. Branding was always a busy day. That was also a time when the local ranchers helped each other.

Since Jan was back to riding, Austin did not require Ted's help as often. There was nothing like riding out together to check on their cattle, and since Mr. Douglas and his henchmen were locked up, they had not lost a cow.

That fall, Ted helped them round up and separate the calves, as they were keep some of the best heifers back for breeding stock.

One morning, Jan and Austin got back into the prior discussion of paying Ted, either with cash, or cattle. Austin did agree that Ted was invaluable, but there was no firm decision made. It was left to Austin to discuss with Ted as to what he preferred. It was the next topic that got rather heated. Jan wanted to dissolve their partnership and put everything in joint ownership, but Austin was being stubborn again and said this was what she original did, and it would remain that was

Ted and Claire stepped right into the middle of it when they arrived. Claire took Austin aside, and at the same time, Ted talked to Jan. It was Ted that finally gave the two of them a lecture.

He did understand Austin's frustration of having to accept financial help. It is tough to be backed into a corner, but he had to admit, it had worked out fine for the both of them. Austin must overcome his damaged ego, and be thankful that Jan loved him enough to bail him out. Even after he rejected her. It was time to let it all go. As Ted said. "It was all water under the bridge. You're one now."

Jan too must put herself in his place, and think of how Austin felt. Maybe she should not push so hard and give Austin time to accept it. No matter if things were left as they were, or if there were any changes to be made. "So," Ted asked, "Is it really worth losing everything you have? Now, I want the two of you to kiss and make up," he said firmly.

Jan looked at Ted, then at Austin, as they sat around the table. Both Austin and Jan knew he was right, but each still had their reason for wanting or not wanting to change the way it was. Austin looked at Jan and said, "Just give me time."

Jan nodded her head in agreement, and that was the end of the discussion.

"Changing the topic, would you mind if I joined in on the round up today?" Claire asked. Jan watched how Ted and Claire looked at each other. It was then that she noticed the ring on Claire's finger.

"Well, congratulations you two," Jan said. At which time Austin looked at Claire's hand.

"Ah, so it ended up to be Claire that finally cornered you," Austin said, going to pat Ted on the shoulder.

"It's all your fault," Ted said jokingly.

"My fault?" Austin asked.

"Yeah, yours and Jan's. You got married," he said.

Austin gave Ted a warning that he had better be good to his cousin or he would be answering to him. He then went to give Claire a hug, while wishing her the best. Austin liked Ted, but he was not sure that he would have chosen Ted as a partner for his cousin. He had been pretty wild in the past.

Jan went to shake Ted's hand, at which time he said, "Come now Jan-you can do better than that," he said, grabbing her then giving her a big hug. But at the look on Austin's face Ted backed off quickly. Austin did not take kindly to anyone touching his woman, and Ted knew that.

"Let's get to work," Austin said, looking at Ted.

Claire didn't seem to mind Ted's tomfoolery. She had learned to accept Ted for who he was.

It was a long, hot, and windy day. Everything went fine, but by the time they were all done, everyone was tired and dirty. Claire had never been to a brand before, so she mainly watched, but she had to admit that it had been fun. Ted looked at her and then at Austin. "We will put her to work at your next branding. Then we will see if she still thinks ranching is so much fun.

"Come on Ted. Don't tell me that you don't enjoy working cattle," Jan said.

"Yes, I admit that when there are two special women around it can be fun, but it's also hard and tiring work," Ted said.

Claire admitted to Ted, that yes, she did know that.

Jan noticed the look Austin gave Ted, so Jan quickly changed the subject. "Have you got a date set for your wedding?

"Claire wants to be a June bride, and we want both of you to stand up for us," Ted said.

Jan first looked at Austin, than said, "We would be happy to do that for you."

Austin did not say too much after the comment that Ted made. He was sure that Ted's feelings towards Jan were that of more than just a friendship. Was that the reason Jan was pushing to give Ted compensation for his help? He had to watch that his jealousy did not come between himself and Jan. He knew that he was very possessive over her, but he had lost her once and had no intention of that ever happening again. He wondered if he should question Jan about his concerns. He hoped that Ted would be faithful to Claire, and that she was not making a mistake.

Claire spent the night at Austin and Jan's. Ted would be back the next morning to help load the calves, and then Ted was going to take Claire back to Calgary. Claire and Jan spent a good part of the evening talking about the up-coming wedding. Her plans were much grander than those of Austin and Jan, but neither Claire nor Ted, had been married before. Austin wondered if Ted was game for all the bells and whistles that Claire had in her plans.

Finally Austin asked Claire about it. She was rather surprised at his question. "Why wouldn't he be?" she asked.

"Well, he was reluctant to get all dressed up at our wedding," Austin told her. "Claire do you know what kind of a guy Ted really is?" Austin asked.

Claire looked at Austin. "Yes, I know he is wild, fun-loving and we love each other," she told him.

"Is that enough Claire? He hasn't the foggiest idea about what church is all about. You know what can happen if you aren't careful. You may think you can change him," he said, putting his hand up to stop her from finishing his sentence. "And maybe you will be able to, but what if he sucks you into his way of life instead?"

Claire was quiet for a moment. "Austin, I know it says in the Bible that we are not to be equally yoke to together. *(Meaning not to marry someone that doesn't believe that Jesus died on the cross, for our sin)*. I understand, and have prayed about it." Then, with tears in her eyes, she said, "I love him, Austin and I can't give him up. He has told me about his wild life and I can accept that as his past. I know he loves me, and all I can do is pray that God will somehow touch him, and save him. I believe God can still do all that before we are married," she said.

Austin and Jan's eyes met. They understood what it was like not to be able to be with the one you loved. "Jan and I will pray to that end. God can definitely change a person and there is always that hope," Austin said, as Jan came over to lay a kiss on Austin's forehead before preparing a small evening snack.

It was the next day, after the calves were loaded and on the way to the Fort McLeod Auction Mart, that Austin talked to Ted about his up coming marriage.

They sat down on a couple of bales near the tack room. Ted sat, quietly listening to Austin's concerns. He told Ted that as a man and friend, he had a lot of respect for him, but as Ted was about to marry his favorite cousin, he was concerned about his life style and the fact that he was not a Christian.

This was a bit new to Ted, so Austin explained briefly what the Bible said. Ted sat there listening for a moment. He then told Austin that he had been watching both him and Jan, and there was something different about their relationship. He also knew very well that things didn't always go smooth for them, but they did seem to be able to overcome each other's shortcomings. That was what he hoped for himself and Claire.

Austin was quiet for a while. He had a question for Ted and he wanted a straight answer. "Ted?" Austin said, looking directly at him. "Are you in love with my wife?" Ted looked up in surprise at Austin's question. "What?" he asked.

"You heard me right the first time, Ted. I want a truthful answer. Are you in love with Jan," he asked surprisingly calm.

Ted was thunderstruck as he looked down at the floor. At that point, Austin knew before he answered.

"Yes, Austin. I have to admit that I had some very strong feelings towards her during the time you two weren't speaking. She is quite a woman," he said, still looking down at the floor. Ted shuffled to take a different position on his bale, while Austin waited for him to finish.

"She didn't realize how I felt about her until the day I took you with me, to help her settle into her new place. She loved you man, and she was very concerned about you losing the ranch after that phone call from your bank. All she talked about was saving your ranch, so you wouldn't lose your dream. Even if you didn't take her back, it was always you. So I did what I could to help her make that come true. Then when she called and said John was after her, I said that I would tell you, but she said no. She didn't want you to be more upset than you already were. I knew from the first time I saw you two together, that you were meant for each other. Then not getting there in time to help her, and seeing what John had done… was about to do…" Ted hesitated than cleared his throat, as he remembered seeing John holding the knife to Jan's throat. He closed his eyes and could still hear her screams, and remembering her lying there with her clothes torn, was almost more then he could take. "Yes, I loved her and wanted her," Ted admitted.

Austin wrung his hands as he listened.

"When you announced that you were getting married, that day I decided that was probably the only way, that I would ever be able to kiss her, like I wanted to. So I went for it." Then looking up at Austin, he concluded. "She's always loved only you and I knew it. I really hope you realize how lucky you are, that you had another chance with her."

Austin just nodded his head in approval.

Ted then added, "I do feel I have to thank you for bringing Claire into my life. I love her Austin, and I promise that I will be true to her. I can't promise you that I won't forget how I felt towards Jan. As you know, we can't help the way we feel, but Claire has taught me what it feels like to be loved in return. I feel lucky to have met her. I hope that clears it up once and for all.

If I make some stupid comments, I hope you will understand why I inadvertently do it. It's mostly from force of habit, and I am sure Claire will continue to reprimand me for that." Ted said, with a grin on his face.

Austin sat, taking it all in. He was very angry for a moment, but Ted seemed to have a way of making things hit home. There was no beating around the bush. He said it as it was, and Austin respected him for that.

"I'd say Claire has her job cut out for her, but maybe a leopard can change his spots," Austin said.

Austin finally stood up and reached out to shake Ted's hand as he asked "Friends?"

"Friends forever," Ted said, also standing up as he reached out to shake Austin's hand, as they laid their other hands on each other's shoulders.

When they went back up to the house, with a clear understanding of each other.

CHAPTER 13

IT WAS THE FOLLOWING SPRING, when two letters arrived for Jan. One was from her sister and the other was from Mrs. John A. Remple, whom she presumed was John's mother, seeing as children were usually given the same names as their parents, or aunts and uncles.

This time she did wait until she got home to open them. Austin was down by the corrals when she returned. She took a deep breath before sitting down with her letters. When she opened John's mothers letter, she expected another lecture on how terribly she had treated poor old John. Well, she might as well get it over with.

It was a very sad letter. John's mother was dying, and her life had been far from a bed of roses. She mentioned how sorry she was to hear about the beating that Jan had suffered, at the hands of her son. She hoped that Jan would find it in her heart to forgive him. He had been brought up with a very abusive father. In her son's younger years, she did her best to teach him that this was not right, but her worst fear was not unfounded.

She continued to say how horrified she was, when she'd heard what he had done. She told Jan that she wished her the best, and that she was sure that young Austin would make her a good husband. It was hard for her to say, but she was glad that Jan had not married into their family. It was with a heavy heart that she realized that she had failed, and that John was following in his father's footsteps. She also said, that she held no ill will towards Jan, for not marrying her son.

Tears filled Jan's eyes, as she thought of what this poor woman had endured, all her married life. Jan's brief encounter with John was probably just a sample, of what his mother had lived through. It was so hard to comprehend. She obviously loved her son and had tried her best to teach him, right from wrong. Now at the end of her life, she had to admit that she had lost the battle. She said she feared for anyone that married John, because they would surely endure the same abuse that she had. She ended with, "I will soon meet my loving God, and then I will be free of all the abuse."

Jan sat there for several minutes just staring at the letter, with tears running down her face. How hard it must have been to admit such a thing to a virtual stranger. It may be that she had very few friends, and just needed someone to know how she felt.

Finally, Jan picked up the letter from her sister. It was a pleasant surprise, but as there had been no contact between them for years, she suspected that it was not good news. Jan opened the envelope, and pulled out a very short note. Mary had probably done this without, the knowledge of her husband Abe.

In it, she said that Mrs. Remple had confided in her, as well as showed her the picture of Jan, that had been cut out of the newspaper. Mary was extremely upset by what she saw. Up until Mrs. Remple had taken Mary into her confidence, Mary blamed Anne (*which was Jan given name*) for all the trouble in the their family. Mrs. Remple had asked for Jan's address. Thankfully she had kept their wedding invitation. She told Jan that Mrs. Remple was now at peace, as she had passed away. She did not know if Jan had received a letter from her before she died.

In case she hadn't, Mary wanted to pass on the message that Mrs. Remple held no ill feelings towards Jan. She hoped Jan would forgive John for what he had done to her. Mary also relayed the fact that their parents were still very upset with her, but someday she would tell their mother what Mrs. Remple had told her.

It was obvious that Mary had not written a lot of letters, because it was hard at times, to figure out what she meant, by the way she had written it.

As for her family, all she said was that every-one was in good health.

Jan was still sitting at the table with the letters in her hand, when Austin walked in.

"Not another letter from your parents?" he said disgustingly, when he saw the look on her face. She handed him the two letters, as she sat staring at the envelopes. She had to thank God for the way things had turned out. What she had done was not right, but it definitely saved her from a life like Mrs. Remple's.

When Austin finished reading the letters, Jan said, "How can people go to church and profess to be so good, and yet treat their partner like that?" she asked.

Austin just looked at her and said, "We have all sinned, and come short of the glory of God, but we must remember that we are answerable for our sins, just as others are answerable for theirs. Sin is sin, and at any degree, it's still wrong," Austin said.

"How true that is, God knows I am far from being perfect, but there for the grace of God, go I." (Meaning, without God's intervention, she could have been in the same position as Mrs. Remple.) Jan said as she picked up Mrs. Remple's letter.

Austin sat there thinking for a moment, and then said, "I guess I should tell you what I did, the day after Ted and I had gone to help you move into your apartment. I was angry with the people back home especially John. So I went for a drive. When I passed the church, there were several cars parked there. I turned around and went in and gave them a piece of my mind."

Jan jumped to her feet and exclaimed, "You did what?" Jan was shocked, as Austin had never stood up for himself when he was younger, and now he was telling her that he actually went to the front of the church.

Austin proceeded to tell her what he'd had said, except for the part about seeing John and what he had told him. "Yeah, it's kind of funny when you think about it. They always said I should go to the front church to apologize. Well, I went to the front of the church as they wanted, but they got more than they bargained for when I did.

Jan was not sure what to think. Then she began to laugh. "I would've liked to have heard what happened after you left," she said.

Austin repeated what he figured they would have said, and also told her the relief he'd felt after getting everything off his chest, once and for all.

After having lunch, Jan told Austin that she was going to ride out to the drop. It was a place of wonder and peace, with the valley below and the mountains in the distance. It was a place that both Austin and Jan would go to get away from the hectic pace of life. Some-times, they would just sit alone, while other times they would ride out together and talk, or just have a quiet time with God and enjoy his handy-work. Austin told Jan not too be to long, or he would come looking for her. He still didn't like her riding out that far by herself, but he knew she probably had a lot on her mind. He also understood that she was upset that there was still no sign of them having another child. As for finding their son, they still had no leads.

On her way out to the drop, Jan rode through the one pasture to check on the cows, as they still had a few stragglers that had not calved. It had rained the night before, and to her there was nothing better then the fresh smell after it had rained. That afternoon, the sun had come out, but a warm jacket was still needed.

When she got to the drop, the ground was still a bit damp. She knew it was not safe to go close to the edge. She was not that fond of heights, especially after that one close call. She could still remember hearing the rocks fall as Austin pulled her to safety. She never again ventured near the edge.

Blaze of Fury

Jan sat on the boulder, with a heavy heart. She thought about Mrs. Remple and what she had endured all those many years, and yet no one knew, or just did not intervene. She surely would have had marks on her. Then Jan thought back, and realized she never once saw Mrs. Remple in anything but a long dress with long sleeves.

Most of the time, she wore glasses with dark lenses. Everyone assumed that her eyes were sensitive to the light, but it was possibly to cover bruises. Jan knew that they had not gone out much. It was all work and no play.

It was a very male-dominated group. Perhaps some men believed that there was nothing wrong with Mr. Remple's treatment of his wife. They may have believed that she had brought it on herself. Whatever the reason, it was not scriptural.

Then there was her sister. As sisters go, Jan and Mary never really got to know each other very well. Jan was almost eighteen when she was sent away, and her sister was twelve. At least her sister now knew what John was really like. Surely she was glad that Jan had not endured that type of life. She hoped Mary had a good husband. She decided that she should wait for a while before replying to her sister's letter. Why was it that her parents didn't know about John's family? They seemed to think highly of them. If they knew, would they still be as angry with her? Yet, they seemed to know what John had done to her. She could not understand them.

Then, as she looked around, all concerns seemed to fall away. She sat there calmly, reflecting on the beauty of this place, while Hope grazed near by. She took a deep breath of fresh air and thanked God for the much needed rain. As she looked down at the valley below, it seemed that the grass already looked greener after the rain. She sat counting the cows as they grazed. Her mind wandered to the past, and how different her and Austin's lives would have been if they had been allowed to marry. They would be sharing this all with their son, though it made her shudder to think that they could be still living within the same old traditional life style. Well, I guess God had it planned differently for them. She prayed for the son she was never allowed to keep, and asked God to someday reunite them.

Jan had just counted the eighty-sixth cow, when she heard a sound from down below. Hope snorted and her ears twitched, so Jan knew that it wasn't just her imagination. She got up and walked carefully across the rocky trail. The treacherous span along the edge of the cliff was approximately two hundred feet, before you were once again on safe ground, but the drop was about a one hundred feet to the bottom. It was one of God's amazing, but dangerous, spots.

A few rocks slid over the edge, as Jan's foot slipped on the gravely surface. After that, she walked extremely cautiously. Little by little, she inched her way closer to the edge. She heard the sound again. Her fear of heights told her not to get any closer than need be, to the edge.

She gingerly peered over, and there to her utter dismay, she saw a man and a horse lying on the pile of rocks below. "Hang on, mister! I'll be down as soon as I can," she yelled. Even though she wanted to turn and run back to her horse, she knew better. She walked gingerly away, until she got close to the boulder.

The shortest way would be to go across the drop and down, but that was too risky with the wet footing. It would take her longer to go back and then down, but at least she could be assured that she would get there alive. Once back in the saddle, Jan tapped the heel of her boot into Hopes side. She wondered who the man was, and why he would be here, on their property.

Jan reined Hope in, before branching off to the right. Their pace was now down to a walk, as they began to descend. The trail was still wet from the rain. Even though she was anxious to get there, she had to be very careful on the decline that lead to the valley below. Once at the bottom, she again nudged Hope into action as they headed back towards the base of the cliff.

She wondered how badly this man was injured, and how she would ever get him back to the ranch. She reached into her

Jacket pocket, and to her relief, she found her cell phone. She had not used it for a while, and was not sure if there was any life left in the battery. Well, she would worry about that later. First she would have to see how badly he was hurt. As for his horse, she was quite positive that it would be dead.

When Jan finally reached her destination, she was off Hope in a flash. She quickly climbed the pile of rocks to where the man lay. He was not moving, and Jan feared that he might be dead. She felt for his pulse. It was slow and irregular, but he was still alive. His one leg was twisted into an awkward position, so she knew it was broken. He had several large gashes on his head, and had lost a fair amount of blood, from what she could see. His face and hands had a lot of scrapes. She wondered about internal injuries, and possibly other broken bones that were not visible.

Jan reached into her pocket and pulled out her cell phone. She gave a sigh of relief when she saw that it was still working. She tried to reach Austin, but with no success. She then tried Ted. She was just about to hang up when he answered.

Ted had laid his phone on the hood of his truck, and had just gone into his garage to pick up a couple of wrenches, when he heard his phone ring.

"Ted, this is Jan." Ted was silent for a moment. Why would Jan be calling him unless something had happened to her or Austin?

"Is everything all right? Did something happen to Austin?" he asked.

"No, Austin is fine, but I have a serious problem on hand and I can't reach him. I'm out at the drop. You know the place," she said.

"What are you doing out there? Did you fall?" he asked, having visions of her lying at the bottom of the drop.

"No, it's not me either, but there is a man and his horse, laying at the base of the cliff. I presume the horse died from the fall, or he shot it, because it apparently has one or more broken legs. This guy is in a bad way. He is unconscious and has one badly broken leg. He also has a couple of bad gashes on his head, and who knows what else," she said.

"Leave it to me, Jan. I'll get help out there as soon as I can. I'll find Austin, so don't worry."

"Thanks Ted. I'll try to make him as comfortable as I can," she said.

"Don't move him Jan," Ted said.

"Yes, I know. Thanks," She said before placing her phone back in her pocket.

Jan took off the bandana from around her neck, before walking over to the clear mountain stream that ran through their property. She dipped the bandana into the water, then squeezed out the excess and returned to the injured man. She knelt beside him and began to wipe some of the dirt and blood from his face. She repeated this several times.

Slowly, he began to stir. He moaned, than tried to move.

"Just lie still," she said, taking off her jacket to put under his head. "Just lay back," she said again, as he tried to open his eyes. He squinted at her for some time, not saying a word. Then he seemed to recognize her as he tried to sit up. He moaned in obviously agonizing pain, before laying back on the soft jacket that she had placed under his head.

"Don't try to get up. I've called for help, so it shouldn't be too long now. Just try to relax," she said, wiping the perspiration from his forehead with her bandana. He was wet and cold, but Jan had nothing else to cover him with. Then suddenly she thought of something. Jan walked over to Hope, took off the saddle, and laid it on the ground. The saddle blanket was all she had. *That will at lease help to keep him warm*, she said to herself, as she laid it over him.

"Why are you helping me?" He asked, gritting his teeth in pain.

"Because you're hurt," she said still wondering where she had seen this man before.

"Who did you call, the cops?" He asked, sneering at her.

Blaze of Fury

Suddenly Jan remembered who he was. It was because of him and his friend that her and Austin had lost their child.

She sat back in silence as anger welled up with-in her, but then as he moved, he yelled out in pain. Jan quickly went and knelt beside him while talking calmly. Her compassion for another person in pain over-came her anger. Even at the thought of what he had done, deep down she knew, this is what God would want her to do. The biblical story about the, good Samaritan came to mind.

She continued to wipe the perspiration and blood from his face and forehead, while speaking encouraging words to him. "Help will be here soon, so hang on," she said.

"Am I going to die?" He asked, grabbing hold of her hand.

"That is up to God," she said softly.

He opened his eyes and looked at her. With the sun shining over her shoulder, her hair seemed to glow. He released his grip on her hand, than raised his hand to touch the side of her face. Then, just as suddenly, his hand dropped to his side as he slipped into unconsciousness.

Jan could do no more, but sit beside him and pray that help would come soon. It seemed like forever, but then she heard the sound of horses galloping. It was music to her ears.

Hope snorted and shook her head. On the hill, Jan saw two riders and, by the color of the horses, she knew it was Austin and Ted. Austin was the first one off his horse. It was then Jan heard the helicopter.

"Are you alright?" Austin asked, putting his arm around her, as she stood up.

Ted looked down at the unconscious man.

"Austin!" Ted called, motioning for him to come and have a look.

It was Jan's jacket under the man's head that he noticed first. Then, when he looked at the man's face, he said. "What is he doing here? Jan, do you know who this man is?"

"I didn't at first but yes, I know who he is," she said stepping back.

"You should have left him here to die," Austin said, angrily.

"I felt that way too when I realized who he was, but then I felt God would want me to do what I could for him," she said. Tears began to fill her eyes at the memory of the child that she should now be holding in her arms. Austin pulled her off to the side, as the helicopter was about to land. Austin then watched her walk over to the creek, where she stood staring down at the water.

Austin and Ted just watched as the medics worked to stabilize the man before placing him in the helicopter. Both Ted and Austin were anxious to know what this guy, had been up to. Perhaps he got what he deserved. After the helicopter left, Ted handed Austin, Jan's jacket and told him that he would leave them alone. He watched Austin walk over and put Jan's jacket around her shoulders. Ted had a good idea what was going through both their minds, as he picked up Jan's saddle blanket and put it back on Hope. After putting the saddle back on Jan's horse, he glanced back briefly before riding away.

"It's cold out here, you'd better put this back on," Austin told her. Jan slipped her jacket on and wiped the tears from her eyes.

"He will be fine," Austin said.

"I wasn't thinking about him. I was thinking about our... our..." Austin held Jan in his arms, as she began to sob. Austin stared out at the mountains and his eyes also filled with tears. Anger once again built up with-in him.

* * *

It was a week late, and Austin had just come home, after being in town. He threw the newspaper down on the table. "Well, Jan, according to your stray cowboy, you are an angel," he said.

Jan looked up from her baking. "What are you talking about?" she asked.

"Read it for yourself!" Austin said, throwing his hat on the chair beside him, before sitting down.

Jan wiped her hands on a towel before walking over to the table. To her surprise, right on the front page, there was a picture of the man she'd found at the base of the cliff. She glanced over the article. He mentioned hearing her soft-spoken voice, as she encouraged him to hang on. He said there was a halo above her head, and her hair shone like the sun. Then when he touched her face, it was as soft a silk.

"He was delirious," Jan, said as she read through it.

"Did he touch you?" Austin asked.

"He grabbed my hand once, as he yelled out in pain. Then he asked if he was going to die, before reaching up to touch the side of my face. Then he passed out," Jan said going to get Austin a cup of coffee.

"Did he say why he was there?" Austin asked.

"No. Actually he spoke very little. He mainly moaned and groaned, but..." she hesitated.

"He must have recognized me at first, because he asked why I was helping him. Then he asked if I had called the police," Jan told Austin.

"Maybe the police should ask him, what he was doing trespassing on our land," Austin said.

Jan wondered if he was up to no good, but she didn't want to get involved in another court case. "Maybe he learned his lesson, Austin. I don't want to go back to court again. We have no proof that he was doing anything, so please, let's just drop it." She said, looking directly at her husband.

Austin knew how hard it had been on her the last time, and he didn't want to put her through all that again. "Okay, Angel. We will drop it for now, but I would like to know what he was doing out there last night," Austin said.

Jan gave Austin a kiss on the forehead. "I love you," she said.

Austin grabbed her and sat her on his knee. "I love you too," he replied, looking into her eyes before giving her another kiss.

"I have to get back to my cookies, or they will burn," she said, laying her hand on the side of his face. Jan went back to work, while Austin went back to reading the paper.

Jan placed some of her freshly baked cookies, in front of Austin, before he said, "It sounds like he was busted up pretty bad. He had broken ribs, a broken leg and arm, a punctured lung, a concussion and lots of cuts and bruises. Well, he still got away luckier then his horse. Maybe this will teach him to stay off of other people's property. Hm… he also wishes that he could see that angel again."

"That is highly unlikely." Jan said while getting some more cookies ready for the oven. Just then, the phone rang. Austin answered it and was obviously annoyed at the caller.

"No! She is not interested in talking to you." He hesitated a moment, "I don't have to ask her," Austin said trying to protect his wife from a media frenzy. "The answer is no!" After a moment he again replied with. "No! You do not have to call back later, as the answer will still be no!"

"What was that all about?" Jan asked.

"That was the newspaper. They want to know if you would talk to them about the guy you found," Austin said angrily.

"Oh my! That is all I need. I hope that puts an end to that!" Jan said, horrified that she would possibly be scrutinized again.

"I hope so too. Well time to get to work," Austin said, giving Jan a quick kiss before heading out the door.

It was a couple hours later when she saw Ted drive down to the corrals. Half an hour later, Austin came up to tell Jan that he and Ted were going out to check the cattle. When she asked about riding with them, he emphatically said no. They didn't need her today. She knew something was up and he was not about to tell her. She became very nervous, which ultimately made her heart beat more erratically. She had been feeling very tired lately, which was very unusual for her. She had made an appointment without telling Austin because if he had any indication that something was wrong, he would get too over-protective.

Jan was getting a bit concerned because Austin and Ted had been gone for quite some time. She hoped, that there weren't any serious problems with the cows. She was deep in thought when the phone rang. It was the police.

Jan's first thought was that something had happened to Austin or Ted, but the officer said it was nothing like that. "Mam, the man you found at the cliff, said he has some very important information for you and, he would only tell it to you in person," the officer said.

Jan hesitated and then said, "I will consent to that, but only if my husband can come with me." The officer said that he would get back to her.

What could he possibly want to tell her, and why were the police involved? Was he under arrest again? Surely she wasn't going to be called to testify at another trial. How she wished Austin would get home. She had to keep busy, so she began to make supper and do some laundry. Life just didn't seem to get any easier.

As she worked, she began to think of the land that they now purchased. The three quarters were under seeded to hay, which they needed badly. The lease could hold another hundred head of cattle, but they were not sure whether they should buy that many because most of the money from the sale of her land had been spent on the new property. They needed a good calf crop this year, and then every thing should be fine. She had the money from her twenty percent of the last crop of calves, so she figured they could buy few more cows head without borrowing any more money. She knew that Austin would definitely not go into debt again. He now made sure that a cushion always remained, so as to not repeat his last mistake. So far as they knew, no one had been told that they had purchased the adjacent land. She shuddered to think of what Douglas would do when he found out.

Then a terrible thought came to her. Did Ted come to see if the rustlers had struck again? Could they have run into problems and that was why they weren't back? She wouldn't be so worried now, if it had not been for Austin's definite no, when she'd asked about her going with them. She gave a sigh of relief, when she heard the men come in.

They were talking about a horse. They had apparently had found something.

Jan stood quietly by the cupboards, and listened to them as they went to wash up for supper.

She was still standing there when they came back into the kitchen. Austin looked at her and then looked down at the table.

"Well woman? Where is our supper?" Austin asked, as he gave her a kiss on the cheek.

"On the stove," she said, still not moving.

"So… could we ask if you would please put it on the table for us? We have had a hard day and we're hungry," Austin said, looking at her. This was strange for Jan. Usually she would have it ready and waiting. "Is something wrong?" he asked, with some concern. Ted also wondered what was up with Jan. It was so out of character for her.

"Well, that all depends," she said.

"On what?" Austin asked, now confused.

"When you left here, you definitely did not want me to ride today, and from the tone of your voice, there was something that you were keeping from me. I had envisioned all kinds of disasters like, trouble with some cows, or a run in with some rustlers. So now, if you want to eat, you'd better tell me what's going on," she told him.

Austin told Ted to have a seat before he went and sat at the table. "We were checking on the cattle. That's about all," Austin said.

Jan looked at Ted. "And what is your excuse?" she asked firmly.

Ted just shrugged his shoulders.

"Well, I'll be. The great Ted Jackson is speechless. Now I know you two were doing more then checking cattle," she said. "Well, okay," she said, putting their supper on the table.

"Now that's more like it," Austin said as he smiled at her.

After Austin gave thanks for the food, they began to eat. The two men just talked about the cows, and how good things were going this spring. Finally Jan had, had it.

"Well, who owned the horse?" Jan asked.

Ted and Austin looked at each other as if not knowing what she was talking about.

"Don't act coy with me, Mr. Klassen." Then suddenly, she said, "It belonged to Douglas, didn't it?"

"Who told you?" Ted asked looking at Jan

"You just did," she said firmly.

"Blabber mouth," Austin said to Ted.

"How am I supposed to know your woman's tricks?" he said.

"What else do you two know that you aren't telling me?" she asked.

"That's it," Ted said, filling his mouth with food, so as not to answer another of her trick questions.

"Well, if you don't want to talk, then I won't tell you what the police wanted when they called today," Jan said, calmly eating her food.

That got both of their attentions, and they stopped eating to look at her.

"What did they want?" Austin asked.

"You first," she told them, calmly before taking another bite of food.

Ted and Austin both, laid their cutlery on their plates and looked at each other.

"I just came to tell Austin about the rumor that Douglas has spread around town," Ted said.

"Shut up, Ted," Austin said.

Jan grabbed Austin's arm. "Ted finish your story now!" She said firmly.

"She is bound to find out, Austin. Douglas is trying to discredit you by insinuating that, there was something going on between you and the guy that, you had found out at the drop, Ted said.

"And so, I suppose the two of you went out there to check and see if it was true? Is that it?" She said, now very upset, as she marched angrily, out of the room. They both got up and followed her.

"Jan, that's not it at all," Ted said.

Austin sat on the bed beside her. "Jan, you know us better than that. We rode out to move the cattle closer. Ted had heard rumors that Douglas may be ready to follow up on his threat. We are sure that the fellow you found was checking things out for Douglas before he strikes again." Austin put his arm around Jan, and told her that they never gave the story another thought. It had only made them angrier at, their neighbor and his dirty tricks.

"I'm sorry Jan, I should kept my mouth shut," Ted said.

"No, it is probably best that I know. People will be looking at me differently now, and at least I will know why," she said sadly. *Would this nightmare ever end*, she thought.

"Let's go finish our meal before it gets too cold," Austin said, standing up and reaching for Jan's hand.

When they had finished their meal, Austin asked Jan what the police had wanted. She passed on her information, to which Austin's immediate reaction was, no way in hell would they meet with him, but Ted's opinion differed.

Ted said, "No Austin. I think it would be a good idea if the two of you go to talk to him. Maybe he has had a change of heart and wants to get things straight. Even if it isn't that, he may give you a clue as to what Douglas is up to. After all, he has worked for the man for several years, and no one would know him better."

The two men then talked openly about the things they had heard, what they should be prepared for and how to prepare for whatever might happen. Jan could not believe what she was hearing. It was like going to war. It amazed her that one man had decided he was entitled to the whole area, because he had been here first. It was senseless.

* * *

A couple of days later, Austin and Jan went the hospital to meet Rod Frame, who was the man that Jan had found at the bottom of the cliff. They had talked to the police and asked how this all had come about, and why the police were involved. They were told that it was because he could be sent back to jail, if it was found that he broke his probation.

He was looking to make some sort of deal to stay out, and one of his requests was to see Jan before he gave them, the information that they required. They were told that this must remain confidential. There would be one officer present, and they would be monitoring the conversation.

Jan was extremely nervous when she and Austin entered the hospital. They asked what room Rod was in and when they got there, a police officer was waiting for them.

When they walked into Rod's room, the sun shone brightly through the window and he seemed to be sleeping. He had apparently undergone some more surgery on his leg, so they were told that he might be a bit groggy.

Jan walked over to the window and was looking out when she heard Rod moan. She turned around to look at him.

When Rod opened his eyes, the first thing he saw, was the angel that he had seen at the base of the cliff. He saw a glow above her head, as her hair gleamed in the light. A big smile crossed his face when he looked at her. He closed his eyes for a moment, and when he opened them again, she was gone.

When Jan saw that he was waking up, she went back to Austin's side.

"Mr. Frame?" Austin said.

Rod turned his head then, looked directly at Jan. He was quiet for a moment, and then said, "Every time you show up, so does she."

"Who is she?" Jan asked.

"That angel. Didn't you see her? She was just over by the window," he said.

"Mr. Frame that, was me. I was standing there when you opened your eyes," Jan told him.

"No, it can't be, because..." he said, without finishing.

"You do look better than when I saw you last," Jan said, as the fear of meeting him seemed to subside.

The voice was the same as what he remembered hearing. He looked at Austin, then at Jan. He also remembered how soft her face felt when he touched her, when she came to his rescue. "Mrs. Klassen, would you allow me to touch the side of your face?" he asked.

Jan looked at Austin, than at Rod, she was feeling rather uncomfortable.

"I don't see what that has to do with what we come here for?" Austin said now thinking that this was all a trick to get Jan here, so he could harass her.

"I was just remembering her talking to me and when I reached up and touched the side of her face, it felt so soft. Thank you Mrs. Klassen for, being my angel. I believe you were sent there to help me. I was sure that I was destined to die there, because of all the bad things I had done." Rod lay there quietly as he reflected on the fact that, Jan had actually come to his aid when he had been such a miserable jerk to her, awhile back.

Jan reached for Austin's hand as they both wondered, what important thing he had to share with them.

"I have to tell both of you that I am now sorry for what happened before. You may not accept my apology, but I do mean it," he said.

They chalked Rod's apology up to the fact that, he was still groggy from the medication he was on.

They stood there in silence, and were about to leave when he opened his eyes, and asked them to wait. There was something else he had to say.

"Just spit it out. We haven't got all day," Austin said, annoyed at having to waste his good time with a guy like him. Did he really think that they would believe that he, all of a sudden had a change of heart? He would have to do better than that, if he wanted to convince them.

"Austin, please?" Jan said, now wanting to know what else Rod had to say. "Let's give him a chance." Jan turned to Rod and said. "What did you want to tell me?"

"You are a lucky man," Rod told Austin.

"I am sure that isn't what we came to hear," Austin said.

"Okay, I just want to warn you that Douglas is going to be trouble for you."

"How?" Austin asked, now all ears.

"He means to break you by stealing a bunch of your cows. He has done it before, but this time it will be big time. He talked about burning you out. That might just be talk, but he has gone a bit mad lately. Keep an eye on my angel for me, if you know what I mean," Rod said.

Austin looked at Jan for a moment, than walked over to shake Rod's good hand. "Thanks, I hope you get better," he said, before turning to leave.

"Goodbye Angel," Rod said.

Jan turned to look at him. Then she walked over and shook his hand. "Thank-you for the information, Mr. Frame," she said.

He held her hand longer then she'd wanted. Then he let her go, while focusing on her eyes. He smiled at her and said, "My name is Rod."

"Okay, Rod. I hope this is a new beginning for you. God protected you for a reason and I hope it was for a good reason," she told him, before walking over to where Austin was waiting for her.

Austin put his arm around her, as they left.

Rod lay there, thinking about what she'd said. If he had been in Austin's shoes, he would have probably sworn at him, and possibly slugged him as well. The Klassen's were different. Maybe she was an Angel. It seemed so strange that, every time she showed up, he got that same vision. His angel was beautiful. He wanted to believe that she was an angel sent just for him. He didn't dare tell any of his friends what he was thinking, or they would think that he hit his head harder then they had thought.

He really didn't care to go back to the Douglas ranch anymore, but if he didn't, they may suspect that he'd squealed. He would bide his time before he left. He would continue doing his job on the ranch, but he would not get involved with any more rustling, or anything worse.

CHAPTER 14

IT WAS A BUSY TIME for Austin and Jan. They spent many an hour fixing fence, and they'd also had been doing what ever they could to help Ted and Claire with their wedding plans. It was only three weeks before the wedding, and Austin decided that it was time to have another chat with Claire, as Ted had still not accepted Jesus as his Lord and Savior. Ted had definitely swept Claire off her feet, and as they say, love is blind. Austin had to admit that it wasn't like Ted had turned a deaf ear, because he'd been to coming, to church on his own. That was something the old Ted would have never done.

As for the trouble that Rod had told them to expect from Mr. Douglas, a couple of months had past, and all was still good. It had been hard to not, continually dwell on what may or may not happen. Austin and Jan had prayed long and hard for God to protect them. God had brought them together and blessed them, and he would watch over what he had given them. It was not that they weren't still alert, but it was no longer wearing on them.

Just as a precaution, the rule on the ranch was that no one ever rode alone. Austin and Jan now always carried their phones wherever they went, and anyone riding on their property was to do the same.

Jan had gone to see her doctor because she had been very tired, and no longer believed that it was just a virus. She wondered if she was pregnant, but then again she had none of the symptoms as before. Perhaps she was just over-worked and stressed out.

It was two weeks before Ted and Claire's wedding that their worst fear was realized. During the night, someone had made off with thirty-five cows, and half a dozen calves. Austin called the police before calling Ted. They had to round up the rest of the herd to see which calves no longer had mothers, and vice versa. Austin was angry and frustrated, and Jan sat crying and asked God why. By the time the police arrived, Ted and Austin had already figured out that someone came in with a cattle liner. They probably hauled in horses to round up the cows, as there was no sign of any one riding onto the property. They checked which direction the truck had travelled after it left their property, but it was not in the direction of the Douglas ranch. Of course Douglas wouldn't be that stupid as to lead the police right back to him. He'd probably stashed the cattle miles away.

Austin and Ted had ridden out to check on the cattle. Jan decided to stay behind, because she was too upset to go riding. So Rod had been right. She wondered if he'd taken part in what had happened.

Austin looked very pale when he returned. Ted did his best to encourage him, but with very little success. He now had twenty-seven calves without mothers and four cows with no calves, and was missing four cow calf pairs. It was definitely a blow to them. Jan asked if there was a possibility that Rod had been involved. Austin did not answer, but Ted told her that Austin had asked the police that question. They had checked that out before they came, and apparently he had been in the hospital for the past couple of days.

Ted was concerned about his friend. "Austin, are you going to be alright?" he asked. In reply, Austin just shook his head no. "I don't know if it's worth the fight anymore," Austin said, looking down at the floor.

"You can't give up now! Something will turn up. We'll get him. I'll be sending out notices to all the auction marts and

Auctioneers so they'd know to be on the look out for them. I'll also call the livestock investigator. Douglas won't get away with this one," Ted said. Ted looked at Jan. Her eyes were red and puff from crying. "I'm going to call Claire to stay with you two. I have to get on the ball immediately, before he can move them," Ted told them.

"We'll be fine. Thanks for your help Ted. I don't know how we will ever be able to repay you for everything you have done for us." Jan said.

"Forget it," he said, before leaving.

That night neither, Austin or Jan slept very well. They were beginning to think that if something wasn't done about that neighbor of theirs, they might have to hire someone to watch the cattle day and night. That could get very costly. Austin got up at three a.m., and went into the living room, and just sat there. He was very quiet the next day. By evening, he was still wondering if it was worth all the hassle. Maybe they should sell, and move somewhere else. Jan thought of that too, but it would mean that Douglas had won. He had to be stopped, or he would just turn on the next family that crossed him. They had to fight this out until the bitter end. Surely God would not let evil win over good, but it was tempting to throw in the towel. The next morning they'd had at least six ranchers in the area, offering them their assistance. They were also told that, through out the past years, many of them have had, problems with Douglas, and in their eyes, he was definitely guilty.

That encouragement did a lot to lift their spirits. They were no longer outsiders. They were finally being accepted as part of the ranching community. They were here to stay. It would be Douglas that would have to leave.

A few days later, Ted brought Claire with him to check up on Austin and Jan. The four of them decided to ride out to check on the herd. Everything was fine for now and, as Ted said, it was not likely that Douglas and his men would try anything so soon again. Jan asked Claire if she would like to ride out with her to their new lease land. Austin and Ted figured it should be safe, but just in case of trouble, they must carry their phones, with them. In the mean time, Ted and Austin went home to pick up some fencing material, as the moose and deer had been pretty hard on fences. They said that they would be back shortly.

The weather was hot and dry, with a fairly strong southeast wind, and they were now in desperate need of rain. The lease land had not been grazed off for some time, so there was a lot of tall grass mixed with new growth. Austin and Jan had ridden out there a couple of times, but they had not rode through it all. Austin was about to check the fence, so they could turn their cattle into this area, when the rustlers hit. Now it was questionable as to whether it was safe to even put their cattle in there, as one side bordered the Douglas ranch.

Jan and Claire rode slowly down one trail, before coming to a fork that looked like the grass had been recently trampled down. They both noticed it at the same time.

"I thought you didn't have any cattle in here," Claire said.

"We don't" Jan replied.

In silence, they followed the trail that led towards the creek. They rode through a dense wooded area and came out at a meadow. From there, a gentle slope led to a sparsely treed area with a creek meandering through it. To the surprise of Claire and Jan, they discovered that someone had manufactured a large make shift coral and had filled it with cattle.

Jan looked at Claire in utter dismay. She pulled her binoculars out of her saddlebag to check and see if there was any one around. "I don't believe it," Jan said after studying the cattle for some time.

"What is it?" Claire asked.

"I think those are our missing cows. Douglas must not have known that we took over this lease, and figured that he could hide them here, until things cooled down," Jan said.

Blaze of Fury

"Do you think you can find your way back to get Austin and Ted? I want to get closer and check it out. I will wait for you here."

"Do you think that is wise?" Claire asked.

"I'll be fine. You just be careful on your way back." Jan was about to call Austin, but her phone showed no service.

"Here-take my phone and give the guys a call when you get on top of the hill," Jan said.

"No, you keep it. You may need it. Besides, I have mine here in my pocket," Claire told her, while making sure that it was still there. "You be careful," Claire said.

"You to." Jan said, as she started down towards the corral.

* * *

Austin had ran into the house for a moment, before heading back out towards the girls. The phone was ringing, and at first he thought of leaving it, but then he changed his mind. It was Jan's doctor.

He wondered why he would be calling. Austin had no idea that Jan had gone in for a check up. The caller asked for Jan, and when Austin told him that he was her husband and would pass on the message, he got some surprising news. He was going to be the father of twins. Austin actually had to sit down. He was thrilled, but now the protective part of him took over. Jan should not be out there right now.

He had no sooner hung up the phone when, it rang again. This time it was Rod Frame. That was when Austin began to break out in a cold sweat. He immediately sensed that something was wrong.

"I just heard you had a bunch of cattle stolen. I told you he would do it. I also heard that he found out that you'd taken over the neighbor's lease. He is madder then hell. I'd advise you and the angel to stay off the lease today," Rod said.

"Why?" Austin asked, his hands shaking so bad that he could hardly hold the phone steady.

"I told you that he'd talked about burning you out. Well, there is some serious talk of doing just that," Rod said.

"Oh no," Austin said in a distressed tone.

"Mr. Klassen? Is your wife is on the lease, right now?"

Austin was so distressed that he forgot that this was the person responsible for the loss of his unborn child. As if thinking out loud, he said, "she is out there, and hasn't heard the news that she is going to have twins. She can't lose her babies. It can't happen."

"Mr. Klassen! I won't let anything happen to my angel. I'll keep in touch," Rod said, before quickly hanging up the phone.

Austin was still holding the receiver in his hand when Ted walked into the house. The look on Austin's face sent a chill through him. Had something happened to the girls? Just then, Ted's cell phone rang. It was Claire. He listened intently, than answered.

"She is doing what? That foolish woman! No, you keep coming this way. We are on our way," Ted told her.

"Austin! We have to get going, and fast. The girls found the cows," Ted said, tapping Austin on the shoulder.

"What's wrong with you? You look like hell," Ted said.

When Austin looked up at Ted, he knew there was trouble. However what Austin told him was worse than he could have ever believed. Especially after what Claire had just told him.

"Let's get going," Ted said. It was then that Ted told Austin what Jan was doing. Ted had never seen Austin look so pale. He was afraid that he was about to have a heart attack. He too, was beginning to shake. Jan was very special to him, and if something were to happen to Jan, he was afraid what he might do to Mr. Douglas. Ted made a quick call to the police and told them where they could meet, and then they galloped at full speed out towards the lease.

* * *

Blaze of Fury

When Jan reached the corrals, she noticed a branding pot and several branding irons. So his plan was to rebrand them, and then probably ship them out of the area. She had to get out of here because it looked like they had everything ready to do it. Well, she would throw a monkey wrench into their plan. She picked up the branding irons, and carried then some distance away, and hid them in an area that had some very dense brush. Then she led Hope down to the Sheep Creek that ran through the lease. Then, after covering her tracks to the best of her ability, she led Hope into the creek and got on. They continued on, in the creek for quite some distance, hoping to disguise their tracks, when she heard some yelling. Someone down by the corrals was obviously very angry, and she suspected the reason why. She nudged Hope on, as they walked farther down the creek before coming out in some fairly dense brush. It was hard to get through, but she had to mask her trail as best as she could.

"Poor Hope," she said patting her horse's neck when she saw the blood on Hope's legs. She got off to check her before continuing on. The scratches weren't that bad. It was then that she heard the sound of horses coming up fast, from behind her. She knew the scratches would be minor, compared to what they may do to her, if they caught her. She was not sure if they found her tracks or were just guessing. She had not gone far, before she entered a sparsely forested area.

She knew she had to move, and fast. The wind was from her back, so she could hear them clearly, where as they, may not have hear her as readily. With one kick of the heels of her boots, Hope was running at full tilt with Jan hanging on. She was now in uncharted terrain. All she knew was that, she would go until she found a fence or an old cow trail. The wind seemed to be getting stronger as the sun beat down on the already dry grass. She had an idea that she may be heading southwest. When she got into, a fairly thick growth of trees, Jan reined Hope down to a walk. Jan wanted to be sure that they were out of site. She stopped and listened. She didn't see or hear anyone. She grabbed her phone and dialed Austin's cell number. He answered almost immediately.

"Jan, where are you?" Austin asked, now very angry with her.

"I'm not sure. I hid Douglas's branding irons, and then got out of there. I followed the creek towards the west, and then came out in some dense bush on the south side. I heard horses coming from behind me so, I headed in what I think is a southwest direction. I don't see or hear them, but they are there. I can just feel it. I'm in a real thickly treed area right now."

"Jan, be careful please. The police are now here at the corrals. I'm coming to look for you. I love you Jan," Austin said.

"Oh no!" Jan said, before she got really quiet.

"Jan! What's wrong?" Austin asked.

"I have go Austin. I see them coming and…" Jan whispered.

"Jan! Jan!" Austin hollered into the phone.

"Austin, I have to go. I think they saw me and… and there is a thick cloud of smoke coming my way. I love you, Austin," she said, before the phone went dead.

Jan did her best to get through the trees. It was thick, and slow going. She finally broke through to another small meadow. Here again, she urged Hope on, as she heard the snapping of twigs behind her. She had to get ahead of them and fast. When she entered another thick growth of trees, she glanced back and could see that, they were gaining on her. She was very stressed and tired. The next time she looked back, she saw that they had stopped chasing her. Instead, another thick cloud of smoke was beginning to roll towards her. It was then that she remembered what Rod Frame had told them. Douglas had talked about burning them out. It looked like he was making good on his threat, and he did not care if he took a life in doing so. Instead of following her, they rode off to the north. Shortly after, she saw another cloud of smoke rising.

Jan had to get out of there. If she now headed northwest she may be able to skirt, the now blazing grass. She had to find her way back to the creek. The wind had fanned the smoke into a "blaze of fury." Her only hope now, was to find the creek but that would not stop the fire. It would jump the narrow creek very easily. She could hear the crackling of the fire, as it entered some trees. Hope was now at a full gallop as they raced across the open meadow. When she looked back, she could already see flames leaping high into the sky as it ignited another patch of dry brush.

This was crazy. *This has to be a nightmare. I will soon wake up in Austin's arms*, Jan told herself. The smoke was now beginning to burn her eyes and she began to cough. When she looked around, she noticed that she was almost completely surrounded by smoke. She had to keep her bearings. She had to find the creek, and soon. Hope began to get very jumpy and nervous, and Jan could not blame her. Jan patted her neck and tried to reassure her, as they came up to some thick brush. The smoke was clouding the area, and it was getting harder to breath and to see. She decided to take a chance, and go through the thick brush. When she first came out of the creek, there was a lot of thick brush like this. Maybe if she got through this area, she might just hit it lucky and find the creek again. Jan began to pray, as she urged Hope through an area that was thicker than anticipated.

"Please, Jesus, please," she continued to say over and over again.

Suddenly Hope slipped, and if Jan had not been hanging on, she would have fallen off. Hope jumped as she unexpectedly plunged into the center of the creek. "Thank you Jesus," Jan said as she turned Hope in the direction away from the fire. It was slow going because the creek was full of all shapes and sizes of rocks. The sun was now partially hidden by all the smoke, and the sky seemed to give off a red glow. Jan knew that they were in trouble, and she may not get out of this alive. She considered going further north, but in the thick smoke she could get lost, and when the fire did jump the creek, there would be nowhere to go. She must stay in the water. She began to wonder if she would ever see Austin again, let alone her firstborn child. This was time lose perspective, as she had to have her wits about her.

Sparks were now beginning to rain down on her. Some of them even burned her skin. Even Hope jumped, and snorted as they began to land on her. Jan began to wonder if she should just get off, and let Hope go free. There was no use for Hope to lose her life to. If Jan let her go, there might be a possibility that she could find her way out of this.

The smoke was now so thick that they could not see where they were going. Suddenly, Hope ran smack dab into a barbwire fence, which sent Jan toppling over her head. Jan landed on a large boulder, sending a sharp pain up her arm and into her shoulder. At that point a hot ember struck Hope. Hope bolted, ripping the reins right out of Jan's hands, as she headed off to the north.

Well, at least she was going in the right direction, Jan thought to herself as she pulled her bandana up over her mouth and nose. The next ember that landed on her arm burned deeper into her flesh. She could feel them land in her hair, and tried to brush them out. She quickly lay down and rolled in the water to soak her entire body, before continuing to walk in the creek.

She did this several times as she continued to search for a spot where, the water would be deep enough to hide under, when the full fury of the blaze caught up to her. She knew that it wouldn't be long now before that happened. There were now flames igniting on both sides of the creek, as the wind carried the hot embers and where they fell, small fires would begin to burn.

Jan began to pray. "Dear God, you are my Lord and Savior. You hold our lives in your hands, and if it is my time Lord, I go willingly. I only pray that, if it is your will for me to I die here, please be with my dear husband. I pray that you will grant me one wish, and that is that Austin will be reunited with the son we never knew," Jan cried.

Just then, Jan stumbled over some rocks and fell head long into the water. As she lay there, a couple of bears ran right past her. She got up and continued stumbling along in the creek. She saw more animals crossing as they fled from the flames. At one point, she was almost knocked off her feet by, several wolves or coyotes-she was not sure which. It was then that she heard the roar of a plane flying fairly low overhead. The fear of animals was not a thing she'd believed she would have to contend with. They were all too busy fleeing to bother with her. They would go running through the creek at full speed, while she trudged on through the water. She had nowhere else to go. She could now feel the heat, and hear the roar of the fire as it closed in on her. She knew that if she didn't find a deep pool, it would soon be the end. Suddenly, she felt herself falling again.

✻✻✻

Austin had tried to search for Jan, but a wall of flames stopped him. He tried several ways to get around, or through it, but to no avail. He returned to the corral, where he dropped down near a stump and just moaned. Claire knelt down beside him. She tried to be strong for Austin, but she could not, and she also began to cry. "It's my fault. I should have never left her alone," Claire cried.

As they heard the sound of the water bombers fly overhead, Austin put his arm around her and told her that it was not her fault. He tried his best to hold back the tears, but he knew no one could go through a fire like this and live. Douglas's men had made sure that the fire would surround her, so she didn't have a hope. He now had lost his wife, and two more children. He could no longer contain himself. He broke down and wept while holding on to Claire.

Ted found a place where no one would see him. He was thinking along the same line as Austin. He couldn't help but feel the pain of the possible loss of a woman that he cared for. He enjoyed going to help Austin and Jan, but he'd had an ulterior motive. He just wanted to be around her once and awhile. He knew that Jan only liked him as a friend, but that was fine with him.

He did love Claire, but it wasn't quite the same. However the fact that she returned his love made him want to be with her more. Right now, he too had to get away to cry somewhere no one would see him. It was hard to say if they would ever find her body, and if they did, how badly would she be burned.

Ted fell down on his knees and began to cry out to God. "Please God, I do believe that you are up there. I know that I have done a lot of bad things, but for some reason you have brought two wonderful women into my life. I ask you to forgive me, and change me. I want what they have." Ted was silent as he cried for a bit before continuing. "I know there is no hope of Jan surviving this fire. Well, almost no hope, but I understand you did some miraculous work when you were down here so, Lord, for Austin's sake, can you do it again? They have gone through so much. Please God protect her. Jesus save Jan, and me too," Ted said now, sobbing uncontrollably.

Suddenly, he felt a real peace come over him. For the first time, he had hope that maybe Jan could still be alive. He had no idea why he felt that way, but he could now go back to Austin and Claire with real true encouragement, that there was always hope. God was in control, and he could protect her.

When Ted found Austin and Claire, he told him about the peace he'd felt after he'd prayed. He now believed that somehow Jan would get through this.

Austin looked at Claire and said. "Well, God did answer one of our prayers. Let's hope he will answer Ted's second one too." Claire had just finished telling Ted that they had been praying that he would turn his life over to the Lord, when Rod showed up leading Hope.

"Where did you find her?" Austin asked, checking over the burns and scrapes all over Hope's body.

"I didn't find her. She found me just northwest of here. It's a wall of fire out there and the smoke is bad, but angels don't die Mr. Klassen, so I know she is still alive. I won't give up until we find her," Rod said, laying his hand on Austin's shoulder.

"Why are you doing this?" Austin asked.

He looked down at the ground. "I've been an outcast from young up, so I felt I had to live the part of the tough guy. My parents were alcoholics and I got a lot of beatings. To get rid of my anger, I started to do the same. I had no friends. I got attention by being malicious, and just down right rotten. I believed bad attention was better than no attention. Then, when I was checking out your place in the rain, my horse slipped, and you know the rest." Rod continued, "I swear to this day, that I saw an angel. She was gentle, and cared for me despite of what I had done. Then I saw your wife. She took over where the angel left off. Even after what I did to her, she still helped me. That was something different than I'd ever known people to do." He hesitated a moment, then continued. "When you came to the hospital that day, I saw the angel again, then your wife. I knew if I told someone this story, they would say I must have hit my head too hard. I figured you guys would understand, seeing you're church going people, and know about things like that. I believe that if I can get to the area where Mrs. Klassen is, I will see the angel again. I'm sorry. I'm talking too much." Rod added. "Just keep thinking angels don't die, and that's why I can tell you that, she is still alive." He turned and heading back through the group of men that had set up camp in the area.

The three of them just looked at each other, not knowing what to make of what Rod had just told them. "God works in mysterious ways," Austin said, not knowing whether he dared to have the assurance that she would survive this.

Chapter 15

Austin was at a loss for what to do next. He and Ted had ridden around to see if there was any possible chance of getting in to look for Jan, but the flames were like a wall and the smoke made it almost impossible to breathe. The fire fighters, who had now arrived in full force, told them to get out of the area. They could see the water bombers drop their loads onto the fire and, for a moment, the flames looked less ominous, but then, fanned by the wind, they would just flare up again. What they needed was for the wind to die down, and a good rain to dampen down the trees and old grass. Their horses were nervous, as they watched the fire grow large and hotter by the minute. Both people and horses began to cough. It was hard to breathe. A cloud of smoke engulfed them, and they knew it was high time to retreat. When they returned to the corrals, where Claire had last seen Jan, the police were waiting for Austin. They told him that he should take his cattle out of the area as soon as possible. They had found the branding irons that Jan had hidden, so they had all the evidence they needed.

The cows were very edgy, due to the smell of smoke that hung heavy in the air. It was difficult for Austin, Ted, and Claire to control the destination of their little herd. They were beginning to think that they might lose some. They needed to herd the cattle off the lease land, and then round up the rest of his cattle, and herd them all the way home, which was as far east as his property went.

Blaze of Fury

Ted knew the four ranches that had just arrived. Two of them, unloaded their horses and began to help, herd Austin's cattle east to a small pasture, near the yard. They all knew how unpredictable a fire could be, so the farther away from the fire the better. If the wind changed, then the fire could turn around and bite you.

Before the other ranches left, they told Austin how sorry they were to hear about his wife, and that the local ranchers had made arrangements, with a fleet of cattle-liners to be on stand by, just in case anyone in the area needed to evacuate their cattle, on short notice. He gave Ted and Austin the phone number to call, if they needed to do so. They also informed Ted and Austin that, there were on their way to the Douglas ranch, where cattle-liners were already hauling cattle out of harms way, as they suspected the wind to shift, and his Ranch could be right in line of the fire.

What an irony they all thought. What Douglas had threatened to do, now may be to his own undoing. Ted and Austin did offer their help. It was not Douglas they were concerned about, but the livestock who could lose their lives in such a horrible way. The two Ranches thanked them, but said that there were already several other ranches there and, in this situation, it may be best that they stay clear.

Austin had high hopes that Jan may have called, by the time he got home, but he was dispirited when he saw that, she had not. There were many calls from concerned neighbors, but none from Jan. It seemed that every one wanted to help. They were all extremely upset at Douglas for his drastic lack of judgment.

Claire had gone back to Austin's house earlier, and had a light lunch ready, when they got the cattle home. She told the men that they must eat something.

While nibbling on their food, Austin and Ted tried to come up with a plan to get into the area that Jan had described. By now, the fire would have devoured everything in its path. They would never be able to find what she had described. The creek would have been Jan's only hope to survive and even then, her chances were slim.

The creek was not very deep, and if the fire weren't bad enough, she would have had the smoke to contend with. Austin and Ted looked at each other, knowing that there was really no hope of surviving in a fire like that. Austin told Ted and Claire that he was going back to the lease. This time he was going with his truck and horse trailer. He wanted to be ready as soon as there was any glimmer of hope that he could start to search for Jan's body. He threw some blankets in his truck, then Claire handed him some sandwiches and a thermos full of coffee. Everyone was hurting, but no one as much as Austin. There was no one that could remove the pain that now overwhelming him.

"I'm so sorry Austin. I wish there was something I could do," she said. Austin said nothing, but just squeezed her hand before he left. Claire was very concerned about him. He did not look well.

Ted said he would follow shortly with his own truck. That was best in case one or the other had to leave earlier.

After Austin left, Ted held Claire in his arms while she cried. Ted had a good idea how Austin felt. Austin had possibly lost, not only his wife, but his unborn children also. The anger he felt toward Douglas was almost over whelming. He hoped that the fire would continue in the direction of Douglas's ranch. The solution to the problem, as far as Ted was concerned, was for Douglas to get burned out for what he did. *As long as the livestock got out, let it burn and with Douglas in it*, he thought to himself. He knew it was not a good way of thinking, but if Douglas took Jan's life, his should be taken also.

Claire and Ted went into the living room, where they looked out at the orange glow with large plumes of smoke rising above. It seemed to be going towards the southwest. The wind was definitely changing. "Maybe this east wind will bring some rain," Ted said, with his arm around Claire. They stared out in disbelief at what was unfolding right before their eyes. How their lives had changed in just a few short hours, and all because of the greed of one man. Ted and Claire talked for a while, and they wondered how that man could live with himself after what he had done. The only problem was that they had no definitive proof of who started the fire, and there had to be solid proof to convict him and his men. Jan was not here to tell them what she seen. It would be Austin's word, based on what Jan told him, against Douglas. Maybe another one of Douglas's hired hands would develop a conscience, and tell the police about who had set the fire and why.

Claire was quiet for a while, as she thought of Jan's family. Surely they would want to know, and be there to support their son-in-law. Then again they did have different ideas. Claire told Ted what she was going to do. The first thing she had to do, was call Austin's parents and his brother, before they found out about Jan on the news. She told Ted to be careful, and that he should take the sandwiches and coffee that she had prepared for him.

"I love you, and I don't want to go through what Austin is," she told him.

"Don't worry. You won't be able to get rid of me that easy," he said, before holding her tight, and then giving her a long passionate kiss. "I love you too and don't ever forget that," he said, running his hands up and down her arms. "Now I have to go. I'll give you a call later," he said, as he grabbed his hat, jacket, and the food.

Claire took a beep breath before calling both Austin's parents and his brother. They had heard about the fire, and that someone was missing and presumed dead, but never in their wildest dreams had they ever thought, that it could be one of their own family. They would all be there as soon as possible. Claire also told them that she was sure that Austin wouldn't mind if they stayed the night, but he would not likely be home.

Claire told Austin's brother that she was going to talk to Jan's parents. She felt they should know. Jake offered to go along, but she said she felt that this was something she wanted do alone. She would wait at Austin's until they arrived. Someone should be near the phone, just in case Austin, Ted, or maybe even Jan called. That was, if a miracle happened and she had survived the fire, but they knew, there was little chance of that.

When Jake and Dianna arrived, the first thing Jake said was, lets pray. Jake asked God to protect Jan and to give Austin strength to face, whatever the future might hold. He continued to ask for guidance for those that were searching for Jan, as well as the protection for the firefighters and that they may get the fire under control soon. Jake then sat on the chair praying silently, while Dianna and Claire sat there crying. After a few minutes Claire and Dianne sat there quietly, reflecting on the seriousness of the situation.

Claire wiped her eyes and said, "Well I guess I better get going and pass on the bad news to Jan's family."

It was a good two hours drive east to the area that Jan's family now lived. What would she say to them? She wanted to remain calm, but firm in what she felt they should do. They were still good people. It was that old hard line that seemed to drive more people away, than it attract. God would have to give her the words to say.

There were so many things going through her mind that she had reached her destination, before she knew it. She decided to go first to Jan's parents place, and then to her sister's. She found it useless to approach Jan's brothers, as they would refuse to have anything to do with Jan, just like their Father. She had to start with Jan's parents.

Claire took a deep breath before she was about to get out of her car. It was then that the strong smell of smoke hit her. She looked down at her slacks and knew that Jan's parents would frown at a woman in men's attire. Why had she not thought to change? *Oh well, the smell of her clothes would be proof enough to confirm her story*, she thought.

It was now evening, and she knew that they may go to bed fairly early, but this was important. Claire walked up to the door and knocked. Mr. Enns was the first one to come to the door. He looked her up and down, and it was obvious that he smelled the smoke that now over- whelm even Claire.

"Mr. Enns, I am Clara Klassen. I don't know if you remember me," she said, using her birth name that, he would recognize.

Mr. Enns nodded his head that he did. At that moment Mrs. Enns approached.

They did not invite her in and that was fine. She had come to say her peace, and then leave.

"I came to tell you about your daughter Anne," she said, also using Jan's former name.

"We don't have a daughter by that name anymore." Mr. Enns said, with a hard, angry look on his face. He was about to shut the door when she stopped him.

"You may be right about that," she said, looking at him. He was obviously annoyed at her brashness. "Anne was caught in a forest fire and there is very little chance that she could have survived, the flames and smoke. We won't know until tomorrow when they will hopefully, be able to send in a search party," Claire said.

Mrs. Enns stepped closer and asked Claire how the fire had started.

"It was started by a neighbor who wanted everything his way, and did not like outsiders. I am sure you know all about that," she said.

Mr. Enns was now, not impressed by this outspoken young woman.

"I just thought you should know. I know all about what happened years ago, but what I cannot understand is your lack of forgiveness. When a man asked Jesus how often we should forgive, he said seven, times seventy. We are also not to judge one another lest we be judged. Maybe I am wrong in approaching you this way. I know you would help if what was happening to Jan, were to happen to a stranger. Well you said that Anne, (using her given name,) is no longer your daughter. So that makes both Anne and Austin strangers. Right now Austin is hurting and could use all the help and support that people can give him. Oh, and by the way, about the same time that Anne disappeared, Austin got the call that she was expecting twins. Put yourself in his place and use some compassion please," she said.

Then before she stepped down off the front porch, she said as tears began to run down her cheeks. "I am really sorry to have to be the bearer of bad news." It was then that she noticed Mrs. Enns wiping tears from her eyes. Claire quickly turned and walked back to her car.

When she drove off, she saw Mr. Enns still standing there, looking down at the porch.

Jan's sister lived only a mile from where her parents lived. Claire tried to get her act together. She had no idea how she would be received but Jan's sister and he husband.

The smell of smoke on her clothes began to over whelm here, so she rolled down the window as she drove. The evening air was still quite warm, which brought back the vivid memories of the wall of fire shooting high into the sky. She fought back tears when she thought of how Jan must have felt as the fire surrounded her. She had to pull over for a while because she couldn't see through her tears. She had to get her emotions under control to continue. She had one more mission to accomplish before she headed back. When she drove up to Jan's sisters home, there was a dim light shining in the house. She walked up to the door and knocked. It was Mary that answered.

"Hi Mary, I am Clara Enns. I came to bring you some bad news about your sister," she said.

Mary immediately invited her into the house. Her husband Abe was sitting at the table. Mary told Abe who she was, but he already knew. He knew who she was. He had not forgotten her, as she was one of their neighbor's children. He had liked Clara, but then the family moved away and that had ended that. He could see that she had been crying, and smell of smoke on her clothes was pungent. He suspected something was wrong, but he made no real move to ask her.

"What happened to Anne?" Mary asked. Abe now seemed to take some interest as to what was said.

"Austin and Anne's neighbor was mad at them for taking over a new lease, and so he set it on fire while Anne was out there, and it will be a miracle if she survived. As of yet, no one has been able or allowed to go look for her," Claire said with tears in her eyes. "I felt I should come to tell you. Austin does not look very well. He could sure use some support from family and friends," she said looking at Abe. "I came to ask if for once, some compassion could be found in your hearts. No one is perfect and it is time for forgiveness. Like Anne said, she knew God had forgiven her for her mistakes. She was very upset that not one member of her family acknowledged the death of her first husband, or her marriage to her true love, Austin. Did you know that she had a miscarriage, when she was thrown from her horse? That and the fire had caused by the same man. He had incited his hired men to do what ever it took, so that he could get a hold of Austin and Anne's land. About the time Anne was trapped by the fire, Austin got a call from Anne doctor, telling him that Anne was pregnant with twins. Put yourself in his place. He has now possibly lost his wife and two children all at the same time."

Neither Abe, nor Mary said too much. Mary continued to wipe tears away, while Abe sat there motionless.

Claire couldn't believe how insensitive he looked. After all, Abe and Austin had been best friends.

It was then that her cell phone rang. "Excuse me,' she said, going to face the door for some privacy. "Hi, Austin? How are things going?" she asked.

"Nothings changed," he said in a defeated tone. "I just called you to talk to someone. I feel like I am going to go crazy."

"Oh Austin. I wish I could help you, but I don't know what to say or do. Just keep praying for a miracle. Maybe God will bring her out of this. I know it looks hopeless but he can work miracles. Austin, keep thinking of what Rod said. *Angels don't die.* How is Ted?" she asked,

"Oh, he is sitting here looking probably as bad as I do," Austin said.

"What's happening with the fire?" Claire asked.

"Well, they moved all Douglas's cattle out because right now he is right in line of the fire. They have been dousing his buildings with the water bombers to keep them from burning. Tomorrow morning, Ted and I are going to take the horses along the creek to see if we can find some trace of her. We will start at daybreak, even if we are told to stay out. I can't sit here and just wait," Austin told her.

"I understand, but it will still be pretty hot and there may be a lot of trees laying across the creek, so you two better be careful. I will be praying for you, Austin." Claire was than interrupted by a tap on her shoulder. She looked up and saw that Abe holding his hand out, for her to hand him the phone.

"Just a minute, Austin. Someone wants to talk to you," Claire said, before handing her phone to Abe.

"Hello Austin."

"Who is this?" Austin asked.

"This is Abe Reimer. I am sorry to hear about Anne," he said.

Austin could not control himself and broke down, upon hearing the voice of his old friend. When Claire looked at Abe, he had tears in his eyes also. *God, please heal the hurt between friends and family,* she prayed.

Abe was also having a hard time talking. "Is it alright if I come help look for her?" He looked at the face of his wife and then added, Mary could help Clara do some cooking?"

"I'd like that very much," Austin told him.

Blaze of Fury

Austin told him what he and Ted had planned. After which, Abe told him that he would be there by five a.m., he then handed the phone back to Claire.

"We are not all as uncaring as you think us to be," Abe told Claire.

With tears in her eyes she said, "I am sure God will bless you for what you are about to do." Claire told them. She said that they would be welcome to stay the night at Austin's, but they politely refused. They would leave early in the morning, and Abe said he would talk to Anne's two brothers. After Claire gave them direction as where to go, she gave Mary a hug, then shook hands with Abe and thanked him again.

It was late when Claire got back to Austin's ranch. She was surprised to see that every one was still up. She excused herself and had a quick shower then changed into clean clothes. It was refreshing to get rid of that suffocating smoke smell. She then made some coffee, found some sweets, and passed them around. She told everyone what she had done and how pleased she was that Abe and Mary were coming. She hoped that this would be the beginning of healing between the families. Only, it may be too late for Jan. "Angels don't die," she repeated over and over again.

Jake looked at her rather strangely. Then she told them about Rod Frame, and also the prayer that Ted had prayed. After talking for quite a while, Claire said that everyone should get some rest. Mr. and Mrs. Klassen could take the one spare room, and Jake and Dianna took the other. She said she would sleep on the couch, as she didn't think she would be sleeping much anyway. Jake prayed for strength for Austin and Ted, as they were about to embark on a painful and dangerous search. God had preformed many miracles before, and he could do it again, but if it was God's will to take Jan home, she asked for strength for the family and especially Austin.

When every one had gone to bed, Claire went outside. Everyone, and everything, was on edge. She could hear how restless the cattle were now, as they occupied the pasture at the base of the hill. There were rustling sounds as they walked restlessly around the pasture. The cows continually called for their calves if they got too far away. At times, it would be a calf calling for its mother and once they were united it would be quiet for a while but then another cow would call until her calf replied, or return to her side.

Claire looked towards the west, where the glow from the fire still lit up the night sky, and the smell of smoke lingered strong in the air. Just the thought, of the fire fighters working in that heat, sent a chill down her spine. They also had families, who would be worrying about them. She prayed for the safety of each and everyone. This had caused enough pain for their family; no one else needs to suffer.

Claire wondered what had been going through Douglas's mind, and what had made him the kind of man he had become.

Rod suddenly came to mind. Where was he? He was a strange man. She began to pray for his safety, as he was also about to enter dangerous territory, when looking for Jan. Little would she had thought, that she would be one day be concerned for his safety, after what he had done to Jan, and Austin.

Then there was Abe and Mary. What she did know about Abe, when she'd lived near him, was that he was a very nice person. Mary definitely got herself a good husband. Yes, good things had already begun to happen. Maybe even Jan's parents would begin to mellow. She was sure that Abe would be talking to Jan's parents and telling them that he was coming to help, where ever could. It would be nice if Jan family could communicate with each other again. She must not give up hope that Jan was alive.

Her mind then turned to her darling Ted. She loved him very much and she knew he loved her too. She wished that he were here beside her. She asked God to keep him safe, and hoped that things would all turn out, so that their wedding could go on as planned.

She tried to put herself in Austin's place. What would she feel like if it were Ted that was missing? She was sure that she would go out of her mind. She would be out there with a flashlight right now, turning over ever tree and rock looking for him. She prayed that God would keep both Austin and Ted safe as they searched for Jan. Something good had to come from this. Then she realized that it already had. Ted had turned to the Lord, and even a hard cowboy like Rod Frame was now talking about Angel's and faith.

Claire knew that she could not sleep. She knew that Austin and Ted would not likely be sleeping either, so she went into the house and found Jan's forty cup coffee percolator. Then she filled it with cold water, and put a few scoops of coffee in the top basket. While she waited for the coffee to percolate, she went to the freezer and took out a variety of cookies that she and Jan had prepared for the extra company that they had expected for the wedding. She was sure that there would be a few fellows out there that may appreciate it.

Claire left a note on the table saying where she'd gone, just in case she was not around when the others woke up. When the coffee was done, she poured it into a very large insulated water cooler to keep it warm. Just before she left, she remembered to grab some disposable cups and the cookies. She decided to take Jan's truck, as it was rather rough terrain for her car. Then she called Ted.

Ted was surprised to hear her voice, as it was already one in the morning.

"Hi Ted, I'm coming over there because I can't sleep anyways, she said.

"Sounds good, but I will meet you at the gate. They are not allowing people past that point," Ted told her.

"How is Austin holding up?" she asked.

"I am not sure. I haven't seen him for a while. I think he may be lying down in his truck,"

Ted said.

"I am bringing some coffee and cookies over. I thought they might be needed by now," Claire said.

"You're a gem. You must have read my mind. I better get going so I can meet you at the gate, Ted said, then hanging up.

When Claire got to the gate, Ted was waiting for her. He hopped in with her and then told her where to find the camp. When she got there, she saw three men sitting on the tailgates of a couple of trucks, but none of them were Austin. She hoped he was getting some rest. When she got out of the truck, she recognized two of the men as the ones that had helped to move the cattle. The third man was another rancher who had come to see if there was anything he could help with. Ted introduced his fiancée to the small group, before she brought out the coffee and cookies. They seemed very happy to receive her small offering.

Once everyone received their coffee and were busy eating their snacks, Claire told Ted that she was going to check on Austin. When she got to his truck, she was surprised that he was nowhere in sight. That concerned her. Midnight was still tied to the side of the horse trailer, so he had surely not gone far. Claire saw that there was a flashlight lying on the seat of his truck, so she picked it up and decided to check around the area. The reddish glow of the half moon that hung low in the sky, gave off a bit of light, even though it was somewhat obscured by the smoke. She wondered if Austin had gone down to the creek. She was almost at the top of hill so it was a bit of a hike down to the corrals. When she got to the corrals she call out for him, but there was no answer. As Claire walked towards the creek, the smoke seemed much stronger. She got an eerie feeling from this location. She could hear the cracking of the burning trees, and the glow of the fire seem even more ominous. Fear now welled up inside of her, and she hoped that she would find Austin here, as she was now afraid to walk back alone. Icy fingers of fear began to grip her body as the thought of how Jan must feel out there all by herself. Claire gave a deep sigh of relief, when she saw Austin sitting on a stump with his elbows resting on a near by branch. His hands were clasped together and his chin was resting on them, as he focused his eyes on the stream towards the west.

She walked up to him and laid her hand on his shoulder. He didn't even seem to realize that she was there. "Austin, you going to be alright," she asked. He did not answer her. Claire stood beside him, not knowing what to say. She to began to stare at the creek. Had Jan reached the creek and found a place deep enough to survive? The creek was fairly shallow here.

Finally, Claire said, "Austin, why don't you come back with me? I brought some coffee and cookies."

Austin looked up at her. "When did you get here?" he asked, sounding totally exhausted.

"Just a few minutes ago. Austin I brought some coffee and cookies, so lets go back and have some," she repeated.

"Oh, okay," he said in somewhat of a daze. Then, as if awakening from a trance, he said, "There isn't much hope, is there?"

"We can't give up Austin. We won't know for sure until she is found," Claire said, taking his arm as they walked up the hill. When they reached the truck, Claire poured Austin some coffee and forced a couple of cookies into his hand, but he did not join in with the other men's conversation. He wished that it were light enough to get out there and start searching. It was killing him knowing that Jan was out there all by herself. Had Jan suspected that she was pregnant? Was that why, she had gone to the doctor? Oh, how he yearned to hold her in his arms.

Ted looked up at Claire as she came over and laid her hand on his shoulder.

"Where did you disappear to?" he asked.

"I went looking for Austin. I found him down by the creek," he said.

Ted turned to look at her. "You went down there by yourself?" he questioned, now very upset. "Don't you ever take off again without anyone knowing where you went. I don't want to have to go looking for you next." He added.

"I am a big girl," Claire told him. The other men got very quiet as Ted gave her a lecture. She promised not to do it again, and at that Ted pulled her down on his knee.

Then, as the others began to talk again, Ted said that perhaps she'd better be getting home. He would love to have her beside him, but just in case the fire turned again, he wanted her at a safe distance. The fire was still heading west, at times a bit southwest. If they ended up with a Chinook wind, they could be in serious trouble. The wind had died down somewhat, but a rain would sure help to slow the fire. It was hard to imagine what Jan was feeling right about now. Ted's hope of find Jan alive was, also beginning to dwindle. He cringed inside at that thought. He had seen fires that were not near as bad, and those people had not survived. He laid his head against Claire. She put her arms around him and they held each other for a while. It was almost three o'clock when she looked at her watch.

"I'd better be getting back, Ted. I forgot that Jan's sister and brother-in-law are going to be at the ranch around five o'clock," Claire said. Ted was surprised to hear that. After Ted had questioned Claire about that, she told him that she had gone to talk to Jan's parents, and then to Jan's sister and brother-in-law.

Ted gave Claire a kiss and told her that she should get some rest. As Claire was leaving, she gave Ted and Austin orders to at least lie down in their trucks, even if they didn't sleep. Ted said he would see what he could do. Claire went over and gave Austin a kiss on the forehead and made him promise that he would lie down for a bit. She told him that he needed to be alert if he was going to find Jan. She also reminded him that Abe would be here in a couple of hours. Before she left, she promised to continue praying for them and wished them the best in their search.

Ted walked her back to the truck, where he took her in his arms and gave her a long, passionate kiss.

"You be careful out there, and be sure to call the moment you find Jan," Claire told Ted. She handed him Austin's flashlight and asked if he would mind putting it back in Austin's truck.

Blaze of Fury

Claire was extremely tired, when she got back to the house. She knew she should have a shower before going to bed, but when she laid down on the couch, she fell asleep as soon and her head hit the pillow. It was someone knocking on the front door and shouting, "Anyone home?" that woke her up.

When she'd first awakened, she thought she'd had a nightmare, but she soon realized this was all for real. She was still groggy when she met Abe and Mary at the door.

Mary had a large basket of food, which she had prepared for Abe to take out to the men that were participating in the search. Claire was just explaining to Abe where to find the men, when Mr. and Mrs. Enns appeared at the door. Claire was speechless. She immediately expressed her pleasure at their arrival.

Mr. Enns said that he was here to help where he could, and his wife would help with food preparation for those that were helping in the search or fighting the fire. "We would do this for anyone that needed help," he told Claire.

Before Abe and Mr. Enns left to find the search party, Claire looked at Mr. Enns and asked if he would say a prayer for the safety of all the men out there, and for a successful search.

He looked at her for a moment, then with hat in hand he, bowed his head and prayed before they left.

"Are Austin's parents here?" Mary asked.

"His father came yesterday and his mother, I believe, will be coming sometime today." Claire said. Mary and Mrs. Enns then began preparing for the next meal.

Claire excused herself and had a quick shower. She felt much better after getting out of her smoke filled clothes.

* * *

Austin was so exhausted that when he saw Abe and Mr. Enns arrive, he broke down. *Why had they not come when Jan was still alive? It would have meant the world to her to know that they cared enough to come to look for her,* he said to himself.

Abe came over and laid a hand on Austin's shoulder. "I am sorry we have to meet under these terrible circumstances, but God will give you strength as you need it," he said.

Austin fought to get his emotions under control. *Men should not cry*, he told himself. Austin reached out and gave Abe a big hug, which Abe gradually reciprocated.

When Austin walked over to Mr. Enns, he reached out to shake his father-in-laws hand, but it was not accepted. "I am glad you came Sir," Austin said, not feeling that he should call him dad, as he had no idea how he would accept that. Austin lowered his hand. Even at a time like this, the shunning continued. However, he had to admit that he was surprised to see them here. Maybe this is what it would take to bring on a change.

Then before Abe brought out the food that the women had prepared for them, Austin introduced Abe and Mr. Enns to Claire's future husband, Ted. Abe seemed much more accepting of this outsider than Mr. Enns was. Ted had been told what to expect from these men.

Before they started to eat, Mr. Enns asked everyone to stand while he gave the blessing for the food. He also prayed for God's direction throughout the day.

They were just finishing up their lunch when Rod showed up.

Austin perked up, hoping that he had something to report.

Rod was totally exhausted, as he sat down on the tailgate of a truck. He leaned back against the truck box, while accepting a cup of coffee and some buns from Ted. He thanked Ted, and said that this was the only thing he had eaten since yesterday morning. He was a fairly large and tough looking man, but right now he was tired and with a discouraging look on his face, he didn't look so tough. He was covered in dirt and soot and he reeked of smoke. Austin and Ted presumed that he had already been searching for Jan.

"Have you heard or seen anything?" Austin asked anxiously.

Rod shook his head, and both Mr. Enns and Abe could see Austin's face drop.

Rod shoved a bun in his mouth and it disappeared so fast that Ted thought he inhaled it. "I followed the creek a ways, but it was hotter than hell out there. Burning trees were laying across the creek in many spots, and even the normally cold mountain stream seemed warm."

Rod washed another bun down with a large gulp of coffee. He grabbed another, then before devouring it, he said. "These are darn good." Then he continued. "There was one time that I was sure that, I got a faint glimpse of my angel, but then she disappeared. I don't know if I seen her for real, or if I just wanted to see her so bad, that I was imagining things," he said. "I didn't see your wife after that, so I must have been seeing things," he added.

"Where was it that you thought you seen her?" Austin asked now more alert.

"It was in the middle of the creek by a small three foot water fall," Rod said, taking another bun, as Ted poured him another coffee.

Austin looked over at the appalled look on Mr. Enns's face. Austin thought he had better explain why Rod talked about angels as he had. After explaining the history of Rod and Jan, Mr. Enns was quiet for a moment before saying; "I guess I didn't know Anne like I thought I did."

"You raised a good girl, Mr. Enns," Austin said.

Austin was anxious to get the search started. He left Mr. Enns and Abe in the capable hands of the organizers of the search party. Austin and Ted told the men that they wanted to track down the places that Jan had mentioned, as well as rechecking the spot that Rod thought he had seen something. The men in charge of the search were none to pleased with the idea of two men out there on their own, but they could not convince them other wise. They were told to be sure and check in every half hour to tell them where they were. Austin and Ted each took a small saw, hatchet and a spade with them. They had no idea what to expect out there. They told the leader of the search part that their first priority was to do a thorough search of the creek that ran through the lease. They would go as far as they could, without running into areas that were unsafe to take their horses. If that failed, they would later go on foot, as Austin was not going to risk his horse getting burnt in the hot coals.

Austin was sure that if they could not find Jan somewhere in the creek, she would definitely not have survived.

All kinds of things went through his mind. Would she have left the safety of the creek after the fire past over? The creek was full of all sizes of rocks. Jan could have fallen and hit her head. She could have been wandering around disoriented and ran into more of Douglas's men. What if they had her? Then he thought of how it would feel to be surrounded by fire with nowhere to go. He had already worked himself into a real frenzy, before they left on their search.

CHAPTER 16

AUSTIN AND TED HAD THEIR horses saddled and ready to go long before anyone else. They mounted up, than trotted off. Midnight was anxious to run after being tied up all night, and Austin let him go. Ted's horse followed suit, as they galloped towards the creek. When they reached the treed area, they slowed down and walked their horses down the hill and into the creek. Austin looked both ways before heading west. "This is probably where Jan started. From here, she would have followed the creek for quite some distance, before coming out at a spot where there was some real thick bush," Austin told Ted, while looking for the spot that she may have gone through.

In the mean time, Ted was checking for any sign of her whether in the creek, or in the surrounding area.

Suddenly Austin stopped. "This must be where she went through," he said, when he saw a lot of broken branches. When he took a closer look, he could see horsehairs in the twigs. "I'll follow as far as I can. You check the creek. I'll meet you up stream somewhere," Austin said, as he urged Midnight through the thorny brambles.

When they got through, Austin checked Midnight for scratches. He found several large ones, but nothing too serious. "Sorry boy," Austin said, patting Midnight on the neck. He led Midnight across an area that he thought could be as Jan had described. This was definitely where she went. He came across horse tracks, and it was not hard to miss the markings of Hope's flawed shoe. The other two tracks were not familiar to him. The thought of a couple of men chasing her infuriated him. He got back on Midnight and followed the tracks right up to where the fire started. The stench of burnt grass grew stronger as Midnight's hooves stirred up the soot beneath his feet. By the time they reached what used to be a thick growth of trees, both he and Midnight were covered the fine black powder.

This had to have been the area where he last talked to her. Where would she have gone from here? She wouldn't have come back because of the men and the fire. She most likely went on through the trees. When he looked around, he knew he would never be able to follow her trail because several trees were still burning and it was way too hot. He saw several fire fighters dousing, trees and hot spots.

From what he'd ascertained, the fire was set both behind, and to the south, of where Jan had been. With the wind blowing from the southeast, she definitely would have gone north or northwest towards the creek. Austin sighed. Maybe there was a chance that she had survived. That was, if she hadn't been overcome by smoke and lost her way. Austin walked Midnight along the edge of the burning trees, all the while looking for some sign. It was a devastating sight. Most of the trees were lying on the ground smoldering, while others were still standing, but now a burnt shadow of their former selves. Every bit of grass was burnt to a crisp. It would take a long time before he would be able to graze cattle in this area. He estimated that they'd lost somewhere in the vicinity of a couple of section's of lease land to the fire. He just shook his head. This would someday grow back, but what about his wife? He felt sick to his stomach at the thought that she could be gone forever.

As he rode on, he came across a couple of smoldering deer carcasses. They were not so lucky as to have survived the flames. Austin wiped tears from his eyes as he thought of the terror that both Jan, and the innocent animals, had faced because of one man's madness. He had to keep his mind clear and not miss any details that might be here. He looked for any sign of tracks, but there were none. When he reached the creek, he saw Ted up ahead waiting for him. "Did you find anything?" Ted asked.

"I found three sets of horse tracks. I recognized Hope's, but the other two were probable the ones that set the fire," Austin said, before filling Ted in on the devastation that he'd seen. He said that he was positive that she would have headed towards the creek.

"I've had no luck so far. It's quite a mess," Ted told him.

They were now entering the area where the fire had begun. Here, too the devastation was appalling. Austin looked over at Ted, and said, "If she went this direction, which I think she would have, she may have come out somewhere up ahead." Austin and Ted sat looking at each other, while thinking the very same thing. It didn't look good, even if she'd gotten too the creek, it was to shallow for her to avoid the fury of the flames.

The bush along the edge of the creek was burnt to cinders. Austin and Ted had to move several trees that had fallen across the creek. Some of the smaller trees, they sawed in half. They sizzled as they landed in the water. They splashed water on the smoldering trees to cool them down, before pulling them out of the way. Their gloves were now getting burnt up quite badly, and so were their hands. With the large trees, they did the same. Only they used Austin's rope to pull them out of the way.

Ted looked at Austin's deteriorating rope. "I hope we don't have to rely on that rope of yours for anything important," he said

"We'll use mine as long as it lasts and save yours," Austin told him, while rolling up, what used to be a good rope. Then, after swinging up into his saddle, they continued on. They could still feel the heat from the smoldering trees, and as the smoke was now getting fairly strong, they both pulled their bandanas over their nose and mouth.

They rode on, scouring the area for some sign that Jan had been there. Suddenly, up ahead, they saw a small waterfall. Only they would have to remove another tree to get to it. Ted and Austin looked at each other as they rode towards it.

"This must be the place that Rod told us about," Austin said, quickly getting off his horse to check for any sign, no matter how small. It was barely a three-foot drop, and with the widening of the creek, the water was spread thin. It definitely wasn't what they would have called much of a falls, as the water trickled lazily over the edge. There were a lot of rocks here. Austin wandered back and forth looking around the boulders and amongst the rocks. It was then that he spotted something almost hidden under some half burnt tree branches. He walked over to it, while Ted sat watching. Austin picked up a branch and threw it, before bending down to pick up a dark object. He showed it to Ted. "Is it Jan's cell phone?" Ted asked.

Austin just nodded his head.

"Well…it's a start. At least we know that she was here," Ted said. Ted got off his horse and began to check the falls itself. The center of the creek was a bit deeper then the rest. He called Austin over to look and see what he thought. It looked like some rocks had been moved.

"Do you think she tried to huddle under here to keep wet while the fire passed over?" Ted asked.

"I don't know what to think," Austin said, looking around. He tried to find any clue, or footprint. They were just about to move on, when Ted spotted her tracks. "It looks like she got out of the creek and it may have been too hot, so she went back into it. She could have been disoriented at this point, because if she had gone down-stream, she would have eventually found herself clear of the fire. Instead, it looks like she went head long into it," Ted said.

They got back on their horses and rode out, and around, the falls before going further up stream. They had gone some distance, when Austin saw a section of old fence that had not been removed. It only went half way across the creek and ended.

Blaze of Fury

They rode over to check it out. The top parts of the poles had been burnt off. *He would have to remember to come out here and remove it before putting cattle in this area.* He said to himself.

"Look!" Ted said, getting off his horse. Ted walked over, and picked up a melted glob of plastic and metal, which he presumed was once a pair of binoculars. "Did Jan carry binoculars with her?" Ted asked.

"Sometimes, but I don't know if she had them with her yesterday," Austin said, looking at them.

Ted took his cell phone from his pocket. He was glad to hear Claire's voice, but she was afraid he was calling, to pass on some bad news.

"We are fine, Claire. Don't worry so much," Ted told her. I just called to ask if you knew if Jan, had a pair of binoculars with her?"

"Yes, she did. I remember her using them to look down at the corral. That was when she first realized that the cattle were theirs. Why?" she asked.

"We found her cell phone by a small water fall, and now, we've found a somewhat melted down binoculars. Hold on," Ted said. Austin told Ted to ask Claire if she would double check in Jan's saddlebag, which was laying on her saddle just out-side by the house, for her binoculars.

Ted passed on the message. After they waited for a moment, Claire informed them that they were not there. The ones they found, had to be Jan's. Ted also told Claire not to expect them back for sometime, as they would be searching until they found her, or until it was too dark.

Austin stood, looking at the fence. Then it struck him. "Ted, do you remember the marks on the front of Hope?"

"Yeah" Ted said, nodding his head.

"It had looked like she'd ran into some barbed…"

Austin began only to have Ted finish what he was about to say.

"Yeah, barbed wire, that explains it. She would have been riding up stream, and with all the smoke, she probably ran right into this fence. Hope could have thrown her, and gotten spooked by the fire, bolted, and left Jan stranded here. She probably had her binoculars hanging on the saddle horn and they fell off," Ted said. He could almost picture what happened in his head.

'Where did she go from here?" Austin asked, looking around.

There was silence as they both tried to figure out what would have happened after that.

"Wait, Austin. If she was riding at this point, but was on foot by the falls, she may have gone back down-stream towards the falls. She probably did stay there for a while, but she definitely left and headed up-stream again. I think we should continue on," Ted said.

Ted looked at his watch. It had been almost an hour and a half since they'd left. They had been so preoccupied, that they'd totally forgotten to check in. Well, at least they had a lead on which direction she had gone.

Ted called into search head quarters and told them what they had found and which direction they were heading. They were warned that even though the fire was classified as under control, the wind was changing and could send the fire in their direction again. They were ordered to call in every half hour, as it was now critical that the search coordinator knew, where they were. They would now intensify the search in their area. When Ted told Austin about the wind shift, he was even more irritable. It was imperative that they find Jan and fast, but as Ted reminded him, by rushing could cause them to miss some crucial details. They continued moving trees out of their way, while looking for clues as to where, Jan had gone or what had happened to her.

When they got to the fence that ended Austin and Jan's lease, they called into search headquarters to find out whether they'd had any success. They where told that the north side of the creek had been checked, and they'd found no sign of her. South of the creek was still burning and too hot to be accessed.

Blaze of Fury

When Ted told them that they were heading farther west into the neighbors property. They were advise that perhaps it would be better left for someone else to do, as that property belonged to Douglas. When Ted told Austin, he got very angry. He took the phone and told them that he didn't give a hoot as to, who owned it. His wife was still missing, and if he had to, he would even search Douglas's house. He told them that Douglas had started it, and if he did not allow him to look for his wife on his property, then he probably had more to hide. With that he handed the phone back to Ted and looked for a place to cross. Most of the fence was down, as the posts were burnt and those still standing were smoldering.

Ted rode up beside Austin. "I know you are upset, but they are just concerned and doing their job," Ted told him.

"Maybe so, but my wife comes before them," Austin said.

It was late afternoon and still no sign of Jan. There were many awkward areas that they had to maneuver through but, when that happened, they just did extra footwork.

They soon came to a fork in the creek. It was already getting late, but the two men were determined to go on. They'd had no indication that she had left the creek, and they were positive that she would not have ventured out of the creek because, everything on both sides of her would have been on fire. After the fire passed over, she would be wet and cold, so there was always the possibility that she went off in another direction. They could have easily missed her tracks when she'd left the creek. They would split up and try to pick up any sign of which way she'd gone from here.

The terrain was getting more hostile, so they decided to search for another half hour before meeting back at the junction. She could have possibly even doubled back, but then the others searchers surely, would have found some sign of her.

Ted decided that when they got back onto Austin and Jan's lease, they should concentrate on the south side of the creek. There were some burnt out meadows that they could start with, but it would be getting dark and his stress was intensifying. He began to understand why Austin had gotten so angry. They were exhausted, hungry and extremely frustrated that the couple of things they'd found, seemed utterly useless now. They were just grabbing at straws. He began to pray. He wondered why he hadn't done that sooner, as God was the only one that knew where she was.

After riding for a half hour, Austin stopped and hung his head. "Why, God? Why have you taken Jan from me so soon after you brought us together? Are you punishing us for what we did in the past? Punish me not her. Please God, let someone find her alive. I don't care who it is, just let someone bring her back to me," he said. Tears began to run down his cheeks, and as no one here to see him, he wept. It was at least fifteen minutes before he gathered his wits about him. Ted would be waiting, so he figured it was time to go back. He was beginning to feel weak, from both lack of food, and lack of sleep.

When he got back to where the two creeks met, Ted was waiting. He didn't look so good either. "Where is she, Ted?" Austin asked.

"I don't know, Austin. I just don't know," Ted said.

Then at the top of his lungs Austin yelled, "JAN WHERE ARE YOU?"

It was then that Ted had an idea. "Austin why didn't we do that before?"

"What? Austin asked.

"Yell out for her every once and a while. If she is lost out here, maybe it will help her find her way," Ted said.

"Well, now you are thinking!" Austin said.

So on their return, every so often, they would stop and call out for her. Then they would sit quietly and listen. They continued doing that all the way back to their base, but with no luck. They would now have to wait until the next morning, as it was dark when they returned.

Blaze of Fury

When they got back, the women had a feast prepared for all the men. Austin was hungry but too despondent and exhausted to eat.

"Eat, Austin, or you will be no good for looking tomorrow," his Father-in- law told him.

"I'm just too tired," he said, dropping down on the ground. It was not long before Mr. Enns handed him a plate full of food and said, "Here, eat it, son."

Austin looked up at him. He was rather shocked that Mr. Enns would use the word son.

God was apparently breaking through that hard core. "Thanks dad Enns, I'll try," Austin replied.

Mr. Enns sat near him and began to talk. "I heard you found a couple of things that belonged to her."

"Yes, her cell phone and what was left of her binoculars, but I just don't understand where she could be," Austin said trying to fight back tears.

"Tonight you go home and get some sleep. You need your rest and strength for when she is found," Mr. Enns told him.

"I just can't go home knowing she is still out here," Austin told him.

"Tonight you go home! I will stay here and wait. If something comes up, I will call you," Mr. Enns said firmly.

"I just can't…" Austin did not get to finish his sentence because Mr. Enns told him that he should learn to, someday listen to his elders. He turned to Ted, and knowing that he also had not slept, gave him the same orders and told Claire to be sure that they both listened.

After eating, Austin and Ted loaded up the horses and took them home. It was time to give their horses a break. After spending the day in cold water and rocky terrain, their legs would be pretty sore. They both gave their horses a good rub down and placed blankets over each of them. They hoped that they wouldn't end up with sick horses in the morning.

When they got into the house, Austin's father, brother and brother-in-law Abe, were sitting at the kitchen table drinking coffee. They had all gotten cleaned up, but looked like a weary lot. Some of the women were washing dishes while others, were preparing food for the next days search crew, or those working on dousing the hot spots.

When Claire looked at Austin and Ted, she hardly recognized them in the dim light. Their mouths were black and their faces were streaked, they were both plastered with soot. She told them both not to touch anything, but to go straight to the shower and get cleaned up. Ted and Austin would rather have just collapsed on the nearest bed.

They both felt somewhat refreshed when they emerged, but still totally exhausted and depressed. Not even Claire could cheer them up, so she sent them both to bed. "If need be, someone could have his bed," Austin said. Austin didn't want to sleep there without Jan. There were too many memories here right now. Austin told Claire that he and Ted would take the beds down stairs, as they needed to get away from the ruckus. Not that noise would've kept them awake, as tired as they were.

It was ten thirty when Austin and Ted went to lay down, but it was much later before Austin fell asleep. Even at that, it was a restless sleep. He kept waking up, thinking that he heard Jan calling him. Finally at four in the morning, he just had to get up.

He made a fresh pot of coffee and had just sat down at the table, when Ted joined him.

"Couldn't sleep either huh." Austin said, before telling Ted to grab a cup of coffee.

"It's rough for me and I can't even begin to imagine how you can hang in there," Ted told his friend.

Austin was quiet for a while. "I have to get back there, Ted. I feel guilty sitting here, with her out there some where all alone, and... well, only God knows what else," Austin said.

They both jumped as Mrs. Enns and Mary walked into the kitchen, and shortly after, Austin's mother joined them.

"Don't think of leaving unless you eat something first," Mrs. Enns told them.

Austin was surprised by how well their families were now getting along, after all that happened years ago. God had been working miracles. If only he would work one more and bring Jan and her babies home safe and sound. *Babies, how nice it would be to have a couple of little ones around.* Austin thought. He could just picture Jan running after two little boys. Well, maybe two little girls, or better yet, a boy and a girl.

"That looks better on you Austin," Mrs. Enns said to him.

"Excuse me? Were you talking to me," he asked, with that same somber look returning.

"You were smiling, and I said that looked better on you," Mrs. Enns told him.

With an ever so faint smile, he said, "I was just thinking about something."

"Well, what ever it was, just hold that thought in your heart," she told him.

After they'd had a quick bite to eat, Austin and Ted prepared themselves for another long, hard day. They both felt like they were carrying the world on their shoulders.

Just as Austin and Ted were about to walk out the door, Austin's Father came into the kitchen. He told them that he'd prayed that they would find her today, than wished them a better day than yesterday.

Austin saw how tired he looked, and ordered him to just stay at home and rest. He had gone out yesterday afternoon and he really shouldn't have, as his health was not that good. He could drive the women over with the lunch, which would be fine. Austin told him that he had enough just worrying about Jan. He didn't need to hear that his father was in the hospital on top of everything else. His mother reassured Austin that they would see he behaved.

"I will send Dad Enns home too. He had a long hard day yesterday, and was out there all night. Be sure he gets some rest," Austin said, before walking out the door.

Just as Austin and Ted loaded the horses, they heard a rifle shot in the distance.

"Another poor animal was probably put out of its misery," Ted said.

* * *

Rod had searched until it was too dark to see anything. He found an area where the smoke was not so strong before rolling out his bedroll in a sheltered area. He lay there wondering where Jan could be. He felt very strongly that she was somewhere nearby. He had checked most of the Klassen's lease with no success. He was now in Douglas's lease, and he knew this area like the back of his hand. He decided that she would have probably walked as far as she could in the creek, trying to get away from the fire. That would mean that she had to be in this area.

He was totally worn out, and needed rest badly. His lungs hurt from coughing. He would start searching again at daybreak. It was just good to get away from all the smoke and finally breath in some clean air. He looked up and wondered about the angel that he had seen, in his past. He just knew that there had to be angels. He closed his eyes and could still visualize the beauty of the angel he had seen at the base of the cliff, and then in the hospital.

She'd shone like the sun and there was always a glow above her head. No one could tell him that what he'd seen wasn't real. He had to remember to keep this more to himself, or people would say he had gone crazy. He found it strange that the angel always seemed to appear just before he saw Jan. As he lay there looking up at the stars, with an occasional cloud of smoke drifting by, he began to think that if there were angels, there must be a God. *God where ever you are, if you are up there, send your angel to show me where Mrs. Klassen is.* Rod thought, before falling asleep.

Blaze of Fury

It was just beginning to get light when Rod woke up. He had now been searching for almost two days. It had led him into all kinds of terrain, so he had spent just as much time walking as riding. He was chilled through and through, and his body and legs ached from walking through the creek and over the rough and rocky terrain. He'd sure be glad to get his soggy boots off.

He saddled up his horse, than tied his bedroll onto the back of the saddle. He rode through more rugged territory, than decided to search on foot. He was positive that sooner or later he would find some sort of a clue as to where she was.

Suddenly, he found what could be her tracks. He came across a spot where the grass had been flattened, as if someone or something had been laying there, but the first real clue was the Kleenex, that had blood on it. It had to be her. He looked for some sort of sign as to which way she'd went. Rod followed the trail that, lead him to a hill, up ahead. The sun was just beginning to come up when he saw something, and this time he was not mistaken. Half way up the hill stood an angel. He stared at her for a few moments, then when he glance down and the back up, she had disappeared. Jan had to be somewhere on that hill. Rod quickly went back and untied his bedroll and pulled his rifle from its pouch. After being out here this long, she would be cold and his bedroll, was all he had to wrap her in.

Rod began to climb the rocky surface of the hill. He couldn't imagine Jan willingly, climbing up this terrain, but that was where he saw the angel. He was just over half way up, when he slipped and fell, jamming his foot awkwardly between two boulders. He pulled free, but knew good and well that he may have busted something. He grabbed a couple of sticks that, he found nearby, and jammed them into his boot, one on each side of his leg. He then wrapped his bandana tightly around the top of his boot. It was a make shift splint and it was the best he could do support it if it was broken. He then continued slowly working his way up the hill. He began to sweat profusely as the pain worsened, but he had to keep going. Rod picked up a dead branch that he thought would work as a crutch. It did help to keep some pressure off his sore leg.

He was disappointed when he got to the spot that he'd seen his angel, because there was nothing there. When he finally hobbled to the top of the hill, he looked around, but he saw nothing. He hobbled to the opposite side of the hill. Rod's hope was dashed when all he saw was some shrubs and a lot of tall grass, waving in the wind. When he took a couple of steps toward the shrub, pain shot up his leg. He decided it wasn't worth his while, but then something caught his eye. He took a couple more steps, and that's when he saw a body lying close to the shrubs. He called Jan's name, but there was no movement. He gave out a big sigh of relief when, he confirmed that it was Jan. He checked to see if she was breathing and even though her breaths were shallow, he knew she was still alive. Her clothes were ripped and burnt. She had some pretty bad burns on her arms, but the worst one was on the side of her face. He checked her over and saw that she had a broken arm, as well as a large lump on her head. He hated to move her, but he felt he should get her into a better spot. Rod rolled out his bedroll and carefully eased her on it. Then, with great difficulty he dragger her out of the tall grass and took her near the trees. Then he covered her the best he could. He picked up his rifle and fired a shot into the air. All he could do was, to hope that someone would recognize it, as a call for help.

*　*　*

It was around six in the morning when Austin and Ted got to the camp. There was a bit of a stir going on, so they went to check and see what the problem was.
The wind had shifted. It was now coming from the west, and occasionally from the south. The fire was still classified as under control, but if the wind picked up much more, they would need to make a fireguard. The priority was to extinguish the hot spots, so it would not flare up again. Another plane flew over,

and dropped its load on the remaining flames. The push was to try to douse it before the wind got too strong.

Austin sent his reluctant father-in-law home when Abe arrived. Austin's brother and his wife had gone home the night before. He wanted to spend another day searching, but he had an important meeting to attend. Jake told Austin that he would be praying constantly for them. Austin thanked him and said that was exactly what they needed now.

Austin and Ted were about to set out on their search, when they heard another rife shot, followed by two more. Austin looked at Ted, and started to say, "I have a feeling that... but then Austin grabbed his rifle.

"What are you doing?" Ted asked.

Austin loaded his rife and shot into the air. Everyone around jumped, and they thought that Austin had lost it. Austin yelled out "QUIET." Sure enough, there were two more shots, heard from the distance.

"A signal," Ted said, now all excited.

Austin fired another two shots into the air, as a reply. All was now quiet.

Austin walked over to the man that was in control of the search party. After a brief conversation, the men all gathered around.

They were told that the search was still far from over. They still didn't know if someone had found Jan, or if someone else was in trouble. For now, they were only going to send four men out to pin point the location of the rifle shot. The four were Austin, Ted, Abe and a man named Jim, who was a peace officer, trained in search and rescue. One of the ranches had offered his horse to Abe, so that Austin would not have to waste time getting one from home.

The four of them set out riding towards the west. Most of the time, they were able to find spots to ride on bare land, but where there had been trees and bushes it was too hot, so they took to the water. They rode up to the edge of Austin and Jan's lease land, where Austin again pulled out his rife and shot into the air. They sat quietly waiting. Had they been wrong? Apparently not as, they now heard the reply of a rifle. It was closer this time, but it was coming from somewhere on Douglas's lease. Austin and Ted knew where they'd crossed yesterday, so it was not long before they were on their way. The smell of smoke seemed to be getting more pungent. The wind had definitely shifted. It was now coming from the southwest. They hoped that it wasn't going to stir up more problems, but just in case, Austin asked Ted, if he would call Claire and tell her to be on stand by, just in case they had to evacuate.

Austin knew Claire would be concerned about Ted, and she may want to know how things were going, so he told Ted to keep her updated, as to what was happening.

They had ridden almost a mile into Douglas's lease, when Ted saw a rider approach.

They stopped and waited to see if perhaps, the rider was coming with some sort of news. Ted watched the rider very closely, then directing his message directly at Austin, he said. "Austin, I want you to keep your emotions under control, understand?"

Austin looked at Ted, then at the rider, and he knew why Ted had said what he did. He knew it would be darn hard, but they were close now, and nothing was going to deter him from finding Jan.

"What do you think you are doing trespassing on my property?" Mr. Douglas shouted.

Everyone sat quietly, while leaving Jim to do the talking.

"We have reason to believe that the person we are searching for, is out in this area," Jim told him.

Everyone tried to stay calm as Douglas pulled out his rifle and pointed it at Austin.

"Get off my property," he demanded.

"Mr. Douglas, just put that gun away," Jim said calmly.

"Not until you get off my property," he yelled.

Blaze of Fury

Midnight got jumpy when he saw the gun waving in front of him. "Whoa," Austin said, reaching down to pat Midnight on the neck.

It was then that the three men heard the crack, and saw the blaze of the rifle, after Douglas pulled the trigger. Everyone was shocked to see Austin on the ground, but still firmly hanging onto Midnight's reins.

Both Ted and Jim leaped at Mr. Douglas, wrestling him to the ground, before he got off another shot. Abe jumped off his horse, but before he got to close to Austin, Midnight began to rear up, and Abe had to back off.

"Whoa!" Austin yelled, while yanking on the reins.

"Sorry Abe," Austin said, getting up with his left shoulder now, covered in blood.

"He is a good horse, but he is very protective. Sometimes too..." Austin was interrupted by another rife shot just a short distance ahead. "Much." Austin said finishing his sentence in somewhat of a daze.

"We are almost there," Austin said, about to get on his horse.

"I don't think you are going anywhere, my friend," Ted said now looking at Austin's shoulder, while Jim finished handcuffing Mr. Douglas. Jim then radioed in to tell his boss to send out the police to pick up Douglas, and why, and that Austin was also in need of urgent medical attention. Only now, they were having a problem getting Austin to stay behind, because it appeared that they were only a short distance from their destination. Jim told them that their options were to either allow Austin to continue on, or tie him up next to Douglas, and at this point, it was not a good idea. He told his superior that he did not think Austin could go much farther, as the wound was bad. In his opinion, a helicopter should be dispatched as soon as possible, to pick him up.

Abe was to stay with their captive, while the other three men carried on. Mr. Douglas insisted that Austin had reached for his rife, but Austin's rife was on the opposite side of the hand that Austin had patted his horse with.

Jim took out his first aid kit and packed Austin's wound, the best he could, to try to stop the bleeding. From what he could see, it looked like the bullet had gone right through. A little lower and it would have killed him. Even though Ted warned Austin of the seriousness of his wound, he could not persuade him to remain behind. Ted understood Austin's feelings, and he knew if he were in Austin's place, he would have done the same thing.

Ted helped Austin get on his horse and they continued on. Austin had felt no pain until they resumed the search. Austin now felt like he had been hit by a wrecking ball, and every step Midnight took, the pain worsened, and he felt like he was on fire. He had to focus on Jan and not on himself, as that was the only way he could get through this.

Austin looked in the direction of Ted's gaze. To his horror, he saw flames shooting high above the trees. They had to get to their destination and fast. Austin began to pray that the rifle shots were because Jan had been found, and that she was still alive. Austin began to slump over in his saddle, as he was getting weaker and the pain was getting excruciating.

"Hang in there, Austin. If it gets too bad use your head and stop. If… I mean, when we find her, she will need a live man, not a dead one," Ted told him.

"I understand," Austin replied, gritting his teeth as they continued over the roughest terrain they had crossed so far.

CHAPTER 17

CLAIRE WAS STANDING NEAR THE coordinator of the search party when the call came in. She stood there listening, while trying to hear if anything was said about Jan. Instead from what she over heard, she knew something was terribly wrong. She was about to ask, what was going on when he hung up the phone and immediately made another call. This time, it was to the police. She froze when he made the third call to request a helicopter be dispatched, to pick up a wounded man. What dreadful thing had happened, and to who? Was it Ted or Austin and how badly was the man injured?

After the man was done talking on the phone, Claire walked over to ask what had happened, but he would not pass that information on to her. Claire was very angry, so she decided to make her own call.

Claire walked some distance from the crowd, and when she was far enough away, she dialed Ted's cell number. It rang for a while before Ted answered. They were in a bad area, so the reception was not good. All he told her was that they were almost to their destination. She asked who had been hurt and by the sound of Ted's voice, she knew it wasn't him. When she asked to talk to Austin, Ted refused to put him on. He made some feeble excuse that Austin was occupied with something else, but when she persisted, Ted decided that making excuses was not going to change, the fact of what had happened. He told her the truth, and then said to keep a lid on it, for now. The family had enough to worry about.

Claire told Ted that she was not sure that it was such a good idea, to keep that from the family. They had a right to know. She promised to tell family only, but she had still no idea how badly Austin was hurt. After all, he was still continuing on with the search. *What else could happen,* she wondered. When she got back to the rest of the crew, she heard an announcement telling them, that the wind had shifted from the south and the fire had flared up again. That scared Claire even more. The search party would be right in the path of the fire, if they didn't get it extinguished and fast.

It was mid afternoon and Claire had managed to work her away around the family, telling them that they should all go home. They could all use some rest, before it was time to bring food over to the men that were still here. Everyone was very tired, so she did not have a lot of trouble convincing everyone, to do just that. She made a quick call to Jake and Dianna and asked if it were at all possible, she would like them to come back to the ranch. She told them that they needed to get together and pray, and that she would fill them in when they got there. She knew Ted would call her, as soon as they found out who was at the other end of that rife. She hoped and prayed that Jan was there.

Jake and Dianna arrived shortly after every one else. As soon as they got there, Claire called them into Austin's bedroom. That was when Claire finally broke. She just couldn't hold it inside any longer. It was like a dam that had burst. Dianna held her as she wept. If only Ted was here to hold her in his arms, and tell her that this nightmare was finally over. She feared for all the men's lives out there, as the fire was still a big threat.

Finally, Claire was able to tell Jake and Dianna, what she had over-heard the coordinator of the search party say. Then, after talking to Ted, her concern was the seriousness of Austin's injuries. Ted would not let her talk to him, and yet, he told her that Austin was still continuing on with the search. She said the only reason that they would have request the helicopter, before finding Jan, was that his injury were serious. She asked Jake to break the news to the rest of the family, as she couldn't do it. She didn't want to worry the family unduly, so she thought it best not to say what she suspected. She told Jake that it was best for the family to know what was going on, but she had a horrible feeling about it all.

Claire went into the bathroom to wash her hands and splash water onto her face. She felt like she was about to go crazy. Never in her life had she felt as much pressure as she did now. When she came into the kitchen, Jake asked for everyone's attention. He asked if they would all stop what they were doing, and meet in the living room. At that point, the entire family had an uneasy feeling. Something had happened. Their suspicion was, that Jan had not survived. You could have heard a pin drop after Jake broke the news of the latest dilemma.

Mary immediately asked about Abe, and she was told that he was fine. He was waiting with the man that had caused the problem, until the police came to pick him up. She was somewhat relieved but still nervous, and rightfully so. Austin's mother was quite up set, while his father sat quietly in a prayer like pose. Jan's parents were also beginning to show a little more emotion. They were now realizing how much time they had wasted by harboring grudges. Only, they knew no real way out of this, without suffering consequences after they got back home. Their only hope was that it wasn't too late to make amends.

Jake started out praying, and was followed by Jan's father and then Austin's father. After that, everyone sat with heads bowed in silent prayer for quite some time. Jake finally closed with a short prayer. After several quiet moments, the women slowly went back one by one into the kitchen, to finish the clean up and work on getting the next round of food together for supper. By the time they got back to the camp, there would surely be some answers to many of their questions.

Book 3 of the *Mountains and Valleys of Life*

* * *

Ted watched Austin as he swayed, dangerously close to falling off his horse, and yet Austin would not give up. They were suddenly in some very rugged territory, with steep cliffs looming above them. It was then that they heard another crack of the rifle. This time it was so close that when it went off, Ted had to grab Austin to keep him from falling off his horse.

"Austin, wait here while we go ahead to find out what's what," Ted said.

"No," Austin said, in a barely audible voice.

Ted took the reins from Austin's hand and said, "Okay friend, just hang on then," Ted said, leading Midnight in the direction of the last rifle shot. Finally, they heard a man shouting.

"Hey, over here!" They had no doubt as to who, that voice belonged to. It was definitely Rod, but had he found Jan?

Austin perked up at the sound of his voice. Rod was on the top of a rather rocky hill, just south of the creek. In a very weak voice, Austin asked Ted to ask Rod if Jan was with him, but just then, another plane flew overhead, which drowned out his voice. They would just have to wait until they reached him. The other side of the hill was more accessible by horseback, which was good because Austin would never have made it on foot.

The smoke was getting heavier, and Ted was now getting very concerned that if they didn't get a helicopter in here to pick up Austin quick, he may not make it.

When they finally reached the crest of the hill, Rod hobbled towards them. Ted and Austin's hopes were dashed, when they did not see any sign of Jan.

"Man! I'm I glad to see you guys. What happened to him?" Rod asked, as he tried to grab Austin, as he slid off his horse and fell down on the ground. Austin was now only semi-conscious.

"Douglas shot him," Ted said putting, his jacket under Austin's head to make him comfortable.

Blaze of Fury

"We had hoped that you'd found Jan," Ted said, kneeling down beside his friend. Ted than yelled at Jim, "get that darn helicopter here now."

"Mrs. Klassen is here, but she is in a bad way. She is just over by that tree," Rod said.

Austin was slowly coming around. "Where is Jan?" he asked, grabbing Rod's pant leg.

"She's over there," Rod said pointing in her direction.

Austin tried to get up, but he had lost so much blood that he was just to week.

"Drag me over there," Austin told Ted and Jim.

"I think you'd better just lie still, Austin," Ted said. He now wanted to run over to see how Jan was, but he couldn't leave Austin like this. Austin should be the one to be near her. Austin was determined to get to Jan, even if it meant his own life.

Austin tried to get up again, so Ted and Jim assisted him over to the spot, where Jan lay on Rod's bedroll. They laid Austin beside her, where he could now touch her. Jim checked her vital signs. She was definitely alive. He did a quick check, and found that she had a broken arm, and quite possibly a concussion, as well as numerous burns, some of which were bad. Both Austin and Jan needed immediate attention.

Jim called back to camp to give their location. He told them they had two critical people and if the helicopter did not get there fast, they could lose one, or both of them. Rod also needed medical attention, but he said that if they got his horse, he could ride out himself. They were then told that two helicopters had been dispatched and were on their way. The coordinator advised them, that they had better get out of the area immediately after they arrived. To their relief, Douglas had been picked up and Abe was on his way back to camp.

Austin was very weak, but he mustered enough strength to get up on one elbow. He touched Jan's face with his fingers. "Jan," he said softly. "It's Austin. You are going to be alright now."

Slowly, Jan opened her eyes and stared at him.

"I love you Jan." Austin said. She tried to smile before passing out again.

Austin dropped down by her side and, as he laid his head against hers, he could no longer fight the weakness within him. At that point, he drifted into a state of unconsciousness.

As Ted knelt down beside Jan, he ran his hand over her hair. It was matted and scorched in spots, and full of dirt and soot. *Oh God, please don't let their lives end like this*, Ted prayed. He couldn't imagine going over to their ranch and Jan not being there. Not only that, Jan would be devastated if she lost Austin now.

He slowly stood up and went over to talk to Rod. "What happened to you?" Ted asked, as he sat on a fallen tree, while Jim checked Rods leg. It was obvious that he had numerous burns, but the worst was his leg. He told them how he'd been hoping to find Jan soon, when he caught sight of an angel on this hill. The vision was clear, so he knew she had to be here. He climbed up the steepest part of the hill and slipped. He fell in between a bunch of boulders and must have landed wrong. "What I couldn't understand was the vision by that falls," he said, rubbing his chin.

"She had been there," Ted told him. "We found her cell phone laying amongst the rocks."

"Darn it," Rod said, slapping his hand on his leg; Only it was the one he injured, and in so doing, he gritted his teeth as the pain shot up his leg. "I should have looked closer that time. If I had, she would have been home yesterday." he said, disgusted with himself.

"Don't go blaming yourself. We are grateful that you found her at all," Ted said patting him on the shoulder.

Suddenly, Ted remembered the families who were waiting back home. He was glad that Claire was the one that answered the phone.

When Ted told her that Rod had found Jan and that she was still alive, Claire yelled, "Hey, everybody! They found Jan and she is alive!" Ted heard a cheer go up from the family. Claire then asked about her state of health, and how Austin was doing. Every family member's eyes were on Claire. When they saw the look on her face, they knew it was not what they had hoped to see. Ted said, that right now, they were waiting for the helicopters to take out the injured parties. Rod also needed medial attention, because he definitely had a broken leg.

"What's the status on the fire?" Claire asked.

"It is getting pretty smoky and I can see the flames above the trees again. I'm sure looking forward to a quiet day, of sitting at home with you. By the way, the camp will be disbanding soon, so you really wouldn't need to go back there. I'll call you later," He said, just as a helicopter came into sight. "I miss you, but I have to go now," Ted said.

* * *

Claire did her best to pass on the message before going outside to be by herself for a while. When Claire looked towards the west, she saw that the sky was now obscured by, a massive cloud of smoke. In one area, she could see the red glow of the fire. "Please, God, let them all get out of there soon and safely," she prayed. The air was warm, but she rubbed her arms as the chill of fear gripped her. Would this nightmare never end?

"They will be alright," Jake said, coming up beside her.

"How can you be so sure? I often wonder what the purpose was in all this. Austin and Jan have had so many disappointments in their lives, and when it finally all seemed to work out something else happens to beat them into the ground. It doesn't seem fair. Will that happen to Ted and I also? Will he get out of there in time, or will it start all over again?" she said as she began to cry.

Jake put his arm around his cousin. "We must have faith that God will bring them out. We may not understand why things happen, but we know God has a reason for everything he does," Jake said.

"Right now, my faith isn't very strong," Claire, stated.

"You are exhausted. You have been trying to be strong for everyone else, and it is time for you to look after yourself. I think you better just get some rest," Jake told her.

"I can't. Not until Ted is standing here beside me," she said.

"I understand, but at least sit down for awhile. I know it is good to stay busy, but you can't keep going without a break. Here, lets go over to the swing and sit down for a bit," Jake told her.

When they sat down, Claire laid her head against Jake's shoulder. The slight rocking motion felt good, and she stared out at what felt like a rerun of an old movie. Claire soon dozed off, but woke up quickly with a jolt. "Ted?" she cried.

"You were just dreaming," Jake told her.

"I heard him calling me. How long was I sleeping?" She asked.

"Oh, about fifteen minutes," Jake, told her.

"It was so real. Do you think that was a sign that he is in trouble?" he asked.

"Claire, it was only a dream. They will get out safely, you'll see," he said, trying his best to encourage her.

Jake and Claire sat, watching the water bombers fly overhead. Finally, Jake said that maybe they should just go in. Watching wasn't going to help Claire's state of mind.

When they got into the house, Dianna told them that the search coordinator had called. He thanked them for all the food but there were only a couple of men on stand by, so they didn't have to bring out lunch because they still had some food left. He also told them that Jan, Austin and Rod were all in route to a hospital in Calgary.

Everyone was now going to converge at the hospital to find out the seriousness of every ones injuries, especially Austin and Jan's. However Claire chose to remain behind, until Ted returned. Jake and Mary said that they would wait with her, but she told them that it would be better if they were with the rest of the family. She and Ted would follow, when he returned.

Claire waited for quite some time, but she couldn't wait at Ted any longer. She left a note just in case Ted came directly home instead of stopping at the camp, but she rather doubted that he would do that, because his truck was still over there. Claire packed up a good portion of the lunch, along with a large amount of coffee, and drove back to the camp. She did not want to waste all this food. Not only that, it helped to pass the time.

When she got there, she counted six men. The coordinator was rather surprised to see her. She told them that the food had been prepared already, so she figured she would bring it over while waiting for Ted. She was glad that she did, seeing as they devoured most of what she'd brought.

When they were done eating, Claire asked if there had been any messages from Ted. All they said was that, they expected them back at any time. Before going over to wait by Ted's truck, she told them that, if Ted did call they should tell him that she was waiting for him here.

The smoke was getting thicker. She sure hoped that the wind would not blow the fire towards Austin's place. Her fear was starting to build again. They had to be right in the thick of it. Claire began to shake as panic set in. She also feared that their wedding plans would be dashed to pieces. It was most likely that Austin and Jan would not be well enough to stand up for them. Even worse, what if something happened to Ted?

Another hour had passed, and still no word. She was told that it was best that she leave the area because of the smoke. They were in the process of moving the camp to a different location. Claire said she would wait for another half-hour. She was told that she could stay only until they had everything packed up and then, when they left, she too would be ordered out of the area. Claire went to the back of Ted's horse trailer and began to cry. She did not know how long she'd sat there, when she heard footsteps. She knew she was about to be told that she must leave.

Without looking up, she said, "I am not leaving here until Ted gets back." Then she heard her name.

"Claire?"

Claire looked up to see Ted standing in front of her. "You're back!" she yelled. Jan's legs felt like rubber as she jumped up and threw her arms around Ted's neck.

"Claire, we will leave that for later. I have to get these horses loaded, and then we'd better get out of here," he said giving her a quick kiss, before going to load up the horses.

Claire felt rebuffed, even though she knew why he had said that. Claire was quiet as she helped Ted put away his tack. Once the horses were loaded, Ted waited for her to go ahead and he followed. She cried all the way back to Austin's. She really didn't know why. Ted was now home safely. When they got back to Austin's, Ted took the horses down to the pasture. He had a bit of problem with Midnight, but he did manage to get him back in the pasture. He put Rod's horse in a separate pen, as Rod had been airlifted out with Austin.

Ted then went back to the house to look for Claire. He found her lying on one of the beds crying. "Claire, what's wrong?" he asked.

"Nothing," she said, turning away.

"Well, it doesn't look like nothing. Can you pull yourself together long enough to take me over to get Austin's truck?" he asked.

Claire finally gathered her wits about her, as she went to wash her face. They were just about to walk out the door when Ted grabbed her in his arms and kissed her.

When he finally released her, he said, "I have been waiting a long time to do that. Now let's get that truck, so I can get back to where we left off." He put his arm around her, as they walked out to his truck. "You drive over, and then I will drive Austin's truck back," he said.

They were both too tired and stressed to talk. It was a relief to finally get back to the house. *One chapter is over and now a new one will begin,* Claire said to herself.

When Claire looked out the window, she began to wonder if this chapter was really done. She no longer saw much for flames. It was now mainly smoke. She began to pray that, somehow they would get that fire put out once and for all.

Claire had supper waiting for Ted when he got out of the shower. He was almost too tired to eat, but seeing Claire now had gone through all the trouble to prepare it, he could not turn it down. He was actually hungrier than he'd thought, so he had no problem devouring what she had put before him. By the time Claire had cleaned up the dishes, Ted had told her all that had happened and what state Jan and Austin were in.

Their original plan had been to go to Calgary, but both she and Ted were exhausted. The other reason Ted felt they should stay behind was, because of the fire. Right now the wind was not blowing in their direction, but if it did, they would have to move the livestock and fast. Claire called Jake at the hospital. He told her that there was no need for them to come, and that he would call as soon as they heard anything. Both Austin and Jan were in surgery, and it would be some time before they found out any results. Rod was still waiting to have surgery on his leg.

Ted sat on the couch with Claire snuggled up against him. They talked about their up- coming wedding, and wondered if it may have to be postponed. They decided to wait a couple of days until they found out, Austin and Jan's prognosis. After talking for a while, Ted got very quiet.

"Ted, it's time for you to go to bed. You have had some long hard days," she said.

Ted looked at her, and for the first time realized how tired she looked. "Claire, I am sorry, but I never realized until now, how hard this has been on you."

Ted took her in his arms and kissed her. Then, slowly releasing her, he said it was time to call it a night before things got out of control. Not only that, he was just plain exhausted.

Claire was one woman that he respected. He now realized that what he had done in the past was wrong although, he also knew that God had forgiven him. He was determined not to take Claire to bed with him until after they were married.

Claire asked about the fire, and he told her that if it did come this direction, they would get a phone call. Ted slept in Austin's room, next to the phone. That way Claire would not be disturbed if a call did come through.

Even though they were concerned about Austin and Jan, they knew that they were now in capable hands.

When Ted and Claire went to their rooms, they said a quick prayer before slipping into bed. They were both so exhausted that, instead of drifting off to sleep, they felt more like they were about to pass out, from shear exhaustion. Finally, they did drift off into a deep but restless sleep.

Ted woke up several times and each time he would have to figure out if he'd dreamt that Jan was found, or if he was still suppose to get up and start searching. At one point, he got up to look out the window. He had to reassure himself that the fire was not heading in their direction. Then, before going back to bed, he looked in on Claire to make sure that she was all right. Once back in bed, he breathed a sigh of relief. Everyone and everything was fine, so he turned over and went back to sleep.

Chapter 18

It took three days before Austin began to really realize where he was. The surgery on his shoulder had been done, immediately upon arriving at the hospital. Then with all the drugs they were giving him, it took several more days before he began to feel like himself. His parents were in the room when he finally became more alert. "Jan…where is Jan?" Austin asked, while trying to sit up.

Austin's mother came over to his bedside. "Austin, just lay back," she said, as his father came to join her.

"Where is Jan? Is she alright?" Austin asked again.

"She is fine, Austin," his mother said.

"I want to see her," Austin said, as the pain tore through his shoulder.

"You'd better take it easy with that shoulder son. You can thank God that you did not bleed to death," Austin's father told him.

"I want to know about Jan, where is she?" He asked again, getting very agitated.

"Austin, really she is doing very well. She does have some burns, a broken arm, and some cuts and bruises, but honestly she is doing quite well." His mother reassured him.

"What about the babies?" he asked.

Austin's parents looked at each other before replying. At that point, he was sure he knew the answer. "They're gone, aren't they?" he said, suddenly feeling like someone had punched him in the stomach.

"No Austin," his mother said, seeing the look on his face. "So far she has not lost them, but she must take it easy for a while. She has been confined to total bed rest. They are monitoring both her and the babies, and if it is God's will, they will all come through this fine."

"I have to see her," Austin said, now extremely agitated.

"Maybe later," his mother told him, but Austin insisted that he would not rest until he saw her for himself. He was very pale, and weak, and near impossible to calm him down.

Austin called the nurse and insisted that he be allowed to see his wife, but they refused because they felt he was not quite up to it. Austin said that he would go with or without their permission. He threatened to pull out all the tubes and go, find her for himself. Finally, they told him that they would try to find his doctor, and see what they could arrange. Austin was satisfied for the moment, and before they left, he did agree to try and have a bit more patience.

It was a couple hours later that Ted and Claire came in to see how he was doing. At that point, they could tell that the nurses were very annoyed at Austin, and he was not looking very good.

The nurse finally came in after Austin had buzzed her for about the sixth time, asking if they had talked to the doctor. She told him that they were doing what they could, and if he didn't quit ringing for the nurses, they would take away his buzzer.

Claire asked the nurse what the problem was.

"We haven't been able to get a hold of the doctor, so he will just have to wait to see his wife," she said, now really angry with her patient.

He was also angry, and because of his restlessness, his shoulder was beginning to burn like fire. At that point, Austin worked his way up to a sitting position, and told Claire that he was going to check himself out. That way he could do what he wanted.

"Don't be a fool, man," Ted told him before turning to speak to the nurse. "Nurse, get me a wheel chair. If you want some peace and quiet, you will have to let us take him, to see his wife. I can't say that I blame him after, everything that has happened. If I was in his place, I'd want to see for myself to."

"Really, we can't do that without doctors permission," The nurse told them. Upon hearing that, Austin tried to get out of bed, and would have fallen if Ted hadn't grabbed him.

"Get the darn wheel-chair, or he will never settle down," Ted demanded.

"Ted, simmer down," Claire, chided him.

"Well, you know he won't rest until he sees her," Ted said firmly.

Austin lay back on his bed, now looking extremely pale. The bandage on his shoulder was turning red, as the blood began to ooze through it.

"Austin, now look what you did. What good are you going to be to Jan, and your family, if you kill yourself?" Claire told him.

It was then that they heard the nurse coming with the wheel chair. Austin was lying there with his eyes closed. The pain in his shoulder was now almost unbearable but he had to see for himself that Jan was all right.

He felt someone touch the side of his face. Then he heard her call his name. "Austin? I hear you are not behaving yourself," Jan said, softly.

Austin opened his eyes. "Jan!" he cried throwing his good arm around her.

"You are not to move that arm," The nurse said when she saw his red bandage.

She went around to the other side of the bed to check it, and then quickly left the room.

"How are you?" Austin asked Jan.

"I am fine, but I heard that you have been giving the nurses a lot of trouble. I asked them to let me talk to you. I assure you that the three of us are doing quite well, but I am a bit concerned about you," she said pushing him back onto the bed. "Your shoulder! It's bleeding! Austin, please behave yourself, or you could cause even more serious problems for yourself," Jan told him. She had a feeling that something was amiss already.

Austin looked up at her. "I am so glad that you are alright," he said running his finger over the bandage on the side of her face. Then he touched the bandages on her arms. "Are you sure that everything is okay?" he asked.

"Yes Austin. It's nothing that time won't heal," she told him.

"Your hair?" He said noticing that it was cut short.

"It was scorched, so I had them cut it off. It will grow back, but you are my concern now," she said as the doctor came into look at his shoulder.

After a moment, they told Austin and Jan that they would have to find out what was happening with Austin's wound.

Jan bent over and kissed Austin. "I will always love you, Austin."

"I love you too. I thought I had lost you forever. Right now I would just like to keep you here with me," Austin told her.

"It will be good to get back home again, but right now you have to behave so we can get well enough to do that," she told him.

Before leaving, Jan asked the doctor about Austin's condition. The fear was that he'd tore something open, because he had been so agitated and did not lie still for it to even begin to heal. Jan apologized for him and promised that he would probably settle down now.

Austin was then wheeled back into the operating room, to fix what ever the problem was.

Claire and Ted took Jan back to her room. She was still quite weak, and tired very easily. The doctor originally had little hope that Jan would keep her babies, but so far he had been proven wrong. She was not really supposed to be out of bed, but as Austin would not rest until he saw her, it was better for her to go to Austin then it would have been for him to come see her.

Jan wished that she could be there for him when he came out of surgery. It was now her time to worry about him. Ted asked if it would be possible for the two of them to stay in the same room, but they were told that it was not advisable. Although, Austin's nurse was all for it, if it would help keep him out of her hair.

Once Jan got back in bed, Claire and Ted told her that they should let her rest, but she asked them to stay until Austin was out of surgery. She also had some unanswered questions.

"I want to know why my parents were here," Jan said, looking at Claire.

When Claire told her what she had done, Jan was shocked that Claire had enough nerve to approach her family like she had. She did thank her and hoped that somehow, she would get a chance to visit with them and thank them for all their help. Claire told her that she was sure that would eventually happen.

Jan said she thought that she was dreaming when she first opened her eyes. The first person she saw was Abe. She did not recognize him at first, as she had not seen him since she was about seventeen. He greeted her, and asked how she was feeling. She was so out of it that, she now wondered if her life with Austin had been just a dream. Then Mary came over to talk to her. That was when she realized that Abe was Mary's husband. She would never have recognized her sister, if she had met her on the street.

When she turned her head, she saw her parents. She remembered starting to cry and her mother told her there was no need for that. She was fine, and everything would be all right now. They only stayed with her for a brief time before they left. It still felt like a dream, but Claire assured her that it was not.

Jan wanted to know about the fire and what had happened to Mr. Douglas, so Claire up- dated her on all that had happened after her disappearance. When Claire told Jan that Austin had been shot, Jan got very quiet and teary-eyed. Claire was surprised that Jan had not been told what caused Austin's injury.

Claire went on to tell her that Mr. Douglas was now out on bail, but the police had charged him with arson, as well as two counts of attempted murder.

A chill ran through Jan's body at the word *murder*. "Why is he charged with two attempts of murder? Did he try to kill someone else, besides Austin?" Jan asked.

"He is charged for trying to kill you also," Claire told her.

Jan looked over at Ted. She saw the tears in his eyes, just before he turned away. After a moment, Jan reached out for Ted hand. "Ted, I don't know how I can ever repay you for everything you've done for Austin and me." Jan felt him squeeze her hand and he held it for a long time.

"You don't know how glad Claire and I are to see that you are alright. You can't even begin to know how worried we all were about you," Ted said, still holding her hand.

Jan slowly pulled her hand away from him, and when she looked into his eyes she quickly turned back to Claire. "I want to thank you too, Claire. I really never got to know you when we were younger. You have been a rock for Austin during this time, and I will never be able to thank you enough. Oh no! What about your wedding?" Jan asked, suddenly remembering.

"We will wait until the end of the week, and decide then. We may have to postpone it," Claire told her.

"I hate for you to have to do that because of us. I know how we looked forward to our wedding. We can't spoil that for you," she said looking at Claire, then at Ted as she saw him winked at his future wife.

"We will survive. The longer we wait, the sweeter it will be," Ted said, still looking at Claire.

Claire stood up. "We'd better let you rest, Jan. We will be back this evening to see how, Austin made out. Don't worry about him. He will come through this. He is a fighter." Claire said.

Ted, laid his hand on Jan's leg for a moment, and said, "See you later."

Jan watched the two of them walk out of the room together. She wished them the best. Her only hope was that Ted would come to accept the Lord. Little did she know that, because of her disappearance, Ted had done, exactly that. Now Rod was also thinking hard about what God was all about.

Jan lay there for quite some time before she dozed off. It was when her new roommate and her husband arrived, that she woke up. They were several years older than her and Austin, but it was so neat for Jan to observe the way they looked and talked to each other. There was a child of about ten year of age with them. She smiled as she thought how nice it was to see a couple their age, still so much in love.

"I am sorry we disturbed your sleep. My name is Dawn, and this is my husband

Nick, and our son Jeffery," Dawn said.

"I am Jan, and you really didn't disturb me," she told them, just as her nurse came into the room.

"Have you heard if my husband is out of surgery yet?" Jan asked the nurse anxiously.

"Yes, he is. Right now he is in the recovery room. He came through the surgery quite well. We only hope he behaves himself this time. I just heard why he was so upset, and I guess it is understandable. I must say you survived that fire better than anyone ever expected," her nurse said, before being called away.

"Are you the women, that they had been searching for?" Nick asked.

"Yes," Jan replied.

"I am so glad that you are doing this well after that horrible ordeal. Many of the ranchers in our area were praying for your family," Dawn told her.

"Why thank you!" Jan said in surprise. "I know God had his hand on me through what I experienced. I still can't understand how I came through it at all," Jan said, as the memory of that seemed to flash before her.

"Did your husband get caught in the fire too?" Dawn asked.

"No, he was shot by our neighbor, when they went on his property to look for me," Jan told them.

"Oh, how awful! They said on the news that he had been hurt, but not how," Dawn said.

"Was that Douglas?" Nick asked.

"Yes it was. Do you know him?" Jan asked.

"Yes, I did years ago. He used to be an okay guy in his younger years, but something sure has changed him. I heard he lost most of his building to the fire."

"Oh, really? I hadn't heard. I guess I missed out on all the details," Jan said.

"Did he really start the fire?" Nick asked.

"I can't say that for sure. I saw a couple of men start it, but I did not see their faces," Jan said.

"Well, we are glad that everything turned out alright for you," Nick told her.

"Thank you. By the way, this may be a strange question, but did they put the fire out," Jan asked.

"From what I heard, it sounds like it," Nick told her.

Jan breathed a sigh of relief, as she closed her eyes. Oh how she wished she and Austin were back home already.

That evening, when Ted and Claire came to visit, they wheeled Jan over to see Austin. He was still groggy, but he was awake enough to know that she was there. He didn't want her to leave, but she told him to remember that they weren't at home, and for now they had to obey the rules. Austin grabbed her with his good arm and held her close as then kissed her.

"Okay, you two, save it for later. After all, there are others around watching."

Ted said jokingly, as Claire gave him a jab in the ribs.

"Shut up, Ted," Austin told him when he finally released Jan.

"I will talk to you tomorrow. Please rest and behave yourself. Don't go undoing something again," Jan told him.

Blaze of Fury

"I promise to behave now that I know you are alright, but I can't wait to get out of here. It will be good to get back to normal again," Austin said.

Before Claire took her back to her room, Jan gave Austin a quick kiss and told him that she loved him, and he did the same. Ted told Claire that he had to talk to Austin about the workings of the ranch before he left. Although it may be hard to do, as Austin would occasionally drift off.

Jan had just gotten back into bed when a woman and a man with a camera arrived. The woman asked if Jan would allow them to interview her, but Jan said no.

She told them that what had happened was just unfortunate, and that she felt it was better forgotten. Claire tried to ask them to leave, but they were very persistent.

"Is there a problem here?" Nick said as he entered the room.

Claire looked up to see a man possibly in his early fifties. He was tall and very handsome.

"Claire this is, my room mates husband, Nick," Jan said.

"Nice to meet you," Claire said, shaking his hand before telling him that they were trying to get rid of some unwanted guests.

"I think you'd better leave and let the lady rest. If she wants to talk to you, she can let you know," he said firmly. At which time, they reluctantly left.

"I hope they won't go bothering Austin," Jan said.

"Well, if they go there from here, I am sure that Ted will soon put them in their place, so don't worry," Claire said.

Jan turned to look at Nick. "I really appreciate your help. Thank you," Jan said.

"Glad to help," Nick replied, before turning his full attention to his wife.

Jan and Dawn began to talk to each other after visiting hours were over. Most of Jan's life she had kept everything bottled up inside. She was not one to share her life's problems, with others, but for some reason as her and Dawn talked, there seemed to be a special camaraderie. They shared some of their life stories with each other, and it was almost like a healing for the both of them.

When Jan fell asleep that night, she had a horrible nightmare. She tossed and turned before calling out for Austin, then a plea for God to help her. It was obvious that she was reliving what had happened.

Dawn got up and went over to Jan's bedside. "Jan," she said softly wiping the perspiration from Jan's forehead with a soft cloth. "Jan," Dawn called again, reaching over to ring Jan's buzzer.

Suddenly, Jan sat up. It felt like her heart was racing a million miles an hour.

"You're safe now Jan," Dawn told her.

Jan lay back with her hand over her heart.

"Are you going to be alright?" Dawn asked, just as a nurse entered the room.

"She had a bad dream," Dawn told the nurse.

The nurse checked Jan's vital signs, and then asked if she was having chest pain, to which Jan indicated that she was. Dawn stayed beside Jan until another nurse came in to do an ECG. Then as her pain persisted, they gave Jan some nitro and gradually the pain began to ease. However she ended up with a terrible headache. Jan lay there with tears in her eyes. She needed Austin to hold her, but that was not possible right now. Jan placed her hand on her stomach. Maybe he couldn't be with her, but his children still were. As she concentrated on them, she gradually began to relax. Her heart rate began to slow down to a more normal pace, but the irregular beating of her heart was still there. When she began to relax, and drift off to sleep, her heart went back to normal.

It was the nurse that woke Jan up the next morning, when she came to take her vital signs. Dawn had already gone for some tests, because of her recurring headaches. Before she came back, Nick arrived with their son and his little friend. He struck up a conversation with Jan, asking her about their ranch, and who was looking after their cattle, while they were in the hospital.

Jan told him that their friend Ted Jackson was doing that, as well as working at the Auction Mart as a brand inspector. She told him that Ted had been helping them to help solve the problem of the missing cattle. Only now, that seemed to have been solved.

Several times during their conversation, Nick had to tell the two boys to stop wrestling and to settle down. Nick offered to do what he could, if they needed extra hand. Jan thanked him, and said that she was sure that they would manage somehow. Jan glanced over at the two boys. Jeffery's friend had an uncanny resemblance to someone, but she could not put her finger on who, it was. At that point, Nick decided to get the two rowdy boys out of the room, before they got too carried away.

After they left, Jan lay there staring at the ceiling, until the nurse came to change her bandages. Some of the burns on her arms had been quite bad and now to top of it all off, she had a slight infection in a couple of them. The afternoon seemed to be very long. She wondered how Austin was doing and how long they would have to stay in here, when she heard a voice from around the curtain.

"Hi Anne."

"Hi Mary! Just pull the curtain back," Jan told her. It had been a long time since anyone had called her Anne, and she knew that her family would never call her Jan.

After Mary opened the curtain, she sat on the chair next to the bed. She was rather shy, and Jan also felt a bit uncomfortable. It had been probably over ten years since they had last talked to each other.

"Did you come alone?" Jan asked.

"No, Abe went to visit Austin. It seems all he could talk about lately, was what the two of them used to do, and the trouble they got into. He never talked about Austin for years, but now since the fire, it is obvious to me, that he really missed his old friend," Mary said. "Are your babies okay?" Mary asked.

"The doctor said they are fine, and I'm looking forward to going home. How are Mom and Dad doing?" Jan asked.

"They were a bit stressed about coming, but seem to be doing better now," Mary said.

Jan and Mary continued talking, and soon both of them felt like, they had been friends for years. Jan asked about the rest of their family and their brothers. It was obvious that her brothers were very much steeped in tradition. The part that was left out was Jan's first pregnancy, and why she never returned. Mary never once brought up the topic of Jan's first marriage. Jan felt bad for Don, as he was a good man, but to her family, it was like he didn't exist. That was probably due to him, being an outsider, and Austin had once been one of them.

"Is there a chance that you and Austin would come back to the church?" Mary asked.

"No, Mary. That will never happen. I really wish you could understand and see that the ways of that church, are not always right," Jan told her. Jan knew her answer had dashed Mary's hope.

Jan told her that God had forgiven her for the past, and that they were going to a church where God's rules were the only ones that she had to obey. It was not that all the rules back home were all bad, but there is a big difference between what was biblical, and what were man- made traditional rules.

After Mary left, Jan felt really sad. It was too bad that there had to be such a wall between her and her family. Would it ever really come down? That evening, Dawn and Jan had another good talk. Dawn was going home the next day, and Jan was going to miss her. Jan had to thank God for sending Dawn and Nick into her life, when she'd needed someone to talk to.

Right after lunch, Jan was feeling very restless. She was beginning to feel stronger and desperately wanted to go home. She was finally allowed to get up and walk around. She decided that, whether they liked it or not, she would go to see Austin. She was just about to leave her room, when Austin arrived pushing his intravenous pole in front of him.

"Where are you off to, young woman?" he asked.

"I was just on my way to see some handsome young man, down the way, but I see he beat me to it," she said, giving him a kiss.

"Now, is that the way you treat all your visitors?" he teased, wrapping his good arm around her. "Are you up for a little walk?" Austin asked

"I thought you would never ask," Jan replied.

As they strolled down the hallway, they talked about Abe and Mary. Austin had been quite happy to see him again. Jan said she actually had a good visit with her sister too. She told Austin about Nick and Dawn, and she was surprised to hear that Nick had also gone to visit Austin.

Then the topic of Ted and Claire's wedding came up. They knew how badly they had wanted to be together, and it was not fair that they should hold up their wedding. It was only a week and a half away, and it was questionable that Jan or Austin would be up for all the excitement. When they got back to the room, Jan's nurse came in to change her bandages. That was when she wished Austin wasn't there to see it. Jan saw the look on Austin's face, as did the nurse, when the bandage was removed.

"Once it is healed, it will not look so bad. If it does leave too much of a scar, there is always the option of plastic surgery," the nurse told her.

Austin touched the side of her face. "I am so sorry, Jan. It must be painful," he said. Then he watched as the nurse undid the bandages on Jan's arms. Austin was horrified at what he saw. He got really quiet as he watched the nurse change Jan's bandages. When she was finished, she placed Jan's arm carefully, back in the sling. Austin clenched his fist as his anger towards Douglas began to build. Even though the nurse said that her wounds were healing nicely, Austin still blamed himself for not being able to protect his wife.

"Austin, are you alright?" Jan asked after the nurse left.

"No, I'm not," he said. Then he saw the sad look in Jan's eyes. "What's wrong?" Austin asked.

"I am ugly. You deserve better," she said, turning away

Austin pulled her towards him. "Look at me," he demanded.

Jan slowly looked into his eyes.

"I will always love you, no matter how bad a scar you may have. You will always be beautiful to me. I love you for who you are, and don't you ever forget that. Wounds will heal, and you're here which is the main thing," Austin told her.

Jan could see in his eyes that he meant every word he said.

"I should have been there to protect you. I knew Douglas was crazy, and after those cattle disappeared, I should have heeded Rod's warning," Austin said, blaming himself.

Jan put her good arm around Austin. After looking at each other a moment, Austin leaned over and kissed her. They were kissing each other, when there was this flash. When they glanced at the doorway, there stood this newspaper lady, and her cameraman. Before either one could say anything, they were gone.

Austin and Jan walked up to the desk and complained about the reporters harass them, and taking pictures. They were told that the news media were not to be taking picture in the hospital, and that they would report it to the police, and have them deal with it. To Jan's embarrassment, that picture made the front-page news the next day. When Austin read the article, he was totally disgusted by the exaggerations of everything.

"Well, I guess that's what sells their papers," Austin told Jan.

It was two days later when both Austin and Jan, with some restrictions, were allowed to go home. Ted came to pick them up. He told them that Claire would be their nursemaid for the next week. Even though Jan could only use her left arm, and Austin's had limited use of his left arm, they still felt that they could manage on their own. Physically, Jan felt good and had regained most of her strength, but because of her pregnancy, the doctor was airing on the side of caution. Her burns were still quite painful, and she knew they would eventually heal, but it was not so easy to get rid of the nightmare, of living through the fire.

Both Austin and Jan were relieved when they got home, but when Jan stepped out of the truck, she could smell the smoke that still lingered in the air. She almost passed out as she began to panic at the feeling of being surrounded by fire. Austin tried to grab her, but was limited in what he could do. It was just good, that Ted was there to catch her.

Claire met them at the door, as Ted carried Jan into the living room. Austin looked very pale, and was wondering if Jan may have been released too soon. Ted lay Jan on the couch, while Claire got a cool cloth to lay on her forehead.

"Jan, are you going to be okay?" Austin asked kneeling beside her.

Jan closed her eyes for a few moments. The room seemed to be spinning.

"Jan, what's wrong?" Austin asked.

Finally, things seemed to settle down in Jan's head, and she blinked her eyes and wiped her tears away. Then she reached over to touch Austin. "I'll be fine," she said.

"What happened?" Austin asked.

"It was the smell of smoke. I just suddenly felt like I was back in... well you know," she said.

"Maybe it would be best if you talk about it, and don't let it build up with-in you," Claire said.

Jan did not answer. She just wanted the memory of it all, to disappear.

Claire brought some coffee and cookies into the living room, and everyone but Jan talked about the past few days. Jan sat eating her cookie and drinking her coffee while trying to blot out anything that pertained to the fire. Jan was surprised to hear that Rod was the one that had found her.

"It was his angel that led him to you, and no one can convince him other-wise," Ted said.

Jan listened to them talk about this angel.

Ted continued by saying, "Rod is convinced that he saw a real angel. He said, she was standing near the top of the hill, while Jan lay unconscious on the opposite side."

They all began to wonder if God did send an angel in answer to their prayers.

No one had seen Rod since that day on the hill, and both Austin and Jan had wanted to thank him. They both had a feeling that, someday their paths would cross again.

CHAPTER 19

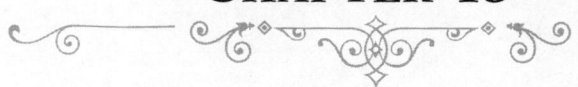

Two months had passed since the fire, and Jan's physical scars had healed quite well, but mentally they had not. She left the house only to go to church, and to her doctor's appointments. Austin was getting very concerned about her. He had tried to get her to talk about what had happened, because he felt that was the key to her whole problem. Mind you, the protective part of Austin was glad, for he at least knew she was safe at home. However it was going too far when she would not even sit with him, on the swing to watch the sunset. She told him that the glow reminded her of the fire, and she didn't want to remember that.

One evening, they decided to watch Ted and Claire's wedding video. Austin put his arm around Jan as she snuggled up to him. Even though Jan and Austin had been somewhat handicapped, they did stand up for Ted and Claire at their wedding. They were unable to stay for it all, as both of them had still tired easily.

The dress Jan wore, had long loose sleeves to mask the bandages and most of the cast on her arm. Her headpiece had a white veil that sort of covered the bandage on the side of her face. Austin sported a black sling around his neck that supported his arm.

"You look quite distinguished," Jan told Austin while snuggling closer to him.

"I must say that you were the most beautiful woman there. Sometimes I have to pinch myself to see if I am dreaming, or if you actually are my wife. It seems like there has always been one thing or another, that tried to separate us, but never again." Austin said holding Jan close to him.

"Your just prejudice," Jan teased, before getting real quiet. When her eyes focused on the bandage on the side of her face, she reached up and touched it. She really didn't want to ever see herself on that video again.

The harder she tried to forget, the more she withdrew from life. Even though the scar had healed, and was not as visible as she'd feared, the memory of the falling tree, and the searing pain as a piece of the burning branch landed on her face, sent chills through her body. The most horrifying moment was when the fire surrounded her as she tried to huddle under the waterfall. All she could do, was call out to Jesus for help. She had been positive that her life was to end right there. When she closed her eyes, she could see nothing but a wall of fire, as it lapped at her and the water. It hovered over her for what seemed like an eternity. She remembered thinking that this must be what hell would be like.

"Are you cold?" Austin asked. Even though it was warm in the house. Austin reached for the throw blanket that lay beside him.

Jan snuggled into the blanket when Austin covered her. He was hoping that she wasn't getting sick. When the wedding part of the video was over, and it got to the part where Jan was no longer in the picture, Austin could feel her relax, and she began to remove the blanket. He had a good idea what her problem was. He felt that they could be in for a rough time, if Jan didn't get some help.

When the video was over, they turned on the television to watch the news. Everything was fine, until they showed a clip of a forest fire. Jan tense up and snuggled deeper into the blanket. Finally, she asked Austin to change the channel or she was going to bed. Austin turned off the television and turned to look at Jan.

"Honey, we have to talk," Austin said.

Blaze of Fury

Jan was a bit confused as to what he wanted. Was it something about the ranch?

"Jan, you haven't been the same since the fire. If you won't talk to me about it, you'd better get some help," he told her.

"There is nothing wrong. Why won't you believe me?" Jan said.

"You call it nothing wrong when you hardly leave the house? I just saw your reaction when you saw the bandage on your face. Then again, when they talked about the fire. You can't handle it," Austin said.

"You don't understand. I just want to forget it," Jan told him.

"Forget is one thing, but you are hiding yourself away, and that isn't going to work. What will you do when our children are born? Are you going to lock them up from the outside world too?" Austin asked.

"Leave me alone," Jan said, jumping up, and heading to their bedroom.

Austin sat there in silence for a while. He had no idea what he should do. She needed someone to talk to. It had to be someone that she felt comfortable with, and maybe someone that was removed from the family. He was about to go to bed when the phone rang. At first, Austin did not know who it was, and then the caller identified himself as Nick. They had met at the hospital.

He told Austin that they were heading down that direction, and wondered if he and Jan would like to meet them for dinner. Austin said it would be nice, but since the fire Jan was having problems and he did not think she would go. However, they were welcome to come out to their ranch. Nick said that if Jan wasn't feeling well, they should perhaps, come another time.

Austin began to confide a bit in Nick, that it wasn't Jan's health that was the problem. Nick told Austin that Dawn and Jan had several heart to heart talks, and maybe she would talk to Dawn about what was going on. Austin told him that he was ready to accept any help he could get, right now.

When Austin got into bed, he knew Jan was not a sleep, even though she was facing the other direction. He turned towards her, and laid his arm around her waist.

"Jan, I know it is hard. You want to forget, but life won't let you. By the way, that was Nick on the phone. His wife was in the same room with you at the hospital. They are coming down this way tomorrow, so I asked them to stop in," Austin said. Austin then kissed her on the back of her head, and at the same time he felt the movement of the babies.

"You know, that was the first time I felt that. It's kind of nice," he said.

At that point, Jan finally began to talk. "You should be on my end of it. They already keep me awake," she told him.

Jan turned to face Austin, and he said, "I love you, Jan. I will do what ever I can to help you. Just help me to understand." He then kissed her.

Jan wrapped her arms around his neck and clung to him. "Just hold me. It's the only time I really feel safe," she told him.

Austin held her, while at the same time being at a total loss, of how to help her get over the trauma she'd gone through.

That evening, they had a light shower, but by noon the sun was out and had dried up most of what moisture had fallen. They would have to start praying for rain, as the pastures were beginning to suffer from lack of moisture.

Jan had been busy straightening up the house, and preparing some food for their guests. She was a bit nervous, but then she remembered how easy it was to talk to Dawn.

Austin was down at the barn, when Nick and Dawn arrived. Dawn's first comment was how pale Jan looked.

Jan told them to come in before calling Austin, to tell him that their company had arrived. She made some fresh coffee before joining Nick and Dawn at the table.

"Where is your son? Jan asked.

"He was spending the night at his friend's place. Today it is just the two of us," Nick said, looking at his wife.

"You two remind me of a couple that are on their honeymoon," Jan told them, just as Austin came into the house. Austin shook their hands, while welcoming them to their ranch. Jan poured everyone a cup of coffee, while Nick responded to Jan's last comment.

"As a matter of fact, you may say that we are still in the honeymoon phase. We have only been married for about 5 years." Nick told them.

"Oh, really?" Jan said, surprised. "But your son is…" then Jan looked at Austin and changed her mind, as to what she was about to say.

"It's alright." Dawn said, looking, at Austin. "Jeffery is my son from a previous marriage. He was three when his father died. Nick and I knew each other in our teenage years. We both got married, but not to each other. Then when we met again, his first wife had already past away. He then remarried. Shortly after, my husband had a heart attack." Dawn choked back a lump in her throat, as that memory flashed in front of her.

Jan noticed it, and understood that moment, where the men were not that tuned into it.

After a moment, Dawn continued. "My son and I moved away, after my husband died. Nick's second wife then died of cancer. Nick was upset and angry at me for awhile, but through different circumstances, well, lets just say everything turned out in the end," Dawn said glancing at Nick.

"You haven't had much luck with your women," Austin said, to Nick.

"Austin!" Jan said, scolding him for saying such a thing.

"Oh, it's okay. You see, I believed God meant for us to be together. I loved Dawn before she got married. I would have preferred marrying her years ago, but I am thankful that it did eventually come to pass," Nick said, smiling at his wife.

"I sort of know where you are coming from," Austin said, as he proceeded to tell them of when he'd seen Jan in the hospital after many years, but she'd disappeared. Then he told them about the incident at the Auction Mart, which had everyone laughing. He then talked about when they both were in the hospital, and how he wished that they could have been in the same room.

Nick and Dawn looked at each other, and began to laugh.

"What's so funny about that?" Austin asked.

Nick went on to tell them of the day he'd brought Dawn back to Alberta from British Columbia, where she had been living. He told them about the snow, and how he had gone out to check his cows before taking Dawn over to spend the night at their older children's place. Only he ran into a bit of a problem.

"Yeah, some problem! I had not ridden a horse since I had fallen off when I was very young," Dawn said. "Well, it was a horrible blizzard and he told me that he wouldn't be long. It was getting dark and he still wasn't home. All kinds of things went through my mind, as to what could have happened to him. He had told me that there was another horse in the barn, and I couldn't just leave him out there. I had a terrible feeling that there was something wrong. I had seen horses saddled up many times, so I wasn't totally dumb when it came to that. Then I heard his horse outside, only he wasn't on it."

"That was when she realized that she couldn't live with out me," Nick told them, with a big grin on his face.

Dawn made a face at him before continuing. "I did get on the horse and, between Nick's dog and I, we did find him. We were frozen by the time we got back to the house."

"What has that to do with the hospital?" Jan asked.

"Well, I ended up with a busted leg and Dawn drove me to the hospital. Dawn was tired and so much in love, that she climbed into bed with me," Nick said.

"Nick you know that you are not supposed to tell lies," Dawn told him.

Jan and Austin laughed, as they listened to the two of them banter.

"They wanted Nick to stay over night, because it was quite a bad break. He didn't want me to leave, and said the only way he would stay, was if I did too. He coaxed me to lie beside him. I did, only I fell asleep. When I woke up, I was pinned between the rail behind me, and Nick in front. Both rails were up and I couldn't move, and neither could he. A daughter of Nick's friend was his nurse. She came in before going off shift and put down the rail," Dawn said.

"Well she spent the night with me, so I had to make an honest woman out of her. We were married the next morning, and here we are," Nick said. Nick began to joke about that day in the hospital and soon he had everyone laughing.

Even Austin and Jan began to share more of how they had gotten together.

Jan told them about the police officer that came to rescue her from Austin, and said that if he didn't behave, she would call him back. Then she began, unwittingly, to talk about the day of the fire. She told them about finding their cows and then hiding the branding irons, before trying to cover her tracks with a branch. She said she remembered seeing that in an old western and everyone chuckled, except for Austin. She continued to tell them that when she heard someone coming, she decided to ride upstream as long as possible to hide her tracks. From there, she went through some thick brush. She rode through an open area, then more bush. She rode for some time, and then when she thought she was clear, she called Austin. Jan looked at him as she continued.

She saw a couple of guys lighting the fire behind her. Then off to the left, they lit some more. She couldn't go back. She had to find the creek. By then, she could hear the fire crackling behind her and the smoke was getting very thick. She rode until she got to the creek and followed it hoping to eventually find her way clear. Then she rode Hope right into a fence and was thrown. She still held onto the reins but then a hot ember landed on Hope, and she bolt and tearing the reins out of her hand and leaving her stranded.

"I tried to cover my face because, the smoke was so thick that, I could barely see, let alone breath," she said. Although she was looking at Austin, she was reliving her nightmare.

"I thought this was how I was going to die. Sparks were falling all around me. At times I had to brush the burning embers off of me. Then I remember falling and I hit my head hard on a rock, and shortly after, the pain in my arm was horrible. I realized that I had fallen over a small waterfall. At that point, the fire was practically on top of me. The only thing I could do was huddle under the waterfall to stay wet. Only, it was very shallow. Burning trees were falling near by and a small branch broke off and landed on my face," Jan said, touching the scar on her face. "I just remember lying there and praying. I don't know how long I lay there. When the fire finally moved on, it was as if someone was encouraging me to go on. I just remember my head and arm hurting when I walked away from that spot. I don't remember much after that. Everything is a blur. At one point, I remember hearing a man's voice and some noise, like gunshots, but... I thought I saw you at one point, Austin," she said, now beginning to cry. Austin got up and took her in his arms and just let her cry.

Nick looked at Dawn then, reached out his hand to her. He could have lost Dawn in that snowstorm. Then there was the time, when she was still married to her first husband that, her life had hung in the balance. He knew that God had a definite hand in their lives as well as Austin and Jan's.

Jan finally excused herself and went into the other room. After a few moments, Dawn asked Austin if she could talk to Jan alone. Austin told her that he would like it if she would.

Austin asked if Nick would like to go down to the corrals with him to check on a sick calf. So when Jan and Dawn came back into the kitchen, they found it empty. Jan did admit to Dawn that she felt somewhat better, now that she'd talked about it.

"Jan, you will have to face your fear head on. It won't go away over night. Just as I had to face my fear of getting on that horse…you must do the same. Only, I would not do like I did. I wouldn't advise you to leave it until it's an emergency. It's better to do it when it is on your own terms." Dawn told her.

"I used to enjoy riding, but I just don't know if I can go out there again," Jan said.

"Jan, if your doctor says it is okay for you to ride, I would do it as soon as possible, or you may never do it again. I wouldn't advise you to go out there alone, of course, especially in your condition. The other thing you may try is, drive out there, if its possible and just walk around a bit, but you must face your fears. God will help you, if you ask him to," Dawn told her.

Jan then changed the subject by asking Dawn about her life. Dawn talked a lot about her first husband, and it was obvious to Jan that, even though Dawn loved Nick now, her love for her first husband had never diminished. Her first husband was her real true love. Where as with Jan, it was the opposite.

Jan confided in Dawn that her love for Austin was far superior to the love she'd had for her former husband. She said that she did care deeply for Don, and they were happy and had a good relationship, but she did feel guilty for feeling as she did.

"Jan, God had a plan for each of our lives, and while it was sad that your first husband died at such a young age, you must remember that he loved you. I understand what you are saying, because both Nick and I felt the same way as you do," Dawn told her.

Jan suddenly looked at her watch. "You will stay for supper, won't you?" Jan asked.

"Oh, we wouldn't want to be a bother," Dawn told her.

"I really want you to stay, and in fact, if I know men, they will be gone for a while and will be hungry when they get back." Jan said.

While Jan and Dawn worked together making supper, Dawn got Jan to talk more about her feelings when it came to the fire. The more Jan talked, the easier it became.

When the men came into the house, Nick was the first to comment on the smell of food. Austin looked at Jan and could sense that she was more relaxed than she had been since the fire. He too was now more at ease when the topic of the fire came up. He noticed that Jan didn't get near as tense, and she surprisingly answered any question about the fire that Nick or Dawn asked her. Austin whispered a prayer of thanks for the new friends that God had sent them.

From that day on, Jan's life slowly got back on track. Even the day Rod came to see how his angel was doing, it did not bother her. She told him that they had wanted to thank him for finding her, but no one seemed to know where, he had disappeared to. Neither her nor Austin recognized him the day he arrived on their doorstep. He was wearing a suit and tie. Rod had turned from his wild life, as a cowboy and troublemaker to a respectable businessman. He was now working for a large oil company. He had apparently worked for them years ago, but then ended up falling into the same rut as many young men do when making a lot of money, and that was, drink and partying. He told them that he had to thank them for who he was now. It all stemmed back to the day Jan found him at the base of the cliff. Austin's brother Jake also had a hand in his new life. They had a long talk when he was laid up in the hospital with his broken leg and a few burns and bruises. He again asked for their forgiveness for being the cause of the death of their unborn child. He said that he would have to live with that for the rest of his life. He also congratulated them on the up-coming birth of their twins before he left.

* * *

It was about a week later that Jan decided that she would do as Dawn suggested. She didn't think she would have a problem riding, but the thought of going to the lease still sent chills down her spin. She decided to saddle up Hope after Austin went to town. This was something she had to do herself, and by riding alone, she could always turn back if she felt she couldn't handle it.

It would definitely be harder to get on Hope, now that she was carrying twins with in her, but she could always use a pile of bales, like Dawn said she had done. Once in the saddle, she walked Hope for some distance before nudging her into a trot and then a gallop. Jan enjoyed the run as much as Hope did, but then she decided to take it slower. She was almost at the gate that led into the lease, when she heard the sound of galloping hooves behind her. Jan froze as she sat quietly looking at the gate in front of her. Was it happening all over again? When she heard her name, she began to relax.

"What in blue blazes, do you think you are doing?" Austin yelled.

"Calm down Austin. I just thought it was time for me to face my fears," Jan told him.

"There is no way I will allow you to go out there alone. I don't want to go looking for you again," he said, now very angry with her.

"Well if you want to come with me, you are welcome. I thought you were on your way to town? Jan said.

"I was, but I forgot to take the empty lick containers with me, and that was when I saw you riding out. I thought we had an agreement that no one rode alone, and I know you haven't got a phone with you. What would you have done if you went into labor?" Austin asked glaring at her.

"I am sorry Austin. I never thought of that. I am feeling fine and just felt it was time to face my fears," she said apologizing. Then she began to think. *Was he always going to scrutinize her every move?* "Austin, I think you should go back and let me do this myself. There is no way that I need you to watch over my every move. It just won't work that way," she told him.

Austin looked at her for a moment and then began to mellow. "No maybe not, but while you are carrying my babies, I am not going to allow you to go out on that lease alone. Later when things are more settled, well then maybe, but it doesn't mean that I won't still worry about you." He said getting off his horse to open the gate. "Come on," he said leading Midnight through then closing the gate behind Jan. When Austin got on Midnight, Jan reached over and grabbed hold of his jacket. She pulled him toward her and gave him a kiss.

"Do you think that will make up for what you did?" he asked.

"Yes," she said before riding in the direction of where she had found their cows.

"You are one stubborn woman," Austin said.

"That started after I met you," Jan said smiling.

They rode through an area where the fire had travelled. Little by little they could see the grass beginning to grow, but the burnt trees still lay scattered through out the area. Austin told Jan that perhaps he and Ted should come out to cut up some of the wood, for burning in their fireplaces.

Jan suddenly got very quite when they came up to the small water fall. Then as they rode a little farther, Austin showed Jan where the fence had been, that Hope had run into. He and Ted had dismantled it so there was no sign of it now. They rode up to the fence that bordered Douglas's property. Jan sat staring across the fence, before asking, "What had happened to Mr. Douglas and how much damage was done to his building sight?"

"Well from what I heard, he will be spending at least a year in jail. As for his buildings, I have not seen it for myself but apparently he had lost his house and several large sheds, and a lot of bales. The building that the ranch hands stayed in was apparently still there, Austin said.

"Who is running the ranch now? Jan asked.

The cattle were sold and no one lives there now. I heard that it could go up for sale, because Mr. Douglas is seventy years old, and it was not likely, that he would rebuild," Austin said.

They talked about how greed and anger can destroy a man, and all he worked for though out his life.

"Nick said that years ago, Mr. Douglas had been a very nice person, but what could have happened that change him so drastically?" Jan asked. Austin just shrugged his shoulders.

Jan had been very nervous out on the lease, and was glad to get back onto familiar territory. She was glad that she had made this effort now, because she would not likely be riding again, for quite sometime.

* * *

The closer Jan got to the birth of their babies, the more she thought about their first son. He would be almost 11 years old now. Austin and Jan had done all they could to find him, but as of yet, they had no luck. The last two months Jan had been ordered to rest and to do very little, which Austin made sure, that she adhered to that.

It was the beginning of December, and Jan and Austin, were in their living room. Austin sat on the couch, while Jan lay beside him with her head resting on his leg. They were talking about their first child, when Jan began to get pains. The babies were not due for another two weeks, but they had been warned, that this could happen.

Austin grabbed his jacket and quickly went out to start their car, while Jan slipped on her coat. Austin returned to pick up Jan's suitcase, which she had packed week's prior. He then put his arm around her, and helped her to the car. He sure didn't want her to slip and fall. Once on their way, Austin gave the hospital a call, from his cell phone.

When they got to the hospital, Austin was directed to fill out the forms, while the nurse took, Jan to her room. After handing in the forms, they sent him to another part of the hospital, where he again was told to wait. Even though he had waited only fifteen minutes, it felt more like an hour.

Jan had told Austin, that she wanted him to be by her side, when their children were born.

Book 3 of the *Mountains and Valleys of Life*

Austin had no problem with that, but now that the time had come, and he seen the pain Jan was in, he was beginning to wonder if he was going to be able to handle this. He had worked with a lot of cattle during difficult births, but this was not at all what he had expected. About two hours had past; when he was told that they would have to take the babies, by cesarean. At that point he got very pale, and had to sit down before he passed out. Austin only was able to gave Jan a kiss and tell her that he loved, before she was rushed away to the operating room.

It seemed like forever, before a nurse came to tell him that he was now the proud father of two sons. It was with a great sigh of relief, when he was told that mother and babies were doing fine. When he asked if he could see her, the nurse said that he should be able to see his new family in about fifteen minutes. At that point he finally began to relax. He would never have believed how hard it was to have a baby.

While Austin waited, he decided to called first his parents, and then reluctantly Jan's parents. Both sets of parents congratulated them, but Jan's parents were still, distant. He had hoped that after the time they spent searching for Jan, things would have change. He thought they were beginning to accept him, but something was now different. When Austin called Ted and Claire, they were over joyed for them, which was more up lifting then his previous call.

Austin then called his old friend Abe and Mary to tell them his good news. It was Abe that answered, and after telling him about his new family members, he began to realize why Jan's parents were so stand offish. Apparently, Abe and Mary had left the old church, and were attending elsewhere.

When Austin was finally allowed to join his little family, he saw the joy in Jan's face, even though she was very drowsy. He kissed her before the nurse, handed him two little bundles. As Austin stared down at his two newborn sons, his heart swelled with pride. They had picked out some names earlier, so as he stood there looking at his children, he asked, "which one in Cody and which one is Casey?"

"I will leave that for you to decide," Jan told him.

Suddenly the pride and joy he now felt, turned to heartache. It suddenly struck him like a bolt of lighting. Jan had gone through the pain of childbirth alone, almost eleven years ago. He tried to imagine what it had been like, for Jan to travel this journey alone. Especially knowing that she would be giving up her first-born child. He had missed the precious moment of holding their first son, and that could never be undone. It made Austin even more determined to find their child.

The *Mountains and Valleys of Life* series

Book 1 - Will Love Conquer All?

Book 2 - Better Now than Never

Book 3 - Blaze of Fury

Coming Soon

Book 4 - The Widow Maker

Printed in Canada